AN UNEXPECTED TURN

Inspired by a True Story

by Ellen Carlisle

Carlisle, Ellen

    An Unexpected Turn
    Inspired by a true story

Library of Congress Control Number: 2019902949

Copyright © 2019 Ellen Carlisle

Author contact: Ecarlisle007@gmail.com

Published by amazon KDP
Cover design by Avery N. Dayton

For Susan
(Who else would read a book three times?!)

and for Kevin,
the sunshine of my life

Table of Contents

Prologue

"Come with me, Trudy..." Still, five years later, I can hear my father's tone, pleading. "Come to South Africa. You'd like Helen, really you would." His voice was barely a whisper. "And Henry, her son...we could all be...be a family..." *A family?* His words continue to echo inside my head, ricochet against the backs of my eyes.

At that time, we were standing towards the rear of my childhood home in the room off the kitchen that had, long before, been the pantry. When I was very young, that room was filled to the brim with all the provisions a family could ever want—flour and sugar for baking, lard for cooking, canned vegetables from the garden. During the war and because we had nothing to store, it became a guest room, first for my aunt and then, many years later, for him.

At his ridiculous invitation, I turned my back to him, pushed the curtain aside, pressed my forehead to the cool window glass. Out of habit I rubbed warmth into the backs of my arms. But I wasn't cold. In fact, his mere suggestion burned my body like hot tea drunk too fast. Helen, Henry...I was having trouble comprehending the situation he was confessing. Could it be that while the rest of us were holding our breath, certain at times it would be our last, he had been enjoying himself? I didn't want to believe he had another life, had been living another life, especially while we had been living in Nazi Hell. I remember trembling with anger; catching the scent of my own sour sweat.

My mind needed a break, time to adjust, and I needed to calm down, so I turned my attention outside. White clouds stretched across a lifeless sky. Water running in the canal at the edge of the field threw off bits of reflected color, blue gems glittering in the sunlight. The garden patch just beyond the back door came into closer focus. My father's recent efforts were visible—shoots of green carrot tops, emerging broccoli stalks, beet stems. Were the vegetables his peace offering? Or was the garden just that resilient, too? My longing for normalcy felt heavy inside my chest. How had my life diverged, again, so dramatically?

I don't remember much before the Nazis infested my sweet five-year-old world. I wish I could remember more. Desperately trying to root out the years of occupation from my mind, I have inadvertently forfeited some of the precious memories I would rather have kept, save for a few indelible glimpses—laughing with my friend, Leah; the taste of a lemon pastry; the warmth of Mom's strong embrace. When life becomes hard, I close my eyes and run those cherished pieces together like animation cels, allowing the snippets to amplify until part of me is living then instead. I used this tactic especially during the occupation. When the bombs were relentless or the hunger unbearable, I'd sift through those cels like a deck of cards until landing on one that allowed me to exhale. I'd hold it up to the light, examine it like a treasure, and then lay that one down and build on it. If I were lucky, I'd be transported into dreams to last the night, or at least until the screech of bombs shattered the silence, and then I'd have to begin the process all over again.

Though my cache of memories is small, I still, even today, hold tightly to a precious few of the privileged life I took for granted. I would like to relive, if only just once more, a family dinner at that massive dining room table. Because I was too young to be helpful, I'd sit quietly, my stuffed bunny, Ribbon, ever-present on my lap, watching bits of dust float in the slanted afternoon sunlight streaming through the windows. Mom and my sisters would pop up and down remembering the cabbage and its serving spoon, the potatoes warming in the oven. Eventually, the table would be full of heaps of home cooking scenting the air. Pop would be seated at the head by the time Mom finally sank into her chair beside him with a contented, exhausted sigh. I'd be beside her, and my sisters, Marike and Maud, across the table. Maud always remained ready to pop up again, her eyes trained on Mom just in case, until Mom smiled at her, and she'd relax and look at her clasped hands in her lap. Marike, quiet for a change, her mouth watering as she surveyed the meal. She'd roll her eyes when reminded to bow her head while Pop said the blessing. He'd thank God for all that we had, which I've since learned was more than plenty, and the seemingly endless supply of food. Lamb and scalloped potatoes, sausages, cakes and rice pudding, Edam and salami—I knew from that pantry, Mom would produce anything we would ever want. Until she couldn't.

My sisters are mostly absent from my cache of cel options. Marike and Maud, the Ms I call them, are six and eight years older and treated me like the annoying afterthought they believed I was. The Ms were inseparable, and although Maud threw bits of kindness my way, her allegiance was to Marike, and Marike kept a tight rein. Instead, I can reliably turn to memories of Mom, who is appropriately at the center of everything good. She is always the right launch when I need to dream—day or night. Usually I push back to age three or four, to a time when my only worries were which fancy dress to wear with my shiny black Mary Janes, or the hope that pastries would be left over from Mom's mid-morning coffee with friends. In my mind's eye, I tuck Ribbon under my arm, grab a lemon pastry from the mound on the flowered china plate, and sit on the cold linoleum floor. I offer the outer edges to Ribbon, "nyum, nyum, nyum," and let the tart gooey center melt in my mouth. I return most of those edges to the plate and find Mom outside. She is kneeling in the dark soil, her sunhat flopped low over her face. A pile of dark red beets already lays warming in the sun beside her, and she is poised to lop green broccoli bunches. She looks up and sees me, drags the back of her gloved hand across her forehead, and offers me an ear-to-ear smile. Her brown eyes dance, and her giggles shake her belly a little. Mom opens her arms wide, and I fall against her soft bosom. I am peppered with kisses, giggling too. Right there I freeze the memory, my arms wrapped

3

tightly around myself, in the midst of Mom's meaty hug. I hear the music in her voice and breathe in her lilac scent for as long as my mind will allow.

"Let's look for Pop!" I'd sing as Mom splayed the blue blanket in the air. It would float on the cool breeze to the ground beside the garden. This was a game Mom was always willing to play during Pop's three-month treks. We'd kick off our shoes and rush to the center of our sea amidst the grass-green expanse. Lying on our backs, we'd search puffy white clouds to find Pop—his face, the sailor's hat he liked to spin on his finger, his oil tanker. The spans of cobalt skies served as the oceans he traveled, stretching forever into the distance. "Where do you suppose he is right now?" Mom would wonder aloud, quizzing me on the ports along his trek to the Persian Gulf. "The Bay of Biscuits!" I'd squeal, mispronouncing *Biscay,* because that always made Mom laugh. Her laugh was pure and contagious, and I loved being the cause of it.

On that blue blanket and with devout reverence, Mom happily relayed stories about Captain Sam VanEck, the love of her life. When they'd first met, her stomach flipped when he just looked in her direction or sat close enough to help with homework. Her eyes sparkled every time she'd relive the story. He was tall, blond, blue eyed. I never tired of hearing that I look just like him, while the Ms have Mom's dark features. When Mom was particularly lonesome for Pop, she would hold my chin in her hands and say, "I have only to look into your face to see him smiling back at me," her chocolate brown eyes welling with tears. I didn't care if she were looking at me only to see him. I was just delighted to have Mom looking at me.

As the story goes, my grandfathers, Opa Mark, Mom's dad; and Opa Sven, Pop's dad, were best friends as well as business partners. Their hope was that their children, Gertrude and Sam, would marry, allowing Sam to take over the successful hardware store the men had built. Only half of that dream came true. Marike loved to loudly blame me for ruining that dream. When Pop's absence was felt hardest, she'd pounce on the chance to remind us all that Pop quit the hardware store and took the Overseas Trading Company's post in order to feed the "unplanned, unexpected, and unwanted third baby." It was my fault he went away for months at a time. I never stopped cowering from her accusations, despite Mom's earnest rebut. Every time Marike lashed out, Mom would proudly remind us all that Pop took the oil tanker job for three reasons: neither Opa was ready to step aside when Pop needed to step in, a tanker captain's salary was very good, and their *second* child was on the way. (She always emphasized the word *second* and looked away while I glared at Marike.) "He wanted to provide for us the best way he could. We were then and always will be his first priority," she loved to say. "Never a more devoted man in the whole of Holland," she'd add vehemently, her chin resolute. And then she'd go silent for a while because her heart ached for him.

Like a picture within a picture, my mind conjures images of the man I hardly knew but learned to love through Mom's stories told on our blue blanket. I thought he was a giant in every way. Even though I've grown to just shy of six feet, in my mind he still seems taller than most. When I was little, I'd hide behind Mom, afraid to be scooped up in his arms and hoisted high off the floor. The Ms would squeal with delight when he'd lift them, but I was torn, wanting so badly to be in his arms yet petrified to be so high in the air. Eventually, he'd seek me out, pry me from Mom's legs. Only when he'd stoop to my level would I dare step forward. He sensed my fear and moved slowly, allowing me to settle, waiting for me to take his outstretched hand. But when he'd bend to me, the Ms would inevitably jump on his back, wrap their arms around his neck, and steal his hat, giggling and shrieking. I didn't blame him for leaving me to chase them, talk with them. They were older, more interesting. My father preferred older, more relatable children, and he didn't make exceptions, even for me.

But the favorite memory I repeatedly draw on stems from the comfort found in Mom's warm reassurance, especially when the Ms were being unbearably mean. Regardless of Mom's efforts, the Ms reminded me I was a mistake and shouldn't be there. Why else would there be only two years between them and more than six until me, they'd smirk. Of course I'd run to Mom, allow myself to be wrapped in a bear hug and soothed by her sweet voice. On the particular day I like to recall, Mom dries my tears and takes my hand, leading me outside by the garden where she unfurls the blue blanket. We kick off our shoes and snuggle close. "I'll say this only one time, Trudy, so listen with your heart," she says, taking my hands and rolling onto her elbows so we're eye-to-eye. Her body blocks the sun which haloes her like an angel. "God doesn't make mistakes, hmmm?" She nods, so I nod. "No, you weren't planned; no, we can't afford you. But at the same time, my dear girl," she says smoothing my hair behind my ear, "you are the most precious gift of all." The words echo against my heart. "Besides," she says, pulling me close, "you know Marike is named for Pop's mom, Maud is named for my mom, and who are you named for?"

"You!" I coo. "We're both named Gertrude!" I whisper the memory softly to myself, my hands over my face so as not to be overheard. "That's right, my love. You have the bigger part of my name and," I hug myself tightly as the words repeat in my head, "the bigger part of my heart."

These are the memories that I fervently cling to. They highlight Mom's optimistic spirit and have molded my faith. The Ms have grown up and live their lives separate from mine, which I guess I expected and ultimately accepted. But the reemergence of my father, the man Mom adored and, because of her, the man I idolized, had unhinged my foundation. When at last he returned home, years after liberation, he stayed on board at the shipyard instead of at home with me. His excuse was that he and Aunt Jenke didn't get on well. *Didn't his need to be with me outweigh his reluctance to be around her? Hadn't he longed to know me the way I'd ached to know him?* At first I was upset and confused, but I calmed myself as I'd learned to do. When he finally did move home and into the old pantry, we attempted to learn each other. Through our talks over hot Droste chocolate, I poured myself onto the table, opened myself up like a book for him to peruse. I repeatedly asked Pop, "Describe how the war has changed you." In effect, I was asking him to tell me who he was and who he is. Because I didn't have a lifetime to glean and assemble the bits and pieces of him, I wanted to stretch out on a new blanket, feel a fresh breeze on my skin, and hear his stories from his own mouth. He revealed little. He spoke enthusiastically about the beauty of the waters he'd traversed. He was enamored with the different blues of the Mediterranean—azure, cerulean, ultramarine, the vastness of the Pacific. And the sight of the emerald green Atlantic crashing and rising above the Indian Ocean has "blessed him for life." He talked about the shift from ferrying oil to fueling the allies and the multiple crews and their troubles.

Though these details were interesting, even impressive, they offered scant about the man I'd longed to know first-hand. Beyond his responsibilities during the war, I wanted to know how he felt about his involvement. Was he frightened? Was he more afraid for his family? And how, most importantly, could he have strayed so far from his family, his country?

In Leiden, the war had dramatically changed everyone in our household—Mom, Aunt Jenke, the Ms; however, all remained steadfastly Dutch. I was shaped, not changed, by the war since I was molded in its grasp not thrown into it fully formed. I was a goldfish surviving in a bowl of murky water, groping hopelessly for something pure and untainted. Everyone lied. From government officials to schoolmates, they lied to protect as well as gain what they valued. Holland believed the neutrality agreement would be honored. Mom believed the mere return of her husband would make her well. And I continue to wait for the return of my childhood friend, Leah. As a result, I am wary of practically everyone. And I prefer to learn things for myself rather than take anyone's word as truth.

Despite my efforts, I didn't know the man standing before me. Instead of revealing himself, he handed me a kist, an intricately carved, large wooden box. In it were stacks of hand-written letters, their parchment paper yellowed with age, tied with twine and bundled by years. "Your mother told you who I was. These letters will do a far better job of telling you who I became," he said. Then he cupped my shoulders with his huge hands, bent to meet my eyes. A tear welling in his caught a glint of light. "Please don't judge me too harshly, Trudy," he pleaded. "Put yourself in my shoes?"

I barricaded myself in my room and devoured the letters, his and *hers*. At first I was shocked, outraged, and grief-stricken. I couldn't fathom how he could live a secret life! He dared to enjoy life while we were hoping to simply continue breathing? While we were clinging to him, he slipped through our grasp unwittingly and did much better than merely survive. He thrived. I couldn't bear the thought of him. I stepped out of my life until I'd read every letter, eating little and rarely coming up for air. When I finally finished reading every one, I was exhausted physically and emotionally. And I wanted to kill him. I had never needed Mom more.

Anger and betrayal gnawed at me for years. Eventually I began reliving the scene with less blame and more curiosity. Finally, I actually heard the words he'd spoken when tearfully handing over the letters. "Put yourself in my shoes," he'd begged. I decided to write down the saga parsed from the letters in order to inhabit each character individually, put myself in each pair of shoes. My hope was to remove myself emotionally, thereby making the story as unbiased and clear as possible. Because the story began when I was very young, I had no memory outside of my small context. I have called on my sisters to help fill in the gaps, provide their memories. My goal was to gather the story on paper in one smooth form, understand the actions of the characters more keenly. Maybe when I step out of myself, read the saga in black and white with all my own color removed, I will begin to appreciate their motivation. And, hopefully, I will be able to forgive.

ONE - Aboard the Janus

1938 Sam gripped the rail of the upper deck, bracing against the cool ocean breeze. He closed his eyes, let the salty air fill his lungs, and smiled into the warm Mediterranean sunshine. Already his fair skin was tinged with pink. This had become his favorite segment of the trip. Endless sunshine, peaceful turquoise waters, and the hint of coral just below the surface thrilled him each time he passed through this area. Eyes closed and face turned upward, he thanked God for his good fortune. The incredible scenery had become his bonus.

Sam's mind drifted to the events that brought him to this moment. When he first began working for the Overseas Tankship Corporation, Sam was in it for the money. But he quickly grew to enjoy the benefits of living on the ship and the implied mystique. When Gertrude became pregnant, his goal was to build a nest egg for a few years during that dreaded baby stage. But after just six months, Sam was promoted to Convoy Leader in charge of his and two additional oil tankers and, indirectly, their crews. The recognition boosted his confidence, and the money was better than he'd imagined. Sam was grinning, lost in his thoughts, when his team joined him.

"I knew to find you here, Captain, creature of habit you are," teased Einer Staal, Sam's Crew Chief. An easy going rounded fellow, Einer had a pocketful of sourballs at all times. Instantly likeable and even-tempered, Einer created and maintained a pleasant rapport with the ever-changing, often multi-national crew.

"Lovely as always, eh, Captain," said Danker, shaking Sam's hand. Danker DeVries, wise beyond his 28 years, served as Sam's very capable assistant. Tall, slim, and charismatic, he reminded Sam of his younger self. Danker became Sam's Senior Engineer when Sam became Convoy Leader, and the pair made a formidable team. They understood each other, often without words, respected each other's abilities, and shared a mounting fondness for their watery route. "Clear sailing through to the Canal, Captain," reported Danker.

Sam smiled, "Now that's the only news I ever want to hear on this bridge," he said, inhaling the salty fresh air. "One day I'm going to dive off this deck into that beautiful water. Have you ever seen anything so captivating?"

The question brought a chuckle from Einer, "not since the last time we made this trek, Captain."

"I know I repeat the same comments every time," admitted Sam. "But it's just so..."

"Incredibly beautiful," added Danker. "It truly is. And you two are the only people who'll hear me say that." He turned and rested his elbows on the handrail. "The last time I described the mesmerizing Mediterranean to Carla, she cried!" he said, looking to the heavens. "You're supposed to be miserable when you're away from me!" he whined in a high-pitched voice. Sam and Einer howled with laughter.

"Rookie mistake. I have not breathed a word to Ger," confessed Sam, tilting his head and dropping his gaze to the deck. "Poor darling is convinced I'm still heartbroken every time we leave. Remember our first few treks? We were terrified!" He tapped his heel to his toe, glancing sideways at Danker and Einer. "Truth is, I do miss my Ger...and the girls. I really do. In a perfect world I'd bring them along with us, have them stow away with the crew." Sam elbowed Einer's arm. "You think the crew would be fine giving up their quarters for my three little ladies, hmmm, Einer? No problem, right, my friend? Bedtime stories in several languages! The girls would love that!"

Einer just shook his head smiling. "Money can't buy enough sour balls for that bribe," he laughed. "I have plenty on my plate convincing them to communicate with *me*!" Einer checked his watch. "Speaking of children, I'd best get back to the crew." He straightened his shirt and smoothed his hair, popping a cherry sour ball into his mouth. "So far, so good, Captain. With the crew, I mean," he said with the sour ball wedged and bulging his cheek. "We've got a good bunch. I hope most of them make the return trip with us."

"Try to get a feel for the situation by the time we reach the Gulf of Aden, Einer. Knowing a replacement count will save time at port," suggested Sam.

"Will do, Captain. See you two below," replied Einer, stiffening to a half salute. The three had long since dispensed with the formalities.

"Right behind you," added Danker. "I expect the radio to be buzzing soon."

"Keep me posted on weather conditions as far out as possible, Danker. And when you can, let Bertie know your best estimate for our arrival in Bahrain. Let's make this turnaround quick and efficient. We are paid by the trek, not by the hour."

"Aye, Captain."

"Maintain routine contact with our convoy mates, Danker. Every four hours should be enough in these pleasant conditions. But take the onus off yourself; if they don't hear from you, let them know you expect them to check in every three to four hours. I'll be in my stateroom tending to the paperwork if you need me."

"Aye, sir," Danker called over his shoulder.

Sam stepped over the coaming and immediately tuned the dial of his small RCA radio. Vivaldi's cello flooded the compact quarters— a small closet, wet bar complete with crystal tumblers, and a sitting area in front of a lightweight metal desk. Thanks to the skylight above the built-in bed, the cabin was bright and warm.

Sam sat on the leather settee, plucked the small silver frame from the end table, and studied the updated family photo Ger had given him when he left. Even with the extra twenty pounds, Ger was still the dark beauty she was as a teenager. They'd planned their future then—two children, a modest home, a fishing boat—a neat and tidy simple life in Leiden. Sam shook his head, marveling at their different reality. In the photo Marike stood erect beside her seated mother, hand on her hip and smiling confidently at the camera. In direct contrast was Maud, skinny and crouched beside Ger, literally and figuratively in the shadow of the other two. Though their personalities differed greatly, their dark hair and eyes made them undeniably their mother's children. *Lucky girls. When the boys start coming around, I'll be very grateful for this job,* he realized. And Trudy. Especially in the black and white photo, her wavy blond hair and light eyes gave her the undeniable distinction of Sam's daughter. Already tall for her age, Trudy would certainly experience an uncomfortably gawky stage as he had. She stood in front of Ger, leaning confidently against her mother's knees. As usual, her sweet dimpled smile stretched across her face. *Someday I'll enjoy getting to know that one,* he thought. "I'll be back in due time, my ladies," Sam whispered, planting a kiss on the glass.

At the desk Sam opened the black leather-bound Captain's log to record their progress, noting their coordinates, weather, average speed, and wind velocity since the last installment in the Bay of Biscay. The Janus had made good progress. At their current rate and barring any delays in the Canal, they would slip into the Persian Gulf ahead of schedule.

That evening cook prepared his special beef stew, and the crew enjoyed it. Maybe it was their satisfied stomachs that helped Einer convince them to stage a talent show. Nearly the entire crew gathered on the aft deck to watch as about a third of the men participated in an hour and a half of pure enjoyment. Among the performers were two men from Norway dressed as clappers, fringe swinging wildly as they danced while the rest of the men whooped and whistled. A juggler from Ireland kept everyone mildly amused while hurling various fruits into the air. And as the setting sun threw streaks of red and orange across the dimming sky, an opera singer from Italy sang so sweetly that Sam fought back tears.

Back in his tidy stateroom, Sam carefully removed his shoes, stowing them side-by-side in the closet. He hung up his uniform, navy pants and long-sleeved white shirt. Soon they'd be in warmer waters wearing short pants and swatting mosquitos. He readied himself for sleep, returning his toiletries neatly into his dobby kit. He wound the alarm clock and set it for 6 A.M., though he was confident the sun would wake him before then. He slipped under the woolen bedcovers and lowered the radio's volume so the classical music could lull him to sleep.

After several weeks in passage, guide planes eased the Janus and her convoy into the noisy Bahrain docks. The long narrow ships slowed alongside wooden walkways undulating on choppy waters until lines were tossed and secured. Here the salty scent of the seas was replaced by the bitter stench of crude, and vast expanses of open sky and seas were replaced by low hanging jungle greens and dense earth. Uniformed men scurried around in tropical hazy sunshine collecting paperwork and shouting to be heard over the drone of engines and the clang of bilge pump connectors. Once the ballast was emptied, Danker would oversee the crude loading.

Sam headed to the office across the sundrenched yard to check orders and collect the ship's mail, swatting at clouds of mosquitoes along the way. As usual, he was greeted by Bertie, the manager. Bertie's pink skin and Irish brogue betrayed his native status. "Lovely to see you, Captain VanEck. A bit ahead of schedule, you are!" A box fan hummed behind him, gently moving white wisps of hair on his head. Bertie had seen Sam approaching and was ready with the ship's mail. He handed Sam the bundled letters from home, orders, and "something from America, Captain," reported Bertie, leaning a meaty forearm on the counter. He made no attempt to hide his curiosity for the contents.

Sam inspected the envelope, turning it over in his hands. The return address read Caltex Corp, 4107 West 44th Street, New York, New York, USA, and was postmarked July 11, 1938. He slid a finger under the flap and withdrew the letter. To appease Bertie, Sam read an excerpt aloud, "...to announce the merger of the Overseas Tankship Corporation with Caltex Corporation of America..." *Please let me keep my position,* was Sam's first thought, but showing concern to Bertie would be like shouting from the rooftops. He continued to scan the letter before meeting Bertie's eyes. "As long as I continue to receive my paychecks, I guess I shouldn't mind too much who signs them," Sam asserted, returning the letter to its envelope. "I do wonder why they chose an American company..."

"Perhaps it's merely an expansion effort, Captain. Nothing to worry about, I'm sure," offered Bertie. But Sam wasn't listening. He'd begun to imagine the larger problems these new orders would create.

Back into the heat, Sam crossed the oil yard to the officers' lounge where the group routinely met once the loading had begun. Stepping into the dim lounge and out of the blazing light temporarily blinded him, and he paused a minute for his eyes to adjust to the smoky haze. He pulled a handkerchief from his pocket, removed his hat, and dabbed at his brow. Ceiling fans attempted to push the thick, humid air inside. He found his group as they spotted him, and he motioned for them to meet him at the topographical map lining the far wall. Each port displayed a similar map, indicating the sea's undercurrents and ridges as well as geographical formations.

The convoy officers, Captain VanDerMeer of the Shell, Captain Sorensen of the Queen, and their officers; Danker, Einer, and the guide pilots all gathered while Sam reviewed the Dispatch Orders. After the men had settled around heavy ebony tables, Sam cleared his throat. "Gentlemen, we are in for an adventure," he began, and told them about the Caltex Corporation's takeover. "The good news is we are all still employed. But we have a new route that will keep us in the Persian Gulf...and south a bit longer. Bahrain will remain our filling port; our service ports will now be in Pakistan and India..." With his finger, he traced the intended route across the waters to Karachi and Bombay on the map. "Once loaded, we will now be directed to discharge in four refinery ports of South Africa as well: Durban, East London, Port Elizabeth, and Cape Town. Any of these, as well as Bombay, can accommodate our drydock as needed. Occasionally, we may be asked to unload in Madagascar, here..." His finger continued to travel south on the map as he spoke, through the Arabian Sea and into the Indian Ocean, landing twice as far from home as they had ever been. Tension in the group thickened like the humidity, as the men stifled coughs and shifted in their seats. Their three-month stints in confined waters instantly became nearly half-year journeys. The men grumbled while Sam explained further. Each time they loaded in Bahrain, they were to receive discharge orders and corresponding suggested routes. "Eventually, we will fall into a routine," he said spinning his hat on his finger. "I'm sure you won't have any trouble devising suitable routes, Danker. Just a matter of time and experience. You have plenty of both."

The men ordered drinks and allowed the news to settle in. Before long they were teasing each other about the inevitable wrath of their wives and families, slapping each other on the back and laughing. After all, these were seafaring men with years of experience. They readily admitted, though only to each other, that they had grown accustomed to long separations from home and family. Eyeing the map and their new ports while sipping a few brown-liquor drinks, they even admitted to a budding seed of excitement for the new seas, lands, and experiences the extended routes held. They sent telegrams home, alerting loved ones of their lengthier absence before dispersing for the evening.

That night Sam slept fitfully. Was it the scotch that pained his stomach, or was it the extended route's issues festering in his gut? He attributed the pain to the anticipation of it all, swallowed two aspirin, and dismissed it.

TWO - Southern Hemisphere

1938 As the fog lifted early the next morning, the convoy motored into teal water on its new trek. Although the route was unfamiliar, the routine of docking and discharging oil was very much the same. The Arabian Sea and upper Indian Ocean held few surprises. But as they approached Cape Town weeks later, Sam stood on deck completely awed. Everything, even the air, seemed different around this southern-most tip. Here the cold waters of the Atlantic crash into the warm currents of the Indian, creating a colorful foamy frenzy. Clear blues and emerald greens dance and overtake each other as the waters tug and give way. Spectacular. Sam squeezed the handrail, shifting his view between the watery dance below, jagged green cliffs in the distance, and the bustle of the city in the foreground. By the time they discharged their load and skimmed along the coast northward to Durban, he could no longer resist South Africa. Durban appeared to be a miniature version of Cape Town, though hillier and more compact, lush and green yet very city-like. The streets were picturesque as in Leiden but busier, and so lively! Buses chugged away from the stop carrying businessmen in suits, women in sunhats held children by the hand. Dark swaths of birds swooped from tree to tree.

Sam left Danker in charge while he ventured out to find a notary to report the weather they'd encountered at sea, as was customary when docking. He felt himself scurrying like a child through the verdant landscape. Billowy clouds moved swiftly in the cool breeze against an azure sky. Jungle green mountains rose unexpectedly in the distance, a dramatic change from Leiden and everywhere familiar. Carefully following directions to the Durban notary, Sam arrived at the one-story white clapboard building. A dark wooden sign read Brown and Dean, Attorneys at Law, in white letters. He pushed open the thick wooden door. Doris, an elderly, pleasantly plump receptionist, greeted Sam and showed him to Joseph Dean's office.

Though an average sized man, Joseph appeared dwarfed by the huge mahogany desk in front of him. Joseph leapt to his feet, reaching to shake Sam's hand. "Good afternoon, Captain. You must be here to report the weather at sea," Joseph surmised, noting Sam's navy blue captain's uniform. His pleasant demeanor and kind face put Sam instantly at ease.

Sam placed his hat on his leather logbook, tucked them under his arm, and shook Joseph's hand. "That is correct, sir."

Joseph motioned for Sam to sit in the upholstered office chair across the desk from him. "What is the name of your ship?" he asked, returning to his chair and rooting through the drawer for the correct forms.

"The Janus out of Rotterdam," Sam announced clearly. He crossed his long legs and balanced his hat on the tip of his finger. "I am Captain Sam VanEck," he announced with pride. Sam never tired of hearing his own title.

"Rotterdam...Holland! My, you are a long way from home, Captain! Welcome to Durban!" Joseph said, punctuated with a warm permanent smile.

"To be perfectly honest, reporting the weather is a duty I otherwise relinquish to my first mate. But I am so impressed with this beautiful area that I wanted to take the opportunity to view the town up close." Sam leaned forward, resting his elbows on his knees as he spoke. "In fact, you are the first notary, make that the first non-shipping-related person, I have met in all my travels! But I just felt compelled to come ashore myself." Sam described the alluring scenery that propelled him off his ship and into the office.

Joseph rested his chin on his clasped hands, fascinated. Listening to Sam's glowing depiction of Cape Town and the surrounding waters made him feel downright patriotic. "Usually, I am reluctant to confess I have never been anywhere else," offered Joseph, "but hearing your description now, I admit it proudly. I used to imagine taking a year or so to live somewhere else, somewhere exotic. But now that I have my wife and son," he retrieved the framed photo from his credenza, "I am certain to live out my days right here. At least that's what she tells me!" He chuckled, handing the photo to Sam. "My wife, Helen, came from England to find me, I like to say. She still feels blessed by her good fortune...in the abundant sunshine, of course!" Joseph's laugh was contagious. "That's our son, Henry, at age three," he said proudly before replacing the photo. Eyeing Sam, Joseph asked, "forgive me, Captain, but you must have visited a variety of beautiful places in your travels. Are you equally enthralled everywhere you go?"

Sam considered the question, aware for the first time of how daft he must appear, but the realization came quickly. He watched as he spun his hat in his hands between his knees. "Yes, I have seen some wonderful sights. But I was always willing to leave them, content in knowing I would eventually be back. The Mediterranean, for instance..." Sam's face brightened, and he smiled remembering his last experience. "The water, particularly near Malta, is just...fantastic. The colors—turquois and azure—are the most beautiful I've ever seen." He hesitated then, reluctant to appear flighty to this new acquaintance. "But from the moment I laid eyes on this area, I felt myself being drawn in as though something were literally tugging on me." Sam cleared his throat and straightened his jacket, stiffening. "Now I am afraid I sound too daft, even to myself! Perhaps we should file the weather conditions," he suggested.

Joseph wrote as Sam read aloud from his logbook—speed of travel, wind speed, distance beyond shore, storms encountered and their locations—and set down his pen. "Now how about joining me for lunch? I do wish my wife were here." He checked his watch. "She should have been here by now, but that's Helen," he smiled.

"She'd enjoy telling you all about glorious South Africa. And with much enthusiasm." Joseph sprang from his chair and patted Sam's shoulder as he rushed by. "Come, come. I'll tell Doris where Helen can find us. I'm sure she'll be along momentarily."

Joseph led the way to Atomba's, a lively lunchtime spot just a short walk from the office. Dark wooden booths lined the walls, and calico curtains dressed the windows. Waitresses scurried by with two or three pitchers of beer in each hand, smiling as foam sloshed over the edge. They eased into a booth by an open window. Sounds of the lunch hour bustle filtered through and mixed with the clanging of silverware and crockery. The waitress took Joseph's order, stew for two, and she returned with two mugs of beer and a mound of warm whole grained bread still steaming from the oven. While they waited, Joseph narrated the scenes of life outside the window. Eventually their conversation contrasted life in South Africa with life in Holland. Sam laughed at the thought of Christmas in the summer heat. "No, I don't suppose you bathe in the ocean during your holidays," Joseph teased. He retrieved a photo from his wallet and offered it to Sam. "This was taken last Christmas. My son, Henry, is just five here, little buggar. Do you have children, Sam?" Joseph asked, replacing his photo.

Sam rooted for a photo in his wallet. He routinely placed the updated shots on top in the silver frame in his stateroom and paid little attention to the photos in his wallet. "Three girls," he said, still digging. "Little angels, really...well, according to their mother. Here it is," he said, relieved. "It's an old one, I'm embarrassed to say." He held the photo so Joseph could see as he pointed out each person. "Marike and Maud are nearly two years apart; they are now..." he thought a moment, "twelve and ten. Marike wears the pants in the family. She's a smart one. I'll be working for her someday, I'm sure. Maud is her right-hand assistant. They couldn't be more different. Marike wants to be a ballerina, constantly spinning about the house on tiptoe. As comfortable as she is in the center of attention directly contrasts her sister's inability to even hold the spotlight. In fact, holding Marike's spotlight is what Maud does best!" They both laughed at his unintended pun. "They are both dark beauties, like their mother." He paused. "And then we had Trudy. She's just four now," he said sheepishly. "Bit of a surprise, that one. But her smile lights up a room. Trudy is named for my wife, Gertrude, the real angel in the family," he said referring to the woman seated in the center. "She has them writing me letters and making pictures and such for my stateroom." He replaced the photo to his wallet. "I'm afraid my poor wife is up to her eyes with taking care of them. But that's the stage we are in. This extended route comes at an awful time for her. I don't look forward to her... disappointment over our lengthier trek."

"No, I don't imagine you do," offered Joseph. "We are lucky to have just the one youngster. And also an abundance of," he spread his hands palm up, alluding to the busy restaurant staff, "help. And quite reasonably too, I might add. Most people employ at least two servants. Keeps the economy going. James, our houseman, has been with us for years." Joseph raised his beer glass as a toast before taking a sip.

"Don't tell my wife!" Sam pleaded, wiping foam from his lips. "Where I come from in-home help is called in-laws, and they are neither inexpensive nor necessarily productive!"

"Look who's here," remarked Joseph, rising to greet his wife. Sam turned to see a petite woman rushing their way, her long auburn hair accentuating her every movement. "Helen, I'm delighted you've come." He clasped her hands in his and kissed her cheek, pausing a moment to smile into her eyes. "Meet Captain VanEck, all the way from Holland! He stopped in to report the weather, and we've been enjoying each other's company ever since." Draping his arm around her shoulder, he looked to Sam. "This is my wife, Helen," he said proudly, eyes twinkling. She grinned at her husband adoringly.

"Please don't get up," Helen insisted, and Sam relaxed back into his seat. She bobbed along the booth bench, and Joseph slid in beside her. "Doris told me where to find you, but honestly, I could have just followed your laughter!" She flashed a big smile at Sam. "Are you telling my husband stories, Captain?" she asked, pulling him into her clear blue eyes.

Sam extended his hand, and Helen shook his. "Do call me Sam," he instructed. "Pleasure to meet you, Helen, and yes, I've had the good fortune to have taken too much of your husband's time today." He inclined his head towards Joseph. "And I am grateful for his warm hospitality. It is very rare for me to stray from the oil yard; I usually stay close to the docks. But as I was telling your husband, the area's beauty compelled me to come ashore and learn more. And I have found a friend in the process. Your husband has been telling me about life in South Africa, and I am fascinated. He also tells me that you are quite the tour guide," he hinted.

Helen beamed at her husband. "Ah, yes, Sam. I suppose because I moved here a little later in life, I maintain the view of a tourist and appreciate my surroundings. Unlike—" she nudged her husband, "those spoiled enough to have been born and raised here who take this beautiful area for granted."

"Helen, my darling," offered Joseph, "do you have the time to give our new friend a look around? I'm certain you'll show him a South Africa he wouldn't see otherwise."

"With pleasure," she said, glancing out the window at the sunny view. "And don't we have the most perfect day! Bright and warm, not a cloud in the sky."

Sam attempted to pay the tab, but Joseph was too quick. The next time would be Sam's treat, he promised. Joseph kissed his wife goodbye and shook Sam's hand as he rose to leave. "Lovely having lunch with you, Captain. And I look forward to hearing your impressions," he said, disappearing in a flash.

As Helen bobbed to the open end of the bench, Sam unfolded himself from the booth, standing to his full height as Helen emerged. She leaned onto her toes and still only reached his chest. She noted his long legs and imagined his stride, deciding immediately against the walking tour of downtown Durban. "Let's take the car," she suggested, smiling up at him.

Helen sped the black sedan through the wide downtown streets, deftly avoiding jaywalkers and parked cars while Sam's knuckles turned white on the door handle. He was holding on for dear life! Helen gestured towards buildings as they sped past, calling out their names and offering a brief history, but Sam heard nothing. His whole focus was on the road ahead of them and the fear consuming him. He'd traveled thousands of miles in the open ocean, often during fierce storms and raging waters. But he'd never been gripped with the fear he felt with this petite maniac behind the wheel. After what seemed like an eternity, they turned onto a narrow street, and the road ahead pitched at an unmanageable angle. Helen smiled at Sam and punched the gas. The car surged upwards, quickly at first. Midway up the hill the engine strained, and Sam leaned forward as though coaxing the car onward, their speed slowing to a crawl. By this time Sam was gripping the dash with both hands, his face inches from the windshield. Beads of sweat gathered at his hairline.

Helen, seeing the fear in his face, couldn't help laughing out loud. "Relax, Sam! I haven't killed anyone yet," she teased. But it wasn't until the car was safely atop the gigantic climb that Sam exhaled. Helen parked the car and turned off the engine. "You'll want to let go of the dash now," she teased, reaching across to tug at his fingers before climbing out of the car. "You can't see anything from there," she called moving away from him. Sam took a deep breath and made the sign of the cross as he emerged from the car. He placed his hat on his head, and in an effort to conceal his fright, checked to be sure his shirttails were properly tucked while rubbing life back into his fingers.

He caught up to his tiny host at the edge of the cliff. Without looking at him, she spread her arms wide, beaming as she spoke. "The most beautiful view in all of South Africa," she declared. Sam gasped in delight. To his right, the Thukela River opened wide. Its indigo water churned and jumped over boulders and branches while rushing straight toward them before abruptly forking hundreds of feet below the point where they stood. Across the carved-out crevasse the vast, green Zulu-Natal spread endlessly. His eye followed a winding path in the brush towards majestic mountains rising in the distance. Lush green hillsides took on a violet hue under clear, brilliant skies.

A flock of long-necked birds soared on the breeze. "Blue cranes!" Helen exclaimed. "Look! Do you see their blue bellies? How gorgeous! Oh you are a lucky one, Captain Sam VanEck!" The birds turned away from them, seemingly on cue, flashing their beautiful underbellies while Helen applauded. As they surveyed the landscape, Helen explained the different provinces and occupations during the country's history. "...They essentially happened upon us en route to India," she said. "At the turn of the seventeenth century, the Dutch—" she caught herself mid-sentence. "Well it's no wonder you feel drawn here, Sam," she joked, her eyes twinkling. "Perhaps you have relatives here already, and they've been waiting a very long time for your arrival!"

They drove on sundrenched roads to Beachwood, a sophisticated cosmopolitan area. Again Sam exhaled after she parked, peeling his fingers off the black side handle, and making the sign of the cross again as he emerged from the car. The streets were bustling with beautifully dressed business people, and Helen and Sam were content to walk among them for a while, absorbing the city's energy. They spotted a bus stop and sat for a rest.

A handsome man in a dark suit hurried past them. "He's meeting his mistress," Helen suggested in a low voice.

Sam looked at his watch. "Three thirty," he whispered, "right on schedule." The man continued across the street, dodging traffic and then disappearing into, of all places, the Samson Arms Hotel. The pair giggled in amazement. Sam scoured the crowd and spotted a dowdy woman with a large tote bag. He nudged Helen and nodded in the woman's direction. "What do you suppose she has in that bag?"

Helen studied the woman waddling slightly, her face downcast, both hands clutching the handles of the bag. "Seems to be very heavy, don't you agree," she thought aloud. "My goodness!" she whispered, "She's robbed the bank!"

"Exactly!" Sam blurted, as though she'd read his mind.

"And who would suspect her? Serves them right, really," Helen continued. "She worked hard for years, and they let her go just months before her pension eligibility. Tsk, tsk," she shook her head and folded her arms over her chest as though truly annoyed.

"I hope she enjoys every cent." Sam grinned, shaking his head. "Poor dear."

"Indeed!" added Helen. "You won't find me banking there, I tell you." She was tickled at his participation. This was a game reserved for her mother or girlfriends. Joseph simply refused. She spotted a young couple embracing across the street. "Oh Sam, look." He followed her gaze to the lovers. "They just can't stand to be apart from each other...married only a month and so madly in love."

Sam added, "And to think they've known each other less than a year. Her parents were not thrilled with the short engagement—threatened to not pay for the party. But look at them, the picture of romance."

"Remarkable, really. What's that saying, 'we don't believe in rheumatism and true love—'"

"'—until after the first attack,'" Sam looked at her amazed. "Marie vonEbner," he said smiling. "I've never met anyone else who knows it."

She grinned at him, charmed by their connection.

From all directions people suddenly collected at their bus stop, and Sam checked his watch. "Apparently, they're right on schedule for the four o'clock bus. And I'm afraid I have taken too much of your time. I should be getting back to my ship," he said, standing and offering her his hand.

She smiled up at him then, noticing for the first time his bright blue eyes. She held them for a moment before placing her hand on his upturned palm. It felt warm and soft under hers. She stood quickly, shoved her hands in her jacket pockets, and led the way to the car. Sam snuck into the back seat and waited for her to notice. Helen arranged herself and started the car. As she bent to look for Sam through the passenger window, she spotted him in the periphery, and a smirk crept across her face.

He exhaled a laugh, "I feel much safer back here," he joked, already feeling comfortable enough to tease her.

"Suit yourself," she trumped him right back and threw the car into gear. Having her passenger safely stowed in the rear only emboldened her. She sped through downtown Beachwood, onto the highway, and through the town of Durban. When they arrived at the office, Sam emerged from the car, crossing himself in earnest, but this time he was laughing along with her. She stepped from the car, and he closed the door for her, tapping it affectionately. "Magic," he said, shaking his head and still chuckling. "The car must be magic."

Doris was on the phone when the bell sounded their arrival, so they slipped past her to Joseph's office. He rose to greet them, delighted by their cheerful demeanor. "Looks as though you enjoyed yourselves," he remarked.

Sam spoke first, twirling his hat on his finger. "I have not enjoyed an afternoon on land as thoroughly as I have today," he said smiling at Helen before turning to Joseph. "Thank you for arranging such an enchanting tour guide, Joseph. Helen has shown me the beauty and the bustle of this glorious area, and she leaves me wanting to learn more."

"Well he's an easy student," Helen offered, slipping her arm through Joseph's. She was relieved he didn't comment on her driving. Joseph wouldn't have been pleased to hear that! She nodded at her husband and added, "There is plenty more to see, Sam. We'd be delighted to show you. How long will you be in town?"

"Only a brief turnabout this time, I'm afraid. But our new route will bring us back soon, I imagine. You have both been so gracious, and I thank you," he said bowing slightly. "Next time, lunch is on me," he reminded Joseph, who conceded, securing the deal with a handshake, grasping Joseph's hand in both of his.

Joseph had become immediately fond of this new acquaintance and truly looked forward to their next meeting. After Sam left he told his wife so. "Interesting man, isn't he, Helen? You can easily spot good character in a person—puts one instantly at ease. Did he strike you that way too, dear?"

"Absolutely. Why I didn't think twice about going off with him, a perfect stranger. In fact, he didn't seem like a stranger at all. Do you know he even indulged in my making up stories while we people-watched in Beachwood?"

Joseph laughed, "Now I know he is a kind soul!" He thought a moment, shuffling papers on his desk. "I do hope he spends some time with us next visit. I'd like to hear more about life in Holland, wouldn't you? Can't imagine living in such a cold environment." He wrapped his arms around his wife. "We have a nice life here in temperate Durban, don't we, darling?" he said, planting a kiss on her forehead. "Let's go home and see what James is cooking up for dinner." He placed papers into his briefcase. "And showing off photos of Henry makes me miss him all the more," he smiled.

Helen hugged her husband a moment; then she placed a hand on his chest. "Let me check my desk for messages before we leave. I'll be along shortly, darling." Ten minutes later they said their goodbyes to Doris and headed home to Merriwold, their haven on the hill.

The Janus remained docked in Durban Harbour for the night. The air became downright steamy, and shortly after sunset, a tropical shower fell. The crew played like children on the wet slippery deck. Sam retreated to his cabin. He didn't mind their behavior, but he didn't want to openly condone it either. He tuned into his lifeline, the BBC, and classical music came through remarkably clear. He poured himself a scotch, sat on his leather settee, and slid his shoes neatly underneath. He sipped his drink, leaned his head back, and closed his eyes, listening to the sounds of his heaven—summer rain, contented crew, Bach, and the rhythmic lapping of the sea against his ship. The next sip brought the now familiar stab of pain to his stomach. Wincing, he abandoned the scotch and let his mind drift through the South African sights, to his new friend Joseph, and ultimately to Helen. He smiled thinking about their antics on the bus stop and laughed aloud reliving her crazy driving. Already he looked forward to the next run.

While loading the ship in Bahrain, Sam and Danker stocked up on whiskey at the local liquor store in case the crew grew restless during the long voyage home. But they were blessed with clear skies and calm seas during their return trek. A sense of relief permeated the ship as they entered more familiar waters. As they cleared the Suez Canal, Sam realized they wouldn't miss all of the holidays. He pushed all thoughts of South Africa aside to focus on the trek at hand and the family waiting at home.

THREE – Leiden

December 1938 "Pop!" Maud squealed at the sound of the front door closing downstairs. Trudy dropped her dolls on their cot and ran to the stairs, her patent leather shoes tapping across the bare wood floor. Marike thundered past her, charging down the stairs while Trudy held tightly to the bannister, placing both feet on a tread before continuing. When Trudy finally caught up to her sisters and Pop in the front room, Marike was pouting.

"You missed Sinterklaas," she muttered, folding her arms tightly across her chest and stamping her foot.

"I am so sorry to have missed your favorite holiday," Pop said, bending to cup Marike's face in his huge hand. His other hand engulfed Maud's shoulder, and she was nearly hidden by his body. "Come now, you must know I tried." He lifted her chin so she couldn't help but see him. "We sped through the water as fast as we could!" He sucked in his cheeks, making his lips look like a fish, his blue eyes bulging. Marike laughed then and wrapped her arms around his waist. "I'm certain your mother treated you well," he said, turning his attention to Mom. She was leaning in the doorway to the dining room, waiting her turn, a damp dishtowel thrown over her shoulder. "You'll have to tell me all about the festivities over dinner," he offered, winking at her, "because I am sure your lovely mother has prepared something wonderful for us." He loosened his grip on the Ms, stepped towards his wife, and opened his arms wide.

Mom fell into them. "Oh Sam!" she sighed, burying her face in his chest, weeping.

"Why you crying, Mom?" Trudy asked, tugging on her skirt. "Why you not happy Pop's home?"

Everyone laughed, and Mom bent to kiss the crown of Trudy's head. "Tears of joy, my darling, tears of joy," she whispered, squeezing her shoulders.

Trudy trained her smile on Pop, waiting. "There's my blue-eyed girl," he said at last, scooping her up slowly in his long arms. She caught her breath and held on tightly. "Trudy, you're growing like a weed! Pretty soon you'll be as tall as Mom!" Despite her fear of being so high off the floor, she held his face with both hands and planted a kiss on his roughly stubbled cheek. He returned her to the floor to wrap his arms around Mom, leading her to the kitchen. "Something smells wonderful, Ger. How I've missed your cooking!" The girls rushed to follow, Marike spinning on her toes; Maud ducking to avoid being hit by Marike's swooping arms.

The massive dining room table was filled—German sausage, cabbage, mashed potatoes—many of Pop's favorites. Just like Sinterklaas but better. Pop was seated at the head of the table, and Mom and Trudy were seated on the side closer to the kitchen. The Ms were seated across from them talking nonstop. Between bites, Pop asked questions so they'd continue talking and allow him to eat. Mom switched her fork to her left hand so she could hold Pop's left in her lap. Every few minutes she'd raise Pop's hand to kiss it. When he winked at Mom, Trudy could almost feel the love thrown in her direction. She hoped some would land on her and kept the smile on her face just in case.

Before Pop came home he'd sent Mom a telegraph that made her angry, upset enough to cry. The Ms approached Mom about it. Maud wrapped her arms around Mom's shoulders, but Mom only dried her hands on her apron, patted away her tears, and waved her hand in the air. "We'll be fine," she exhaled. "Just a bit longer route now, that's all."

Later that night, after Mom had calmed herself completely, Trudy found her mother in the front room on the sofa and climbed onto her lap. Holding Mom's face in her little hands and looking into her deep brown eyes, Trudy asked, "Why you sad, Mom?"

Mom curled a wisp of Trudy's hair around her finger. She looked at her small child, searching for the right words. "I miss Pop a lot. And I know you girls do too." She thought a minute. "Let's just say you're going to have to memorize a few more ports on Pop's route, Trudy. You think you can do that?"

"I can do that, Mom. You help me?" Trudy searched her Mom's eyes. "Then you won't be sad anymore?"

Mom tilted her head. "I am so happy to have your blue eyes to look into, Trudy, my love," she said, smoothing Trudy's hair behind her ear. "We will be just fine, won't we?" She forced a smile then, but Trudy could see the sadness shift in her tired eyes.

Since Pop's return, Trudy wanted to learn more about this new route that had made Mom so sad. About three weeks into Pop's stay, she got her chance. Mom asked the Ms to clean up dinner so she and Pop could talk in the front room. After putting away all the food and wiping down the table, Marike danced to the sink to wash dishes, and Maud stood ready to dry. Trudy tiptoed from the kitchen into the dim dining room, her woolen socks sliding on the bare wood floor. Concentrating on the voices coming from the other side of the staircase, she heard Pop say he didn't have a choice and something about a new company in charge. "How much longer," Mom continued to ask. And then, because she'd raised her voice, Trudy clearly heard Mom say "no more." But Pop was shushing her because she was crying again. Trudy, upset at the sound of Mom's crying, dissolved onto the floor clutching Ribbon, her stuffed bunny, tightly. Clearly, she heard Mom say "worry," and then "German," and thought about the dinner sausages. But food is nothing to worry about, and Pop was telling Mom not to worry. He said "new trek," but Trudy was too naive to make the connection.

"OK, ok, shushhhh," he soothed her. "One more run, Ger," he conceded loud and clear. "I'm here through spring...." Then he lowered his voice again so only bits and pieces were audible, something about the holidays and Old Year's Night.

By the time St. Nicholas Eve arrived, mistletoe hung everywhere. The air was drenched with the sweet aroma of Mom's constant baking, and the Ms had decorated mounds of sugar cookies—pink angels, red bells, green trees. There had never been so much food in the house! The sideboard in the dining room held stacks of tins bursting with cookies, cakes, and pastries of all kinds. Trudy licked the spoon from the chocolate cake batter while the Ms washed the pans. The delicious chocolate scent of that cake would call out to Trudy all evening.

"Come, come, let's go!" Mom clapped her hands, hurrying everyone along. Mom poured hot cocoa into five metal thermoses, one for each of them. The girls were bundled into wool coats, knit hats, new boots, and warm mittens. Mom wrapped a pink scarf around Trudy's neck so only her bright blue eyes were visible under her hat. Thermoses in hand, they headed to the town square to join the neighbors. Not Leah, of course, but many others gathered around the pavilion to hear the church choir sing Christmas carols. The notes floated on crisp air and bounced off the clapboard shops and red brick apartment buildings lining the square. "Saint Nicholas, my dear good friend...now me something give..." they sang, their breath rising in puffs of white over their heads. A gigantic fir tree stood behind the choir, bright lights and baby's breath decorating its branches. Afterwards the grownups merrily talked with friends and neighbors while little ones became overheated chasing each other. All the while, the Ms and their friends tried to look disinterested. Pop and Mom had grown up in this town and knew everyone in it. Lots of *happy Christmases* and *good new years* were heard above the din of conversation, the accordion, and children's squeals.

The Ms claimed they were too cold and wanted instead to get ready for St. Nick's visit the next day. Pop instructed them to take Trudy along home; he and Mom would join them soon. They were enjoying themselves too much to leave just yet. Maud tucked her thermos and Trudy's into the crook of her arm and reached for Trudy's mittened hand. Marike took Trudy's other hand, and the three scurried along icy streets to home, with the wind whipping at their backs. Trudy grinned all the way. At home they giggled with anticipation as they placed wooden clogs on the front stoop. Trudy pressed her hands together and closed her eyes, praying that St.

Nick would bring only dark chocolate this year. Inside, the M's unraveled Trudy's scarf and hung her wool coat on the peg. In return she hugged them, reaching her little arms around their waists and laying her head on their stomachs, as long as they'd allow. Then they helped themselves to thick slices of that delicious chocolate cake.

On New Year's Day when the sun shone brightly overhead, the family bundled up again and headed out back to the canal for the annual parade. The Canters were among the crowd, and the parents visited comfortably together. Leah, Trudy, and all the young children shrieked with excitement as colorful boats glided by. Some boats held choirs in dark velvet costume, their voices traveling easily across the water. Others shot bands of red, green, and blue water into the sky. A nativity scene with live animals floated by on one boat, and another, rimmed with flames, held jugglers tossing fire into the air. At last a smaller vessel came into view carrying a man dressed as St. Nick. All the children tumbled over each other laughing and scurrying to claim their share while he threw candy to the crowds along the water's edge. Afterwards up in Leah's room, the two friends pooled and divvied up their treats—nougats for Leah, dark chocolate for Trudy. They agreed to have just one candy a day so it lasted longer, completely unaware just how scarce candy and carefree days would soon become.

FOUR – Durban

In early July of 1939, the Janus was gliding once again in Rotterdam's cool waters, heading towards the southern hemisphere. Just before dawn that morning, as crimson seeped into the charcoal sky, Ger stood on the front stoop wrapped in a cotton blanket. Her breath became bursts of fog as she uttered prayers for her husband's safe travels into the cool morning air. She shifted her weight against the wooden rail as she watched his silhouette grow smaller in the distance. She felt as though her heart were tied to his feet, and each step ripped another piece from her chest. At times, watching as he left over the years, the pain was excruciating. Finally, he turned the corner and disappeared from view. He would catch the bus to the train and the train to Rotterdam. "This will be the last run," he'd promised. She had reminded him often of that promise throughout his stay.

As usual, Danker met his Captain on the bridge while inspecting the ship. Although the air was chilly, they crossed their arms and lifted their faces to the warming sun. Later the two met in Sam's stateroom to catch up. Sam poured them each some tea in china cups, and they settled in for a chat while the BBC provided Tchaikovsky. Sam wondered how Danker's family felt about the lengthier route. "They are content with my traveling profession," Danker reported, "for as long as I am." Sam searched his face expectantly. "And I am," Danker continued haltingly, rubbing his rugged jaw, "but not like you, Captain. You seem to enjoy the seas more and more. I would like to have a wife someday and a home, maybe a family...but all of the above will definitely be on land!"

Sam sank into his leather settee, holding his teacup and saucer in his lap, eyes to the ceiling, remembering the promise he had made to Gertrude. He met Danker's eyes. "At first the idea of being a seafarer nearly repulsed me. Live on a ship for months at a time?" he said swatting the air with a dismissive hand. "I truly couldn't imagine being so far away from Ger and the girls. And although I adore the sea, living atop it is something else entirely. And," he shot Danker a smirk, "the bugs around the Gulf were an unexpected treat." Danker chuckled at the sarcasm, imagining the bird-sized flies. Sam's smile faded as he grew pensive. "The world is huge, isn't it, Danker?" he said, intently sitting upright. "We've been blessed by the chance to step outside of quaint little Holland and catch a glimpse. And the more I see, the more I want to see. Everywhere we go my eyes are opened to different cultures, amazing sights. The world is brilliant! Each time I'm home, the seas pull me back, as though I am tethered to the tides. And I am increasingly—" Sam caught himself, unwilling to say the words aloud. He downed the rest of his tea and set the cup and saucer aside. Sam leaned toward Danker, elbows resting on knees, hands rubbing. "Suffice it to say, Danker, that one never knows what life has in store. We stay true to our mission, but an errant storm, a false reading occurs, and we are yawed off course." He sat back, draped a long arm on the back of the cushion, and found his friend's eyes again. "Or are we? Perhaps what we perceive as an unexpected turn is actually our intended path." He watched his thumb rub the opposing palm before continuing. "I never planned to become a seafarer. And I certainly never expected to be grateful for this life, but there you have it. I am hooked." He looked up through the skylight, let the statement hang in the air. "But this arrangement is killing Ger. I told her this would be my last run."

Danker gasped. "I can see how this situation is weighing on you, Captain, but in order to change command, well, there's simply not time."

Sam raised a hand. "You're going to tell me there's protocol, and the process takes weeks, months, Danker, I know. I realize that, my friend. But—"

"But Gertrude doesn't know that."

Sam leaned forward on his knees. "I just need more time to make the arrangements. Now that the decision is made, I just have to act on that decision." He eyed Danker. "And I'll recommend you to replace me, Danker."

"Captain, I don't know if I—"

With a raised hand, Sam interrupted him. "Take the promotion, man, and the added salary! And then find something else. But your resume will thank you." Sam could see he was making sense to Danker. "When we dock in Bahrain prior to our return, I'll get with Bertie to initiate the paperwork. With any luck, I'll get another trip before hanging up my cap. In the meantime—" Sam looked at Danker, who merely nodded. He understood this was to be kept confidential.

With the help of guide planes, the Janus and her convoy mates were navigated through rough waters in dimming late afternoon light into the Bahrain docks. Sam hurried away from the noise and stench and towards the office.

"Ah, Captain," Bertie's smiling pink face greeted him. The two shook hands, and Sam removed his hat. "I trust you had pleasant holidays at home?"

"Wonderful, Bertie, thank you." Sam patted his belly. "And lovely to have my wife's cooking, too." Sam's hat spun on his finger while he waited for Bertie to fetch the mail. In his ship's pile were the orders: Cape Town, Elizabeth, East London, Durban—all South Africa. Sam could hardly believe his good fortune.

"Good news, Captain?" asked Bertie.

Sam hadn't realized he was grinning. "The best" was all he said as he scurried out the door.

Several weeks later under clear skies, the Janus pulled into the docks in Durban's Harbour. After months at sea, Captain and crew darted off ship towards land like school children headed for recess. The southern hemisphere's spring was evident in the crisp shade and warm sunshine. Sam left his ship in Danker and Einer's capable hands.

Sam found his way quite easily this time to the Brown & Dean law offices. He smoothed his shirt and made certain his belt was straight. He removed his hat upon entering and was warmly greeted by Doris. She showed him through the teak-lined outer office to Joseph's, and he leapt from behind his desk to welcome Sam. "Good to see you again, my friend!" he said, shaking Sam's hand with his right and clutching Sam's elbow with his left. "Helen and I were wondering when you'd return...she'll be delighted, as am I. How was the journey?" he asked, motioning for Sam to sit and resuming his seat behind the desk. He rooted for the necessary forms to record the weather. They knew to take care of business before moving onto friendlier topics. Sam spouted technical terms while Joseph wrote quickly. Finally, Joseph set down his pen and clasped his hands in front of him. "Now tell me, how have you been? And how were your holidays? As I remember, you were quite keen on getting home in time. Were you successful?"

"Yes, well, almost," Sam's hat spun around in his hands as he spoke. "My oldest girl, Marike, was not pleased I'd missed her favorite, Sinterklaas, but she forgave me pretty quickly." The thought suddenly occurred to Sam that Joseph might recommend a doctor to check on the increasing pain in his stomach. If extended care were necessary, as he was beginning to suspect, he could easily arrange it and a drydock period simultaneously. And Ger would be grateful if he took care of himself rather than add to her burden. So grateful that she'd accept another "last" run perhaps. "Forgive me, but I just had a thought..." Without going into too much detail, Sam acquired a recommendation for a doctor who worked out of Addington Hospital. Joseph's confidence was all the assurance Sam needed. Sam wrote the information on a piece of paper and slid it into his pocket, thanking him. He would make the call as soon as he returned to the ship.

"Well, look who the tide washed in," Helen exclaimed, recognizing the back of Sam's blond head. He rose to greet her, extending his hand, but she pulled him in for a hug instead. He caught a hint of her sweet flowery scent. "Lovely to see you again, Sam." She stepped back and smiled up at him, her blue eyes dancing, her soft face beaming. "Please sit; do you have time to spare?" she asked, propping herself on Joseph's desk and swinging her silk-stockinged leg.

"I was just about to tell him about our holidays, my love," Joseph said. "But now that you're here," he gestured to her with both outstretched hands, relinquishing the stage. Joseph cupped the side of his mouth and spoke to Sam. "She tells a much better story," he said, his light eyes twinkling.

"Oh they were lovely, just lovely. And I can hardly wait to start them all over again soon! We decorate every inch of our Merriwold—that's what we call our home—happy world in an obscure German translation. I have some German from my mum's side." She spoke with her hands waving in the air, and her blue eyes sparkling with enthusiasm. "Anyway, Christmastime is my absolute favorite time of year," she said, clasping her hands in her lap and smiling broadly. "We host a traditional luncheon on Christmas day for neighbors, family, and friends—" She shot a glance at Joseph. "Before Henry arrived, our tradition was to host a wonderful party two nights before Christmas that always lasted into the wee hours, didn't we, darling?" She smiled at him and rolled her eyes. "But those days are over, and we are very content with our daytime event. There's lots of music and drink, of course. James and I prepare for weeks, and I think we have as much fun preparing as our guests do that day." Joseph nodded in agreement. "But the true delight is in watching Henry on Christmas morning." Her face glowed at the mention of her son's name. "His favorite gift by far was a book on bugs, of all things! He is forever chasing salamanders and toads, anything that crawls or creeps in the dirt. Makes a frightful mess of his clothes!" Her face lent such expression to the story, captivating Sam, who hung on every word. She continued talking until the phone's ring interrupted her. Joseph motioned for privacy with a finger to his lips, so Sam and Helen tiptoed into the quiet hall, closing the door behind them.

"May I take you two for lunch?" whispered Sam, bending close to her ear.

"Please do!" she whispered back with a giggle. "I forgot to eat breakfast, and I'm famished!"

Forgetting a meal was unthinkable to Sam, and he couldn't help but laugh. "How does one forget to *eat*?" he shook his head and turned his hat in his hands, smiling. Her manner surprised and delighted him. "Are you saying your petite figure is by accident?"

"Believe me, I love to eat! The last thing I plan to do is skip a meal!"

"Well now I am concerned that I can afford your lunch," he teased. "Perhaps we can find a pastry shop instead?"

Joseph abruptly opened his office door looking very serious, briefcase in hand. "I'm afraid that was the courthouse calling. Judge Jacobs is having a difficult time and asked that I get there straight away. I am terribly sorry, but I must go now." He shook Sam's hand. "Of all the days to have an emergency, Sam, I do apologize." He straightened and thought before continuing. "Honestly, I have looked forward to your return since you left, Captain. Are you able to meet later, come to the house for dinner perhaps?"

"I am afraid not, Joseph. But I thank you for the invitation. These longer treks take a bit of getting used to for the crew, and we will be leaving shortly. I will arrange for our next drydock in Durban, so I can plan for that personal issue we discussed and have more time to spend here as well. Go take care of your Judge. If it's alright with you, I'll take your lovely wife to lunch and look forward to seeing you next time."

They shook hands again. "That sounds like a perfectly good plan, Captain. I'll look forward to then." He turned to his wife, inclined his head toward hers. "I do wish I could join you. Enjoy your visit, and I will see you here in a few hours. I'll call Doris to look up any information that I don't already have," he said patting his leather briefcase, his mind already on the task at hand. He pointed to Sam, "safe travels," he cautioned. "And do let us help you when the time comes." Sam was sure he would be able to count on Joseph when needed.

The Corner Café was just a short walk from the office. The food was not great but would suffice for the limited time they had. The weather was cool and breezy, so they sat inside at a table for two in the rear. The place was clean and bright, and the ruffled blue curtains gave it a homey feel. The waitress brought chicken salad sandwiches for them both, and Helen dove in, quickly devouring half her sandwich before Sam barely made any progress at all on his.

"I don't know you well enough to say this, but I'll venture a guess that the last five minutes at least equaled your longest stretch of silence to date."

The comment caught Helen by surprise, and she was tickled by it. She covered her mouth with her napkin as she laughed. "How do you know me so well already?" she grinned, not expecting an answer. "Sometimes I'll be half finished with a meal before Joseph even begins. It's terrible! But rare." She straightened and feigned seriousness. "Usually I eat slowly and very lady like," she teasingly assured him.

But Sam's mind repeated her question. How do I know you so well? He'd wondered that himself. Perhaps it was her husband's obvious endorsement that enabled her to reveal herself so candidly. He decided not to spend too much time thinking about the reasons and just delight in the fact that he had friends at a fantastically beautiful port on the other end of the world.

Helen finished her sandwich and chatted on easily about Henry while Sam ate his.

"I look forward to meeting him someday," Sam said between bites.

Then Helen remembered Sam's words to her husband. She looked at Sam and smiled, laying her hand on his forearm. "Please don't think I'm terribly rude," she began. "But if you don't mind my asking, what personal issue were you referring to when you were speaking with Joseph?"

It took Sam a moment to remember. "Oh...it's nothing, really." But he could see she wouldn't be satisfied until she heard the details. He put down his sandwich and took a sip of lemonade. "I'm having stomach issues and asked for a recommendation. Nothing serious." By the look on her face, he knew she still wasn't satisfied. He finished his sandwich and wiped his hands on his napkin. "I am afraid I'll need some medical attention, and just in case, I can arrange for the ship to be attended to at the same time. Living at sea has some disadvantages, you know." He grinned, hoping that would be the end of the discussion.

In one long breath she said, "What type of attention? Will you need time to recuperate? You'll have to come to Merriwold and stay with us so we can take care of you."

Sam raised a hand, "Now hold on a minute, your imagination is much too vivid, and you are too kind. No one said anything about recuperating. It's just a hunch that something is even the least bit amiss."

"Well if there is something wrong, Captain Sam VanEck, you'll be coming home with us. Plan on it. And we won't take no for an answer," she said defiantly.

Sam could see the subject was closed. He was enormously grateful, and the thought of spending time with them in their home made him hope for the worst, silly as that seemed. They ordered apple pie a la mode for dessert with chocolate sauce on Helen's.

The time passed too quickly, and when he did glance at his watch, Sam saw he was close to being late and became flustered. He reached for his hat and searched for his wallet. "Helen, I am delighted you were able to join me today. You are a joy to be with," he said motioning for the waitress and paying the tab. He promised they'd have more time during his next visit. He followed her out the door and into the sunlight. He adjusted his hat, checked his shirt was snug before quickly setting off in the direction of the office. Helen struggled to keep pace with him. She slowed him with a hand to the crook of his arm, and he whirled around to look at her, his attention already back on board. "Sam, let's say goodbye here and go our separate ways. Wouldn't that make more sense?" He squirmed and checked his watch. "I am impressed that you feel you need to walk me back, but no need. Thank you for lunch, my friend. Now go, shoo, before I make you look bad to your crew."

He reached for her hand and bent to kiss it. "Thank you, Helen. You are most kind. Once again I thank you for sharing your time so generously, and I look forward to seeing you next time." He knew he should run off, but he simply didn't want to leave her. "I really must go," he said, his eyes locked on hers. She looked so beautiful to him, especially the way the sunlight played brightly off her auburn hair. He noticed for the first time that her eyelashes were the same bright auburn, saw the freckles faintly spilled across her nose. Everything about her was bright and light. After an awkward minute, Sam realized he was still holding her hand. He dropped it clumsily and let out an uncomfortable laugh. Blushing, he felt like a teenager. "Please excuse me, Helen. I really must go. Till next time." He doffed his hat and took off in long, determined strides.

Sam found Danker waiting patiently. Together they inspected the ship before he checked the paperwork. All was in perfect order, and he thanked Danker for a fine job. "You are quite capable, my friend. Next time we'll drydock here, and you can try your hand at captaining a while longer."

"But Captain—"

"I know, Danker, this was to be my last run. It just became my second to last."

But when they arrived in Bahrain, Sam collected the ship's orders and learned how wrong he was. Rumblings of the German army's escapades had been taken too lightly. *Surely the British would easily thwart the Germans if necessary* had been the general opinion. Hitler's threats had become real, and he was moving too close to home. Nazis had invaded Poland, owned the North Sea, and the expectation was that the Netherlands could be next, regardless of their Neutrality Agreement. As a precaution in this worsening situation, Caltex ordered the Janus and its convoy mates to maintain only a southern route until further notice.

Sam gathered the convoy captains and their first mates to the officers club. As Sam delivered the news, he saw chins drop, mouths gape open. These fearless teammates appeared pitifully frightened. They had all been aware of Hitler's dalliances and dismissed them with the rest of the world. But now his threats were real, and they were completely powerless to stop him. If they were able to commandeer a ship and return to their loved ones, they would immediately do so. But the thought was ludicrous. Any of their ships required a full crew to operate, and they could not endanger the crew's lives in what could well be a suicide trek. They had no choice but to follow Caltex's orders and stay south. Realizing this, the men's grumbles grew louder, their palms rubbing palms and foreheads as eyes held each other's for only a glint.

Malta and Port Said became the Janus's northernmost ports, and new southern ports in Sri Lanka, Australia, and New Zealand were added. The ensuing six months were spent servicing these new ports while the realization, *We can't go home*, repeated in everyone's minds. All chatter came to a deafening halt. They were in constant fear for their families and friends back home. The crew became edgy and short tempered with each other as a result, and squabbles broke out routinely among them. Sam's stateroom became his refuge; his crew and yardmen, his only human contact. The world's focus turned to a small monster, and the monster threatened his family and his country. Sam kept his little radio tuned to the BBC round the clock, and his officers often joined him to listen to reports of the horror unfold. All the while, Sam sent desperate letters and telegrams to his family in Leiden with little response. In May of 1940 Sam's biggest fears were realized. Holland, despite her neutral claim, immediately fell to Hitler's siege. All hope of communication was lost.

Each night before bed Sam held the photo of his family and prayed until he fell asleep. He tried to keep his mind from imagining what they could be going through. Angry frustration gnawed at him from the inside. Schemes and thoughts constantly circled in his mind for months. Finally, he surrendered to his hopeless inability to help and, instead, began to fervently pray they'd merely live through it. There was nothing else he could do.

FIVE – Durban

Mid-morning, 8 November 1939, Helen stood on her second floor veranda absorbed in the vast Indian Ocean below. Crashing waves kept beat with the throbbing inside her head. She didn't feel summer's warm breeze. She hadn't felt anything for nearly three days. She heard the soft then loud knocks on her bedroom door, but she didn't answer, hoping to prevent the day from unfolding. As the knob turned and the door pushed open, white sheers moved with the breeze, skimmed the whitewashed wood floor. Helen concentrated harder on the thundering surf below.

"Helen?" Her mother's hushed voice sounded distant, muffled. Abigail gently approached her daughter, turned her by the shoulders to face her. Helen appeared frail and shrunken under the black hat, her dress hung lifelessly from slumped shoulders. Abigail's heart ached as she folded her petite Helen in her arms. She'd watched with pride as her daughter matured over the prior ten years. Watched the happiness seep into her life, rooting out traces of the hard life she'd known before Joseph. Now her blue eyes were devoid of life, her face drawn and pale. Although they had already experienced more than their fair share of sorrow, death was one lesson she wasn't yet prepared to teach.

Back in England, Helen's father had left them when Helen was a child. Abigail was too grief-stricken to deal with her impish daughter, and Helen grew into a rebellious youth. Her good looks and quick wit helped her sail through school effortlessly, allowing too much time for fun.

When her pregnant eighteen-year-old daughter eloped with an RAF pilot, Abigail was neither surprised nor particularly devastated. His orders took them to South Africa, where he promptly left them. Stranded in a strange country and with a three-month-old baby, Helen begged her mother to come to Durban. When Abigail arrived, baby April was placed in her arms like a peace offering, and Abigail was dubbed "Grannie." As the two women peered into April's round cherub face topped with a shock of black hair, the bitterness melted away, and they started anew. The subsequent years drew them into a dependable alliance that blossomed into a strong friendship. They continued to work on their mother-daughter relationship.

"Mother, the tears won't come. What's the matter with me?"

Grannie pulled her daughter to her soft bosom. "Oh, my baby girl, you are in shock," she said stroking her back. "We'll get through this," Grannie assured her. "We'll get through this together." She squeezed her daughter's hands twice, their signal for *all is well*. "The car is here now. Shall I get the children?"

Helen willed herself to move towards the door. "No, I'll get them," she sighed. "Please tell the driver we will be down shortly." Grannie slowly walked along the long hallway and made her way down the stairs unsteadily, favoring her bad leg. Helen approached Henry's room and took a deep breath before entering. Henry sat on his bed, head down, feet dangling several inches above the floor, hands tucked under his thighs. "Hello, Henry," Helen whispered, sitting beside him. She wrapped her arm around his small shoulders, and he fell weeping into her lap. "Shhh, my love. We'll have time for tears later. Let's try to get through this morning together, shall we?" Henry slid off the bed and stood before his mother, wiping his eyes with the back of his hand. His dark hair was cut close and slicked in place, thanks to Grannie's efforts. Helen ran a finger down his cheek, wondering if he would ever be the same happy child he was before his daddy's death. How much of his youth had the last few days erased? She held her young son's face with both hands, "Be strong, my little man." She searched his sad pale eyes. "Grannie is waiting for you downstairs. Will you go to her now? Tell her April and I will be down directly?"

"Can Floyd come too, mama?" Henry held up the stuffed rabbit from under his arm.

"Of course he can, my darling." Helen knelt on the braided floormat and hugged her son. He felt tiny and limp in her arms. "I love you," she whispered, restraining her own tears. Then she tapped his bottom to send him on his way. He reluctantly obliged.

Helen knocked softly on April's door and entered the small room. April stood quickly and stopped brushing her thin brown hair at the sight of her mother. She had grown into an awkward girl and, at sixteen, had the social grace of a two-year-old but none of the confidence or enthusiasm. She wore a black blouse and tights; her gray linen skirt lay on the bed.

"April, you're not ready? The car is waiting," her frustration obvious.

April rubbed her hands nervously and mumbled, "Mother, I . . . I wasn't sure . . ."

"Speak *up*, April," she spoke softly, rubbing at the sudden pain in at her temples. Her patience exhausted in an instant. "What did you say?"

April looked away from her mother. "Joseph wasn't . . . I wasn't sure if you . . . wanted me to come," she said clearly at last, pinning her deep-set dark eyes squarely on her mother's.

Helen folded her arms across her chest. "April, Joseph was the only father you have ever known. Of course you should be there. And I could use your help with Henry. He's just so...little," her slow, steady voice suddenly caught in her throat as she spoke, clearly concerned for her six-year-old. Helen rubbed at her throbbing head, "I have enough on my mind today, April, please don't add to it. Now do hurry; we are all waiting," she chirped, her frustration climbing.

The little church couldn't accommodate the funeral cortege, so two hundred white folding chairs were set up on the grass, and the service was held graveside. The day was already hot, but a welcomed breeze silently moved the leaves in the trees. By the time Helen's car arrived, every available chair was filled, and several people stood. The community had suffered a loss, and people gathered to console one another. After the pastor's eulogy, former clients and peers took turns at the podium sharing stories and farewells. Acquaintances paid their respects; childhood friends cried openly. Joseph had touched so many lives and helped each person there in some way. The tribute was overwhelmingly beautiful.

Finally Helen was left to talk with her husband one last time. She placed an unsteady hand on the casket. "My darling Joseph," she whispered, crying bitterly. "I don't know what you saw in that wreck of a girl, but I am forever grateful you noticed." She held Henry close. "I will raise our son to be just like his Daddy. And I will love you forever." She kissed her hand and transferred it to the casket. Henry tugged on her skirt and led her to the car.

The last visitor left Merriwold at dusk. James had organized the flowers in various vases down the center of the dining room table. He prepared a light supper of cold salads, which Grannie, Henry, and Helen sat down to eat.

"Where did April run off to?" asked Grannie.

"Oh, mum, I don't know. She must have gone off with David. Where else?" She sighed and attempted to rub away the tears welling. "At least she was able to jolt me from shock. Don't know if I should be grateful..." her voice trailed off and she blew her nose again. "Do you know she hadn't planned on coming today?" She looked at her mother incredulously. "Never occurs to her to be helpful to me." Shaking her head she added, "The girl is just like her father." She set down her fork and rubbed her temples again. "I can't...I don't know how..." She looked across the table at her son, his shoulders hunched, leaning over his plate, pushing food around but not taking a bite. She wondered how they'd continue breathing.

"I was astounded by the number of people there today, Helen," Grannie offered in a cheery voice. "Never dreamed so many people could be acquainted with one person," she said, hoping to raise their spirits.

But Helen's attention was on her son. "Hear that, Henry? Your daddy was a very special man," Helen began but quickly saw Henry was too tired to listen. She moved from her chair and knelt on the floor beside him. "I was proud of you today, my little man," she said kissing his head. She pulled him out of his seat and hugged him close. "Get ready for bed, and I'll be along to tuck you in." She tapped his bottom, and he slowly left the room. Helen watched after him. "Will we ever be able to fill the gaping hole in his life?" she cried. "He's just so little . . .I really don't know how we'll survive, let alone have Christmas this year..." Her voice broke as tears thickened in her throat. She crossed to her mother and placed a hand on her shoulder. "Thank you for being there with me today." As Helen kissed her mother's waiting cheek, Grannie covered her daughter's hand with her own and squeezed it twice. There were no words yet to comfort her grieving daughter.

With great effort Helen dragged her tired body up the stairs. Henry's muffled sobs were audible as Helen entered his dimly lit room. He looked so tiny in the light of the small lamp on his bedside table. The bookshelf held mostly picture books, a set of jacks, dominoes—pieces of a childhood he wouldn't get to finish. She knelt on the floormat beside his bed and smoothed his brown mop. She wanted to take away all the pain, snap her fingers, and shake them from this nightmare. She prayed for the words to soothe her aching son, but none came.

"April said Daddy's never coming back," blurted Henry, tears flowing.

Helen rubbed his back and hushed him. "That's true, sweetie. But let's do our best to never let him fully go away." He rolled to his back, making room for her to sit, comforted by her familiar scent. "Close your eyes," she urged. "Imagine Daddy's open arms as you jump into them. Do you see his face smiling at you? Can you hear his hearty laugh?"

Henry scrunched his eyes tightly shut. "Yes, Mama, I can see him, I can hear him," he said with a hint of excitement.

"Good! That's good, my love. Then you will always keep him right here," she kissed his forehead, "and right here," she patted his chest. "Always remember how so very much Daddy loves you."

Henry's deep blue eyes met Helen's. "If Daddy loves me so much, why did he go away?"

Helen smoothed the hair away from his face. Such a sweet innocent face. "Oh my darling little boy," she cried. "Daddy didn't *want* to leave us. Sometimes things just happen, and we don't get to choose. Some things are just...meant to be."

The sound of the heavy front door slamming downstairs jolted them. Helen felt her chest tighten as April padded up the steps and latched her bedroom door.

"I want Daddy," Henry cried.

"Me too, darling, me too."

When Henry fell asleep, Helen tucked Floyd under his arm and pulled the plaid blanket up over his shoulders. She kissed his head and tiptoed out of the room. Helen saw light spilling under April's door, but she didn't have the strength to talk to her. She slipped inside her own room and locked the door, locking out the world. The full moon threw slices of light into the dark bedroom. The radio played Mozart's "Moonlight Sonata," slow and somber. Helen stepped out of her black dress, released her auburn hair, and slid a white cotton nightgown over her head. She sat on the veranda floor, wrapped her arms around her knees, and let the tears flow. Sadness mixed with anger, and she cursed God for taking him. She cried in self-pity, and in gut-wrenching sorrow for Henry. Slowly the moon's glow faded to misty morning light, and Helen crawled under the covers and floated into a deep sleep.

For many months Helen's world remained murky. Everything she touched, everything she looked at seemed to be just beyond her reach, out of focus. She forced herself out of bed in the mornings to see James send Henry off to school and resisted the urge to climb back in once he'd left. Friends and neighbors were wonderful. They nourished her body with homemade treats and fed her soul with faithful attention. Eventually, Helen allowed herself to heal, and the fog surrounding her head began to clear. Her grief peeled away a layer at a time. Helen welcomed the healing and the glimpses of her personality resurfacing from distant hiding places. Her sense of humor finally reemerged too, and her friends' reaction to that return did just as much to cheer her as the humor itself.

"Good to see your old self again, Helen," George Stuart loved to say. George and his wife, Elizabeth, had befriended Helen soon after she'd arrived in Durban. He was warm and reassuring to her from the start, and she learned quickly to rely on his steady disposition. "When are you coming to work for me at the rooms?" he asked more frequently now. Helen honestly did not want to go back to Brown & Dean without Joseph. A few years after his death, she found herself considering George's offer. Not only had they been good friends, she had a tremendous respect for the way he ran the medical facility in town. She held his offer in the back of her mind, knowing she'd first have to deal with the Dean half of the Brown and Dean Law office.

SIX – Leiden

1941 The whistle jolted the household awake, and they held their collective breath, gripped in fear, until the bomb exploded in the distance. So began another day. Fully awake now, Trudy tried to shake off the remnants of her latest nightmare. Shivering, she snuggled into Mom's back, tucking her knees into the bend of her mother's until body heat warmed them both. Trudy pressed her face to Mom's back and asked to hear her mother's dreams, but Mom said she has stopped dreaming. "Tell me about Pop then," she pleaded. Mom rolled to her back, covered her face with her hands. After a while she turned to her daughter, her dark eyes searching. Words seemed to catch in her throat but wouldn't spill out. The stories flowed easily at night when the day was done and they tried desperately to choose their dreams. But dreaming was nearly impossible in the morning, when there was no escaping the day ahead.

"Let me, Mom!" Trudy whispered, "I'll tell you about Pop!" Trudy's little arms embraced her mother while she contemplated the right story to choose; she knew them all by heart. "Pop," she began slowly in her best mom-voice, "is a good man, kind, thoughtful, loving. Your fathers worked together and wanted you to meet. You were in Grade 10, and he was in Grade 11. You were having trouble with maths, so your father asked him to help you. And he said yes!" Trudy hugged her mom close. "You blushed when he sat very close to you, and you hoped he didn't notice. But you didn't want him to move away, did you, hmmm?" she teased. "He showed you how to do the first problem, and you understood right away!" Trudy leaned in and touched her forehead to Mom's. "That's because you're smart, like me!" she said beaming eye-to-eye. "Anyway, he said you were sharp as a tack, and he smiled at you and patted your hand. And when you looked into his eyes, you knew you would love him the rest of your life! Isn't that right?"

A tear escaped as she pulled Trudy close and kissed her forehead. "Oh Trudy, what would I do without you?" Mom asked, cupping Trudy's cheek. It never occurred to Trudy to ask what she'd do without Mom. "What a lovely way to start the day," she smiled, her dark eyes full of love. Then she pulled her tired body from the bed and headed down the cold bare stairs to find something suitable for breakfast.

Aunt Jenke, Pop's sister, had come to live with them the year before. The Nazis had taken her house, leaving her nowhere else to go. So Trudy moved into Mom's room, shared her bed. Aunt Jenke moved Trudy's old bed to what had been the pantry off the kitchen. Instead of tinned fish, jars of homemade jam, rice, beans, and everything needed to bake delicious desserts, the otherwise empty shelves held the clothes and odds and ends Aunt Jenke was able to bring with her. The extra mouth to feed added to the tension. Aunt Jenke's muffled crying scared Trudy at home, and the soldiers everywhere, including the school, frightened her all day. She didn't want to go to school, but she was more afraid not to. When Maartin and Peter Hagedorn refused to go, soldiers went to their house and dragged them the four blocks. They lost their slippers along the way and had to then cram their bloodied swollen feet into their shoes the rest of the week.

Trudy had been growing and steadily outgrowing her own clothes, so she'd begun dressing in Marike's old clothes. The pants had to be rolled up at the bottom, and the waist was big enough to allow a tucked-in sweater. Marike had grown tall enough to share Mom's clothes. Maud's clothes continued to fit her though everything was just too short.

Trudy knocked and called to her sisters, "good morning." The Ms were somberly getting ready for school. They didn't want to go either, but arguing proved useless. They tiptoed down the cold wooden steps to find Mom in the kitchen. One by one she rubbed warmth into their arms before they sat. Today they'd have tea without sugar and a poached egg. "Mom, you're still the best cooker in the world," Trudy declared, smiling.

Trudy took her dishes to the sink and then quietly unlatched the door to the old pantry. Aunt Jenke snored softly, her wiry gray hair tucked into a wool cap. "Good luck today, Aunt Jenke," she whispered. After the girls left for school, Mom and Aunt Jenke would stand in line for whatever groceries they could find—flour, eggs, powdered milk. Real milk was no longer available because the Nazis liked beef, Mom explained. Afterwards, the women would bake bread. This had become their dreary routine.

Once the sisters were sufficiently bundled and kissed, the three gathered their books and stepped into the frigid, sooty morning, leaning into the wind on their walk to school. Windmills had been either bombed or burned, so the polders overflowed, muddying the streets. The smell of burnt metal filled the air. The girls slogged through mud, dodging soldiers in jeeps who beeped and yelled at them to watch out. *Achtung!* They'd shout and laugh as their tires sprayed them with dirt.

Before she was old enough, Trudy longed to go to school. She craved books, wanted schoolwork and projects just as the Ms had. But most of all, she wanted to walk to and from school with Leah, her best friend. The two used to dream about eating pastries at her house after school and working on *their work* together. But now that Trudy was old enough to go to school, Leah was not allowed. Jewish children were banned from public school. In fact, they were forbidden to simply be outside much of the day. Until the Nazis came, Leah and Trudy had spent most every day together. Even when the air was cold, the two could be found deep in little girl conversation while creating sidewalk chalk masterpieces on the pavement between their houses. Leah would always make pictures of colorful fish while Trudy made fields of pink tulips. Now, Leah's parents felt keeping Leah inside all the time was best. Trudy missed her friend desperately. She couldn't help thinking how much better life would be with her best friend at her side. Watching her sisters and then Leah go to school used to make her ache to be bigger. Now she wished she were tiny, no, smaller than that, small enough to disappear.

Eins, swei, drei, vier... The class counted aloud to ten. When at home, Trudy and the Ms sang the numbers and facts to familiar tunes to make the learning stick. All students were required to learn the German language as well as that country's history. But there was no singing in Frau Reusing's classroom. Using a metal ruler as a baton, Frau Reusing would instruct the class to hold their mouths tight and follow her tempo. When Maartin Hagedorn stumbled over *acht,* she railed at him. The sound of metal against his knuckles reverberated off stark walls, marble floors. Though the pain was piercing, he didn't dare cry.

Constant sniffles and coughing echoed around the classroom. The children were pale and sickly, and all of them shivered from fear, though unsure of what exactly. At lunchtime they'd sit quietly still in their seats. Trudy unwrapped the handkerchief holding her meal, a biscuit with a hint of Mom's blackberry jam spread in the center. Her eyes darted around the room to see the other children's meager meals were no better. The children avoided eye contact as though they were ashamed. The *tick-tock* of the clock echoed endlessly.

Students kept their arms stiffly at their sides and faces toward the floor while walking single file to an empty classroom. Soldiers' boots sounded like bullets ricocheting off the school's marble hallways. The children were separated into groups and given numbers. One day in particular, Trudy was Number 4. Each group had to run as fast as they could across the room and back. Some of the soldiers stood along the far end of the room, making sure each student touched the wall before turning back. The whistle made a short shrill sound, and the children raced, hearts pounding from exertion, to the far side, sure to touch the wall before turning and racing back again. Running used to be joyful outside under clear skies. Now the skies were constantly gray, and the wind sent ash and soot swirling. Herr Koehler, the newest teacher, eyed the results of his stopwatch making notes on a clipboard. The children lined up again, hands at their sides, no talking. As usual, Pieter Smit was the fastest in the class. He was summoned away from the other children to the corner of the room by Herr Koehler. Herr Koehler wrote on his clipboard as Pieter spoke, his face flushed and serious, panting from exhaustion.

After school the girls met up and slogged their way through the mud and wind in silence. Mom had warned them to never call attention to themselves. They were a household of females surrounded by soldiers. They had enough trouble without inviting more. "Keep your heads down and never make eye contact with a soldier," she warned them repeatedly.

Silence was easy for the girls as they walked. There was nothing to say. For a year and a half they had complained, whined, cried, and prayed. None of it brought comfort anymore. Twilight's chill seeped through their coats and leeched into their bones. The winter sun barely poked through the gloomy sky, and the few street lamps still standing didn't light. A vee of planes roared overhead, rattling their chests. They hardly flinched. They kept their eyes to the muddy ground and stayed close together until their house came into view. Then they'd sprint in a race to the door. Marike always won.

Inside, the house was dark and reeked of ammonia. Aunt Jenke had spent the day cleaning again. They found Mom in the kitchen making biscuits with the powdered milk and eggs she was able to score earlier. The radio aired German music on the only station that came in clearly. She was focused on her baking so didn't look up when she asked about the day. This was the routine they had fallen into. The girls sat at the metal kitchen table taking turns reporting their days' events at school—Marike, then Maud, and then Trudy. When Trudy told them about Pieter Smit's victory, Mom stopped, dropped her chin to her chest, and made the sign of the cross. No one asked why she did this. All had learned to not ask the questions they didn't want answers to. Mom didn't want to tell them that Pieter will join other strong blond boys who will train to be Nazi soldiers, fighting against fellow Dutch in a war they're too young to understand.

Simmering on the stove in the big aluminum pot was a bone. From the garden Mom had dug up an onion and the last of the carrots and added them as well. They'd have small bits of this soup for as many days as possible. Mom made a game of stretching the soup. The last batch had fed them for ten days. Even Marike had stopped whining aloud about these pitiful meals. She had stopped dancing too, and the still silence was deafening. But they had all learned complaining only worsens the mood. Often Trudy would crawl into bed at night, her stomach twisting with hunger. She'd squeeze her eyes shut and search her mind. She could almost remember the full taste of Edam cheese, the meaty smell of Mom's stew, the weight of a sweet pastry on her tongue.

Mom began going to bed early too. There was nothing else to do, and she was tired anyway. They were forced to keep the house dark, and had no choice but to keep it cold. She and Trudy were grateful for body heat and snuggled close to talk about Pop. They used to lie on a blanket in the back yard, point at the sky and imagine where he was on his route in the clouds, count the days until his return. Now dark clouds blended into gray skies, and they had no idea where he may be. The game's focus changed. Instead, Trudy wanted to know her father, this figure from another life who had disappeared, the man Mom desperately clung to. "If only Pop were here..." Mom would always say, as though he could magically stop the war by raising his big hand. So Trudy would ask, "Tell me about Pop?" And to start, Mom's words were always the same: "Your Pop is a good man, kind, thoughtful, loving. If he were here, he'd know exactly what to do. He'd be calm. He'd hold us up with his big capable hands, and our world inside our house would be a haven from this miserable life." She'd squeeze Trudy tightly when adding "...and I have only to look into your smiling face to see him grinning back at me." And Trudy would smile into the darkness as Mom told stories of both their past life and of their someday life.

SEVEN - In the Southern Hemisphere

1942 The Janus's tanks were topped off with gasoline, and the young Bahraini stood at attention, saluting like a soldier, tiny beads of sweat collecting above his upper lip. "The convoy is full, Captain. Can I be of further assistance to you, sir?"

Sam straightened his hat and placed his hands on his hips. "You could gather your friends and replace my blasted crew." Sam eyed the young man closer. The boy was probably tall for his age, but the peach fuzz on his chin betrayed him. "But I'm afraid your mum would miss you. How old are you, son?"

"Eighteen, sir," he lied, snapping again to attention.

"And too eager to be fighting this war, aren't you?" The boy held his breath now, standing tall. "Count your blessings, son. With any luck those damn Nazis won't take your home as they've done mine!" Sam rubbed his jaw. "You're a child; be a child! While you still have that luxury!" The boy simply stood at attention, afraid to move or speak. Finally, Sam collected the boy's paperwork and dismissed him. The boy scampered away.

Sam hurried to the officers' lounge. He had the convoy's new orders and was eager to move on with the ever-changing route. As the fighting spread throughout the Mediterranean, the convoy's route had been altered accordingly. The team was relegated to Pakistan, Sri Lanka, and India. When Hitler's armies oozed into the Soviet Union in the Fall of 1941, Caltex ordered Sam to change ports and purpose. Instead of carrying crude to refineries, they supplied gasoline to fuel allied ships. The resulting route caused the convoy to dodge mines and risk their lives to maintain ports in Madagascar, Australia, and New Zealand. But after too many bombs hit Australia in 1942, Caltex finally deemed that area too dangerous, and the route changed again.

He removed his hat, tucked it under his arm, and ducked inside the dark and smoky officers' lounge. He dragged his handkerchief across his upper lip, dabbed at his forehead and behind his ears while fans spun furiously in a futile attempt to disperse the heat. Danker sat with the other captains and first mates. Cut off from all ties to home, this seafaring family had grown close-knit. Danger and constant worry cleaved them to each other, bound by patriotism, loyalty, and fear.

Danker had Sam's whisky glass waiting at the table. With the first sip, Sam winced in pain. The others had increasingly noticed this reaction. "When do you plan to have a check, Sam?" asked Captain VanDerMeer. Van was ten years Sam's senior and a well-respected friend. "I must say you're not looking too chipper."

Sam realized the problem had gotten much worse, bad enough that others noticed his discomfort. "As luck would have it, our orders have finally changed for the better. After a last discharge in Kenya, we'll be servicing again the South African ports of Cape Town, Port Elizabeth, East London, and Durban. I have a friend's recommendation for a doctor in Durban." Sam absent-mindedly took another sip of scotch and winced again. "I'll be making that call today," he tried to joke, pushing the glass out of easy reach. "I do appreciate your concern, Van. Not to worry," Sam said patting his friend's forearm. Looking at the men around the table he had to laugh. "But honestly, this is the first time in four months any of us has stepped foot on land. We all look positively ghostlike." The group exhaled a chuckle glancing at each other and realizing Sam was right. The tension dissipated somewhat. "I half expect this damned crew to jump into the Gulf rather than get back on board." He rubbed his chin. "Which may not be entirely bad..."

"Still no better, eh, Sam?" asked Captain Sorensen. Sam shook his head and squeezed his fists. He had repeatedly asked Caltex to replace the whole lot of them. Even Einer Staal, who normally had trouble with no one, threw up his hands in defeat. "We are nothing but chess pieces to Caltex, I feel," he complained, anger quickly simmering. "I almost don't mind being sent all over this globe, but for God's sake, equip me with a crew to handle the task!" His team muttered in agreement. But his complaints landed on deaf ears at Caltex, and Sam had no recourse. "They tell me all the capable, honorable men are busy defending their fellow countrymen." The men grew silent at that.

Only a sliver of moon lit the convoy's path across the Arabian Sea. Thankfully, the water was calm, and Sam could hear the rhythmic sounds of the engines' hum and the water lapping against the ship. Looking into the moonlit water, as he so often did during his treks, he wondered what his children were doing, if they were safe and warm, if they were fed. And how was Ger faring under the added stress? She had always been rather dependent, and she seemed so tired during his last leave at home. *This experience would either strengthen her or...* Sam shook the thought from his head and turned his attention to two neat stacks of the day's paperwork. The radio aired a Brahms piece, but before long the news interrupted, and Sam raised the volume. The German army emanated in all directions from the Black Sea, stretching the fight to the Crimean Peninsula and northern Africa. "Vervloek deze oorlog!" he shouted, pounding the desk. *Curse this war!* His home, his beautiful Mediterranean, his employer, and now his watery back yard—Sam's whole world was now at war.

"Enter!" Sam shouted to the knock on his door. Einer nearly stumbled over the coaming and stood at attention. His khaki uniform was impeccable, except for this expanding pocketful of sourballs. He steadied a lemon ball between his teeth while he spoke. "Good evening, Captain," Einer marbled almost inaudibly.

"Let me guess, Einer, the crew is upset." Sam dropped his pen and rubbed his forehead.

Einer cleared his throat. "Worse than that, sir," he began, tucking the candy in his cheek, "two jumped overboard, and one was missing when we sailed from Bahrain. His mate disguised his absence, sir."

Sam stood and slammed his palm on the desk blotter. Turning his back to Einer, Sam peered into the black water below. "And the two that jumped?"

"The Bahrain police fished them out, sir. They were pretty soggy, but they'll be alright."

"I suppose we should be grateful the rats didn't sink," Sam said as he poured scotch into a rocks glass. "We'll be stopping briefly in Mombasa, Einer. No one sets foot off this ship." His gaze was piercing. "Do you understand? Plenty of time will be available when we drydock. Tell them if they all behave in Mombasa, they'll get a week on land in Durban." Sam crossed to stand within inches of his crew chief and at least a half foot taller. Einer kept his eyes straight ahead, squarely on his Captain's Adam's apple. Sam leaned in closer to make his point. "And Einer," he warned in a low voice, "do not disappoint me."

"No sir! I won't, sir!"

Sam regretted his overbearing tone. "Einer?" he added, softening, "sink your teeth into that sourball before you choke on it." He paused, waiting for the crunch before dismissing him.

Sam downed half his scotch and felt the instant retort in his stomach. He dropped himself onto the leather settee, removed his shoes and kicked them underneath. He stretched his long legs in front of him. From the side table, his four silver-framed females smiled at him, and he raised his glass, "Cheers, girls." Downing his drink enraged the fire in his stomach, and he cried out in pain. He slumped against the leather and gratefully allowed Beethoven's "Symphony No. Three" to wash over him.

Rain came down in torrents as the Janus discharged its cargo at the Mombasa docks. Night fell early, and Sam was content to stay on board, while the rest of the crew was required to do so. As a safeguard, Sam had Einer announce that the recent malaria shots were not yet effective. Sneaking off ship could render them and their shipmates deathly ill. In truth, Sam didn't want anything to interfere with the scheduled drydock in Durban. He was anxious about his upcoming medical check-up, eager to see his friends at Brown & Dean, and surprisingly desperate to find his land legs again.

EIGHT – Durban

1942 Helen took a deep breath and entered. This stately office had always impressed her. All available wall space was consumed by leather-bound volumes, their nostalgic scent as soothing as an old friend. A relieved smiled crept slowly across her face as she inhaled the comfort. During the three years since Joseph's passing, Helen hadn't been emotionally able to stand in the space she had shared with her husband. But today she felt oddly at peace.

Doris emerged from Mr. Brown's office and wrapped a meaty arm around Helen. "You are looking well, dear, and I am so glad!" Her obvious relief touched Helen's heart. They sat in the two upholstered chairs while Helen brought Doris up-to-date on the family, and Doris reported on her growing grandchildren. "I'll leave you to Joseph's office now, dear. I'm going out for a bite to eat, but I'll be back shortly to check on you. Mr. Brown won't be in until two o'clock, so just let the phone ring," Doris called over her shoulder as she left.

Except for the usual stacks of work in progress, Joseph's office was just as he had left it. His chair was pushed under the desk, and as always, the teacup sat ready to be filled. His diplomas were displayed on the wall, and on the credenza were his three favorite photos—the two of them on their honeymoon, a larger photo of Henry proudly modeling his Grade One uniform, and the smallest frame held his parents who had been gone for years. Helen stepped out of her shoes and pushed up her sleeves. She grabbed a box and began rooting through drawers for anything of sentimental value. She was finally in the frame of mind where she could distinguish between useless and priceless. Her plan was first to tackle his office before deciding what to do about her own office there.

The front door chimed, and remembering Doris had left, Helen reluctantly headed to the outer office. The sight of Sam, standing tall, handsome, and uniformed, took her breath away. Completely surprised, he stopped turning his hat in his hands. "Why Helen! I expected to find Doris." He crossed the room and hugged her, quickly sensing her tension. He took a step back saying, "Helen...Sam. I know it's been a long time, but—"

"Sam, I know you, of course. Don't be silly. You simply caught me off guard, that's all." She moved to one of the two upholstered chairs facing Doris's desk and motioned for Sam to sit in the other. She watched her right thumb gouge her left palm, blinking back tears. She felt a wave of nausea, and her heart grew heavy. She thought she wouldn't have to relay this news anymore. "You have not been here for quite a while, Sam." She took a deep breath. "I am terribly sorry to say...about three years ago..." She took a moment to compose herself before continuing. "Joseph suffered a heart attack...and...and died. It was sudden and quite a shock." Helen watched as her fingers turned her wedding ring round and round. Although the words still hurt to say, they didn't carry the sting that had accompanied them just months earlier. "I am here today collecting odds and ends. I haven't actually worked here since his...passing." As she finished, she felt the tension trickle from her body.

He reached for her hand. "I am so sorry, Helen. What a shock! You must be in such pain."

"Joseph spoke so highly of you, Captain. Though we didn't know you very long, we considered you a treasured friend." The news warmed his heart; he felt the same way about them both.

"How are you managing?" he asked sincerely. "And how is your son faring?"

Helen looked to the floor and then to Sam. "Day by day in the beginning," she said frankly. "But we're doing much better, especially in the last few months. I feel I've certainly turned the corner." She forced a smile. "I've had to be strong for Henry, thank God. My mum helped me realize he'll fare only as well as I do."

"You have a double blessing in your son—not only a reason to continue but to thrive. And you both owe it to yourselves to do so." He squeezed her hand. "Give yourself time, Helen. It is the best healer."

"You are right about that, Sam. I have already come very far. And I don't want to continue mourning. I'm a party girl at heart, Captain," she reminded him, forcing a smile and letting her eyes glance at his. "And I do look forward to being happy again."

"May I help?" asked Sam, forcing his voice to sound bright. "Let me take you to dinner," he suggested. "I'll even let you drive," he teased. Helen considered his offer before accepting. He was, after all, more of a friend to her than to Joseph, she realized. And Joseph would have encouraged them to have a good time as he had on their prior outings. They agreed to meet at the Caister Hotel at seven. The restaurant inside was one of Helen's favorites and located near the shipyard, an easy walk for Sam. "It's a date then," he said standing, adjusting his hat under his arm. "In the meantime, I've got to report the weather to someone, and it looks as though we're the only ones here," he said glancing around the empty outer office.

"Mr. Brown will be in shortly. He'll record your information. Meanwhile," she grinned, tilting her head, "give me a hand?" They worked together at an easy pace, taking time to ask about and explain photos and the significance behind mementos around the office, especially those concerning Henry. "Look at this, Sam," she said holding up a clay piece. "This is Henry's tiny three-year-old hand, isn't it darling?" She wrapped it in newspaper, then gently placed it in a box. At times Helen fought tears, but mostly she enjoyed the memories, relaxing enough to laugh despite the situation. She searched through the bookshelves, plucking intermittent novels from the reference books and taking anything with gilt-edged pages. "To me they are fourteen carat gems," she said running her fingers along the smooth gold of the paper.

When Mr. Brown returned, Sam followed him to his office and filed the necessary paperwork. Once finished, he again found Helen in Joseph's office, kneeling on the thick carpet. Her shoes were beside her, and she was reaching into the lower cabinet of the shelves. She pulled out a few more leather-bound tomes and placed them into a box. "That will do it!" she said, wiping her forehead with the back of her hand. "Feels good to be done!" she exhaled. "Now I'd better go have a lie-down before our dinner engagement."

Sam helped her to her feet, and she stepped into her shoes. He carried three boxes to her one into the outer office where she stopped to set down her load and hug Doris goodbye. "I'll be in touch," she assured her. Outside Sam placed the boxes in the boot of her car, and she thanked him for his help. "It's Providential that you should come in today of all days and after such a long time," she commented as she placed her box in the boot. "Why, I myself have not been here in years." She looked up, squinting into the afternoon sun. "Quite amazing, don't you think?"

The thought had already crossed his mind a few times. He smiled at her then and closed the boot with a thud. "Remember, Helen, I've not been here during the same three years, so yes, positively Providential. Now go rest up, and I'll see you tonight," he said helping her into the car.

Sam hurried out the door and walked briskly towards town. Since he was a little boy he felt he could hurry time along simply by rushing. Just as he'd always felt too that slowing down his motions could almost make time stand still. His mother would often find him floating in the lake near their home; arms and legs stretched akimbo, the sun warming his face, thick water magnifying the heartbeat inside his ears. He would claim he'd been there for days. But today he wanted time to fly. He felt buoyed with anticipation. How many months had passed since he'd had a conversation with anyone other than his crew or a naval man? And when had he last spoken with a woman? "Oh dear heavens!" he stopped abruptly when he realized it was when he was last home nearly four years before. He hoped he hadn't appeared like the nervous schoolboy he felt like inside. Sam rushed through the day's appointments, including the pre-admittance checkup at Addington Hospital.

The Caister Hotel was a veritable palace. The lobby's teak-lined walls stretched fifteen feet tall with arched windows flanked by golden taffeta drapes that pooled onto needlepoint rugs. Helen, already fifteen minutes late, raced across the marble foyer. She had been disappointed with all the dresses in her closet and finally settled on a sapphire chiffon with fitted bodice. The restaurant was crowded with men in dark suits or various uniforms and women in dresses cinched at the waist. Waiters in black scurried amid the white linen-topped tables. Through the commotion Helen spotted Sam coming towards her. He was dressed in his starched white uniform. His shirt's epaulets had gold stars, there were three stripes on each sleeve, and he wore a navy blue tie. His shoes gleamed, and his overall impression was neat, tidy, and incredibly handsome. He led her to their table for two by the window.

"You look absolutely lovely," Sam said and meant it. He felt privileged tucking her into her seat. They settled across from one another, at first catching each other in awkward glances, unsure of where to begin. Helen took in the view of the marina, touching the back of her hair. The boats gave a colorful foreground to the dark ocean beyond. The setting sun tinged everything with an overall rosy glow.

Though they had met several times and spent hours together, he hadn't fully captured her delicate beauty before then. With fresh eyes he noticed the glow of her soft skin, the way the corners of her mouth turned up always ready for a smile, the almond shape of her eyes. At last Sam smiled and reached his hand to cover hers. "I am delighted you are here," he began, and the conversation flowed easily from there. Like childhood friends reunited as adults, they talked for hours. Helen gave Sam a synopsis of her life, her fading recollections of England, the husband that brought her there, and the life that kept her there. He marveled at the enormous strength inside this outwardly delicate woman; how she had managed to survive heartache after heartache yet maintain her enthusiasm, especially when she spoke of Henry. There was so much to tell about the imp called Henry. When she spoke of him her eyes lit up, and her smile stretched ear to ear. Sam was enchanted. Her stories brought giggles from them both—hers at the recollection and his for the sheer delight in watching her relay them.

They shared a bottle of Pinotage, Sam sipping cautiously. She ordered sea bass, and he had filet mignon, rare. Somewhere between the delicious meal, the smooth wine, the easy laughter and flowing conversation, they became completely enamored with the person across the table. He wanted to know every detail about her, yet at the same time, he felt the reassuring calm of having known her his entire life. Sam told stories of his travels through the beautiful waterways and the many countries where he had docked and visited. He talked about how the war had strengthened the bonds with his fellow tanker men, and he told amusing stories of the crew trouble he had dealt with over the years, though they had not seemed at all comical when they'd occurred. Never before was he able to laugh off their antics, and that night he and Helen laughed until their sides ached. Admittedly, she had not laughed, really laughed, since before Joseph died.

They agreed to share vanilla ice cream with hot chocolate sauce for dessert. When Sam reached for the goblet, Helen noticed his wedding band. She sensed an unexpected pang of jealousy and felt foolish because of it. Throughout all the storytelling, he never mentioned his wife, and she wondered why. "Sam," she began tentatively, "we've been talking for hours, yet you never mentioned your family. Joseph told me you have three children, is that right?"

"Yes, that's right." Sam retrieved his wallet and showed Helen the photo of his family. "This was taken four years ago; I haven't seen them in almost as long." Sam motioned to the waiter for the check, paid it, and gathered his thoughts. Resting his forearms on the table in front of him, he continued, "I've had no communication with my family since before the Nazis took Holland three years ago." He straightened, pausing to rein in his emotions. "I cannot even be sure they are alive." Sam turned to the dark water below, hesitant to continue. "I have seen too much death in this God-forsaken war. Mines have claimed other tankers and their crews. The ocean swallows up soldiers blasted off patrol boats, God rest their souls. If I allow myself, I will easily be overcome with grief." He hadn't said these words aloud, and they sounded foreign to his own ears. "Instead I have become numb. Even the news of Joseph's death hardly registered a pang of sorrow for myself; only for you." He caught himself and looked into her eyes, wishing he could retract that statement. "I am sorry, but it's true," he admitted. "Now, I know I have—may have" he corrected himself, "a family that I may or may never see again. It is my duty to love and support them, and I do. I swear to God in Heaven, I do." He hesitated, shifting in his chair; then decided he had gone this far. "But does that mean I am required to live out this horrendous limbo in agonizing worry? This limbo could very well constitute the rest of my life as well." He held her gaze for just a brief moment. These pent-up thoughts seeped out of him like air leaking from a tire. He felt deflated, exhausted.

Helen returned the photo, and Sam replaced it in his wallet. He leaned forward on both elbows, laying his hands palm up. After a brief hesitation, she silently obliged, placing her hands in his. Their mutual attraction was undeniable. "Seeing you today shot energy into this tired man's soul, Helen. I haven't felt...alive...in quite some time. And I believe you feel the same way." He squeezed her hands. "Please, Helen, don't be upset with me. I am being honest with you. If I don't talk about my family, it's because they have fallen silently into the background." He locked his eyes on hers. "I forced them there, made myself push them into the recesses. For my own survival." He searched her face. "Can you understand that, Helen? As callous as that may sound, it's the truth." He sat back in his chair, certain he'd said too much. But once he'd begun, he couldn't stop. The admission was liberating.

Helen watched Sam's eyes as he spoke. They were clear and honest, and they never wavered from hers. She wondered how she'd feel in his situation, not knowing. She realized that Joseph had been gone the same amount of time. Tonight she'd allowed him to slip into the background as well. She had decided to no longer be consumed by grief, so she understood his choosing not to be consumed with worry. She recalled fretting constantly while her first husband flew. What a silly waste of time, she'd finally understood. She decided to trust Sam's decisions, to accept his rationale. And, more importantly, she decided against marring the most delightful evening she'd enjoyed in years.

Outside the sky had grown dark, and the cooler air was a pleasant change from the summer's daytime heat. He put on his hat and checked his shirt was neatly tucked. They walked to her car, his long strides almost doubling hers. She slid behind the wheel and rolled down the window. Sam squatted to eye level. "When can I see you again?"

She thought about that question, about him, about the evening. She needed time to consider her options without his handsome face just inches from hers. "I don't know, Sam..." she looked away and then glanced back at him. "How long are you here for?"

Sam's coy smile slowly appeared. "It just so happens I'll be here for a few months, beginning with a short stay in the Addington Hospital." Her concern flashed quickly across her face. "Now don't you worry, just some routine stomach nonsense. But I'll be able to recuperate while the ship is in drydock. And if necessary, they will sail without me until I am fully recovered." He reached in and pushed her hair off her shoulder with the back of his hand, sending tingles down her arm. "I want to see you again, Helen. May I call you?"

She searched her purse for paper and pen and scratched out her phone number. "Will you be taking visitors in the hospital?" Helen offered. "Though it depends on Henry's schedule, of course," she quickly added, leaving herself an out just in case.

"Better give me a few days," Sam suggested, not wanting to appear too eager. But he prayed she would come. After some awkward silence, they agreed they should part. It was getting late. Sam watched as her car sped away into the navy blue night.

Helen parked in the garage. Moonlight illuminated her steps up the short rise to the house. Crickets chirped loudly in the garden as she passed, nearly drowning out the roar of the ocean. Inside, the house was dark and silent. She checked on her sleeping family— Grannie, April, and Henry. She closed her bedroom door and stepped onto the veranda. The waning moon spread a silver path along the dark ocean, straight to her. Leaning on the railing, she asked the sea, "What have you brought me now?"

In his stateroom, Sam settled under a lightweight cotton coverlet. He set an early alarm on his clock and he turned off the music, oddly content in silence. He lay on his back in the dim space, reviewing the events of the day and growing increasingly excited like a little boy awaiting Sinterklaas. The more he considered their coincidental meeting today, the more he believed it was destiny. She had been in Joseph's office only briefly and on the same day he had happened to arrive after an extended absence. A smug smile crept across his face. Already he had strong feelings for this woman, and viewing their serendipitous meeting today as providential made those feelings all the sweeter.

NINE – Leiden

1942   A hint of gray morning light seeped under the blackout curtains. Mom felt Trudy fit herself into her back as they waited for the warmth their bodies would eventually create.   She pulled Trudy's arm like a blanket across her middle, counting on their heat to melt her into action.   When she'd gathered enough energy to face the day, she kissed Trudy's palm, pulled her own weary body from the bed, and wrapped herself in a worn flannel robe.   She watched as Trudy dragged Marike's old pants over woolen tights and added a dark sweater.   Trudy caught her Mom's eyes and smiled.   Neither spoke, but they knew both would rather lie back down and sleep the day away.   If they could sleep until the war's end, they surely would. But a mother needs to be strong for her children, smile, and attempt to set a better tone.   She was thankful that although Trudy's eight-year-old mind couldn't explain it, she somehow knew her Mom relied on her smiling face to continue trying.

Before autumn turned the leaves brown, Mom had collected dozens off the trees, dried them, and stowed them in the dark, cool cupboard.   She boiled them in water, one clump at a time, for what she called mystery tea.   She handed each girl a full mug as she entered the kitchen and sat at the table.   Trudy felt the liquid spread its warmth inside her chest, and let the mug warm both cupped hands.   She closed her eyes and allowed the steam to warm her face.

The room was still and quiet because the radio was gone.   Soldiers had taken it and everything else they wanted one dreadful night.

Trudy tried to shove away the memory, but often she could think of nothing else. Always the planes roar overhead. But that evening they were flying so low that the ground shook and rattled everything from the floor to the dining room chandelier. Pictures fell from the walls. The noise of rattling pots and pans echoed off the linoleum floor, the plaster walls. Cracks in that plaster grew like climbing spiders. Upstairs, the cot bounced around, throwing the dolls in all directions. Trudy was gathering them when she heard the front door bang open. Mom screamed. Aunt Jenke's screech was louder. Boots hammered the wood floor as they swept through the house. There must have been four or five, all shouting. Trudy grabbed Ribbon and ran to her sisters cowering in the corner, clinging to each other. "Go see what's happening," they ordered her, pointing with an outstretched arm to the door. "The soldiers won't bother you, you're too little." Trudy whined and refused, frozen by sheer terror. But the commotion continued downstairs so they pushed her shoulders, her back until they slid her straight-legged, her shoes sliding on the wood floor, out the bedroom door. Trudy heard the lock slide into place.

Trudy's heart pounded hard in her chest as she slipped off her shoes, tucked Ribbon under her arm, and crept silently down the stairs. Her socks made no sound at all as she breathlessly made her way from one step to the next. She went just far enough, stopped where the banister started and the wall ended. She peeked into the front room and saw no one. The soldiers stormed into the dining room then, just on the other side of the wall. Trudy held her breath while her heart continued pounding in her ears, out of her chest. Mom's silver serving pieces clanged as it was stuffed into a large canvas bag. All the while they shouted, laughed. More hammering, clanging, and an ensuing loud crash as the brass chandelier hit the table. Mom yelped. They swarmed back into the kitchen, and Trudy heard more clanging as they picked over pots, silverware, dishes. Trudy squeezed Ribbon tight, afraid to move, afraid to breathe. Their language sounded disgusting like snarling, fighting cats. All at once they were rushing through the front room, booty in tow clanging in canvas sacks. Trudy pressed herself into the wall, attempting to hide. The soldiers were charging out the door as quickly as they'd come. But then one stopped abruptly. He turned for a last look at the front room, making sure no prize was overlooked. Suddenly, his eyes landed on Trudy's. As he stepped toward her, she wet her pants sending a tiny rill in his direction. He barked at her cowering, quaking body, a deep guttural sound. Certain he intended to hit her, she raised her hands to shield herself. The seconds were so painful. "Kacke!" he shouted, plucking Ribbon from her fingertips and stomping out the door.

"Trudy?" She was thankful for Mom's voice dragging her from that awful night. Trudy finished her tea, wiped her sweaty palms on her pants, and slid into the coat Mom held. The sleeves pinched her armpits at the top, stopped inches above her wrists. She had grown taller but not wider, so she was able to button it closed. Mom tied the wool scarf around Trudy's face and planted a kiss on her head. Trudy easily wrapped her arms around Mom's waist. Her chubby middle had completely disappeared. The girls slid their small packets of lunch into their pockets before beginning their walk to school in the bitter ashen morning. Sleet pelted their faces, and wind whipped their backs. They leaned into the cold and made their way through stiff muddy streets. For a while their cheeks remained red, the only color in their dreary world.

While the girls were at school, Ger and Jenke stood, ration cards in hand, in a long line at the market, stomping life into their freezing feet and hoping for food. With hushed whispers and watchful eyes, they also learned the progress of the collaborators in their midst. There was a war going on within the war, Dutch against Dutch, collaborator against resister, monster against Jew. And the resistance was outnumbered two to one.

Trudy's stomach growled as she unwrapped her scraps of lunch. Talking was forbidden, so her eyes darted around the room, hoping to make contact with some of the other children. No longer embarrassed by the misery they shared, the children hoped for some hint of connection. She caught friendly fearful glimpses from a few girls. And then she noticed something confusing. Most of the children were as thin as she was. But for the first time, Trudy saw a few who didn't appear thin at all. In fact, Ryker Petersen looked almost chubby in comparison. He was hurriedly eating something. Could it possibly be a sandwich? As he took a big bite, he caught her staring at him. A smug smile stretched across his face. He cupped his hands around his open mouth to reveal meat and cheese and bread. Trudy wanted to scream. She had been dreaming of Edam and salami for years! He wiped his mouth with the back of his pudgy hand, chuckling. She snapped her head away, unable to look at his fat face. Feeling defeated, Trudy peered at the crumbs of stale bread in her hand. Slowly, she raised her palm to her open mouth, catching the bread with her tongue. Instead of chewing, she let the crumbs gather on her tongue until the bread turned soft. A few minutes later it would turn sweet, and she would close her eyes and pretend it was dark chocolate from Sinterklaas.

After school the girls met to walk home. They silently raised their collars and leaned into the wind as twilight engulfed them. In the distance black smoke rose into a widening cloud. Bitter cold seeped up through the icy slush and into the bottoms of their boots. The morning sleet had turned to snow, covering everything like a dirty blanket. They used to turn their faces to the falling snow, laugh while catching big flakes on their tongues. Now they kept their heads down, imagining this snow would taste no better than the mud off Nazi shoes. They walked to the house carefully in the twilight and the snow. No running race today.

Once inside the girls inhaled the welcomed scent of food. They dropped their books on the dining room table and rushed to the big aluminum pot on the stove, breathing deeply. A large bone simmered with potatoes, onions, and beans. Mom stood slicing a large loaf of white bread. A very successful day at the market.

As usual, the girls told about the events of their days. The reports have shortened over time, but Mom insisted they continue to talk about their life. Focusing on the present helped keep their minds from wandering to the past and also from fretting about the future. Marike spoke first, as usual, providing snippets of her day. "We had a test on German history. Maud and I studied for days!" she said crossing her arms and stomping her foot. "Why do they make us study the whole book if all they want us to know is found on four pages? We memorized Chancellors, Emperors, dates..." her face to the ceiling in frustration. "All we have to know starts in 1933, as though Germany didn't even exist until Adolph Hitler became Chancellor—"

"Fuhrer," corrected Maud. "He prefers to be called Fuhrer." The Ms rolled their eyes in unison. "We were tested today also," added Maud. After all our studying, for our test we had to sing the anthem!" Mom laughed at that, helping ease the tension. "I guess that is silly, isn't it?" Maud chuckled then, too. "I can barely pronounce the title, Das Leed der Doot-shen," she attempted.

Marike, harder than everyone, was laughing now too. "Oh my Lord! You must have failed miserably!"

"I'm sure I did! But I don't mind." Maud hummed the tune and marched around the sparse room, straight-armed like a soldier. Everyone laughed until Maud raised her arm and called "Heil Hitler!" and the room snapped into silence.

Mom rushed to her and gripped both arms down at Maud's sides. "Never again, not even in jest," uttered Mom in a low voice. "The man is a monster. He has taken everything, literally and figuratively. This is our haven. We will not allow him inside ever again. Understood?"

"I'm sorry, Mom. I didn't mean it. It's just that we were laughing...I didn't...think."

Mom quickly pulled Maud in for a hug. "Hush, hush," she soothed, "it's okay, Maud. I'm sorry to overreact, my love." She held Maud's face and looked into her eyes. "We heard some news today that made your salute hit a sore spot." She kissed Maud's forehead then looked into her eyes. A forced smile spread itself. "Get the bowls?" she asked.

"What news, Mom?" asked Marike. Jenke and the girls took their servings and sat at the table.

Mom brought her bowl and bread to join them. They inclined their heads while she spoke in a low voice as though she may be overheard. "We are all aware the Nazis have singled out the Jews, say they're awful people and don't deserve any rights. That's why

Leah can't go to school, and her mom can shop only between certain hours of certain days?" Mom looked into their eyes and saw they were well aware. "A Nazi named Seyss-Inquart has forced all Jews to register themselves at the Office. Because he doesn't believe they will all do this willingly, they are enlisting local help identifying the Jews, including physically escorting them to the Office to register." She hesitated before continuing, "That means our own countrymen are voluntarily helping the Nazis. Some of them are actually taking their side *against* the Jews. Can you imagine? They don't see anything wrong with helping the blasted Nazis and potentially hurting our Jewish friends!" She quickly covered her mouth with her hand and then shot it back into the air. "And for what, an extra portion of food? A few guilders?"

"What's wrong with being Jewish?" demanded Trudy, thinking only of the Canters. "And why do they have to register? We are Catholic. Are we registered too? What does it mean to register anyway?"

"First of all, there's nothing at all wrong with being Jewish! We all know this; everyone knows this...except that monster Hitler and his cronies." She thought a moment. "And I cannot, for the life of me, comprehend what he's got against them either. Why, how can one's religious beliefs alone, with no associated action mind you, make an entire group a target of—" she caught herself just in time, "—of frustration?" She shifted in her chair, eager to move on. "As for the word, *register*..." Mom searched for an explanation. "If you're Jewish, you have to go down to the Office and put your name in their book called a registry so the Nazis know how many Jewish people live here and where. They like to keep statistics, I'm told," she added, not wanting to worry Trudy. She found Marike's eyes and Maud's eyes, silently confirming with them to keep the real truth quiet. "Now there is a growing number of people called the Resistance. They try to thwart the Nazis at every opportunity. They do things like let the air out of the tires of their jeeps, steal radios to listen to the real news and then spread what they've learned. They get under the Nazis' skin like fire ants," she said grinning. "But they are small in number. For every one Resister there are two who actually aid the Nazis. Those monsters are called collaborators." She dipped a piece of bread into her soup and put it in her mouth, savoring the bite for the slightest moment. "I will never understand why anyone would willingly help the enemy."

"For food!" Jenke piped up. When people get hungry enough, they'll do anything to feed their families." She looked at Ger who shook her head. The two obviously disagreed. "Today I was able to get a ham bone," she motioned to the pot on the stove, "but Mrs. Petersen got a whole pig!"

At the mention of the Petersen name, Trudy's ears tingled. "So that's how Ryker gets to eat sandwiches!" She pictured him licking his fingers and patting his full stomach. Trudy patted hers only to silence the growls. "He's actually getting fat!" she cried.

Mom placed her hand on Trudy's forearm, and warned, "You mustn't speak to him, Trudy," she said in a stern voice. "Do you understand? He's not to know what we've just talked about, not one word!" She held her daughter's eyes until Trudy nodded her understanding. Mom pushed thin soup around in her bowl and then let her spoon drop. "Let him get fat, let them all get fat!" she said in disgust. "At least then we'll know who the traitors are. Oh it's easy to recognize the Nazi enemy in his uniform. But the real enemy looks like us, talks like us, dresses like us. And they'll smile to your face and then stab you in the back! So ladies," she added touching Trudy's shoulder on her left and Jenke's arm to her right, "we are going to remain loyal to Holland and, unfortunately, suspicious of *everyone* around us. Helping the Resistance is too dangerous, but I'd rather starve than help the damn Nazis!" she said, banging her fist on the table for emphasis. They finished their meal in heavy silence.

In bed that night Mom wrapped Trudy in her arms. She regretted the necessity of their dinnertime talk, and she wanted Trudy to rest well. "How was your day at school, my love? You didn't get to tell us at dinner, and I'm sorry for that." She squeezed Trudy tightly and kissed her head. "Did you have a test like your sisters?"

"I don't know if it was graded, but we all were passed a piece of paper and a pencil and were told to make a swastika."

"Were you able to draw one?"

"Yes...but I didn't want to. It's so ugly! Looks like a big spider on the page. Nothing but black, Mom..." her voice trailed off as she began to cry.

Mom pulled her daughter close, rested her chin on the top of Trudy's head. "Go ahead, tell me all about it, Trudy, my dear, sweet love."

"I miss my colors, Mom." Trudy whispered pitifully. "I want to draw tulips outside with Leah!" she sobbed, covering her face. "And I want to lie on the blanket with you and find Pop in the clouds... Will we ever be able to do that? Will the sky ever be blue again?"

Mom was unable to think of a single word to soothe her aching daughter. She wanted to tell her the sky would be clear in the morning, but she knew tomorrow would be just like yesterday, gray and dismal with only a hint of sun through the murky haze of war. She wanted to tell her she would buy her crayons at the market tomorrow, but Trudy would know that's a lie. And she wanted to tell her someday soon she'd be outside again with Leah and that before long their world would be back to normal. But she was painfully aware theirs would never again be the same carefree life they would try desperately to remember the rest of their lives. She knew that the war would overshadow every aspect of their lives going forward. And she knew she would never be able to comfort her sweet daughter when the inevitable happened to Leah.

TEN – Durban

Early December, 1942   Sam walked gingerly down the sterile hospital corridor, leaning heavily on a handrail along the wall. The tan marble floor chilled his feet through leather slippers, and every painful wince echoed off white plaster walls. The ulcer operation had gone smoothly. Aside from a few dietary restrictions, he was told to expect an easy recovery after, of course, several uncomfortable days.

As he lay back onto the bed exhausted, Helen entered the room, her arms filled with flowers. "Sam!" she gasped, "you look positively awful!"

He laughed, which made him wince again. "And to think I hoped...*prayed* you'd come!" He slowly pulled himself to sitting and patted the bed. "Won't you sit down and tell me more?" He cocked his head and grinned at her. "The flowers are lovely, and you are an angel to bring them. Thank you, Helen," he said, tapping his chest.

She arranged the flowers—green stems of yellow, pink, and purple blossoms—in the water pitcher, and stepped back to admire her work. Then she pulled back the curtain and let the sun stream into the room. Satisfied, she kicked off her shoes and hopped onto the foot of the bed. During the last few days she'd thought often about this man, about their most recent chance meeting. She remembered, in particular, their people watching on the bus stop in Beechwood the first time they'd met. The recollection made her laugh aloud. She thought about the few lunches they had shared, and how quickly Joseph felt a kinship for this otherwise stranger. She allowed their easy-going rapport over dinner to warm her heart. While she did not like hearing about his detachment from his family, she appreciated his view of the situation. And she appreciated his honesty. The more she learned about him, the more she wanted to know.

He took her hand, easing her closer, and she let him kiss her palm. "Looks like you have time for a chat, my friend." The conversation flowed easily all afternoon, sharing stories of themselves, their families, their dreams, and the war that impeded all of the above. But good comes from everything, they acknowledged. And being constantly aware of so much death makes one more fully appreciate life.

As the sunlight faded, the room grew dim, and Sam became obviously tired. "Sam, you need weeks to recover fully. Won't you please consider spending them at my home, at Merriwold? We have an extra room, plenty of space really. And I hate the thought of your spending Christmas on your ship."

He remembered the offer she made when they'd last met, and he was surprised and delighted to have it extended again. But he had concerns. He pulled himself to a more upright position, arranging the sheet neatly over his lower half. "I'd hate to intrude on your holiday traditions, Helen. Will your family object to having a stranger in the house, especially during the holidays?"

"Until Joseph died we had wonderfully large parties. We South Africans love our parties! And as I've told you, I adore this time of year. The family used to be well accustomed to having strangers in the house. They'll warm up to your staying with us as soon as they meet you, I'm sure. And you will get all the rest you need," she promised. She stepped into her shoes and tucked her purse under her arm. "It's settled then." Helen wrote her phone number again with the address on a slip of paper, Seven Fairway, Durban Heights. "Or you can ask to be driven to Merriwold. Give us a ring so we know when to expect you. Now I really must be going. Henry will be home from school soon, and I'm sure he is full of beans." She glanced at her watch. "Probably driving Grannie and James a bit crazy about now. Which reminds me," she dropped herself onto the bed again, her eyes bright. "You'll need a bit of guidance when meeting the family...ooh but this will have to be quick. Maybe just two warnings. "Henry will want your attention constantly. You must be firm from the start. And," she said standing, "don't address Grannie as 'Grannie' until she invites you to do so. A little pet peeve I cannot explain, but there you have it."

Sam extended his hand, and Helen placed hers in it. Hers felt soft and tiny in his large, calloused paw. He slowly pulled her to him. "I have so thoroughly enjoyed our time together today, Helen. Thank you for...everything."

She patted his chest and touched a kiss to his forehead. "Such a pleasant afternoon, Sam. I enjoyed our time as well. Now you rest, and we'll see you at Merriwold."

Helen scurried down the wide white marble stairs. In the hospital foyer stood a ten-foot-tall Christmas tree bedecked in red balls and white ribbons. The holiday spirit was everywhere, and she hoped it would be again at Merriwold as well. She felt confident inviting Sam to Merriwold was the right thing to do. But she was equally skeptical the family would agree.

"Mummy is home!" Henry squealed, abandoning his building project on the lounge floor. "James, is dinner ready? Mum is home, and I'm starving!" Henry wrapped his arms around Helen's waist. "I'm so glad you're here! I'm starving!"

"Lovely to see you too!" Helen bent to deliver a kiss on her son's head. "And what smells so good?"

"Chowder, I think!" Henry's bright eyes warmed Helen's heart.

Grannie and April joined them in the dining room. As Helen sat in her usual seat, she glanced at Joseph's empty chair and wondered how he'd feel about the impending visitor. A few years ago Joseph wanted to share this table with Sam as a friend. Now this friend had become something much more.

The table was set with red and white crockery on a yellow cloth, and the fish chowder was served from a large white tureen. "Everything looks and smells wonderful, James. Thank you." James tipped his head to her and took his post in the doorway, arm bent at the elbow, a red kitchen cloth draped over his forearm. His worn white shirt appeared bright and crisp against his dark smooth skin. He was contradiction personified. James had much to say but spoke only when asked. The lessons he had gleaned from his spot in the shadows must have made him a wise man, though, and Helen knew that. She wondered what he'd say about their visitor.

Henry didn't know what to do first, so he filled one hand with bread and filled his mouth with the other. He was reaching for more bread when Helen scolded him. "Henry! Where are your manners?"

"You act as though he had some to lose," April muttered under her breath. Helen quickly reacted, shooting a glare at April. Since Joseph's death, April had adopted an increasingly sour demeanor. She seemed to enjoy even the negative attention she drew. But Helen decided to let the comment pass after all.

After Grannie told everyone about her afternoon playing bridge, Helen created her opportunity to tell them about Sam. She took a deep breath, and avoiding all eye contact, began. "We're having company for the holidays, isn't that lovely?" She raised her water goblet and sipped nervously.

"Aside from the usual for Christmas lunch?" asked April. Anyone out of the ordinary would easily put April on guard. Since Joseph's death, she was relieved the guest list had been whittled to a faithful few for the traditional brunch—Dr. and Elizabeth Stuart, the Wilkes, the Roberts, and her mother's cousin, Martin, and his family.

"Yes, April, in addition to our usual guests. Do you remember our talking from time to time about Captain VanEck, the oil tanker captain from Holland?" Grannie and April searched their memories and came up blank. "We had intended to have the Captain here, but his schedule always precluded the chance." Helen shifted in her chair. "Well, he is recuperating in hospital from a stomach operation and needs a bit more time to recover." The speed of Helen's speech increased as she spoke. "I offered him our spare room. He'll be staying with us through the holidays," she blurted then quickly gulped her water.

"Staying here?" asked April incredulous, her eyes wide. She dropped her fork and tucked her hands under her thighs, her eyes darting between her mother and Grannie.

Grannie eyed Helen. "Why can't he take a room somewhere? How well do you know this man?"

Helen kept her voice calm and even. "I feel I know him very well. He's a good man, mother. I hate the thought of Joseph's friend, anyone for that matter, in a hotel room for Christmas, or in his case, on a ship that's being repaired." She shook her head, "can you imagine the noise?" Helen quickly turned to Henry and touched his arm. "Having Daddy's friend here will be fun! Maybe he'll help trim the tree. Would you like that, sweetie?"

Henry pointed to himself with his thumb, "But *I* put the star on top!"

"Of course, my darling, that's your job," she assured him.

April mumbled at first. "This is just too strange, mum" she objected.

"You're forgetting that I do know him. I know him very well and so did Daddy." She set down her glass, shifted in her seat. "Once you meet him, you'll see, we will all be just fine." Helen smiled, knowing their worries would disappear immediately. "He arrives Friday and will be with us until he is ready to sail with his ship. Not long, really. Now we have only three days to ready the gray room." Helen shot a glance to James, who seemed to be waiting for it to land on him. He conveyed his understanding with the slightest nod. "Yes, well then, all settled. Plan to meet him at dinner here on Friday. April, invite David to join us if you'd like," she offered absent-mindedly, returning to her supper.

April and David had dated for years. The two latched onto each other on their first day of secondary school. Both misfits in their own way, they clung to each other, becoming quickly comfortable as an old pair of shoes. The only child, David enjoyed escaping his mother's grip at Merriwold where no one was watching. Conversely, April delighted in the overflow attention poured onto David at his house. Over the years, however, David grew into an attractive and driven young man while April remained awkward and sheepish. Helen explained their continued relationship as his laziness. They behaved more like siblings than lovers, and the notion of a relationship without sparkle baffled her completely.

Early the next morning James's son arrived to give the guest room a fresh coat of gray paint. James and Helen teamed up to ready the house for Sam as well as the holiday visitors. James stocked the pantry and liquor cabinet, and Helen baked cranberry scones, mince pies, and butter cookies. She filled a basket with fresh mangoes and plums and placed it on the kitchen table. Together they hung mistletoe and garland everywhere and a red-bowed wreath on the front door. The aroma of fir and pine gave the house a welcoming air.

While all the work was being done, April busied herself with schoolwork, and Grannie played bridge incessantly in order to *stay out of the way*. Even when Henry was little, she would quickly volunteer to read him to sleep rather than help with the evening chores. And once Henry learned to read for himself, Grannie would volunteer to listen until she herself fell asleep. That was her grandmotherly duty, she'd explain. And she was very dutiful those three long days.

At last Friday arrived. Henry burst through the heavy front door squealing, "I'm on holiday! No school for a month!" He found his mother in the kitchen baking cookies and took her hands in his. They spun around the kitchen in a cake flour fog.

"Henry," Helen tried to calm him with a soft voice, "do you remember our guest Captain VanEck arrives today?"

"Oh yes, mummy! When is he coming? I want to play marbles with him. Do you think he'll play?" Henry paused long enough to sample an angel cookie.

Helen ruffled his hair. "Just one cookie," she warned. "I'm sure the captain will want to play with you, but," she cupped his chin in her hand, "let's make this a quiet and relaxing time for him here at Merriwold, shall we?" She locked onto his blue eyes. "You must be more quiet than usual, is that understood? Can I count on your very best behavior?"

Henry rolled his eyes. "Yes, mum," he agreed. He took another cookie and headed toward the foyer. "I'm going to wait for the Captain outside," he announced. Ashes the cat scampered outside too, and the door closed with a thud behind them.

As Helen continued baking, she felt the butterflies in her stomach warring with pangs of fear. She wondered how well she'd be able to mask her growing fondness for Sam in front of her family. Family! How would she ever explain his? She assaulted the dough with her rolling pin, and the oven timer sounded. Helen slid a metal spatula under each cookie, and transferred them onto the cooling rack. They were perfect shapes of Christmas—bells, stockings, stars, and angels. She paused, scooping up an angel, and holding the warm, sweet shape eye level. "Help!" she pleaded.

Outside, Sam unfolded his long legs from the hired car, tucked in his shirttail, straightened his hat, and absorbed the setting. Merriwold, a modest whitewashed stucco made grand by opposing upper and lower verandas with bright pink flowers cascading from white iron railings above to the railings below, sat perched on a bluff overlooking the ocean against a brilliant blue sky. The garden, brimming with color, began just outside the front door, meandered along the front, turned the corner and exploded into a beautiful collection of trees, shrubs, and glorious flowers. Two metal rocking chairs waited beneath the syringa tree, its white and yellow blooms creating a carpet on the ground. The sound of the surf, birds floating on the breeze, and a home amidst it all. Incredibly lovely.

He thought of his own home and ached for them—Ger, Marike, Maud, and Trudy. Safe travels, she had bid him. If only she knew how far he'd gone. He slipped his wedding band into his chest pocket and headed toward the house.

Henry caught up with Sam as he reached the top step to the lawn. "Captain VanEck? Is that you?" Sam set down his suitcase and removed his hat. Henry stretched his cupped hands toward Sam. "He was green when I caught him, but now he's looking a bit dull," Henry said, peering with one eye between his fingers.

Sam bent at the waist, hands on his knees. He peeked inside Henry's hands. "Well, look at that, a salamander," he said, enthusiastically. "Yes, I am Captain VanEck, and I am delighted to meet you, Henry." He studied Henry's round face and saw glimpses of his friend in the set of his eyes, the corners of his mouth. His heart hurt for this young child who would grow up without his father. Sam placed his hand on the boy's head. "Is your mother inside, son?"

"She's baking cookies! Let's go have one!" Henry freed the salamander and reached up for Sam's elbow. "She has been baking for days. Oh I love when company comes!" He led the way along the walk and up four more steps to the front door. He pushed it open with a shove, and it banged against the doorstop. "He's here!" Henry yelled. "Captain VanEck is here!"

Helen emerged from the kitchen, untying her apron. She placed an arm along Henry's shoulder. "Hush, Henry. Is that any way to announce a guest?" She smiled up at Sam. "I see you two have met?" Then she whispered in Henry's ear, "Go wash your hands and have yourself *one* cookie." He quickly disappeared, leaving them alone in the foyer. Helen touched her hair nervously. "You're looking well, Sam. How do you feel?"

"Wonderful, thank you," he said turning his hat in his hands. All thoughts of Leiden had vanished, at least for the moment. He set his hat on his suitcase and took both of her hands. "I am thankful and very happy to be here, Helen." He lifted her hands and kissed them. He could not deny his feelings for her, but rather than risk sounding foolish, he chose to not voice them just yet.

"Mummy," Henry's voice startled them both. "When can we have dinner? James was wondering." Henry looked awkwardly at Helen. "Your face is red, mum, are you ill?"

Helen felt herself flush. "Quite well, my love," she said smoothing her hair and checking the waistband of her skirt. "Please tell James we'll have dinner at seven. That will give us time to show the Captain around and let him rest." She looked to Sam, "is that alright with you?"

Sam lifted his bag and hat. "Helen, I am grateful just to be here. I plan on being a good guest and doing precisely as I am told. Now, where would you like me to put my satchel?" Sam followed Helen through the lounge and to the upstairs hall, stopping at the first room on the left. The gray bedroom smelled of fresh paint, even though the windows had been left wide open. Ocean breezes pushed the white sheers against a dark mahogany chest of drawers. A matching arched headboard framed the top of a double bed. Sam watched Helen as she spoke, and the sight of her near the bed was nearly overwhelming.

"...hanging space here, and the upper three drawers are empty...Sam? Are you alright?"

He cleared his throat. "Yes of course. Plenty of space."

"I'll leave you to unpack. Please let me know if you need anything? When you are ready, join me in the lounge for a drink?" she caught herself, "of coconut milk, of course." Helen had felt the electricity as well, and she was eager to leave the bedroom. Her emotions hadn't been stirred in quite some time, and the strength of her urge caught her off guard. "I'll be downstairs, Sam," she said, avoiding his eyes as she slipped past him and closed the door behind herself. Safely alone in the hall, she leaned against the closed door and exhaled. She waited there until her heartbeat calmed to a normal rate.

Helen knocked on April's door across the hall and let herself inside the bedroom, startling April. "School work?" Helen observed, sitting on the bed. April spent most of her time in her room where she felt most at ease, claiming to study though her grades didn't reflect the apparent effort.

"Yes," she moaned, turning in her chair to face her mother. "After the holiday we have another paper due on Hitler and the Nazi aggression. We're supposed to guess what will happen between now and this time next year."

"Captain VanEck arrived a short while ago. Perhaps he can offer some insight," Helen offered.

"Here? He's here already?" Her voice jumped an octave, and she rubbed her hands as she spoke. "Must he stay just across the hall? How long will he be here?"

Helen jumped up to close the bedroom door and hushed her. "Don't be rude, April, he'll hear you! He'll stay until he feels ready to get back to his ship. He's had an operation, April. He'll be with us at least through the holidays, as planned."

"Why here, mother?" her voice was strained.

"April, calm down," Helen said dismissively. "We talked about this, remember? He has nowhere else to go. He was a friend to Joseph and to me, not a stranger." She stood with her arms folded, unsmiling.

"But he is a stranger!" April was up and pacing now, her arms squeezing her own thin frame. "Living four feet from my bedroom door!"

Helen exhaled an angry whisper, "His visit shouldn't bother you so!" as if telling her daughter how to feel would magically make her do so.

April stopped abruptly and lowered her head. Her shoulders slumped as though the air inside her had escaped. "Would Christmas be so dreadful if you had only your immediate family to share it with? Must you always be the hostess, entertaining your guests?"

Helen was taken aback. "April, you are not making any sense. Having company offers a distraction from those who are missing." Helen stood squarely in front of April. "I'm tired of feeling lonely. I want to get on with my life. Can you understand that? You are nineteen now. Where is your compassion, April?" She searched her daughter's face, but April wouldn't meet her eyes. "Do you ever think of anyone beside yourself?" It was more of a statement than a question. Helen smoothed her skirt and touched her hair. "Dinner is at seven. Make it a pleasant evening, April." Helen opened the door and looked back at her slouching, unkempt daughter. "And stand up straight!" she quietly seethed. "People will think you're unhappy."

An hour later, Sam found Helen curled up in her blue upholstered chair by the wide picture window. She was completely absorbed in the view of the ocean. "You look too peaceful to disturb."

"Oh Sam," she said, rising unsteadily onto stocking feet. Her right foot had fallen asleep and was tingling. "You are not disturbing me at all. Make yourself comfortable," she said, motioning to a chair like hers. "I'll tell James we're ready." She stomped her foot as she walked. "Pins and needles," she called aloud.

Sam sat and immediately saw Helen, Joseph, and Henry smiling at him from a teak picture frame. He lifted the photo to get a better look.

"That was taken just before Joseph's heart attack. We are very fortunate to have it," Helen said, taking her usual seat and tucking a leg underneath her. James had followed her in and set down a silver tray of drinks and hot hors d'oeuvres. Helen made the necessary introductions.

"Pleasure to meet you, James." James nodded and returned to the kitchen. "Beautiful family, Helen. Joseph was a lucky man."

"We shall always miss him," Helen said. "But time is a powerful healer. And life has just taken a positive turn." She cocked her head and offered him a brave smile which he warmly accepted. "Now let me warn you, for lack of a better phrase, about the people you are about to meet."

"Uh-oh. Should I take notes?" Sam asked, straightening to attention.

Helen moved to the window. "Wouldn't do you any good, I'm afraid. The minute you figure everyone out and learn what they want from you, poof," she snapped her fingers, "everything changes."

Sam chuckled. "Sounds like your family keeps you on your toes." He helped himself to a mushroom canapé and glass of milk.

"Indeed. We'll begin with my mother. Her given name is Abigail Adler, but everyone calls her Grannie, even her bridge partners. But don't assume she will allow you to call her Grannie, remember. She has a problem with her hip and drags her leg a bit, but never acknowledge that she's dragging it, or she will hate you for it. But don't worry. She's at the age where she usually forgets most everything a day later anyway." They laughed at the idea. "All joking aside, I honestly don't know what I would have done without her in those early years. She was a rock I clung to dearly.

Henry you already met, so you already know him. Such a joy. I don't know how I would have survived Joseph's death without him. An afternoon with him is like being suspended in time, though he has far too much energy for one small body, and the noise level is quite extraordinary." She ran a hand through her hair and exhaled. "He truly wears me out. But that is the best kind of exhaustion." She looked at Sam and smiled.

Sam nodded in agreement. "From the instant we met I felt..." he searched for the right word, "tired." The two laughed out loud until footsteps descending the stairs caught their attention.

"April," whispered Helen.

"Who?" asked Sam.

April entered the lounge tentatively, like a bug afraid to be swatted. Sam rose to greet her.

"Sam, this is my daughter, April. April, meet Captain VanEck," instructed Helen then watched closely to be sure her daughter behaved appropriately.

April's eyes finally found Sam's, and she nervously placed her hand in his. Her long brown hair was pulled back loosely, and she absent-mindedly touched it before adjusting her navy linen skirt. "Pleasure to meet you, Captain," April mumbled, glancing out of habit at her mother to acknowledge her compliance.

Sam felt completely stymied. *Daughter?* This dark, almost masculine looking girl was a direct contrast to her mother's light, softly feminine looks. "What a nice, er...how very nice to meet you...at last, April. Please tell me again how old you are?" *And who are you and where did you come from?* He wanted to know.

Thankfully, Grannie and Henry burst through the front door. "Mum! Mummie!" Henry called.

"We are right here, dear," offered Helen calmly. "Come in, Mother, I want you to meet Captain VanEck."

Sam extended his hand. "You must be Grannie." The instant he said the word, Sam realized his mistake. "I mean, Mrs. Adler." Too late.

"Humph," Grannie snorted and moved toward the sofa.

"Dear Mrs. Adler," Sam pleaded. "I apologize. I should have waited for your permission to call you such an endearing term. Why, I have no business being so presumptuous, especially on our first meeting." He glanced at Helen for moral support. "Helen has told me so much about you, I feel as though I already know you." He took her hand again and covered it with his other. "I do trust our relationship will grow in that direction."

She was putty in his hands. Grannie felt herself soften, though she didn't fully melt. "No harm done I suppose," Grannie sniffed. But his response revealed the budding romance, and the clue did not go unnoticed. She poured a glass of sherry and lowered herself onto the sofa, extending her bad leg straight in front of her. As soon as Sam found his seat, Henry quickly climbed onto his lap and made himself comfortable.

"Well, young man, nice to see you again," Sam said, readjusting Henry's weight away from the operation site.

"April showed me Holland on the globe. Did you really ride in your boat all that way?"

"That's a funny way to put it," Sam chuckled. "Yes, we certainly did! But we left Holland about four years ago. I travel to other places now. Let's have a look at your globe, and I'll show you," Sam offered, helping Henry to his feet. Henry retrieved the globe from the desk, and Sam knelt beside it. "This is the Persian Gulf, where oil is drilled. Crude oil is used to make gasoline and diesel for ships, tanks, and planes. We take on oil here and deliver it to places like Bombay." He traced a route through the Gulf of Oman and into the Arabian. "Sometimes we went to Port Said and into the Mediterranean Sea, but no longer. Lately we run along the coast of Africa—Port Elizabeth, Cape Town, and out to Madagascar. You know all those places, right?" Henry nodded silently. "And here we are in Durban."

"I know Durban!" Henry squealed.

"We're having a geography lesson, David." Rather than interrupt, David had slid into the room and listened patiently while Sam spoke. His emerging wanderlust fed off Sam's descriptions.

"David," Helen said, "I want you to meet our guest, Captain VanEck." The two shook hands. "Sam, this is April's fiancé, David Williams."

"Pleasure to meet you," Sam said, standing to shake David's hand. "Henry asked about my travels, which are much easier to explain with a globe."

David straightened to his full five-foot-ten-inch height, though still easily four inches shorter than Sam. He strengthened his firm grip on Sam's hand before letting it drop. "An honor, Captain. I understand you are an oil tanker captain. You must have plenty of war stories to share. And I'd like to hear about all the places you've seen."

"Do you ever get lost, Captain VanEck?" interrupted Henry.

Sam felt completely lost. Not only does Helen have a grown daughter, but she's engaged to be married! He wondered how the whole subject of April had not surfaced in any of their meetings or in the hours they'd spent talking just the other day at the hospital. "Maybe once, Henry."

"Kos is op die tafel," announced James in his native Zulu. *Dinner is served.*

The group moved into the cozy sage green dining room and stood behind their seats. James had set the table with white crockery on a striped crimson cloth that complimented the needlepoint chair pads. Oversized serving dishes were filled to the brim and arranged on the buffet table by the large picture window. Helen raised her water glass and proposed a toast, "to good food and friendship and to the end of the war. May God bless us all." With that everyone filled their dishes and settled in place. The evening went well, thankfully. Dinner was delicious, and the conversation, lively. Even April, who was normally painfully withdrawn around strangers, could not resist Sam's charm. David was particularly interested in hearing Sam's views on the war in general. April had fed David questions in order to acquire information for her paper, and Sam eagerly obliged. Sam vehemently hated the war, and he loathed Hitler. He had strong opinions about the Nazi gangsters that invaded his land and his neighbors', but he fought the urge to unfurl the extent of that emotion that evening. He made a concerted effort to keep his stories as light as possible, avoiding the doom and gloom he most often felt. Instead, he spoke optimistically about the United States' involvement and his admiration for Churchill and Roosevelt.

Helen allowed herself to relax and enjoy the charged atmosphere. She quietly observed Sam's charming manner and the way he held Henry's attention. Even Grannie enjoyed hearing stories of Sam's travels. Like a maestro conducting a symphony, Sam seemed to tap those listening with his invisible baton, reassuring each that they were vital to the evening's production. From across the table that night, in front of unsuspecting witnesses, Helen fell hopelessly in love with this already smitten sailor.

Hours later, Sam assured his captive audience he had more stories to share at another time. He followed Helen and Grannie into the quiet lounge. Helen snapped on a lamp and put Cole Porter's "Anything Goes" on the phonograph. Sam felt suddenly exhausted and made his excuses. Helen crossed the room to him. Only then did she realize the time, and she regretted letting it slip by unnoticed. "Not to worry, Helen. The evening was too delightful to cut short. And I know once I sit down with you lovely ladies, I won't be able to leave." Sam took Helen's hands and, bending at the waist, kissed them both. "Thank you very much for a most enjoyable evening." He paused with his face near hers.

Helen's heart raced. "You are most welcome, Captain. Sleep as late as you can in the morning. We won't disturb you." She made a mental note to remind her son of that promise.

Sam reluctantly let go of her hands, then turned and bowed to Grannie. "Good night, Mrs. Adler. Lovely having dinner with you."

Grannie waved her hand. "Call me Grannie; everyone else does."

Sam and Helen exchanged a victory glance. "Good night, then, Grannie."

From her chair in the lounge Helen heard Sam bidding good night to April, David, and Henry in the kitchen. "Good night, Cappy," called Henry, and an outburst of laughter followed. Sam slowly climbed the steps to his room.

Grannie chuckled. "He's an interesting fellow, Helen. What is it about him that made you feel inviting him to stay indefinitely was...ok?"

Helen thought about how to answer that question. It was the same question she had been asking herself. She sat near her mother on the sofa, resting her arm on the top of the cushion and tucking her feet under her so they could be face to face. "Joseph has been gone a long time now it seems. He was good to me, spoiled me really. I miss the attention." She wasn't being completely honest, and they both knew it. Helen heard the door to the gray room close. The children were still laughing in the kitchen. Helen thought about Sam. "There is something about him," she began and smiled to herself. "He's like an old friend," she said remembering the quote they'd shared during their first day together. She changed tact. "Have you ever met someone whom, from the first encounter, you felt you'd known all your life?" Abigail patted her daughter's hand and smiled. "It's more than that, mother. He's like a puzzle piece that fits snuggly into place," she said lacing her fingers.

Abigail took her daughter's hand and squeezed it twice. "Whatever makes you happy, Helen." She sipped the last of her sherry. "I hope this little...encounter is a stepping stone to get you out in the world again. But remember, he'll soon be off to his dangerous and intriguing life, and where will that leave you?" She rose unsteadily to her feet. "Perhaps you'll find a local man to date like that nice Mr. Benson, the pharmacist. He is always asking about you." She headed to the stairs. "Good night, Helen. Enjoy yourself today, but think hard about tomorrow."

"Good night, mother," Helen called to the back of her aging mother. There was a time when Helen was awed by her mother's ability to read her mind. Now she found the talent irritating. The group emerged from the kitchen, David and April, hand in hand, and Henry looking exhausted. David thanked Helen for the evening, and April showed him to the door. "Good night, you two," Helen called to the couple. "You are done for the day, young man," she said to Henry. "Let's go!"

Helen tucked Henry into bed with Floyd fitting snugly under his arm. She kissed his head and pulled the coverlet around his shoulders. He didn't think to ask for a story; Sam had more than filled that requirement. "Shhhh, remember?" she whispered with her finger to her lips. "The Captain will be resting in the morning when you wake up," she reminded him while tiptoeing quietly out of his room. With renewed energy, Helen went back downstairs to the kitchen and made the dough for James to bake bread when he returned at dawn. Then she applied polish to the silverware for James to buff. Finally exhausted, she climbed the steps, ready for bed. She paused outside Sam's closed door. All was quiet. Despite her mother's warning, Helen felt wonderfully content. All the beds in her home were full, and the family had shared a magical evening with a wonderful guest. She was still smiling as she climbed into bed. She turned on her tiny bedside radio. The song "Yours" emanated softly as she drifted off to sleep.

ELEVEN – Durban

Late December, 1942 South African summers bring changeable weather. While at sea, Sam was skillfully in control, regardless of weather. On land he remained at Mother Nature's mercy. He napped lazily during storms and walked briskly in the breeze as they cleared. The change of pace, as well as the submission to it, healed him quickly. One morning Helen found Sam seated in the painted rocker on the lower veranda; a cotton throw blanket on his lap, his hat pulled low over his face. For the moment the skies were gloriously clear. A cool breeze ruffled the syringa casting dappled shade over Sam, who was, in fact, asleep. Four years ago this man was merely a friend, an afterthought from the life she shared with Joseph. How quickly he'd grown to inhabit Helen's heart as well as her house. Is this fate, she wondered, or did she just wish it so? As she set the tea tray on the small table beside him, he stirred. She added three sugar cubes to his tea, two to hers, and waited for him to wake fully. "You look like the picture of health to me, Captain. Let's go into town? Christmas is only days away, and I still have a few gifts to find." She patted his knee, teasing, "that is, if you can leave this chair!"

Sam sat upright, adjusted his hat, and took the tea. "Perhaps I've become too comfortable," he confessed.

"You most certainly have. Why look at those shirttails!" she laughed.

Sam delighted in her teasing. "I like to look my best for those I want to impress," he reminded her, laughing at himself. "Honestly, Helen, you have been so kind to me. I feel like a new man." He smiled and patted his stomach. "I cannot thank you enough for sharing Merriwold, this slice of heaven, with me."

"You are so welcome," she calmly assured him, pouring a little milk into his cup. "Shall we leave at ten? That will give you plenty of time for your breakfast, which I've noticed you cannot do without, and we can get ourselves to the market before the afternoon rush. This close to Christmas it will be crowded, I promise you that."

"Then we will finish before noon," he stated. "A crowd is the only thing I dislike more than shopping."

Helen raised a hand in warning. "Don't even think of trying to get out of this, Captain. Merriwold is my ship, I give the orders here, and we have a mission!"

Sam straightened to attention and saluted. "Yes ma'am! I will be ready, ma'am, on time!" They laughed, but then Sam turned serious. He stirred his tea. "Helen, I've wanted to ask you something." He set his cup on the tray and leaned forward, his forearms resting on his knees. "Meeting your daughter was quite a...surprise. You had not mentioned her before she entered the lounge the day I arrived. The photographs, well, the ones I've seen...she's not in any. Will you tell me about her? That is, if you want to. I don't mean to pry." Sam watched her reaction carefully, but she was motionless and matter-of-fact, which confused him even more.

"Surely you are mistaken, Sam. She is my daughter after all. Joseph must have mentioned her too. Perhaps you've forgotten," she said dismissing him. She crossed her legs, the upper one bobbed forcefully. "She is certainly no secret; she is nineteen years old for Heaven's sake!" Perhaps he had forgotten, he reassured her, though he was certain he had not. He wanted to hear April's story again then. Helen clasped her hands and looked up into the syringa tree, obviously uneasy. "I was married, briefly, as you know, to a pilot," she began flatly. "But the marriage was a painful mistake.

He kept his plane, and I kept April. Simple as that." The bitterness was still fresh in her voice. "He never looked back." She paused for a moment, turning her ring. "To be honest," she began, "Oh I don't like talking about this..." she hesitated, searching the sky, but he did not let her off the hook. She focused again on her ring. "That was the biggest failure of my life. My relationship with him caused so much pain—for me, for my mum..." her voice trailed off, and her gaze settled on the ocean. "Because of me and my mistake, we uprooted from our native country. Can you imagine?" She shook her head in amazement. "Do you know my mother never complained? She abruptly abandoned her entire life to come here, because the undeserving brat that I was asked her to do so. I made the biggest mistake of my life, and she agreed to come help me care for it the result the rest of her life." Sam wondered whether she meant the rest of Grannie's life or April's. "But," Helen continued, shifting in her seat and crossing her legs the other way, "what began as a mistake turned into a happy ending. Actually, it was Joseph who handled my divorce, and you know the rest of that story." She attempted an uneasy smile.

"Yes, I do! And the happy ending continues to unfold," he said with a wink. "But I still don't understand why you neglected to mention her," he insisted.

She sipped her tea, choosing her words before speaking. "When April was a baby, my mother and I delighted in her. But as she grew older, she became more and more like...him. Isn't that amazing? They've had absolutely no contact since her infancy, yet she increasingly took on all his mannerisms as she grew." She shook her head, studying her ring. "By about age twelve she became a true replica of him, unfortunately." Old anger simmered quickly. "He deserted me; deserted us! What kind of man walks out on his child?" she asked bitterly. "The entire mess has all blurred into a dark and miserable time in my life." She sat erect. "Look here," she began, pulling the hem of her skirt just above her knee. "Do you see this scar?" Sam readily saw the colorless rounded mass just below the kneecap. "I took a terrible spill as a youngster onto a smoldering log. The pain was unbearable, and I was inconsolable. While the wound has certainly healed, I have only to look at it to remember the disaster." She replaced her skirt, crossed her legs, and let her foot bob. "April is a scar that will never heal," she said, her face resolute. "In any event, April will finish school this year and marry David the next. There's nothing else to know, really." She looked at him defiantly. "Did you have any more questions?" she asked, crossing her arms over her chest.

Raising both hands in surrender, Sam suggested they go inside for breakfast.

The market was a sensory thrill, an open-air display of local craftsmanship and produce arranged in stall after stall. Brightly colored batiks and fabrics hung on display. Textured wooden carvings, and intricate jewelry begged to be touched, while aromas of scented soaps, spices, and baked goods filled the air. Helen picked up a pair of tea light holders. "Aren't these exquisite, Sam," she said running her fingers along a stripe of carvings in the wood. "I just adore candles." He offered to buy them as a thank you gift, and she accepted. "Quite naughty of me to go off Christmas shopping and buy something for me first. But often that's the best part about Christmas shopping, isn't it!" She spotted a conch shell and put it to her ear to hear the ocean waves mimicked inside. "I never grow tired of that sound," she said offering him a listen.

"Then stow away with me on my ship," he said, pressing the shell to his ear. "The sound is much more varied and beautiful on the sea than in this shell."

She dismissed him with a coy smile. "Now let's see. Who else is on my list?" She pulled a piece of paper from her purse. "April is next. Pity. She is so difficult to buy for. I never know what she would like. She doesn't seem to have any preferences at all, so I usually buy her something I like. That way when she rejects the gift, which she inevitably does, nothing is wasted." She crossed to a display of silk scarves and plucked an emerald green one from the table. "Beautiful, isn't it?" she asked, laying it across her shoulder. "Brings out the blue in my eyes, don't you think?" Helen paid for the scarf and stuffed it into her sack. "Now I'm afraid we must go our separate ways while I find something for you." Sam objected vehemently, but her mind was set. They would meet near the produce area in thirty minutes.

Alone and amid the wonderful handmade gifts, Sam's family filled his thoughts. How would they observe the holidays? He thought of poor Marike missing her beloved Sinterklaas. Celebrating, he knew, was out of the question. But he hoped they'd find some joy, maybe in singing carols, telling stories of the past, clinging to hope of better times ahead. He often wondered what their days were like, did they have enough to eat, were they safe and warm. He kept himself from wondering if they were alive; he simply told himself they were and dismissed all other thoughts. Though his family was often in his thoughts, he'd learned to push them to the alcoves of his mind. Since he was powerless to affect their situation, keeping them below the surface was his only way of coping.

He picked up a few items and met Helen on time. She noticed his sacks and wondered if they were gifts for his family or hers. When she asked him, he lowered his head and walked away from the crowd.

"Don't think they haven't been on my mind," he said, perching himself on a bench. He let out a sigh. "Remember, we have not communicated. I have tried contacting the authorities myself, I've begged Caltex Headquarters to get me information. There is just no way in or out," he said, his shoulders slumped. "If I were to send gifts, chances are slim the girls would ever receive them." He looked away from her. "I've been a seafarer for years, and they are accustomed to life without me. I used to find that comforting. Knowing they were managing sufficiently without me allowed me to focus on my job, even enjoy the route, lonely as a seafarer's life may seem." He placed his hands on his thighs, squinting at her in the sunshine. "Now it's frightening."

He reached for her arm and led her to the spot beside him. "So I learned to stay focused on our treks—all business; nothing personal. When my crewmates gather in my stateroom, we listen to the BBC broadcasts, discuss the war's progress and our part in it only. Discussing what-ifs proved counterproductive." Sam met Helen's eyes. "And until we met again, my fine lady, I was quite content in my solitude." The sun lit her hair bright red. "You are like an angel, *mijn engel,* sent to rescue me." They had so much they wanted to say to each other, yet neither knew the acceptable words or where to begin. It was too soon to voice what they both felt. Their hearts pounded as they dove into each other's eyes.

Finally, Helen whispered, "Let's get something for mother." Reluctantly, Sam rose to lead the way. "Let's get her something noisy to wear so we can hear her coming." Their laughter relieved the tension. "Then lunch. I'm ravenous."

In the farmer's market area they bought mangoes, dates, berries, and breads and then headed to the sandy beach. Just outside of town they found a secluded spot with a full view of the sea and spread their blanket. Sam stretched himself across the quilted expanse, one hand behind his head, and let the warm breeze wash over him. Helen sat near him with her legs folded beneath her. "If only we could freeze time, make it stop right this minute." Her voice was edgy.

Sam propped himself on an elbow, and she slid in near him. "What a gift we've been given in this time together. Don't let worries snatch away our precious moments. With the world at war, we have only today for sure." Helen began to speak, but he hushed her with a gentle touch to her lips. Then he pulled her to him and kissed her as he'd wanted to since their visit in his hospital room. They spent the rest of the afternoon like that, holding each other, kissing, napping, and not caring who might see them. Their lifetime of memories would have to be built one snippet at a time.

On Christmas morning Sam awoke to Judy Garland bidding everyone a merry little Christmas from the phonograph. He followed the sound to the lounge where James brought a tray of tea and mince pies in porcelain dishes. Grannie, April, and Helen filed in groggily. Henry, on the other hand, was an elf with a mission and tore his way through the robed group to the tree standing in front of the big picture window. He spread his arms wide and let out such an enthusiastic "Merry Christmas!" that even April lit up, and high-pitched chatter ensued. They each took a seat near the tree.

Henry's child-like greeting also stirred a spot in Sam's heart. He couldn't help but ache for his children, his home, and his own childhood traditions. He longed for snow instead of sand, to be surrounded by it falling on carolers in the town square, to be warmly welcomed by old acquaintances on Sinterklaas. He wondered how his children were spending the day. Was Ger able to make their traditional meal? Would Christmas bombs replace the chime of bells? Would they have the strength in their hearts to sing? Would his children ever be able to erase this horrible time from their minds? Would they live through it?

Helen noticed him drift off and handed him a thin wrapped square. "For your new memories," she said. Inside was a copy of the Judy Garland record currently playing. "To remember your first holiday at Merriwold with us."

He tilted his head and patted his heart. "You know me well. Thank you." A smile attempted to make itself evident.

Brown paper and ribbon cluttered the room. Among the gifts were tin measuring cups for Helen, a new record album for April, and dice for Henry. April sincerely loved the silk scarf and let out an uninhibited "Thank you, Mummie!" and Helen laughed out loud. Emboldened, April approached Helen with a small wrapped box, certain she'd again found the perfect gift for her mother, the one that would bring them closer. "This is for you, and I hope you like it," April offered sincerely. But before Helen could open the wrap, Henry let out a cry. Ashes, the cat, had scratched him. As Helen rushed to him, the box slid behind the chair cushion and out of sight.

Helen sat back in her chair, pulling Henry onto her lap. She wrapped her arms around Henry and kissed and rubbed the scratch while April watched and waited. Finally, April picked up another gift and presented it to Grannie, who welcomed the present and her granddaughter with open arms.

Sam delighted in watching everyone opening gifts, and then he reached behind the tree for a handled bag. "Merry Christmas, ladies," he said, handing gifts to both Grannie and April. "I hope you find these useful."

Grannie ripped open the package and let out a squeal. "What a perfectly beautiful gift! Helen, did you choose this?" She held the topaz pendant to the light, and it sparkled.

"Only because I wanted to be certain you'd like it," Sam interrupted. "And topaz is much more fitting than rain sticks," he added with a wink in Helen's direction, who was stunned into silence. She had no idea Sam had bought gifts for them.

With some effort, Grannie rose from her chair. "Thank you, Captain. Helen, I'm going to get dressed so I can wear my new jewelry. Merry Christmas, everyone!"

"Captain," April started, "I don't have anything for you," she confessed.

"Nonsense," replied Sam. "Enjoy," he insisted. As April slowly unwrapped her gift, Henry snatched the empty bag.

"What about me, Cappy?" he asked, peering inside the bag and then back to Sam.

"What about you?" Sam teased, sitting to be eye-to-eye with him.

"Haven't you got something for me too in that bag?"

Sam peered into the empty sack. "Doesn't look like it, sport. Were you expecting something?" Henry's shoulders fell. Sam patted the breast pocket of his bathrobe. "Oh, what's this? Could this be for you?" Henry lit up and clasped his hands together. "Couldn't forget young Henry, now could I?" Sam tickled Henry's middle while he climbed into Sam's lap and reached into Sam's pocket for his treasure.

"A compass!" blurted Henry, his eyes wide.

"To help you stay on course," explained Sam.

Henry jumped off Sam's lap. "Thank you, Cappy!" He grabbed Sam's hand. "Now come show me how this works!" As soon as Sam pulled himself out of the chair, Henry was out the front door, the cat at his feet.

April was less effusive. "Soap. I guess everyone can use soap," she mumbled. She wondered if he were somehow telling her she needed to bathe. "Thanks, Captain." Crumbling the brown paper she announced she was off to dress for David's house. "Seems we're all wrapped up here." She smiled to herself at her choice of words.

"That's fine, dear," said Helen, oblivious. "Will you and David be back for lunch?"

April stopped short. "Um, yes. You were expecting us, right?" she asked, heading up the stairs.

"Be here by one," called Helen after her. "And remember to wish David's parents a Merry Christmas." She turned to Sam and apologized for her daughter's lack of enthusiasm. "She's always been a bit...ungrateful."

"Cappy, are you coming?" Henry had burst through the front door and stood with his hand on his hip.

"On my way, skipper!" Sam turned to Helen and squeezed her hand. "Join us?"

"Compasses are for sailors," she said. "I prefer my feet firmly on the ground, thank you. I'd better go talk with April. Wish me luck?" Sam kissed her on the cheek and cinched his robe tightly before hurrying outside.

Helen knocked loudly on April's bedroom door and without waiting for a response, entered.

"I didn't say come in," April hissed.

"What's wrong, April? You seem a bit...off." Helen sat on the bed and folded her arms in front of her. "Are you angry with me?"

Helen's directness, not to mention her concern, threw April completely off balance. "Well, I'm not really angry with you, mother." *Mother.* The word hung in the air out of place.

"Feels good to be called 'Mother,' no matter what the tone."

"If you behaved like a mother instead of a love-sick teenager—" April gasped as the words escaped from her mouth; her face flushed. She avoided her mother's eyes and nervously rearranged tiny wooden figurines on her bureau.

Apparently, her feelings for Sam were obvious. Helen attempted an explanation. "Joseph has been gone a long time. I deserve love in my life. Would you deny me that?" April ignored the question. "You love David, right? Knowing how that feels to be in love, would you deny me that chance?" she repeated.

"Love, love, love!" April shouted, spraying the miniature menagerie to the floor with a sweep of her arm. "You've always had plenty of love in your life, right mother? My father, Joseph, Henry, and now him! But there's never enough, is there..." hot tears streaked her face. She turned her back to her mother and stood at the window, arms wrapped tightly around herself.

Helen slowly approached her. This was new ground for them. Helen reached a hand toward her daughter's back, but then let it drop. "Love isn't doled out in measurements to be used sparingly, April. There's always enough, more than enough. In fact, the more you love, the greater your capacity to love."

April whirled around to face her mother. Her tone was acrid, "I suppose, then, that I should be grateful you love him. Go on, keep on loving *everyone*, so perhaps someday you'll have the capacity to love—" April hugged herself tighter, eyes on the floor, tears flowing.

"What is it?" Helen demanded.

"Me!" she shouted, her arms open wide. "Me! The inconvenient, constant reminder of the man who walked out on you!" The words were out, indelibly. "I certainly don't look anything like you, so I must look like him. I know that's dreadful, but I can't help that! Maybe I even behave like him, I don't know. But I am *not* him!" She spat the words. "Do you realize you've made me pay for him my whole life? Ironic, isn't it, *my* paying for *your* mistake?" Seething now, "You've cut off the hand of the victim instead of the thief!" April collapsed into a heap on the bed, tears burning. "Yes, I am his child. But. I am *your* child. Too. I am yours, too. How can you so easily dismiss that fact? Dismiss *me*?" she pleaded between sobs. After a while she propped herself on an elbow, calmer. Setting her eyes directly on her mothers' April continued, "You make time for this stranger; move him into our home? You have time for everyone else. Henry. Grannie. Guests. Anyone really. Except me."

Helen was stunned. She had no idea her feelings were so transparent. She dropped onto the edge of the bed, shocked. After a very awkward silence, she offered an excuse, backpedaling. "April, try to understand. Imagine two very different mothers raised you and Henry in two very different families. Your mother was inexperienced and frightened. Here I was in a new country with the added responsibility of raising a child. Your father had left me completely alone. Can you imagine how devastating that was for me?" Helen folded her arms tightly, crossed her legs. "You were just a small child. I was in a very sad state. Why, I was heartbroken. I'd been abandoned." She pouted in self-pity. "By the time Henry came along, so much had changed. His mother was settled and mature...and loved." She found April's eyes and sat more upright. "But you must know that I did the best I could under the circumstances," Helen declared, in an effort to convince her daughter and herself.

But April's heart was not softening. "Abandoned? I know all about being abandoned, and you never left the house!" April's anger boiled quickly. She bolted to standing. "The best you could? Who are you fooling?" April crossed the room and snatched her purse off the door handle. "I really don't want to argue on Christmas. I'll go to David's house, you'll prepare for your beloved guests, and I'll see you at one. Oh and before I forget," she crossed to the closet and retrieved the green silk scarf her mother had just given her. "Mind if I wear this once before you reclaim it?" she snapped, draping the scarf around her neck and glaring at Helen. She slammed the door behind her.

April sailed down the stairs, her scarf trailing behind her. She went directly to Helen's chair. Plucking the gift from behind the cushion, she took a moment to weigh the situation. Finally, she threw the present under the tree and headed for the door.

At first, Helen sat panting as though she'd been physically attacked. Feeling suddenly cold, she rubbed her upper arms and thighs, her mind doing its best to reassure herself. *She can't possibly know how I feel, how I felt. I make her pay for his mistake? Ridiculous!* "How dare she speak to me like that!" she said aloud, her anger beginning to simmer. "I hope she has an ungrateful child of her own someday, I really do," she muttered, smoothing her hair. After a few minutes she stood, adjusted her skirt, and wondered how she had raised such a self-centered child.

By one o'clock Merriwold was a flurry of activity. As guests arrived, Helen delighted in introducing each one to Sam. Dr. and

Elizabeth Stuart were the first, as usual, followed by Cousin Martin, his wife, Phyllis, and their two children, and finally the neighbors from either side, Muriel and John Wilke and Emma and Tim Roberts—all eager to resume their traditional great time. The house and meal reflected Helen's enthusiasm for her favorite holiday. Background Christmas tunes and mouth-watering aromas filled the house and set the tone. Red and white candles, ribbons, and poinsettias were everywhere. Full, fragrant wreaths graced the doors and mantle, and mistletoe hung from every doorway. Red and green homemade quilts, garland crockery, and Christmas drinkware filled with grog and champagne were in abundance.

Sam adeptly filled the role of host, mingling easily with everyone. When he became tired, he sat down to a long conversation with Martin, George, and Tim. Helen delighted at the uproars of laughter coming from their corner of the room, certain Sam's storytelling was the culprit.

Late in the afternoon, Helen noticed Martin's off mood and cornered him. He confessed he had not wanted to dampen the party, but he had been called to active duty. He was scheduled to leave the next day for the desert in Northern Africa. "Oh Martin, how awful," she said, hoping the party atmosphere would not be affected. "Surely they plan to keep you in a safe place, barking orders to the enlistees?"

Martin shrugged, "I should think something like that." He glanced toward his wife. "Phyllis is taking it pretty hard. The children are old enough to be aware of the risks but still young enough to think their daddy is invincible." He winked at his cousin, and she hugged him.

"You *are* invincible, Martin. Remember that." She held both his hands. "Promise to write me often?" He promised he would, but the mood for him and his family was irretrievable. They made their excuses and left. The rest of the guests took Martin's lead, and the party drew to a close much earlier than expected.

"I am sorry your party ended so soon, but I am delighted this beautiful evening is still young," confessed Sam. "Let's take a walk on the beach, shall we?"

April was playing her new record album, and Henry and David were wrestling on the lounge floor when they ducked outside. The evening was warm, and the ocean breeze, dry and soft. They carried their shoes and walked side by side, caressed by cooling sand and sounds of the surf. Once out of Merriwold's view, they joined hands and continued in comfortable silence.

At last Sam spoke. "April seemed upset earlier today. Is everything all right?"

"Everything is fine, I suppose. Seems she feels neglected somehow. Must be the age." She said, dismissing the topic entirely. "How do you handle your girls?"

Normally Sam's family was not discussed, but neither could deny their presence today. "I leave the child rearing to Gertrude. I must admit a seafarer doesn't make for a very good father." Sam led them to a dried log on the sand. "Or perhaps that's why I became a seafarer in the first place," he admitted. The sun was just beginning its descent, giving everything a two-dimensional glow. "Originally, my cargo route was manageable, and my cause was supporting a family, not a war. When Hitler spread his cloak of terror over Holland, my choice was not simple: return to occupied Holland against company orders and be forced to work for the Nazis, or join the fight by ferrying fuel to allied forces. Each mile took me farther from the family I was responsible for and the only home I had ever known. If I am ever allowed to return, all will be dramatically changed, and in ways I can only begin to imagine."

He stared at the massive sea. "My girls hardly know me," he confessed. "I was so busy being their provider that I neglected to be their father." He lowered his chin to his chest, his broad shoulders hunched forward. "To be honest, the worry constantly tugs at me. After all, it is my duty to protect them." Small frothy waves pushed forward and receded. "But when the world is at war, who am I to magnify the wellbeing of only four people?" He gouged the sand with his heel. "The saddest truth is...I hardly miss them anymore." He tilted his head and peeked at her through anguished eyes. "A hideous confession, I know," he whispered.

Helen watched her own polished toes make swirls in the sand. "You cannot ask me to be your judge and jury," she said softly. "I don't know what I'd do in your situation or how I'd feel. You are separated from your family by miles and circumstance." Recalling her daughter's outburst, she admitted, "April and I live in the same house, yet we create our own abyss." Helen exhaled a cleansing sigh before finding Sam's eyes. "Joseph has been gone a long time now, and I find myself missing him less and less," she confessed. "I think our emotions have a mind of their own, and we cannot control them. They rule us, and we have no recourse but to succumb to them." Standing beside his seated figure, the emotion burned strong between them. "You talk about your girls, Sam, but what about your wife? Are you afraid to talk about her with me? To tell me how very much you miss her?"

He pulled her close and sat her down beside him. "Where do I begin?" he said. "My father made quite a name for himself in our very small town of Leiden. He developed a hardware business. Honestly," Sam chuckled, "I don't know how he made money. Anytime someone needed a loan or was short on cash, they knew he'd just reach into his pocket to cover the debt. That was the kind of man he was. Honest. Dependable. His wealth and his esteem grew in tandem, but he didn't do it alone. Ger's father was his dedicated partner. The two were inseparable." He looked at Helen and shrugged. "It was just expected that their children would marry. I never thought twice about it. Ger was intelligent, pretty, hard working. She is a fine human being. But love? Oh I loved her while we were growing up in school, but adolescent love doesn't always make for a strong foundation, as you've learned as well." He rubbed the back of his neck. "I was naive. I assumed we would grow to love each other over the years, and we certainly did! At least I thought that was love...until now." A breeze pushed a tendril of hair across her face, and he gently pushed it aside, searching her eyes. After a moment he lowered his head. "And then the girls came...I took the tanker job..." He shot his legs out in front and crossed them at the ankle. "You must think I'm terrible."

Helen reached her arm across his shoulder. "Sam, you were simply doing as you thought you should, as did I." She stood between his knees. "Instead of condemning our actions, let's thank Providence for bringing us together. Just think. If you were hopelessly in love with your wife, you may not have given me even so much as a glance."

Without taking his eyes from hers, he lifted her hands to his mouth and kissed her palms. "I am falling in love with you, Helen," he said. "And not the puppy love I've felt in the past. I...I never knew love could feel like this." She wrapped her arms around his neck and kissed him.

As they walked back along the sand, Helen began humming "Till We Meet Again," and Sam joined in. Two-part harmony, heart and soul. They reached Merriwold just as the sun set and lit the sky with a glowing bright pink. Holiday music emanated from the lounge. As they climbed the front stairs, Henry pulled open the door and yelled, "Merry Christmas, Cappy! Merry Christmas, Mum!"

"Merry Christmas to you!" they happily responded. "Did you beat David in wrestling?"

"Of course I did!" he bragged. "Didn't I, David! Dave, Dave, you're my slave!" he teased, squealing with delight when David chased him. Henry ran around the dining room table, through the kitchen, and then charged full speed into the sofa. "I'm tired!" he said, wiping his forehead.

"Me too," announced Grannie, emerging from the kitchen. "Let's go, Henry, you need a bath, young man." Henry kissed everyone goodnight, and gave David a passing smack on the head. David feigned an attack, sending Henry shrieking up the stairs.

"Well I suppose we'll go to David's house. Wouldn't want to intrude," April said pulling David to his feet. She would have done anything for an invitation to stay. *Let's get acquainted*, she longed to hear, for only the four of them were left, a perfect opportunity. She held her breath, hoping, but what she heard was:

"Merry Christmas to you both and to your parents too, David." *How considerate of her to leave us in peace*, thought Helen.

"Thank you, Mrs. Dean. And thank you for the lovely lunch today." He turned to Sam and extended his hand. "Pleasure to see you, Captain," David said, his dark eyes twinkling. "I look forward to hearing more of your stories next time we meet."

"I look forward to then," said Sam. "Good night to you both," he called after them.

Sam and Helen sat by the tree, recounting the day's activities. Sam noticed a remaining present hidden behind the tree and handed it to Helen. It looked familiar. She turned it over in her hands and recalled April's handing it to her. Inside was a tiny jar of black ink and a writing pen. The note read, *Looks as though you'll need these. Merry Christmas, April.* "How very thoughtful of her, and such a surprise." She smiled up at Sam. "Now I have no excuse but to write every day to my sailor," she grinned.

Sam crossed to her and sat at her feet. "But tonight we have each other in the flesh," he said. "Merry Christmas, my darling," he said, handing her a wrapped square.

"Sam, thank you," she said, tearing off the paper to reveal Perry Como's record album. She popped up and placed it on the phonograph. "We'll meet Again" began, and Sam rose to his feet, extending his hand to her. He held her close as they moved to the music, suspended in time.

With the pressures of Christmas behind them, Helen and Sam were free to spend the next week as though they were on vacation. They took Henry to the beach, played croquet on the lawn, strung flowers, shopped the market, rode the bus to town, and pretended they had the rest of their lives ahead of them in Durban Heights. They often ended their afternoons outside in the garden sipping beer at the little metal table set under the syringa tree. They were seated there when the telegram arrived from Danker. The Janus would be ready to leave the next day. Tears welled immediately in Helen's eyes, and he pulled her onto his lap and forced a smile. They decided to welcome the New Year in style.

The ballroom in the Ambassador Hotel was decorated elegantly for the occasion. Marble columns were draped with garlands of gardenias. Yards of soft white fabric hung gracefully in each doorway. Floor-to-ceiling windows overlooked the marina, and the backdrop sky was magnificent in crimson and gold as fading sunlight melted into the sea. The eight-piece band played "The Way You Look Tonight," and Helen and Sam left their table to dance, her champagne colored evening dress moving placidly in her wake. The sight of her put a lump in Sam's throat, and he could hardly speak. He bent his tall frame to embrace her tiny figure as they moved to the music. "You're lovely," he sang in her ear, "never, ever change..."

Helen knew she was the luckiest woman there. Though the room was crowded, Helen believed she was the only woman there, thanks to Sam's undivided attention. They held each other tightly, collecting embraces that would have to sustain them until next time. Heavy silence crept in during dinner though. Their separation was imminent; their reunion, uncertain. They searched each other's faces, silently noting every detail. They left the hotel before midnight and walked along the sand carrying their shoes. The full moon danced on the ocean. "Moonlight on the water is deceiving. Tonight its beauty captures us, and tomorrow it will release me on my sad journey away from you," Sam said, holding her by her shoulders.

By the time they arrived at Merriwold, everyone was asleep. They tiptoed passed April's closed bedroom door, and stepped quietly inside Henry's. Lying on his side, he was calm and still, a marked change from his waking demeanor. Helen grinned, pointing to the compass Sam had given him, clenched in Henry's palm. Floyd had been relegated to the floor. They crept quietly from the room, and Helen took Sam's hand, leading him to the end of the hall and into her room. She closed the door behind them. The tea candles cast dim light and soft shadows on the walls. Sam approached Helen from behind and slid his arms around her waist. Bending, he gently kissed her neck, and she closed her eyes, softening under his touch. He carried Helen to the bed, and they made love for the first time but as though it could be their last.

Shortly before dawn Sam awoke. He gently kissed Helen's forehead, pausing briefly to admire the serene face of the woman he loved. He tiptoed back to the gray room. Before falling back to sleep, he praised God for the soul mate he felt was created just for him. The thought of leaving her ripped holes in his heart. For the first time the lure of the seas and distant shores revealed a greater purpose. And for the first time in his career, he was not eager to get back on board and out to sea.

Grannie was cordial, Henry was tearful, and April was thankfully absent when Sam said his goodbyes. Henry held his compass in his outstretched hand. "Please take this, Cappy. So you can find your way back here!"

Sam knelt on one knee and hugged Henry tightly. "You keep that compass; I have one on my ship, Henry." Henry gripped Sam around the neck. "Take good care of your mum. I'm counting on you." He patted Henry's back, and Henry saluted Sam while tears streaked his face. "And kiss your sister goodbye from me, will you?"

"Yuck, do I have to?" Henry screwed up his face, wiping a tear with the back of his hand.

Sam turned towards Abigail, extending his hand. "Good bye, Grannie. Lovely of you to make me feel so welcomed." She quickly pulled him in for a hug. He had gotten under her skin during his visit, and she had obviously grown to enjoy his company. "When will we see you again, Captain?"

"Just as soon as I can," he winked at Helen. "Though at least a couple of months, unfortunately."

"Be safe then," she instructed, furrowing her brow in earnest.

They parked near the dock, and he quickly retrieved his bags. He was dressed in full uniform, and Helen saw that he had already mentally resumed the part. "You know the address?" she asked. He tapped his pocket. "You'll write and let me know where you will be getting your mail?"

He let bags drop and set his hands on her shoulders. "Helen, my love, I will see you before you know I'm gone," he said, attempting eye contact. He cupped her chin until she met his eyes. "Would Providence bring us together at last only to keep us apart? Of course not! We'll be tethered across miles of ocean," he said, bending to wrap his arms around her petite middle. "I love you, Helen Dean.

With all my heart and soul." He kissed her, and she wrapped her arms around his neck.

"I love you, my sailor," she declared through tears. He held both her hands to his chest and drank in her brilliant blue eyes with a long last look. "We'll meet again," he sang from the Perry Como tune. "Now, come, come. Long goodbyes can be too painful." Then he picked up his bags, straightened his hat, and headed toward the ship. He didn't look back until he had ascended the plank to the deck, when he gave her a final tip of his hat before disappearing from view.

Everyone missed Sam and his stories, his sense of humor, his calming presence. He'd charged Merriwold's atmosphere with electricity and then took the plug with him. Like a plant without water, the house, and everyone in it, drooped. April greeted her with kindness, knowing how much her mother was hurting. Helen said goodnight early and retreated to her room, eager for the day to end. She clicked on the small radio by her bed. Appropriately, she heard *Darling, Can't You, Won't You Hurry Home?* Helen, seated at the antique writing table with her heavy smooth ink pen in her hand, began her first letter.

TWELVE – Durban

1943   The first weeks of the New Year passed slowly as Sam's absence left a dull void Helen couldn't seem to fill. One morning she dressed in a navy lightweight knit dress and pearls and went downstairs for breakfast. Henry, dressed in his khaki uniform, was ready for his first day back to school after the Christmas holiday. "Good morning, mum!" he greeted Helen, wrapping his arms around her waist. He fixed his wide blue eyes on hers and, again, asked when Cappy was coming back. "Soon, Henry, soon," she told him, though she wished she knew for sure. She turned down the top of his lunch sack, placed a kiss on his forehead, and patted his bottom sending him to James who was waiting to take him to the bus.

"You're looking very smart today, Helen," remarked Grannie. She poured a cup of steaming hot coffee for her daughter and carried it to the dining room.

Helen sat at the table and added cream and two lumps of sugar. "Mrs. Peterson phoned again," she said flatly. "You know George Stuart has been after me for months to work in his hospital rooms. I thought I'd give it a go. We could use the extra money, and I could use the distraction." She tentatively sipped her coffee.

Grannie tried to make her voice sound pleasant, "Aren't two children and this home distraction enough, dear?" She reached across the table and touched Helen's hand. "I think April could benefit from your focused attention—"

"Don't start, mother, please," Helen interrupted, raising her palm. The day had just barely begun, yet already she wanted to climb back into bed for the night.

Grannie took another approach. With a softly calming tone, Grannie covered Helen's hand with her own and said, "The Captain left weeks ago, and you haven't smiled since. You cannot wrap your life around someone who isn't here, Helen. You don't even know when he'll be back, or if he'll be back for sure." Neither noticed April enter the room with a plate of breakfast until she lit a cigarette; then all attention swarmed to her.

"Don't let me interrupt," she said, enjoying the scene.

"Since when do you smoke?" Helen demanded through clenched teeth. "That is a disgusting habit, you look horrible, and the stench! If you must smoke, do it outside!" Helen grabbed her purse and was out the front door. Neither Helen nor April had spoken about April's crying outburst on Christmas day, though April prayed for some evidence of concern from her mother. In her wildest hopes she imagined Helen's approaching her, asking her why she felt the way she did, offering time to work things through calmly. "You're wrong, April, of course I love you!" April heard in her dreams. She had bared her soul, and her mother simply stomped on it like a dreaded bug. The longer things went unspoken, the tighter April sealed herself shut. Once Helen left, she extinguished the cigarette in her plate. In truth she hated the taste of cigarettes and the way they made her hair and clothes reek. But she knew her mother hated them too. At the very least, she caught her mother's attention.

Outside, Helen deeply inhaled a calming breath of fresh air. Then she tucked her purse under her arm and headed down the hill to the bus stop. The summer had been hot, and the foliage wilted pitifully. Big heads of shriveled blue hydrangea hung lifeless on long stems. Tall gladiolas stooped unhappily. The normally lush green landscape looked as though God had taken an eraser to the whole area. She climbed onto the bus and took a seat by the window, watching the sights of the city creep into view. The bus slowed to a stop by the city park. Helen walked through it under the shade of massive leopard tree canopies to the hospital rooms.

Helen enjoyed waiting in George Stuart's office. Large windows were framed with blue pinwale corduroy curtains. His furniture was heavy and honey colored, and the chairs opposite his desk were upholstered and inviting. Bookshelves lined one full wall and were filled not only with medical journals, but novels as well. Head tilted sideways, she was reading the titles when he arrived. "Most people assume they are all medical and don't get close enough to learn otherwise. Feel free to borrow one anytime," he offered, hugging her.

As they sat in the upholstered chairs, Helen said, "There's no greater comfort than a warm bed and a good book." She smiled at her old dear friend. He was one of the first people she'd met nearly twenty years before. "Well, George, after all these years, we're finally going to work together. Tell me what you need me to do."

George crossed his legs and placed his index finger against his nose. His hazel eyes danced as he spoke. "Around here we need to lure people into the healing process, and often that takes more than a good book. Human touch, Helen, along with emotional connection, is so important. I know you can easily pitch in with the routine duties, but I need you here for your compassion, Helen. And I need your sparkle to light up this sorry atmosphere." Helen looked away, blushing. "It's true! Can I count on you, Helen? Besides," he winked, "working here will help fill the time between visits from a certain sailor, am I right?"

Helen immersed herself in the job, grateful for exhausting days that passed quickly. She had arranged her schedule to coincide with Henry's. Because of escalating petrol prices, Helen rode the bus to and from work, saving the car for intermittent pleasure trips. After work she'd hurry across the park to catch the afternoon bus to Mercer Street. There she'd intercept Henry on his way home from school, and together they would climb the hill to Merriwold. This quickly became their routine. At last the summer's heat subsided, allowing the grass to resume its deep green hue. The lantana bloomed profusely, and Henry snagged an orange cluster, blowing to disperse the tiny petals. As usual, they peeked inside the mailbox and were delighted to find a telegram from Sam.

Dear Helen STOP Will be at Merriwold on Saturday STOP Hoping you are free for the weekend STOP Too late to stop me if you are not FULLL STOP

"Tomorrow!" Helen gasped, her hand to her mouth. She and Henry squeezed each other. "Cappy is coming tomorrow!" She heard him repeat over and over as he ran inside the house.

All fatigue evaporated. Helen set to work baking bread and a pear pie, and then she polished the silverware and had James press the yellow table linens. After a brief break to eat dinner, she skipped upstairs to tidy the gray room. In his absence she had ignored the empty room; now she threw back the curtains and opened the windows wide, inviting the fresh ocean air. She polished the mahogany furniture and cleaned the floor. She filled a small vase with orange and blue flowers from the garden and set it atop a white lace doily on the bedside table. Leaning in the doorframe, she admired the results. Only then did she notice the clock beside the bed—midnight! Bone-tired weariness seeped in. Helen climbed into bed, propped herself on two pillows, and opened the book, *Cottage Pie*. The next morning she awoke in the same position to a knock on the door. "Mummy," Henry called, "When is Cappy coming?"

Seven-thirty! "Come in, Henry," she called, pulling herself more upright and feeling as though she'd just gone to bed. "Let's say dinnertime."

Henry threw himself onto the bed and stretched out his arms. "I don't think I can wait that long," he moaned, rubbing his face with both hands. His striped pajamas pinched his belly, and the pant legs just barely skimmed his ankles. *How can he be growing so fast?* Helen wondered.

The front door slammed shut with a thud, and Helen and Henry held their breath, listening for James's steady footsteps ascending the stairs. "Master Henry," he called softly, "someone is here to see you," he sang.

Henry bolted upright. "Cappy!" he whispered into his mom's face. "Cappy, Cappy, Cappy!" he called running down the hall and barreling down the steps. Nearly ten years old, Henry was like a newborn colt, all limbs and wild enthusiasm.

"My goodness, you've grown already, Henry!" Sam bent eye-to-eye with Henry's beaming face. "Where's your mother?" But Henry, too excited to stop, chattered on about school and friends and the crickets he had caught in seemingly one long exhaled sentence. Sam knew stopping Henry's babble was impossible, and Helen would appear when she was good and ready, as usual. Sam followed Henry into the lounge. *Precious Merriwold*, he thought, inhaling the smells of baked goods, curry, and dried flowers. Home. James emerged from the kitchen with a tea tray. "So good to be here, James. Thank you." James simply smiled and tilted his head.

Upstairs, Helen dressed in a frantic hurry and dabbed on sweet perfume, slowing finally as she descended the last few steps. As soon as she saw him sitting in the lounge, her heart raced. "You really are here!" she called to him. He'd heard her footsteps and rose to greet her, scooping her off the floor in one smooth motion. He fought the overwhelming urge to kiss her. Henry joined the embrace, easily circling his mother's waist with one arm and raising the other to Sam's hip. Even the cat joined in, rubbing herself on Sam's leg. "Henry, why don't you finish your homework?" Helen suggested, her eyes still fixed on Sam's. But he proudly announced he had finished. They suggested he help James with lunch, but he didn't bite.

Finally, Sam leaned forward and took Henry's hand. Lowering his voice to a whisper, he said, "I'll bet you have quite a bug collection outside." They had started their secret bug rendezvous in the garden at Christmastime. Glancing nervously at his mum, Henry then brought his face closer to Sam's, nodding. "You go get it ready for me to see, and I'll be out shortly. Shhhh," Sam said, raising his finger to his lips. Henry charged outside, slamming the big door shut behind him. At last Sam engulfed Helen in a warm hug, repeatedly kissing her neck, her cheek, her lips.

"Welcome home, my captain. I've missed you so," she whispered into his ear before landing a kiss there.

"Cappy, are you coming?" Henry's shout pierced the room.

"Hold that thought, my love," he whispered before kissing her palm. "He will have to sleep sometime," he winked.

Sam found Henry in the garden under the shade of the Sweet Thorn tree. Its limbs were heavy with ripening fruit, thanks to the temperate weather. He crouched down and grabbed a handful of warm earth then let it fall slowly through his fingers. Being on land felt increasingly gratifying. "What have you got, young man?" Sam expected to see an array of beetles, moths, perhaps a grasshopper. Henry stood solemnly still, knees touching, hands clasped behind his back, blue eyes intently focused on Sam's. Finally, he stepped aside and looked to the ground. There lay a beautiful spotted bird. Sam leaned in for a closer look. The bird's head and underbelly were pale yellow. Neat rows of white spots contrasted against sleek black feathers, and his crown gave him a serenely regal quality. A black eye stared vacantly. One wing protruded awkwardly from the otherwise smooth, compact body.

"It's a crested barbet," Henry said sadly. "James says he belongs farther north, maybe Jo-burg," he said squatting beside it and petting the underbelly. "James said our garden lured him here. But then he broke his wing and couldn't fly home." Henry looked up to Sam, squinting in the morning light, "Do you think he was sad when he couldn't go back where he belonged?"

Sam crouched closer and gently stroked the bird's silky feathers. "Maybe he wasn't sad at all," he offered. Instead of Jo-burg, maybe he felt he rather belonged here, in your garden?" He searched Henry's expectant eyes, "Maybe he didn't want to go home after all."

Henry tapped his index finger to the side of his face, considering Cappy's explanation. A moment later, he smiled, decided he liked that reasoning. "Let's bury him right here in the garden then!" he suggested. He retrieved a spade from the garage and handed it to Sam, who dug a shallow grave next to the bird. Kneeling beside the bird, Sam lowered the stiff body into the ground. Henry mounded fresh soil over the grave and patted it down with his fleshy hands.

That night, long after dinner and after Henry, April, and Grannie had gone to bed, Helen sat cuddled in Sam's arms on the lounge sofa. The sky had turned pitch black, thanks in part to the blackout restrictions. The ocean's presence was evident only by the sound of waves lapping against the shore. Helen suddenly noticed that Sam was still in uniform. He looked himself over; apparently, he hadn't noticed either. "I was just so eager to be here," he confessed, squeezing her tightly. "Merriwold has become my haven, and you and Henry, my family. Do you know that, darling?" He looked into her eyes, "I want you to know how very much you mean to me."

They sat for a while in contented silence. "Let's go out to the sand," Helen suggested, jumping up and extending her hand. Although he was tired from a long day, he knew by the twinkle in her eye his objections would get him nowhere. He followed her out the door, careful to not let it slam, then across the street to the sand. Engulfed in darkness, the ocean seemed like a massive oil slick. Only glints of light reflected the crescent moon on the dark sea, peeking from behind thick clouds. Helen reached up and slid Sam's jacket off his shoulders, then worked at the buttons on his shirt.

"What are you doing?"

"Lovely night for a swim, don't you think?" She let out a flirty giggle and scurried away from him, disappearing into the night. Then he heard splashing and her giggle rising and mixing with the water. "Sa-am," she lured.

He peeled off his clothes and ran toward her voice. "Helen," he called into the inky darkness.

"I'm here!" she sang across the water. A flash of moonlight caught in her hair, and he dove towards her. The water felt thick and cool on his skin as he paddled to her. Her hair was slick against her head, and her skin glistened. She moved to him and wrapped her arms around his neck. Their wet bodies slid against each other with the current, her breasts flattened against his chest. His hands drank in every inch of her smooth skin. When he couldn't resist her any longer, he carried her to the water's edge, and they had their fill of each other under the midnight blue sky.

So began their February visit. Sam returned in March and April as well. They grew to feel as though they were living the normal life of any couple, ignoring the fact that their dates were monthly, and their brief separations actually set them oceans apart from each other. When they were together, they simply picked up where they had left off. Daily letters, usually delivered in weekly bundles, kept them abreast of each other's lives. They continued to fall madly and deeply in love, completely content in their routine, while all around them people complained bitterly about the war and its effects— rationing, blackouts, death. Letters from Martin tugged at Helen's heart. But if it took a world war to keep Sam in her life, so be it.

Their monthly visits ended by May. Each passing week drained another ounce of Helen's enthusiasm. She grew worn, easily tired and blamed her lack of energy on the change of season. Summer's heat gave way to cooler breezes by the end of July, but the change had little effect on Helen's mood. All around her the foliage offered brilliant color but she didn't notice, focusing instead on the pavement at her feet as she'd drag herself up the hill after a long day at work. Henry was on holiday. Rather than meeting her to ride the bus, he intercepted her on the hill as she neared Merriwold.

"Hello, Mum!" he called, wrapping his arms around her waist.

"Hello, love," she sighed before placing a kiss on the top of his head. They continued the climb while Henry chatted on about the day, his hands punctuating the air. They stopped at the mailbox, delighted to find another telegram waiting.

Dearest Helen STOP Mechanical difficulties necessitate drydock in PE STOP Please join me STOP Have booked your room at the Marine Hotel for three weeks STOP Hoping to see you 5 August STOP Please respond FULL STOP

"Is Cappy on his way?" asked Henry, seeing the excitement on his mother's face.

"Not exactly." She stopped and eyed him closely. "You know, working for Dr. Stuart is very tiring!" she giggled, suddenly filled with energy. "I need a vacation. If I were to go away for a little while, would you be a good man and take care of Grannie and April?" She lowered her face to his. "Could you do that for me?"

"I can do that!" Henry said proudly, scurrying now to keep pace with his mother. "We're home!" Henry announced when they entered the house. They found Grannie in the lounge, sipping her late afternoon sherry.

Helen kicked off her shoes and sank into her blue chair. "What a week!" she sighed. "I may never get used to this!"

"Mummy needs a vacation!" Henry blurted. The women laughed, though Henry didn't know why. "She's going away, and I'm going to take care of you while she's gone." Grannie's jaw dropped immediately, and she looked to Helen, who shooed her son out of the room.

"Mother," Helen began, holding up the telegram. She tucked her leg under her and continued. "Sam has asked me to meet him in Port Elizabeth, and I've decided to go."

"Helen, you can't," Grannie scowled. "What about Henry and April...your job? Have you thought about any of that? And how am I supposed to explain your absence?"

"Mother," Helen began calmly, "Try to understand. We didn't choose this. How could an oil tanker captain from Holland choose to fall in love with a woman in South Africa, thousands of miles away?" Helen moved to the sofa beside her mother and wrapped an arm around her plump shoulder. "Fate chose us." She searched her mother's eyes and saw no mercy, no understanding. "I won't ask for your blessing then, but I do ask that you take care of Henry while I'm away. Say whatever you please to your bridge friends, I really don't care. Tell them I am visiting Joseph's mum in Port Alfred if you must." She found her mother's eyes again, "Please, just be happy for me, mother? He has become the love of my life."

Grannie sipped her sherry and sighed, tilting her head. "Okay," she said reluctantly. "...all right then, but" she hesitated, "why don't you ask me to care for April too?"

Helen tucked her foot under her, crossing her arms over her chest. "Mother, I hate to say this, but I have nearly given up on April. I could try to get through to her for *another* twenty years and still get nowhere." She rubbed at her temples.

"She doesn't hate you, you know. She wants only your attention and approval. She wants to know you love her, Helen."

"No amount of attention is enough," Helen stated with a dismissive wave of her hand. "She is a greedy sponge. Apparently, I don't have what she needs, and I'm nearly through trying." She clenched her teeth, and her jaw pulsed. "Perhaps when she is married and has children of her own, she'll appreciate what I do for her instead of always...looking for more!" Helen pulled herself up from the sofa and smoothed her skirt. "I'm tired, mother. I'm going to take a bath."

Helen met George in his office early Monday morning and told him about her plans. "I have been wondering about you and your captain but always hesitant to pry. You work it out with Mrs. Peterson and Mrs. Milne. We'll manage without you—not happily, mind you." He smiled at her, "just remember to come back!" She would ostensibly be visiting Joseph's mother, she told him. "You'll have a tough time convincing people that twinkle in your eye was put there by your mother-in-law!" he teased. Helen replaced the two books she had borrowed and found another for the train. She planted a kiss on his cheek before scurrying out the door.

THIRTEEN - Port Elizabeth

1943 The train ride to Port Elizabeth seemed maddeningly slow. After trying to read, nap, and write, Helen finally gave up and watched the beautiful scenery outside her window. Lush green hills in the distance jutted abruptly from the plains, yet the deep blue ocean remained almost constantly in view. Closing her eyes and clasping her hands, Helen prayed for strength and guidance. At last the whistle signaled their arrival at Naucopoort Station. The train slowed and, with a cough of steam, eased to a stop.   Helen disembarked into the afternoon light and spotted him immediately. Sam stood tall in full uniform, clutching a bouquet of proteas. He spotted her too and moved towards her through the crowd. As he embraced her with his free arm, she dropped her bags, and he lifted her off the ground. "You are my angel, my love," he whispered. Unafraid of being recognized there, they kissed openly. He set her down and hoisted her suitcases, leading the way to the hired car.

The Marine Hotel lobby was elegant yet welcoming, awash with pastels and parlor palms. Fans hung low from the white paneled ceiling and pulled damp ocean air through the plantation shutters. Sam retrieved two room keys from the desk clerk and easily managed Helen's bags as well as his own. The couple walked up a flight of steps and along the corridor, not touching or speaking, as the unexpected awkward tension rose around them.

"We have Rooms 34 and 35 with balcony and ocean views," Sam said setting the bags on the floor between the doors. "You choose which room you'd prefer," he said, unlocking Room 34 and pushing open the door. Helen stepped into the floral sitting area and twirled around, taking a quick look. She reached into the hall, took hold of Sam's lapel, and gave it a tug. Stepping inside, he wrapped one arm around her waist and pulled her in for a kiss. "I'll get the bags," he said. He hung the Do Not Disturb sign on the door and bolted it shut before leading her into the bedroom. They opened the windows to let the ocean's breeze fill the room and pulled back the blue cotton bedspread. He held her close.

"Love me forever, Sam," she whispered.

"I already have, my darling." He lifted her onto the bed, and they made up for lost time. Exhausted, they dozed off to restful sleep. By the time they woke, night had fallen. They slipped into white cloth robes and stepped onto the veranda. Countless glittering stars dotted the night sky, and the moon reflected a silver path on the dark ocean below. "The moonlight on the water is the most beautiful sight," he said. "And I find great comfort knowing we are seeing that same sight, no matter how far apart we are." He turned to her and saw the moonlight glimmering in her hair. He reached out and ran his fingers through silky-soft tresses. "I was afraid you might not come."

Sam pulled her to himself and rested his chin on her head. He closed his eyes and smoothed her hair. "Helen, from the moment I saw you in the office that last time, I knew Providence was playing a hand in my life. I had not thought much about destiny before, but now I find myself wondering what fate has in store for us." He took a deep breath. "Do we dare to dream of a life together? Often I feel I am too selfish, that I am more harm than good in your life."

"Hush, Sam, don't say that!" she said touching a finger to his lips. "I couldn't bear my life without you in it." She tilted her head to look up at him. "Surely, you must know that?"

He gently cupped her face with both hands and looked into her eyes. "I am thrilled and grateful you feel that way, my love. I pray you always do." He kissed the top of her head. "Let's pretend the world is at peace, and this is the start of our forever, just the two of us in beautiful Port Elizabeth without a care. We must live for the present, Helen, without regret."

In the beginning of their three-week stay, they were able to pretend the outside world didn't exist. They began each morning wrapped in robes, sipping hot tea in the chilly air on the balcony, planning their days. They visited museums, parks, local attractions, or just sat together enjoying the sunlit balcony absorbed in novels they'd share and discuss. But little by little, reality seeped in, and Helen couldn't ignore it. They had been shopping in town and found a café for a cup of tea. "Sam," she began, "these few weeks have been pure heaven. But in a few days I'll return to my life, unable to pretend anymore. Where will that leave us then?" She kept her gaze steady as he leaned towards her.

"Don't you see? We'll be exactly as we have been, only apart." He gathered her hands in his. "Now that our souls have found each other, nothing can separate us! We are bound together, Helen. I love you more than life itself. When the war ends, we'll be together forever, just as we are meant to be." He kissed her fingers, one at a time, and smiled at her.

Helen had never loved anyone so deeply, but under the circumstances... "When the war ends, when the ship docks...I'm afraid I'll spend my life waiting." She caressed his arm but averted his eyes. Letting out a long breath, she began in a low voice, "We long for the war to end, but when the war does end, won't you be sent back to Holland? To your wife and children?" She searched his eyes then, "where does that leave me, Sam?" He let his eyes move briefly away from hers, and the hesitation was painful. Helen snatched her purse and jacket and hurried out of the café. By the time Sam gathered their things, she was across the street and on the beach, shoes in hand. He caught up with her in long easy strides, and they continued for a minute walking briskly in silence, leaving deep heel marks in their path.

At last Sam slipped his arm around Helen's shoulder to slow her, calm her. "Helen, please," he said, stopping and setting down the shopping bags. He held her by the shoulders, but she defiantly looked away. "Only a scoundrel would leave his family, shirk his responsibilities, so I have been afraid to state my intentions." He smoothed wind-caught wisps of hair from her face. "Darling, you know my marriage has been dead for quite some time, was never really alive, I now realize. And I have been away so long. My children, they scarcely know me. But perhaps that's what makes this right." She looked at him quizzically, not understanding. "The same sea that took me away from them brought me to you. The timing is perfect when you look at us that way." He lifted her chin with a gentle finger. "Let me phrase this plainly. I've come a long way to meet my other half, Helen. Don't even think of turning me away now."

Helen fell into his arms. "Sam, if only it were as simple as you make it seem. How will I find the strength when you are not with me?" she pouted like a schoolgirl.

He smiled down at her. "But I am always with you, my darling. Right here," he kissed her forehead, "and right here," he covered her heart with his hand, "and especially here," he kissed her on the mouth.

The remainder of their days together was spent with picnics on the beach, scenic drives along the shore, late-afternoon lovemaking, and naps before dinner. Just prior to their last day they woke to rain pounding on the metal roof above them. With a touch of his large hand to her heavy eyelids, he encouraged her to sleep some more while he showered and dressed in full uniform. With a cup of tea in hand, he sat on the edge of the bed. "Don't wake me," she whispered, eyes shut tightly and kicking the sheets. "If I open my eyes, my dream will end!" She reached out a hand, and he held it. "I'm at Merriwold in the garden. The syringa is in full scented bloom, the sunshine is warm and glorious, and I'm planting flowers in black earth. I hear your voice," she continued, smiling with eyes shut, "and turn to see you coming up the steps, suitcase in hand. 'I'm home, Helen,' you say, 'I'm home at last.' She hugged herself. "Then you pick me up and—" she opened her eyes and was startled to see Sam in uniform. Bolting upright, "Why are you—We still have one more—What a terrible way to wake from a most wonderful dream!"

"Not to worry, darling, shhhhhh. I just need to check on the ship," he explained, setting her the teacup in her hands. "Danker has been doing a wonderful job, but the captain needs to be seen from time to time, especially if we are to set out tomorrow. I'm afraid I can't avoid it any longer." He reached his hand to lift her chin until she looked in his eyes. "Let's meet here at say," he glanced at his watch, "one o'clock?" She nodded. He bent and placed a kiss on her forehead before heading out the door.

Helen showered and dressed in Sam's favorite, a blue cotton shirtdress and matching cardigan. She admired herself in the mirror, pleased with her trim waist and the way the blue of the dress highlighted her eyes. By the time she reached the market, the rain had stopped. Gusty winds quickly made way for blue skies, and the sun's heat caused steam to rise from the black streets. Helen filled her sack with fresh bread and fruit, cheeses, olives, dates, a thick slice of smoked ham, and a bottle of red wine. As she headed towards the hotel, she breathed in the clean, fresh air. Her head felt as clear as the rain-drenched skies.

Helen made herself another cup of tea and placed her final routine call to Merriwold. She reminded her mother to have James at the station when she returned and sent kisses to Henry, as usual. She felt encouraged yet slightly offended at how well they seemed to manage in her absence. She hung up the phone and glanced at her watch; time enough to read on the sunny balcony. She dried a chair and put her feet up on the small table, crossing her legs at the ankles. Sam returned and changed into civilian clothes before joining her out there. He dried the stubborn drops and pulled the chair beside her. Beaming at him, she said, "I almost forgot I have something to show you," she said pointing to the metal table at her feet. Sam glanced at the familiar writing paper. Holding it up, he saw neat little rectangular holes in the paper before he recognized his own handwriting. "What in the—?" Censors had deftly cut out every location reference, and the result left the paper looking moth-bitten.

"I've been meaning to tell you," Helen laughed, "but I wasn't sure how the censors would react to even more information in our letters. We really must do something about that! "Together they devised a plan, a code for Helen to know of Sam's whereabouts without being censored. Sam scribbled all his possible locations down on paper, and they named each one accordingly: Bombay—Bill; Bahrain—Bertie; Durban—Dorothy; East London—Elsie; Port

Elizabeth—Peter; Cape Town—Catherine; Mombasa—Mary; Matadi—Mike; Colombo—Claire; Karachi—Kathleen; Calcutta—Clifford; Madras—Margaret; Australia—Alec; New Zealand—Nick. They made two lists, one for each of them. "I hope we see a lot of Dorothy!"

He took her hand and kissed it. "Let's get in the car and see where it takes us." They drove along the coast towards Mossel Bay, far from town crowds, and parked near a deserted stretch of beach. Helen spread the flowered quilt, and Sam set down the sack of food. Then he turned to the ocean, and stretching his arms wide yelled, "I love the ocean...!" and sweeping her up in one arm continued, "...for bringing me to you!" He wrapped her in a bear hug and kissed her neck in short staccato bursts. "You are so precious to me, my *engel*," he said. "These last weeks have been heaven on earth." He took her by the hand, and they walked barefoot along the water's edge, careful not to let the cold water touch their toes. The sun still hung high in the sky and warmed them through. Helen collected bits of shells and sea glass, and when her fist couldn't hold any more, they returned to their blanket.

Propped on one arm, Sam stretched out his long legs and crossed them at the ankle. "Your long South African days confuse me" he said unpacking the picnic sack with one hand. "My stomach screams dinnertime, but the bright skies swear it's too early." He rolled to sitting cross-legged and uncorked the wine. "Just something else I'll have to adjust to." He poured them each a taste in the borrowed hotel glasses. Clinking their glasses together, they locked eyes but words caught in their throats: *to us, to our future, to your safety,* nothing seemed appropriate or enough.

Helen turned away first and cleared her throat. "I'm glad the sun sets later here. Makes our last day all the longer." Last day. The words brought tears to her eyes, and she quickly wiped them away. "Let's have our supper, shall we?" They ate the dates, and Sam sliced the ham, and for a while they continued in heavy silence.

Sam refilled their wine glasses. He unfolded his long legs and studied the view. The sun had reluctantly begun its descent, washing the sky in deep orange. The water below grew considerably calm, and the air turned cool and salty. Slowly, he turned to her, and his heart raced just looking into her face. He reached and gently ran two fingers down her soft cheek. She looked at him adoringly. How could he feel anything but love for this angel of a woman God sent him half way around the world to find? His voice was a whisper, pleading, "How I wish I were free to marry you, my darling Helen," he confessed.

With her eyes focused on his, she covered his hand with her own and kissed his palm. "Then marry me," she challenged. "Right here and now, with the sea as our witness." With that she stood, hands on hips, compelling him to join her. He did so gladly.

Sam searched his pocket and produced a small ring, laying it in his palm for her to see. "I planned to give this to you tonight, Helen, as a promise of my love." He slid the ring onto her middle finger and held both her hands to his chest. "I have no right to ask you this, Helen, but," he searched for the words and lowered himself onto one knee. "Please, Helen. Please wait for me?" His voice cracked with emotion. "I have loved you my whole life, Helen, from the beginning of time. Let this ring be a symbol of our constant devotion, my lovely wife."

Helen knelt in front of him and, unclasping the gold chain from around her neck, she slid off the "H" pendant. She placed it in his hand and folded his fingers over it. She held his fist to her chest. "I will always be yours, my sailor husband. In God's eyes we are already one; I believe that. And I also believe that someday we will spend all our tomorrows together. Until then, keep me always in your breast pocket, close to your heart." A tear escaped down her cheek. "From now on I consider you my husband, and I, your devoted wife."

Her words were music, and she was speaking a symphony into his heart. He lowered his lips to hers. They sank onto the blanket as the fiery sun melted onto the ocean. As the night seeped in around them, they gathered their things and made their way back to the hotel. Once inside, Helen peeled back the drapes from the balcony doors, and the moonlight spilled inside. Meanwhile, Sam tuned the radio. "Till We Meet Again" came through clearly, and they danced wordlessly caressing each other, allowing the echo of their vows to continue.

"All aboard!" The ticket clerk's call stabbed Helen's heart.

When Sam touched her shoulder, Helen threw her arms around his neck, tears streaming down her face. He dropped her bags to wrap her in both arms. "May God bring you safely back to me soon, my husband." Sam kissed the top of her head and held her tightly to his chest. Tears brimmed in his eyes. Every parting could be their last; every goodbye, final. Leading her by the elbow, he directed her to the train. She paused on the first step, turned and offered one last kiss. Seated by the window, she found him again. Pressing her hand to the glass, she mouthed, *I love you* as the train pulled slowly away, dragging Sam's heart with it. He stood on the platform, hat in hand, until the train disappeared from sight and its husky chug was replaced by the sound of his heart pounding in his ears.

The miserable captain boarded his ship. Instead of his usual prayer on deck, he prayed for her safety and a quick reunion.

The orders read Land's End: Bahrain, and the convoy glided quickly through deep waters. Sam, at the helm, motored away from the woman he loved and the life on land he now longed to live. Surely his heart would break. The joy they shared together more than equaled the misery they endured apart. He longed to hear her voice, watch her eyes twinkle as she spoke, feel the warmth of her touch. And always, his arms ached to hold her. The next evening he wrote to her, thanking Providence for bringing them together. And they continued to write faithfully, allowing their feelings for each other to augment on paper.

FOURTEEN – Leiden

1943 Trudy slowly shifted from sleep to wake. Sunday. No school, thank God, and already the day was half over. Between Mom's coughing and planes shrieking throughout the night, she had hardly slept. Mom was sleeping beside her, her emaciated frame rising and falling with short breaths. Trudy snuggled into her warmth, draping an arm in the trough of her middle. She pressed her face to the back of Mom's shoulders, where her skin stretched taut like a painter's canvas. A cough rattled Mom's insides, but still, amazingly, she didn't wake.

Downstairs, Trudy pulled on her boots and wool coat and wrapped her scarf around her face. Marike and Maud were wrapped in blankets reading German history books. "I'm going to Leah's," she called to them, not giving them enough time to try to stop her. Trudy had been warned against visiting Leah's home. If she were seen, she may be tagged as part of the Resistance, or worse, a Conspirator. Mom said as hard as it was to not see her best friend, avoiding her was best for everyone concerned. But the morning was foggy, and Trudy couldn't resist the chance. The dim quiet street was just too tempting. Being without Leah left a gap in Trudy's chest that painfully spread and darkened as time dragged on.

At first no one answered Leah's door. Suddenly, the little door covering the peephole slid opened and quickly shut. Leah pulled Trudy inside and slammed the door behind her. The two hugged each other tightly. Months had passed since Trudy had last snuck into her friend's house. Leah's eyes were huge and sad, and her skin, a ghostly white. As always, the yellow star with *Jood* in black ink was pinned to her left chest. Trudy wondered why she bothered to wear this, knowing the girl didn't dare go outside, not since Jews were banned from school and most public places, even their own market.

Trudy followed her friend into the kitchen, rubbing her hands for warmth. From years of visiting, she automatically hoped to find something delicious leftover from the store. But the counters that had always held pastries and treats were bare. This house that had always been filled with the aroma of baking cookies and bread now had an odd odor, like the time she and Leah brought in a dead rat from the canal. They sat at the kitchen table. "I wish I could offer you pastries, Trudy," Leah rubbed her palms together nervously. "Like the old days."

Trudy clapped her hands together, threw her head back, eyes closed. "I dream about your mom's pastries...and her latkes! Remember the time—" Leah's chin had dropped to her chest as she wept quietly. "Leah, what is it?" Trudy dropped to her knees and searched Leah's trembling face.

"Oh Trudy!" she exhaled. "My father says a man named Seyss-Inquart has turned our lives into a horrible mess." Trudy was familiar with the name. Mom and Aunt Jenke relayed stories they'd heard at the market about this man they called the devil. He was the one insisting Jews wear the yellow star and register at the Office. Leah wiped quiet tears with the palm of her hand. Her knee bobbed nervously; then finally she leveled her red-rimmed eyes to Trudy's. "We have to move, Trudy. Just because we are Jewish, we have to move," she cried. "We were all upstairs packing when you came."

"Noooooo," cried Trudy. "What do you mean you *have* to? Where will you go?" She hugged her friend, not understanding any of it.

"My father isn't sure. Probably Amsterdam. There are two other cities we are allowed to go to, but we're hoping for Amsterdam. Otherwise," Leah took a deep breath, rubbed her palm with her thumb, "we may end up in Germany." With this Leah dissolved into sobs, her body cowering against the thought.

"Leah!" Trudy cried, "all the way to Germany!" She frantically searched her friend's face. "You must stay here in Holland!" She thought a moment, then whispered. "When the fighting stops, you'll come home, right?"

But Leah couldn't think beyond that minute, let alone when the war might end. What neither girl knew was that the Canter's house no longer belonged to them. The Nazis had taken it and all their money and possessions, along with those of every other registered Jew in Holland. They had taken the store long ago, but Mr. Canter kept that from Leah, too.

Upstairs the girls found Leah's parents in their room. They were hunched and old looking, skinny like most everyone, and frail. They turned and looked at Trudy when she greeted them but didn't smile. Fear had etched deep creases in their faces. Trudy ran to Mrs. Canter first and wrapped her arms around her waist. "You are my second mother," she cried. "I will miss you all so much!" She turned to Mr. Canter, and he pulled her close to his chest, stroking Trudy's hair. She thought she heard his heart snap in two.

In Leah's room Trudy helped Leah sort through her clothes. Her mother had told Leah to take only what was most important because she'd have to carry her own suitcase. Leah had laid out a week's worth of underclothes, three shirts, two pairs of pants and two sweaters. She would wear all of it under her coat in order to fit more into her bag. When she couldn't squeeze another thing into the bag, she turned to Trudy. "Take the rest, Trudy. Wear my clothes until I come back...If I come back," she added grimly. "They won't fit me by then anyway..."

"Don't talk like that, Leah!" warned Trudy. "You and your parents will be back soon!" she insisted, though deep down she felt she wouldn't see Leah for a very long time. Leah tossed her friend a thick sweater. It felt warm and soft in Trudy's hands, and she rubbed it against her cheek. "I'll take good care of your things for you," she promised, searching her friend's face for some sign of hope. Trudy scanned the room, looking to see what else Leah was leaving behind. In the corner of her room stood the two-door cabinet that used to overflow with Leah's art supplies—colored pencils, stacks of drawing paper, paints of all colors, and brushes. She saw the paints had dried up, only nubs remained of the prettiest colors, and but a few slips of paper were left. Trudy lifted the bucket of colored chalk and was flooded with memories of coloring the concrete outside with her friend. "We were so young then," she said, peering at her friend.

Leah understood what Trudy meant. They had grown old in the few years since the Nazis came. And at only nine and ten, they both dreamed of sweet, simpler times. Could they ever be carefree again?

Eventually, the room grew dim, and the cold seeped through to their bones and into their empty stomachs. Being outside after dark was forbidden, so in the last twinges of light Trudy said goodbye to her best friend. She found it hard to realize she'd spent the entire day there with Leah. They held each other tightly and promised to be careful. They would see each other soon, Trudy tried to assure her, though they both felt that was impossible. With a heavy heart, Trudy gathered the extra clothes into a bundle, and they slowly walked downstairs. "Write to me as soon as you're able!" Trudy said, and Leah promised.

One foot inside her house, and Trudy smelled burnt bread. She slowly made her way to the kitchen, where everyone was gathered. Soup simmered in the big aluminum pot on the stove. Trudy looked from the blackened brick of bread on the counter to Mom, whose face was buried in her hands. "All those ingredients..." she moaned.

As Trudy set the clothes on a chair, all attention shifted to her. Tears steaked her face. "They're leaving," she whimpered. "The Canters have to go away." She dropped herself onto the chair, and Mom and Maud rushed to hug her, attempted to ease the pain. Trudy relayed Leah's story. "Please tell me they'll go only as far as Amsterdam and come right back when this stupid war is over!" she whined, pounding the table with clenched fists.

They all tried to console her, but their efforts proved useless. Aunt Jenke had been hearing rumors of deportation at the market as well as talk of labor camps and gas chambers. But of course she hadn't shared any of that with the children. The Ms did their best to cheer their sister, but there was little they could say. They served her soup and cut away the burnt outer edges of bread for her. Mom encouraged her to eat, but Trudy, for once, wanted none of it. She stood, slowly met their eyes with her own red-rimmed eyes, and then turned and gathered Leah's clothes. Sad and incredibly lonely, she climbed the stairs.

When the dishes were clean and the pot was returned to the otherwise empty refrigerator, Mom headed upstairs for bed. She heard Trudy's muffled sobs under the blankets and slid in beside her, wrapping her up in her arms and resting her chin on Trudy's head. "Let it all go, my love. Just have yourself a good cry," she said rocking her daughter gently. "Life isn't fair sometimes, and it's ok to be angry...for a bit."

"I hate this!" Trudy wailed. "I hate the soldiers...and the planes...everything smells rotten!" Mom squeezed tighter. "I want to play outside! I want to play with Leah! And I want to eat pastries and chocolate and drink MILK! REAL MILK!" she sobbed into her mom's chest, hands clenched into fists. "What will I do without Leah?" she groaned. "She looked so scared..." Mom rocked and soothed, rocked and soothed until Trudy's breath evened and her tears slowed.

Mom held Trudy's face in her cold hands. "I know you're sad and more than a little bit mad," she said, her sweet brown eyes inches from Trudy's. "And it's good to let go of that anger once in a while, purge your body of—" she turned her head for a coughing fit "—all that nastiness. But being angry won't help anyone, not Leah, not her parents, and certainly not you." She cleared her throat again. "Anger will only eat up your insides. We have learned this, right?" Trudy nodded, and Mom kissed Trudy's forehead. "I am so sorry, Trudy, my love, truly I am. I don't have any answers. No one does." Mom turned her head away to cough again, a deep exhausting cough. She lay on her back, wiped her mouth with the back of her hand, and continued in a raspy voice. "We will pray for them every day, okay? I'm afraid that's all we can do."

After school the next day Trudy met the Ms to walk home. As they approached, Leah's house already seemed different. Trudy ran to the door and pounded on it, ignoring Marike's pleas to stop. She pounded again, harder, and the door gave way. The Ms caught up with Trudy, and they all stepped inside the cold, dank house and softly called Leah's name. But she had already gone. Trudy ran upstairs to Leah's room. Her bed covers were fixed just so. On her art cabinet she'd left a drawing of her family. The three of them, each holding a suitcase and crying big tears. Everything was black and gray except for the little yellow stars on their chests. Trudy rolled it up. At home she hung it by the front door so it would be the first thing for Leah to see when she came home.

That night for dinner they had a rare treat. Though she claimed to be just lucky that day, Jenke scored three sausage links and an apple. She divided the booty into three and made a week's worth of suppers from each portion. Ironically, she would be the only one to suffer a stomachache that first night. Mom asked her what else she'd eaten, but she insisted she had nothing more than everyone else that day.

Before the day was over in the trailing evening light, a van parked outside Leah's house. A team of ten men quickly took every bit of furniture, art, and clothing from the house and fitted it all stacked and tidy into the other loot in the van. Local Nazis would take first pick of the Canter's miscellaneous belongings. Anything deemed valuable would be shipped back to Germany and added to the Fuhrer's collection.

FIFTEEN – Durban

1944 Early in February, Helen received a cable from Sam. He would be there for April's wedding! She and April had been working steadily on the plans for her big day, and their enthusiasm kept Merriwold buoyant in anticipation. Helen's energy overflowed. She worked more hours in the rooms to exchange for the anticipated time off, and at home she spent time washing linens, baking, and cleaning out cupboards. Joseph's desk caught her eye. She hadn't opened a drawer since his death. She ran her hand over the slanted mahogany front and realized how far into the past he'd receded. Sitting on the floor, she pulled out the drawers one by one and emptied the contents beside her. She found little worth keeping—a few ink pens and an old photograph of Henry, until she discovered a cardboard box. Inside were the letters she had written to Joseph when they'd first courted. He saved every one. Reading them over, Helen had to smile reliving that time in their lives. Joseph had been handling Helen's divorce from her first husband, so they had put their feelings on paper rather than be seen together in public. He was a good man, she knew, and she felt fortunate. But that life was over now. She didn't want anything to impinge on the life she planned to share with Sam. She gathered all the letters and bits of trash and brought them outside. The weather was too hot for a fire inside, so she dug a hole in the sand and burned each one. Then she went upstairs for a bath.

When Sam arrived later that afternoon, they sat in the garden sharing a cold beer in the shade of the syringa tree. Soft, warm breezes were barely noticeable. She told him what she'd done with Joseph's letters. "That part of my life is behind us," she said. "I must be getting old," she laughed, "because I never want to go through that getting-to-know-you stage again!" Helen set her beer glass on the little table and slid onto Sam's lap, slipping her arm around his neck. "I love you more than I've ever known how to love, Sam. I shall always love you and only you." He kissed her then, and for another brief snippet in time, all was right in the world.

The household woke early to Big Band music. April had instructed James to blast the music at precisely 7 A.M. to set the tone for her wedding day. "Emphasize the horns and trumpets," she'd said. The aroma of cinnamon scones wafted upstairs and drew everyone eagerly to the dining room. April beamed. Already she was showered and dressed in her getaway dress. She would finish getting ready at the Beachwood Yacht Club. Her pale yellow wedding gown hung from the door top. A small suitcase held everything she'd need for the day and following week. The couple planned to spend their first week as husband and wife in Port Elizabeth, at Helen and Sam's suggestion. Afterwards, they would return to Pietermaritzburg where the newlyweds had bought a little home on a neat square acre of property.

"What a lovely day for a wedding!" exclaimed Grannie. "The sky is brilliant, and there's a beautiful breeze. Low humidity too, thank God!" She looked at April's shining face. "And won't you be the most beautiful bride!" she exclaimed kindly.

April gathered her things. "Don't be late!" she warned, smiling. James carried her suitcase to the car. He would take her to the Club and come back for the others.

Helen helped Henry tame his hair. He looked quite handsome in his tan linen suit and bowtie. He joined Sam in the lounge-turned-waiting room where he was ordered to *stay clean* while Helen and Grannie put the finishing touches on themselves. Sam had dressed in full uniform—white slacks and four stripes on each cuff of his double-breasted navy jacket. The star on his brimmed and corded hat matched the stars on his lapels, and the result was utterly handsome.

Helen floated down the stairs, grinning into Sam's smiling face. "It's not nice to outshine the bride," he scolded.

Helen twirled in a circle for her adoring fan. "After today, April's happiness is no longer my concern," she said smiling brightly. "Let's pretend this is our wedding day too."

He folded her into himself, resting his chin on top of her head. "Your freedom has been a long time coming. I do hope your changed role brings a change in your relationship as well." He loosened his hug to see her face. "Would you be receptive to that, Helen?"

"Sam," she grinned, "my hopeless romantic is ever optimistic." She patted his chest. "There is always hope, I suppose. Why, Grannie and I became friends after I was married and she moved here from England." She shrugged. "I suppose anything is possible." She slipped her hands into his. "I am excited for us though. Imagine not having to worry about April showing up unannounced?" she whispered into his ear, leaning forward onto her toes.

Grannie made her way down the stairs. She was handsomely dressed in a two-piece linen suit and wore the pendant Sam had given her his first Christmas at Merriwold. She beamed at him, expecting compliments, and he did not disappoint her.

The small crowd of guests gathered in the Yacht Club gardens for the brief ceremony. The couple stood under the gazebo, and the ocean spread far and wide behind them. April held a bouquet of blue hydrangea and white nerines, their delicate fragrance sweetened the air as she passed. Her simple gown moved easily in the breeze. David appeared confident in his dark tuxedo. From a distance they looked picture perfect, a magazine-quality union of the handsome slick man and his innocent, young bride. But up close there was something listless about his staid demeanor in direct contrast to her broad smile. No one noticed the disparity, least of all Helen. She had anticipated this event for years, and she came to celebrate. Mingling arm in arm, Helen and Sam left cupped hands and whispered comments in their wake, but they chose not to care. This was their coming out party, they'd decided. They plucked hors d'oeuvres from silver trays and danced to live big band music. And for a gracious five hours, bride, groom, and guests were allowed a respite from the world's troubles.

All too soon Sam was back on the Janus. As the war intensified in the Mediterranean and Northern Africa, Sam was kept increasingly busy ferrying crude to refineries and gasoline for the Allies. His convoy route included Matadi, about 80 miles inland on the Congo River, a convenient refueling location for what had become American-led troops in Northern Africa. Because the Janus was about 100 feet shorter than the newer T-2 Tankers, she was a bit more maneuverable on the river, making turnaround faster. Though the distinction made Sam proud, it also kept him from Helen. Four times he sailed past Durban on his trek around the Cape of Good Hope and up Africa's west coast. Four times he passed her returning to Bahrain. Hugging the coast, he flashed his lights towards Merriwold, just beyond his reach.

Progression of the war throughout 1944 brought an end into view, with the Allies firmly taking control. For months the crew worked around the clock. Each day Sam and Danker recorded the tonnage loading and disbursement. Sam knew the impressive record would someday prove personally useful. Increasingly dangerous conditions prevented any shore time leave, making everyone on board irritable. So in the evenings, Sam would gather Danker and Einer to his stateroom and pour them each a drink. With classical music playing in the background, they'd escape their troubles by discussing their ever-changing plans for after the war's end.

Meanwhile, Helen's job duties increased as she began to assist during surgery as well. Her days grew longer and more demanding. She found herself writing sad scripts to Sam, remembering their time in Port Elizabeth. *Our PE visit was heaven on earth, but now it seems just a dream I've awakened from. No matter how hard I try, I cannot get back to that beautiful dream!* she wrote. *I fear what will happen to us should this separation continue or the war end...*

On Saturday mornings, Helen would sit in the garden on her metal chair and imagine Sam in his. As the seasons changed, she continued to work hard in the garden, hoping to impress Sam. But as their separation dragged on, being in the garden only intensified her loneliness. Instead of cheering her, the colorful gerberas and cascading yellow jasmine cried out for Sam's compliments. Eight months after the wedding, Helen sat alone in the garden. She must have been terribly lonely because, surprisingly, a tiny yearning for April's company began to gnaw at her.

SIXTEEN – Leiden

1945 Trudy woke early to Mom's hacking cough, which seemed to have steadily worsened. They did what they could to stay warm, but the cold weather hadn't broken long enough to allow her to get well. There was no heat in the house, and when the firewood ran out, they began burning the furniture, piece by piece. Mom said they were blessed to have the massive dining room table. The thick legs and top kept the fire burning all winter. Mom said the chairs would warm them till summer's thaw. Trudy regretted the kitchen table was made of metal.

Trudy gently rubbed Mom's washboard back as the cough shook her body; then she doubled the blanket over her and rubbed warmth into her arms, shoulders, and back before heading down stairs. In the kitchen she found the Ms smearing a jam of sorts on a piece of bread. Silently, they pointed to the one they'd made for her. Aunt Jenke had steeped something in a pot to warm them. Trudy wrapped her hands around the mug, blew into the steam, and inhaled the savory scent before letting the hot liquid spread inside her chest. Today, Jenke would be given coupons to last the month. Trudy prayed there would be something left in the market to trade for them. And she prayed her aunt would learn good news from the others gathering there. For months they had been encouraged by stories of the Canadians beating the Nazis nearby. Every night they bowed their heads and prayed the allies would continue winning. Meanwhile, the planes maintained their presence roaring like rolling thunder overhead day and night, increasingly, it seemed. Black smoke and ash filled the sky, so thick at times they wondered if it were day or dusk.

The girls walked to school in silence dodging mud and soldiers in jeeps until suddenly they all saw it and stopped abruptly. They traded quick glances but did not point or acknowledge the bits of green poking through the dead earth just over there, on the other side of the street, near what had been the hardware store. Bulbs! Through all the mud and rubble a determined green tip emerged. Even the Nazis can't squelch hope forever. Trudy knew that after dark that night the Ms would make her sneak to that spot and rip open the earth for whatever bulbs could be found. "You're too small to be bothered with," they'd say. "The soldiers want their girls older, like us," so of course they couldn't take the chance.

The day dragged because Trudy was at once hopeful that no one else had seen the green bits and incredibly fearful she'd be caught stealing them. When school finally ended, the girls met to walk home. Without turning her head, Trudy searched and found the bulbs poking ever so slightly through the ground. She mentally noted the exact spot.

After dinner Trudy and the Ms practiced German in the front room. They called goodnight to Mom as she slowly pushed herself upstairs. They pretended to work in the room's dim candle light until Aunt Jenke said goodnight and closed the pantry door. Trudy shook with fear as Marike tucked Trudy's light hair into the dark wool cap and pulled it low on her face. "Be strong," she coaxed, raising the coat collar to Trudy's chin. "Get the bulbs, and we will eat like kings for a week!"

Trudy glanced at Maud and saw the fear in her wide eyes. Marike opened the door a crack. The uncharacteristically clear road waited. Marike shoved Trudy outside, snapping the door shut behind her. Trudy felt the butter knife and soupspoon in her pocket and prayed the tools would work. The night was moonless, and for the moment, quiet. Trudy scurried across the muddy street. Her breath against the scarf felt warm while the rest of her shivered in fear. Silently, she raced to the exact spot, dropped to her knees, and began pawing, digging, tearing at the earth. If there were two bulbs, there could be many. And there were! She continued digging, digging, digging and uncovered at least twenty bulbs! Her pockets bulged. She wanted to take off her hat to hold more, but she was afraid her blond hair would be easily spotted against the dark night. She shoved bulbs far up inside her coat sleeves. As she continued rooting in the black dirt for more bulbs, she heard the jeep.

Quickly, she dove behind the remains of the old brick storefront and waited for the jeep to pass. The headlights cut the black night and glinted off something metal in the dirt. She searched her pockets and realized the knife was missing. The soldiers saw the glimmer too and slowed to a stop. Her heart beat so loudly in her ears, she was afraid they could hear it. One of the soldiers hopped out and bent to pick up the shiny object. The smell of him reached Trudy, and she was reminded of the night the soldiers came into their house, Mom's fright, and Ribbon. She thought of Leah and wanted to scream. From this short distance she could see he looked well fed while all in her family were ghostly skeletons. Here she was risking her life to eat a tulip bulb! Her hands balled into fists, her rage rising like vomit in her throat. She wanted to kill him. And she suddenly realized she didn't care if he killed her for trying.

The soldiers called to hurry him along, and he laughed while slipping the knife into his pocket, sauntering toward the jeep. At last they drove off. Trudy waited until they were far away and until she felt her shaky legs would hold her. She stood unsteadily, gathered the few bulbs that had fallen, and ran back home as fast as she possibly could. The Ms were quietly hurrying her through the cracked door, waving their hands in a frenzy. As soon as Trudy was close enough, they yanked her inside. "We saw the jeep! Did they see you? Did you get the bulbs? Where is the butter knife?" They pelted her with questions while she quietly emptied her pockets and let bulbs fall from her sleeves into a muddy beautiful pile on the floor. A triumphant smile stretched across Trudy's face. "Mom will be so happy!" they crooned, hugging her. Trudy soaked in the awe evident in their eyes. For the first time, Trudy felt important and appreciated by them. And she felt loved, just as her mom had always insisted she would.

They never told Mom where they came from. Eventually she stopped asking and began calling their appearance the Blessing of the Bulbs as though they were dropped from heaven. Aunt Jenke made dishes that lasted for weeks, their earthy essence apparent in each one. She sliced, diced, grated, and steamed them. And, of course, she made soup. And they thanked God for one more meal.

As the months passed, they began to believe the Nazis were leaving at last. During their morning walks to school, the girls noticed fewer jeeps of soldiers crowding the streets. Teachers were absent more and more, so classrooms were combined. The Ms were put in the same room together even though they were supposed to be in different grades. It really didn't matter, Mom said, because they hadn't been taught anything worthwhile since the Nazis arrived. "Someday we will get real schoolbooks and start these years over," she began saying with regularity. Trudy was so happy to be talking about *someday* again. The word hit her in the belly and sprouted optimism throughout her body. Seemed everyone had begun cautiously looking ahead lately. Rumors spread about the Nazis finally being defeated everywhere and retreating to Germany. However, that truth was inconceivable to the Nazis, and they were furious. They didn't go away easily. In their angry wake they burned buildings and bombed bridges and roads so relief couldn't easily gain access. People were starving everywhere. Many would starve to death.

One glorious day in the middle of July, Heaven really did drop blessings from the sky. Mom was too sick to go, but Aunt Jenke gathered the girls and took them to the field, walking arm-in-arm. The air had been steadily working on cleaning itself, evident in bits of blue sky poking through the gray haze and bringing the scent of a happier past. Hunched, haggard-looking people gathered around the makeshift fences. On the field were painted huge white Xs. Jenke and the girls politely bumped their way through the amiable crowd to the fence. They heard the engines then and turned their faces to the sky. Trudy had to remind herself to not be afraid, they shouldn't be carrying bombs, but she couldn't help but tremble. As the planes approached, people pulled their hats lower against the wind, raising frail, boney shoulders. Some covered their ears from the noise. All kept their eyes on those planes as their bellies opened and huge parcels fell near and on the Xs. Sheets of paper also fluttered from the sky, warning them to eat slowly and only a little at a time. Food! People pushed against the fences until the field was safe, and at last the fences were laid down. There was plenty for everyone—powdered eggs and milk, biscuits, flour, and oh God, chocolate bars. They could hardly believe their eyes. Everyone was crying and cheering, hugging and laughing. Maud wrapped her arms around Trudy and lifted her off the ground. And then Trudy, six years younger, easily lifted Maud off the ground. She was as light as a feather. When Trudy hugged Marike, she was afraid to break her, she'd grown so gaunt. Aunt Jenke took Marike's hand and Maud took Trudy's as they made their way through the crowds to the spot. Everywhere people silently wept and hugged each other, clinging at times to each other instead of crumbling to the ground from pent-up exhaustion. Jenke and the girls gathered their fair share of parcels and went home to Mom.

Mom had increasingly been staying in bed, and her coughing continued not just at night but throughout the day as well. Aunt Jenke made them all some powdered eggs, and they took some and a biscuit upstairs to Mom. With effort, she pulled herself to sitting. Maud helped her sip water from a glass. Mom's hand shook as she sipped and coughed, sipped and coughed. Trudy sat on the bed and set the dish of food on Mom's lap. She looked at the eggs and biscuit, then to Trudy and over to the Ms and at last to Jenke. "Well, girls," she smiled through tears, "we made it." They all huddled on the bed to sit close. For years they'd wished away the war. Now that it appeared to be over, they were all having trouble believing the news. One look outside, and they realized life would never be the same. Like a chicken spared from slaughter, they were not sure of where to begin, what to do next. She didn't know why, but Trudy was weeping. She looked around the bare room at her family. Each one was pale and terribly thin, but they were alive. And she began to recognize an inkling starting in the pit of her stomach and slowly rising towards her chest: hope.

"Mom, what about Pop?" Trudy could see by her smile that her mind was already there. "I wonder if Pop knows the war is over for us. Can he come home now? How can we find him?"

Mom set down her empty plate. "I have thought about this day for nearly six years now," she said, tears flowing easily. "Can you believe that small lifetime has passed since he was home? And what miserable years they've been!" She coughed for a long while, a hacking wrecking cough. Maud offered her more water. "There is no mail, no telex office, no telephone service yet," said Mom. "We have waited seven years; I guess all we can do is...wait some more." She smiled through her tears, and her eyes found Trudy's. "We have been to Hell and back, girls. What's a little more waiting?" She opened her arms wide, and they all fell in for a hug. "We did it! We survived! Soon we will be a family again!" she said confidently. They hugged until Mom's coughing worsened, and she wearily lay back down to rest. The others left the room, but Trudy stayed a few minutes to rub Mom's back until she fell asleep, praying for God to heal her and for her father's safe return.

SEVENTEEN - Aboard the Janus

1945 Sam stayed tuned to the BBC broadcasts whenever possible. Danker and Einer often joined him in his stateroom, sipping whisky from crystal tumblers and listening as the war slowly knitted to a close. Together they dreamed of life after the war back on land, back home. News of the "Black Sea" meeting between Roosevelt, Churchill, and Stalin raised everyone's hopes. The world held its collective breath as Allied forces continued to defeat the enemy in Europe. Hitler's suicide confirmed their hope and raised their spirits. Finally, the war was officially declared over on 8 May 1945, Victory Day in Europe. Word of the German surrender rippled through the Janus like glorious thunder in summer's drought. Whoops, hollers, popping champagne corks echoed throughout the ship—a unified heaving sigh of relief. Many nationalities had served on or were served by this ship—Chinese, Italian, Dutch, Indian, African. Today they were all equal parts of a cohesive team. Today they were partners in peace. With each slap on the back and heartfelt toast, they took pride in a job well done. Six years, sixty-three round trips, and over a million miles later, the Janus's wartime service had ended. Celebrations continued for a week.

During the ship's three-day discharge in Port Elizabeth at the end of May, Sam, aching to share his joy with Helen, convinced the guide pilot to fly him to Durban. He cabled Helen that he was coming and was surprised when she wasn't waiting in the garden. When James answered the door, Sam fought the urge to kiss him.

Instead he held him by the shoulders and beamed into his face, "Good to see you, James! You're looking well!" Then he flew passed him calling Helen's name as he charged up the stairs. He burst into her room, "I'm home, my love, I'm home! The war is over!" Helen stood motionless in the doorway to the veranda. He picked her up and spun her around. And saw her tear-streaked face. "What could possibly be wrong? Darling, we have waited so long for this! Our time has come, Helen, don't you see?"

She fell against him, allowing him to wrap his arms around her for a moment. "Sam," she began, "the war is over, and so must we be." She unhooked herself from his embrace. "You must realize the war was our lifeline, Sam. Because of the war, you are kept here, in my half of the world. Now that it's over, you'll be sent back to Holland and reunited with your family. After all these years...I know you, Sam. You'll feel...obligated." He couldn't object, and his silence confirmed her statement. "I've known this day would eventually come. I've implored you to tell me, Sam, when the war ends, where will that leave me?" He opened his mouth to speak, but she raised her hand to hush him. "I blame myself, Sam, not you." She held his hands to her chest. "I have loved you with all my heart and soul, Sam, loved you like no other, and I will never love another."

"Helen, please don't say these things. Not today. The war is over, Helen!" He cupped her chin and lowered his face to hers. "First and foremost we need to celebrate that. Senseless killing will stop. Bombs will cease. And yes, people will be reunited with their families and loved ones. This is wonderful news! It's not about just the two of us! Not today." He led her onto the veranda and sat her on his lap. "Of course I've thought of my family, my children. Of course I want to know they are safe and fed. I am their father, after all. My country has been torn up! I need to do whatever I can. But believe me when I tell you, my precious better half, you are the one I yearn to look after, Helen, day and night." He hugged her against himself and smoothed her hair. "Yes, I will return to Leiden, but only to visit, a detour on my way home to you. And I pray to God that you will still have me." She smiled at him through tears, holding his face in her hands. "But now is a time for celebration, Helen. I wanted so desperately to share the news with you, not with anyone at Leiden. I will be here sometime in August for a long visit, my love. I have arranged to take leave, and we will start our life together then, without fear of war or mines or past lives. I love you, Helen VanEck, and only you."

Three days later, Sam was back on his ship wondering if his brief stay at Merriwold were real or just another beautiful dream. At last the lines of communication opened for Holland, and five-pound food parcels were quickly arranged. Sam handed money to 4th mate Steensma with his home address for weekly dispatches for the ensuing two months. As soon as telegrams were possible, Sam sent his first words home in six years: *Congratulations on liberation Stop Arranging local agents commence weekly food parcel drops Stop Anticipate airmail usual address Stop Sam* All he could do now was wait for a response.

Although the war was officially over, Sam's ferrying duties had certainly not ended. As they maneuvered the ship toward Bahrain, the temperature warmed to an oppressive 92 degrees. Sam checked in with Bertie at the local mail station; no word yet from Holland. The convoy continued to Bombay and arrived again in Bahrain at the end of July. This time Bertie retrieved the airmail envelope when he saw Sam approach. Sam tore into the envelope. Gertrude's once beautiful handwriting was hardly recognizable. His chest tightened as he read...*Please excuse my writing, but the conditions over the years here have wrecked my nerves. I know your safe return will heal me. The children are in great need of food. Maud seems to have suffered the most for lacking the essential things. At present we are in need of sugar...* His resurrected family appeared in his mind's eye. They were crippled by hunger and deprivation, and there was little more he could do from his refuge thousands of miles away. As he read on, he realized they were needier than he had allowed himself to imagine, and he was flooded with guilt. He felt suddenly sick to his stomach and ran out back, retching by the trash cans. He wiped his sweaty palms on his pants and pulled his handkerchief from his pocket to mop his face. Feeling frantic and disoriented, he made his way to his stateroom and closed the door.

Inside his cabin Sam opened his dresser drawer and placed the folded letter under his socks. Closing the drawer, he stopped short at the sight of Helen smiling at him from the frame on top. He stood frozen in place like a schoolboy who'd just been caught stealing.

EIGHTEEN – Durban

1945   Danker and Einer gathered with Sam in his stateroom listening to reports of Hiroshima's devastation. "I just thank God the Nazis didn't have this equipment," Einer repeated over and over.

"Hasn't our planet seen enough suffering already?" pleaded Danker. "What a tragedy that mankind had to use the fruits of science in this way. I just hope that evil yellow monster now realizes that crime does not pay!" he said, slamming his fist on the desk.

Sam didn't offer much. He was becoming immune to even the most horrific events of the war. "Gangsters get what they deserve," he'd always say. He had his own battle taking shape. Holland vs. South Africa—all prisoners, no victors, and he the only gangster. He stepped onto the outer deck. Already the air felt different, cleaner. Unlike the dreary days of wartime blackouts, lights now dotted the coastline giving off a welcoming glow. He inhaled deeply. What a relief to feel and smell the crisp southeast trade wind again. He closed his eyes and imagined Helen in her hilltop home. He pictured her leaning in the doorway to the veranda searching the ocean for her sailor husband before settling into bed. He longed to be climbing into that bed with her. When he returned to his cabin, Einer and Danker had gone, but they had left the radio on. Beethoven's "First Symphony" aired, and he was sure Helen was listening too. "I'll be home soon, my love," he said aloud, unbuttoning his shirt. He climbed into bed and turned off the light.

He could almost feel her warmth beside him, the comfort of her head on his chest, his fingers sifting through her soft hair. He drifted off to sleep as the music played on.

By the end of August, Sam was seated in the garden at Merriwold. Spring's thaw was slow, and the metal chair's cold seeped into his bottom and the backs of his thighs. He was sipping the traditional beer, its cold carbonation shivering in his chest. He checked his watch and tapped his foot; crossed his legs one way and then the other. The Japanese had suffered a second atomic bomb, further declaration of war, and the humiliation of unconditional surrender. He felt no pity; Helen was late. Grannie was off visiting with April and David at their new home. Perhaps that was why Henry was so chatty. He had been babbling on about school, bally scouts, and *The Phantom of the Opera* play they'd seen recently. At first Sam heard nothing as Henry pranced about chattering. When Henry finally bent to Sam's level, held his face between his two pudgy hands, Sam finally allowed Henry's youthful enthusiasm to calm him. Sam exhaled and smiled before standing and wrapping his arms around the boy. The deep love he felt for this child continued to amaze him. In the recent years he had witnessed more of Henry's short life than that of his three children combined.

Helen steered the car into the garage, and Sam and Henry hurried down the slope to greet her. He whisked her up off her feet and held her there. His throat tightened, and he blinked back tears. The stress of impending peace had snuck up on him, caught him off guard. Their future was now uncertain, and he loved her more than ever. "So good to be home, Helen," he whispered.

"So good to be held by you, my love," she whispered back, her arms wrapped securely around his neck. When Sam placed her feet on the ground, she greeted Henry and pulled him in for a hug. They walked toward the house, and it was then that Sam noticed the garden was in full glorious bloom. The purple blossoms of the syringa tree gave off a musky perfume, and the kafir boom had dropped a crimson carpet by the chairs he'd just been seated in. Sam and Helen stayed in the garden while Henry ran to help James with hot tea.

As soon as he left, Sam pulled Helen onto his lap and quickly kissed her. "I've waited too long for that kiss. I've missed you terribly, my love. I think the war's end has made me a bit unsteady." Helen simply hugged his neck and kissed him again before slipping off his lap and standing beside him. "The garden is amazing, Helen, you have been working very hard. The flowers are beautiful, and I see more coming."

Helen smiled and looked over her handiwork. "You know I find working in the soil very soothing, comforting really. I suppose it's obvious then how desperately I've needed to be consoled." She looked at him squarely. "What will become of us now? You are expected back in your other life, Sam. And I must continue mine." She reached to touch the side of his face, tilting her head as his face softened. "But, heart of my heart, how can I ever let you go?"

After dinner Helen was clearly exhausted. She had worked extra hours in the preceding weeks in order to take some time off during Sam's three-month shore leave. Sam insisted she go enjoy a hot bath. He'd be up soon to say goodnight; he and Henry had some catching up to do. His manner left her no choice, and she gratefully obliged. Sam and Henry talked with James a while, then went up to say goodnight. Helen was dressed in a white nightgown, sitting on the edge of the bed and smelling of gardenia soap. He pulled back the coverlet for her and fought the urge to climb in too. "Nap now, my love. I will see you later," he whispered in her ear. As Henry said goodnight, Sam looked around the tidy room—the writing desk and inkwell where she wrote him faithfully, the silver hairbrush on the vanity, the sheers moving gently in the evening ocean breeze—noting them all indelibly in his memory.

Henry and Sam visited for over an hour in Henry's room. Sam sat on the bed while Henry showed Sam his scout uniform and newest additions to his bug collection, a locust pinned to a board with an orange monarch butterfly below. Henry talked excitedly about weekly visits with April. All the while Sam marveled at the youngster before him, whose whole world was comprised of a handful of people, his only concerns were those in his own back yard.

At the first hint of Henry's yawn, Sam sent him to the bathroom to clean his teeth. "Off you go, young man. Tomorrow is another day," he said hoping to hurry the boy along. When Henry returned, he uninhibitedly wrapped his arms around Sam's neck and kissed his cheek before nestling his head on Sam's shoulder.

"G'night, Cappy," Henry slurred, yawning.

Sam held him close, closing his eyes as he wrapped his arms around this sweet boy. He held the plaid bedspread so Henry could climb in underneath; then pulled it up over his shoulders and kissed his head. "Tomorrow we'll search for bugs in the garden," Sam promised, laying his big hand on the side of Henry's head.

Down the hall in the gray room, Sam unpacked and readied himself for bed, killing time. When he was certain Henry was sound asleep, he tiptoed to Helen's room and was happily surprised to find her awake. "Come here, my love," she said with outstretched arms.

Sam had not been granted such a long leave since his operation three years earlier, when they had fallen in love. They'd been so eager to spend this leave together, but their three months seemed to pass as quickly as the briefest stay. Breezy spring days brought plenty of sunshine as well as intermittent evening storms, and they spent a lot of time lounging on the beach across the street, digging in the garden, or feeling the mist of the rain on their faces under the covered veranda. When Henry returned from school each day, he knew to find them sitting on the metal chairs under the syringa, most often sharing a beer.

One day Helen and Sam joined Henry and his friends on the beach. The boys splashed in the water while Sam and Helen watched from the sand. Helen sat in a short chair mending socks with Sam stretched out on a blanket at her feet. So much had happened in the world in the six years they'd known each other. How many lives had been lost and begun? Sam watched the boys playing, and his mind drifted to his children in those same years. How they must have struggled with fear in a crowded house, air raids, lack of food, an ailing mother, an absent father...or had they even noticed he was gone? In their desolation did their prayers include him, or was the docket full with their own grief? He had so adeptly avoided their grief, too easily turned his back and closed his eyes. He listened to the boys' laughter, saw gulls flying overhead, felt the cool ocean breeze, and watched this angel of a woman darning his socks. Merriwold, completely unchanged by it all, welcomed him from its hilltop perch. Guilt spread within him like cancer cells left unchecked.

Helen sensed his distance. "Meet me in town after work tomorrow?" Helen's sweet voice jolted him. "An English company is presenting Shakespeare's *The Merry Wives of Windsor* at the Criterion Theatre, and I want to see it." She didn't look up from her sewing. "Doesn't that sound wonderful? You can drop in on George before we go."

As the men finished their chat, Helen appeared in Dr. Stuart's doorway. "Thank you again for taking such good care of Helen, George," she heard Sam say. He was holding George's hand in both of his and bent at the waist to meet eye-to-eye. "Five o'clock, right on time," he said flashing his blue eyes in her direction.

"I never keep a handsome man waiting. Besides, I'm famished!" Helen said unbuttoning her white jacket. Underneath she wore a tailored navy shirtwaist. "We have just enough time to grab a quick bite at the Playhouse Grill."

They shared a sandwich and pot of tea and hurried to the show. They sat through the play holding hands, laughing aloud, completely absorbed. Afterwards, they took a long walk on the beach, dodging moonlit waves in the cool evening air. "I want us to have this life. I want to be able to walk on the beach with the woman I love and not worry about where I'll be sent next. I want control of my life, Helen. I rarely take leave, the crews have been lousy—we lost two more, did I tell you? One drowned; the other took a three-hour pass and his tools and never came back." They laughed at this. "Can you blame him? I'm ready to do the same!" Sam stopped and pulled her close. "I will be eligible for my pension in a few short years, Helen. Will you wait for me, my love?"

She brushed sand off his jacket and gently laid her hands on his chest. "Sam, we will never have complete control of our lives, you know that. We don't know what lies ahead for us. I do know that I love you as I have never loved before. When you are away, I merely survive until you return." She ran her hand down his leathery cheek, and he leaned his head towards her palm. "But Sam, if we want to be together, we cannot simply wait for fate to make that happen for us. You are going to have to take action; create the opportunity for us. Do you see that?" she asked peering into his eyes. "I'm afraid you are so accustomed to being *sent* everywhere, that the thought of your making your own plan is too foreign." She waited until the thought registered on his face. "Caltex will never send you here permanently; you're going to have to request that when the time comes. Better yet, create the right time to make that happen," she rose up on her toes, eyes wide on his, "make *us* happen."

Back at Merriwold, Helen lit the treasured tea candles Sam had given her while Sam poured them each a sherry in short stemmed glasses. He sat in an upholstered chair, and Helen sat on the carpet near his feet. She leaned her head against his knee while he stroked her hair. "When you are home, I feel as though you've never left," she began. "I have no doubts, and the world is...wonderful." she spread her arm in the air. "When you are with me, I am full of hope for our future." She sipped her sherry and set it down; then kneeled to set her eyes on his. "And when you are not...well, that makes for a different world completely." She sat on her heels and placed both her hands on her thighs. "What will become of us, Sam, if you don't take steps to change our situation?" His leaving inevitable, she wanted desperately to know when they could start their lives together.

He held her eyes. "Someday, Helen, I will step off that ship and never go back, I promise you. But I have to do so properly. I cannot afford to jeopardize my pension because that impacts our future as well. And I have the three girls to think about. They are my responsibility, and I must provide for them, especially now that their mother is ill." He held her head to his chest and rested his hand on the side of her soft face. "I have been such a lousy father; it is the least I can do." He sipped his sherry. "You are an angel, Helen. You are whom I live for, only you. Someday we will have the rest of our lives together, right here in Merriwold. Do you believe that, my love?"

She looked into his eyes, "What else can I do?" she asked. "You are my life."

"The stars are incredible tonight!" Henry called as he swept passed them and out the front door, taking the room's tension with him. Sam quickly decided to seize the opportunity to speak with Henry alone. He kissed the top of Helen's head and followed him to the garden. Henry had pulled a metal chair to the lawn, out from under tree limbs. His eyes were pinned to the sky. The night was cool and humid, and crickets chirped in the distance. Lazy waves slowly brushed on shore and retreated. Sam carried the other chair and sat beside him. Bright glimmering stars spattered the midnight blue sky. They both gasped and shot their arms upward when they glimpsed a shooting star, laughing at their mutual reaction.

"Make a wish," Henry urged, standing and pulling Sam to his feet. They shut their eyes, and the silence closed in around them. Sam made his wish quickly, of course. It was the same wish he had repeated several times a day for years. He opened his eyes to see Henry, eyes squeezed tight and lips pressed together, still working his magic. He had witnessed the transformation in him from boy to young man, and his heart ached at the thought of leaving him. Henry opened his eyes and locked them on Sam's. Volumes went unsaid between them. They shared a kindred bond that they were not entitled to own. Though their relationship had not been sanctioned by marriage or legal document, their commitment was as strong as father and son. Henry reached inside his pocket and pulled out his fist. He cleared his throat, extended his hand, and dropped his compass into Sam's upturned palm. When Sam looked at Henry quizzically, Henry said, "You gave this to me three years ago, and I've treasured this compass ever since." Henry chuckled and pushed his thick hair off his face. "Did you know I used to sleep with it?" Sam smiled, recalling the compass clutched in Henry's small hand. "I want you to have this now, Cappy, so that you know I want you to find your way back to Merriwold, to Mum, and to me."

Without hesitation or inhibition, the two embraced each other as father and son about to be separated for a very long time.

The next evening at dusk, Helen stood on her veranda. She spotted the guide planes first and then the convoy and knew the Janus was leading the way. The flashes—two rapid, two slow—were hardly discernable in the nebulous light, but she knew that had to be Sam's signal. She turned her little lamp on and off and hoped he had seen. The moon was rising behind her hilltop, making a path to him. She wanted to run along that illuminated path and sail away with Sam. Instead she snapped the sheers shut, lay on her bed, and had a good cry.

The Janus set the course, and her convoy mates followed. The rhythmic sounds of the engine welcomed Sam back on board. Once underway Danker and Einer joined Sam in his stateroom, sat in the leather chairs across from Sam's desk, and brought him up-to-date on the events of the prior three months. They popped up and down with papers to be signed, orders to be addressed, and looked over his shoulder reviewing the latest discharge orders.

Business over, Danker took three tumblers from the cabinet and Sam's whiskey from its hiding place. "Gentlemen," he said, pouring each two fingers' worth, "I'm about to be a married man. Carla said yes!" The three clinked their glasses.

"Are you sure she'll be able to stand having you under foot all the time?" Einer teased. "You know she's quite accustomed to your travel schedule," he said with a wink.

While Danker talked excitedly about his and Carla's plans, Sam's mind wandered. He felt increasingly isolated, surrounded by people whose lives were taking direct paths to bright new futures, while his own future grew fuzzy and more uncertain.

Sam drifted over to the leather settee turned on his small radio. The Nuremberg Tribunal was in progress. "Those gangsters have the cheek to plead not guilty! What scum!" With that the conversation turned to world events, and as usual, an inspired Sam led the conversation well into the night.

After loading in Bahrain, the convoy made its trek north for the first time in almost seven years. Throughout the trek, the atmosphere was buoyant. All around him fellow Dutch talked of seeing loved ones again. But instead of eager anticipation, Sam's heart sank further with each mile. His heart was in Merriwold, not Leiden. While the Janus docked in Port Said, Sam bought six packages of silk stockings and had them sent to Helen. News spread on ship that a fellow tanker, the Nykerk, hit a mine and sank while enroute to Antwerp. Imagining the same fate, Sam's only fear was never returning to Helen.

They spent three days docked at Humber and Tyne. During the daytime, Sam searched for supplies for Leiden—sewing materials, fountain pens, schoolbags, and bicycles—and had them sent on ahead. He hoped they'd arrive before he did. Perhaps the diversion would allow his heavy heart and soul to slip past them unnoticed. In the evenings, the captains and first mates gathered in the officers' lounge for a drink and wartime stories. On the second evening two Dutch Shell tankers arrived. The captain of one, Tom Andersen, was an old friend of Sam, though the two had not met since 1936. During conversation, Sam learned that the Queen of London had decorated him and his colleagues the year before for continuous Atlantic trade services. Tom was surprised Sam had not at least received the Dutch Merchant Service Campaign Ribbon as he himself had. Sam felt slighted and underappreciated, and the feeling began to erode the fierce loyalty Sam had served Caltex with throughout this miserable wartime stint.

NINETEEN – Durban

1946 Henry and Helen waited patiently while Grannie deliberately and slowly placed both feet on each step from the train to the platform. Hampering her further were two carry-alls loaded with produce that she struggled to maneuver through the narrow exit. "Ooo, it's hot!" she said, "seems cooler at April's house," she wheezed, unloading her bags on Henry. "You really need to see their home, Helen. You'd be so proud," she said easing herself, backside first, into the car. "All that produce and those beautiful flowers are from her garden. I never knew she had such a green thumb!"

"Can we go to April's, mum?" Henry pleaded. "We were supposed to go with Cappy when he was here months ago, and we didn't," he reminded her.

"As a matter of fact, Dr. Stuart has asked me to take a ride with him to the PMB to check on a patient. You can come along and keep April company while we work. I believe he's promised to go in two weeks, while you have summer holiday."

By the time the women made their way up the rise, Henry had April on the line making plans. He held the phone out to Helen when she entered the house. "She wants to talk with you about the details."

"Hello, April. Grannie says you have quite the garden. The flowers are beautiful, did you really grow them yourself?" April assured her mother she had. They set plans for the fifteenth of December. The doctor and Helen would drop Henry off to stay with April while they made their rounds. After a short visit with April, they'd make the drive back home. April offered to serve dinner, but Helen refused, sure Dr. Stuart would want to get home.

The sky was already bright when Dr. Stuart arrived at 5:30 that morning. Evening rain had left wet paths on the pavement, and the air smelled fresh and clean. The three rode quietly until they turned inland, and the ocean slipped out of view. Helen looked into the backseat at her sleeping son. "You can take the boy out of the routine, but not the routine out of the boy, they say." She studied his face, so carefree and trusting. "We were all innocent like him once. I wonder when we learn to be cynical and suspicious."

George gave Helen a quick sympathetic glance and reached across the front seat to pat her hand. "It's a slow educational process," he said.

Under Helen's direction, George finally turned the egg shaped car onto the long driveway. The property was lovely, flat near the house while green hills rose in the distance. Flowers bloomed in bunches of vivid color spilling onto the walk and driveway and promised more behind the house. April emerged from the house as they parked. A little dog yipped around her ankles as she hurried towards them.

"Welcome! I'm so happy you're here!" she called. April opened the car door for Helen, who stepped out and offered her daughter her cheek. Henry bounded towards her, nearly knocking her onto the ground. "You are a small horse, aren't you?" But Henry's attention was on the pint-sized brown and white dog, wagging his stump of a tail and sniffing Henry's hands. "This is Buddy. I think he likes you!"

"He's kissing me! I didn't know you had a dog!" Henry giggled, ginning ear-to-ear.

April scooped up Buddy. "David brought him home so I won't be lonely when he travels. And he travels all the time, doesn't he!" she said, kissing the dog. "Come inside. I want to give you the grand tour."

The place was rather small and wide, not deep. Lots of dark wood and light braided rugs. Beyond the foyer was a sun-lit gathering room overlooking a modest yard and fields beyond. Morning newspapers were strewn across an old farm table, the sawed-off legs transformed it to a large coffee table in front of the dark leather sofa. April swept them into a pile as she passed, and as she did, a key fell to the floor. April picked it up and studied the house key, puzzled, because it was not hers. Dismissing it, she pushed it into her pocket and turned to the dog, "Let's show them out back!" She led them through the kitchen and opened the glass door from the kitchen nook. Surrounding the adjacent patio were flowers wild with color—brilliant yellow, vibrant blue, bright orange, lime green. Herbs overflowed from chunky pots near the black iron parlor set. On the other side vegetables grew in neat rows—red tomatoes hung heavily on green vines, squash and peas were staked and housed. Everything looked freshly delicious. Back inside the efficient, square kitchen, April placed the key on the windowsill above the sink that overflowed with dirty dishes. A beautiful bunch of fresh flowers stood tall in the center of the white kitchen table. "Those flowers are from my garden, right, Buddy?" She kissed the dog and placed him on the floor. His hind end wagging as she led the group back to the gathering room.

"Well you certainly do have a green thumb!" said Helen. I don't remember your taking an interest at home..."

"I saw how much pleasure the garden gives you, and I've always wanted to try vegetables. Most of the flowers in the front came with the house, but the gardens around back are all mine." April suggested they have some tea, but Helen muttered something about muddy shoes, and said they must be going, business before pleasure.

April promised to have afternoon tea ready for them when they returned. "That will be an interesting first," Helen grumbled as the engine roared to a start. You'll have to vouch for me, George, Sam will never believe me," she laughed.

Helen read the directions as George drove to three patients—a heart attack victim, a hip surgery patient, and a bedridden elderly man whose many family members waited on him hand and foot. George said the man was too happy to die and assured Helen he would be there every time they ventured to the PMB. She believed him whole-heartedly. Helen assisted George as he deftly performed routine tests—drawing blood, warming the stethoscope before placing it on their backs, pumping the blood pressure cuff. He asked questions and listened intently to each patient, scribbling notes.

The car stirred up dust along April's long driveway in the late afternoon sun. At the sound of their approach, April emerged to greet them with Buddy and Henry in tow. "David will be along in an hour," she said. "Won't you please join us for supper?"

Helen tightened her arm around Henry's shoulder, and without looking to George for concurrence, declined. Long day, long drive. "I supposed you've learned to cook as well?"

"Yes, and I love it! Especially vegetables from the garden, everything is so fresh and lovely." April was exuberant.

"You seem very content here, dear," Helen said approaching her. "I wish you continued happiness in your home," she said sincerely, offering her cheek. "Our best to David. We'll see you both next week for Christmas lunch then."

Emotionally exhausted, April stood in the driveway waving as the three drove away. *Yes, I'm here to stay, so now can we be friends?* she wondered, remembering Grannie's stories.

Again Henry stretched himself out on the back seat and slept during the return trip. George spoke little, so Helen's mind wandered. She thought of her own newlywed days when her world was a garden and she sewed seeds for their future. Even April's father made her happy in the beginning. But the buoyancy of new love often becomes weighted by life's details. She wondered how long this phase could last for April, who always seemed more comfortable with misery than joy. She thought about the newlywed relationship she and Sam shared and wondered how it would evolve if he actually stayed forever. Would their love eventually become cumbersome? She prayed they'd have the chance to find out.

Helen refused to be swept up in the Christmas spirit. Of course she went through the motions of decorating, baking, and the traditional luncheon with the usual guests. At the party she noticed everyone glancing at an empty chair, tentatively looking around the corner for Sam to suddenly appear. Like school children about to hear the recess bell sound, they longed for their tall storyteller to make them laugh or dream.

Late that night, long after the guests had gone, Helen lay in bed with the covers pulled up to her chin. The BBC was hardly audible as the rain pounded the roof and veranda and overflowed the downpipes. She thought of all the work she and James had done in the garden that week and was sick to think it might be ruined. Most of her time had been spent pulling out old plants and turning over the soil, making way for ferns, hydrangeas, and a bit of portulaca along the edges. She wanted the garden to be beautiful for Sam's next visit, whenever that might be; now she wept quietly at the thought of wasted precious time.

The phone's ring jolted her. April was sobbing bitterly on the other end. A car had hit and killed the dog. Helen thought of the cute little animal and how attached April appeared. To make matters worse, David had tried to comfort the dying animal and was bitten so badly that he needed to have an anti-tetanus injection at the hospital. She tried desperately, but there was nothing Helen could say to ease April's pain. As April continued to cry, Helen's heart began to melt. At last she just gave up and cried along with her aching daughter. Helen's tears and compassion helped soothe April's pain in places words could never have touched.

TWENTY – Leiden

1946 The Janus settled at Wilton's Shipyard on the Maas River off Schiedam. From the moment the ship was visible in the distance, Wilton's employees had been alerting the families of her progress. After a routine customs check, the crewmen gathered their meager belongings and anxiously shuffled into summer's still air. Timidly, they stepped on home soil, set down their bags and breathed in their homeland for the first time in more than seven years. They eyed each other with mixed emotions, joyful for their safe return yet fearful of the scenery waiting to unfold beyond the gate. All were eager to see their loved ones yet hesitant to see first-hand the war's devastation. They simply shook hands and exited the yard in search of transportation.

Fuel was scarce, and public transportation, iffy, but Sam was fortunate to find a bus and then a tramcar to start. Both were crowded and stifling hot despite the open windows. Sam offered his seat to a woman and stood with his satchel between his feet. It bounced as the wheels hit ruts and potholes. Then his luck ran out, and he carried his satchel the final three miles. All around him was evidence of war—remains of buildings protruded from the ground, charred and pocked farmland, eerily abandoned homes. The stench of something burnt—rubber, wood, human hair?—hung in the air. He sat to rest on a bench and to slowly absorb his surroundings. The devastation was astounding, worse than he had ever imagined. His beautiful countryside, continually swathed in brilliant color, appeared dead and hollow like an old log washed ashore after a storm. He continued towards home, avoiding gaping holes in the pavement and growing more anxious about his girls with each step. It was clear to him now he could never fully comprehend what they must have endured. He had been able to evade these thoughts too easily until now.

"He's on the way!" Aunt Jenke declared, replacing the receiver. Trudy rushed to hop onto Mom's bed, making sure she'd heard the news. Aunt Jenke followed her into the dining room, which had become Mom's bedroom when she could no longer climb the steps. "Remember he'll have entry formalities and a three-hour trek at least, mind you. And that's if he can find available transportation."

Trudy squeezed Mom's hand and helped her to sitting. Already she was weeping, her frail body trembling. She'd grown weaker and terribly thin. Her cough rattled her insides. "Oh Mom, you have waited so long for this day! What do you want me to do? How can I make it the perfect day you've been dreaming about all these years?" Giddy laughter made her cough. Trudy held the water glass to her lips. Mom settled down and smoothed her hair, obviously nervous about her appearance. "You are still beautiful, Mom. Nothing can change that, especially in Pop's eyes!" Trudy assured her, touching her forehead to her mother's.

"I'll be well in no time," Mom whispered. "You know that, right, Trudy?" For years Mom had been saying all she needed was Pop's safe return to make her well. Now Trudy prayed that were true. She helped Mom into the bath and carefully washed her hair while Aunt Jenke changed the bed linens. After a bit of supper, Mom fell exhausted into bed for a nap. As Trudy leaned in to touch a kiss to her head, Mom took her hand and smiled with the same loving brown eyes Trudy had known all her life. "We are almost whole again, Trudy, my love. Our house will be the right kind of full soon," she said, her eyes smiling with sweet anticipation.

Finally, close to 11 P.M., Aunt Jenke opened the door and stepped back to allow Sam into the quiet house. The girls didn't quite know what to do, how to behave. They'd been dreaming of his return for years, and now that he was home, they suddenly felt lost. They looked at each other, watched their feet tap the floor and slide to and fro. The last time they saw him, they were children in every way. They had since grown far beyond their ages—twenty, eighteen, and twelve. They watched uneasily as he removed his hat, apprehensively let their eyes meet his. He scanned their faces, and then, overcome with emotion, sank to his knees, weeping. Trudy moved first, and they all fell into his embrace. "My dear little girls," he cried, wrapping his arms around their skinny frames. Then he held them by the shoulders, one by one, and studied each girl. He looked into Marike's dark sad eyes and smoothed her dull, limp hair. He could still see her confident spirit hidden just beneath the surface, but he couldn't at all imagine her dancing around the room. He slowly let his arms drop and reached for Maud, wincing at the touch of her emaciated frame. Searching her sunken eyes, he whispered repeatedly "I'm so sorry." He let go of Maud, opened his arms to Trudy. She had changed the most, grown tall, terribly thin, of course, with cascades of thin blond waves. Expectation was evident in her clear blue eyes. She wrapped her arms around his neck and laid her head on his. She was hopeful for a normal life, for food in the pantry, church bells in sunshine and, most of all, a healthy mother. She took his hand and led him to the dining room.

"Mom has been waiting such a long time for you, Pop."

The room was dim and had a faint medicinal odor. Someone snapped on the lamp, and Mom struggled to pull herself to sitting. Their letters had hardly prepared him for her condition. Gertrude was literally a ghost of her former self. Painfully gaunt, she was almost unrecognizable. Her once lustrous hair had fallen out in patches leaving bits of string gone wild. A maze of blue veins was visible through paper-thin skin. Her once beautiful shiny eyes were sunken, dull. Mom wanted to avoid his eyes, but she had waited so long to see him, to touch him. She trembled with anticipation as he gingerly lowered himself onto the edge of the bed near her. "Hug me, Sam. I don't care if I do break." Slowly, tenderly, he embraced her bony frame as her silent tears streaked her face. Gently rocking, he let his tears flow too. They stayed like that for several minutes, but to Ger, it seemed like a second.

Finally, Sam cleared his throat and, with a large hand behind her shoulders, gently guided her back to the pillows. "Rest now," he instructed. "We'll talk more in the morning," he promised, kissing her forehead and avoiding her eyes.

"Tomorrow starts a new day, a new chapter," Mom whispered, clasping his hand in hers. "Lovely to have you home, Sam," she beamed. "I feel better alre—" she began until a coughing fit overcame her.

Beginning the very next day, Pop continued the daily six-hour round-trip commute to the Wilton Shipyard while his ship's overhaul was being assessed. Years of hauling cargo and hasty drydock repairs left the Janus in very poor condition. He'd leave the house early and return at suppertime. At least they would have that time together, to get to know each other, Trudy hoped. Mom would rest all day to have the strength to join them at the kitchen table, never taking her eyes off Pop. He talked on about the different ports and the countries that seemed so mysterious—India, Japan, Madagascar. They all participated in those stories, asking questions, making comments. Trudy could see that Mom was in her glory, having lively chatter again in the house. And then he turned the talk to the girls, asking for details of the past seven years, and they all fell abruptly silent. No one wanted to relive a moment.

One day the girls accompanied their father to the shipyard. On the bus and train Trudy sat beside him, feeling comforted by the touch of his thigh against hers. Pride dripped off him as he toured them around his domain. But when they behaved like children half their age, running along the deck, jumping on casings and hanging on the handrails, he corralled them below to his stateroom. They stepped over the coaming and scanned the neat and tidy room, partitioned by furniture into different functions. They were impressed by the leather and crystal, but the walls were oddly bare. Of all the pictures and letters they had sent him over the years, not one was on display.

Seemingly as quickly as they'd arrived, they began their three-hour return trek home to find the packages Pop had arranged for in England. The girls squealed with excitement to find two new shiny bicycles sitting on the porch! They laughed taking turns riding them in circles on the street. At first they were awkward and nearly toppled over, but the Ms kept at it and were riding up and down the street effortlessly in a short time. Trudy had never ridden a bicycle before. Realizing this, Maud stepped off the shiny white bicycle and offered Trudy a ride. With the least bit of instruction, Trudy was on her way. The breeze in her face was exhilarating, and she welcomed the free, unrestricted feeling. She pedaled and shot both legs akimbo, beaming into the sinking sun. She wanted to ride all evening, but Pop called them to the house. "Girls, do well in your schoolwork, and I'll join you for Sunday afternoon rides," he promised.

For four months Pop continued his long commute. On the weekends, Mom would smile with delight as Pop carted her out to the backyard for fresh air. "Sit with me, my love," she'd ask, motioning to the back stoop. "Isn't this a beautiful day!" Her world was brightening, but all he saw was absolute devastation. The garden Mom had cared for meticulously had gone to weed. The sound of church bells was ominously absent. The canal was muddy and uninviting. All this sadness was new to Pop. Every time he looked for a favorite windmill or saw a demolished building, he felt the violation and anger rise in his chest. But these were scenes his girls had grown to accept. He didn't dare bother them with his sadness. They had already suffered more than their share. But he couldn't pretend he didn't feel violated, angry.

"Ger, I don't have time to just sit. Look at this place! There is so much to do—mending the house...and I really must install a garden before the weather steals my chance." His expression was disgusted. "You rest here, breathe in the fresh air, get well," he'd say, squeezing her shoulders briefly before hurrying off to one project or another, head down in concentration.

Trudy wanted so desperately to see Mom smile, hear her laugh. She wanted him to make her well again, as she believed he would. Mom didn't complain. She seemed to patiently wait her turn. But having him home just didn't feel like anyone had anticipated. Mom improved very little, and she didn't seem nearly as relieved as Trudy had imagined she would. "We just need more time to make happy a routine again," Mom explained, tapping Trudy's hand.

Unexpected word came from Caltex headquarters. "After reviewing various bids," Pop read aloud, "Todd's Shipyard will perform the required work on the Janus." Pop continued scanning, "...estimated at over a million dollars," he looked at the girls wide-eyed, "the vessel needs 1,700 tons of new steel, and Holland's depleted supplies simply can't afford them. Captain VanEck, you are hereby ordered to take the Janus and her convoy to New York, USA, for a full overhaul." He lowered the paper, mouth gaping open. "I'm going to America," he stated with wide-eyed amazement.

Trudy was heartbroken, not for herself but for Mom. Immediately, she grabbed hold of Mom's cold hand. Five months had passed since Pop's return, and she was no better. "When will you be back?" Trudy demanded. But he didn't hear her. His mind had already sailed.

The words were a hot poker scalding Ger's chest. "Noooo," she cried, her voice barely a whisper before coughing took over. "How can this be, Sam? They know you've just been returned to us!" Ger fought tears at first, but they won. Weeks from now she would wonder if his visit were just another dream, another trick of her ailing mind.

Sam knelt beside Ger. "No one could have predicted this, Ger. I just never thought..." his voice trailed off, unable to find the words. "I don't know how long, how many months a full overhaul will require." His focus returned to Ger. "I'm truly sorry. It's not fair, you're right. But no one else can take my place," he explained. Ger was far too familiar with that truth. She had learned it, lived it for the past eight years. And she agreed. No one else could take his place.

In the morning before he left, Pop gathered the girls around Mom's bed in the dank dining room for a proper goodbye. Embracing each one, he muttered his apologies for the chain of events—the war, their situation, his unavoidable lack of involvement, his sudden emergence and disappearance. No, he didn't know when he would return. Jenke brushed him off with a quick hug before excusing herself to the kitchen. Marike and Maud remained solemn. Another goodbye to the father they hardly knew didn't stir much emotion. They let him hug them and then ran upstairs to their room.

But when Pop let go of Trudy, she began to cry and curled back into his arms. "You're supposed to stay here forever now, never to leave again!" she managed between sobs. She was afraid of what would happen to Mom once he'd gone. "You were supposed to make her well again, Pop," her voice pleading. "Please stay and make Mom well again? Pop!" He shushed her, stroking her hair. She turned from him and ran part way up the stairs until she was hidden by the half-wall. She dropped herself down on the step.

"I am so sorry," she heard him say again. And heard only muffled sobs in response.

TWENTY-ONE – Brooklyn

On 18 November 1946, the Janus and her convoy mates began the long and icy journey from Wilton's Shipyard in Rotterdam, Holland, to Todd's Shipyard in Brooklyn, New York. Danker's replacement, Graham Willems, along with Einer, met their captain on deck and, together, inspected the ship. While the crew was unenthusiastic about the trans-Atlantic voyage in winter, Sam was excited by the new adventure, eager to see America, and ready to escape the confines of the deceitful life he had created in Leiden. He wanted desperately to reunite with Helen, if only on paper, fall back in sync with the tides and the rhythm of their letters. He wished she were there with him. His stint in Holland left him lonely and withdrawn.

Brisk winds kept them alee during most of the trek, especially while motoring through the northern Atlantic. But as they neared America's eastern shores, Sam, Einer, and Graham couldn't resist. Protected in the Hudson River, they stood on the bridge bundled against the bitter cold air, marveling at the Manhattan skyscrapers. "They look like flaming pillars of diamonds!" cried Graham, seeing thousands of windows reflecting the afternoon sun. Rooftops spouted marvelous plumes of white steam.

Upon their arrival, the convoy officers were shuffled to the yard office, where men shook their hands and patted their backs, congratulating all on a successful trek. Sam's longtime friend, Captain VanDerMeer, had retired at the end of the war. When the convoy returned to the Netherlands earlier that year, he stepped off his ship, swore to never leave land again, and happily relinquished control of the Shell to Captain Jorgen Timmer. Tom Sorensen, however, continued to captain the Queen, and his familiar presence provided Sam some comfort. The two men embraced and smiled into each other's eyes. They remembered easily that steamy officer's lounge when Sam first announced their lengthier route.

After Customs officers declared the vessels free of narcotics, the officers crowded themselves into a yellow cab and headed uptown to 4107 West 44th Street, the Caltex Headquarters. The office was modern and sleek with tall narrow windows letting in beams of sunlight. Drawings, blueprints, and photographs of seafaring ships of all kinds were framed and displayed on dark paneled walls. A secretary dressed in a tailored pantsuit let them into a large conference room where they sat at a dark gleaming table. Coffee was promptly delivered; tea wasn't offered. There they learned that while the officers would stay in a boarding house, the crew would remain on their ships until they were reassigned to one of the newer T-2 vessels, thereby saving Caltex the lodging expense. At hearing this, a delighted Einer winked at Sam and tried to stifle a grin. He'd be able to explore this new area without his usual babysitting responsibilities. Beaming, he pulled a lemon ball from his pocket and popped it in his mouth. What no one knew at the time was that Einer would be leaving with his crew on the first outward-bound T-2 tanker available.

After the officers were given directions to Clara's Bed & Breakfast on Washington Avenue, they returned to their ships to collect their belongings. In his stateroom, Sam folded his uniforms and packed his things neatly into his satchel. Pausing to lean against the doorway, he absorbed the details of his stateroom. The space he had called home for fifteen years was about to change completely. *Change is good*, he assured himself. He pulled on his white hat, raised his collar to the cold, and walked uphill the short distance to Clara's.

Clara pushed open the door to his room and handed him the key. "No women and no hot plates," she said before briskly turning and walking away. He stepped inside and quickly took in the scene. The room was small with dreary graying plaster walls and a metal framed bed. Sam bounced himself on the mattress and was relieved to find a bit of give in it. The floor was bare dark wood, and the only window overlooked Flushing Avenue, three floors below. He opened it and leaned his head into the cold air, turning to face one way then the other. He could not hear the water. How would he sleep without the sounds of the sea? How would he breathe without salt air to fill his lungs? Sam plugged in his little radio and turned the dial, immediately landing on Grieg's "Holberg Suite," clear as a bell. At least he'd have his constant companion, the BBC. Smiling, he bent to set his whiskey and scotch bottles on the closet floor and hung his uniforms and overcoat neatly on the rod above them. The rest of his belongings went neatly folded into a four-drawer chest. He wiped the top with his sleeve and propped Helen's photograph against his radio. He studied another framed photo of the two of them. Running a finger along the glass above her face he whispered, "How I long to hold you, my dear Helen..." He would have given anything to have her there with him.

For the month of December the Nederland Club was bedecked in red, green, and orange and continually crowded with uniformed Dutch seamen. Sam celebrated Sinterklaas and Christmas there in Dutch fashion but with a New York twist. During both holiday celebrations the champagne flowed and lively music flooded the room. Though traditional Dutch fare was replaced with prime rib and pasta, as at home, pastries and chocolates were abundant. After another New York-style feast on Old Year's Night, a crowd gathered at the floor-to-ceiling windows to watch the fireworks show staged from the roof. Sam stood with Tom and Jorgen watching the colors light up the sky and feeling the explosions in their chests. The display was more colorful and lasted longer than any they'd seen.

Holland, six hours ahead, had already welcomed the New Year. "The celebrations were outstanding at home, according to my wife," said Jorgen. "Everyone is so eager to leave the past behind, optimistically looking ahead," he beamed. "These fireworks are amazing, but can you imagine what they are feeling at home?" Colors bounced off the glass in front of them and spread into the night sky. "I'm going to call her again," he said, shaking Sam's hand goodnight. "I'm sure she'll be awake."

After a while, Sam stood alone in the crowded boisterous room. Over the big band music he caught bits of giddy laughter, saw couples kissing openly, and heard heartfelt best wishes. Two weeks earlier he'd sent a parcel home to Leiden—a silk scarf for Jenke, a soft woolen blanket for Gertrude, and Silly Putty and pink tulip bulbs for Trudy. He felt odd sending the bulbs back to Holland, but after hearing the Blessing of the Bulbs story, he would forever associate tulips with his youngest, bravest child. He began to feel out of place. On the main floor he found a manager who helped him send a cable home. He sent them his best, his love, and his prayers. His words fell hollow, even to his own ears.

Two months later, Sam again found himself in the crowded club. This time the dark wood paneled rooms were decorated in orange, and crystal vases on every table held bunches of white lily of the valley flowers. Nearly three hundred people crowded the two floors, and the atmosphere was joyful as the Dutchmen welcomed the arrival of Princess Maria Christina, Queen Juliana's fourth daughter. They shook hands, patted each other on the back, hoisted glasses to toast the baby's arrival. The event signified the rebirth and renewal the country desperately needed. Sam sat at a white linen-clad table with his old friend, Tom Sorensen. They compared stories of their travels in wartime, the countries they'd visited and the sights they'd seen. They honored fellow captains lost at sea. And they talked of the devastation at home and the families they missed. They confessed to the guilt of being absent through their families' darkest days, and although they were unable to say the words aloud, they couldn't help but feel a tiny bit grateful to have been duty-bound elsewhere.

Every morning Sam walked briskly down the hill to the shipyard to write notes on the Janus's overhauling process. The sequence, streamlined and methodical, amazed him. Tugs shifted her from one berth to another as she progressed. Gangs worked diligently on the main deck often well past midnight. Lightbulbs in steel cages swung from rafters spraying work light into the damp, dark space.

Rivets dropped from bulkhead-deck connections clanked against steel buckets. At the same time, other crews worked feverishly taking the engines to pieces, their greasy parts laid in neat rows on raised shelving. The empty steel hull reverberated with the pounding of metal on metal, and the noise was deafening. Rubbing his forehead, he wondered how any crew could stand it sixteen hours a day. These relatively brief visits gave him pounding headaches, often to the brink of nausea. Surely the crew had resorted to stuffing cotton in their ears.

Information noted, he'd then walk up another hill to the Caltex headquarters. There he'd meet with the same uniformed officer and relay from his notes the ship's progress. Routinely, Sam spoke with anyone in charge to discuss the possibility of transferring to South Africa. Spinning his hat on his finger, he'd lean towards the officer of the day, stating his request. But he was met with dropped jaws and screwed up faces. "Weren't you just away from your homeland and family for...years?" they'd remark quizzically. They'd shuffle papers, adjust their ties, and clear their throats. But the answer was always the same: wait until retirement; then see what you can do. Eventually, he gave up and became a tourist.

Sam spent his afternoons venturing into the city alone. He marveled at the abundance of everything—throngs of people bustling like ants at any hour of the day or night, towering buildings housing businesses and people, stores offering everything under the sun. He walked amid this abundance craning his neck to soak in every detail—the gargoyles looking down at him from their perch in the mortar, gleaming brass doorknobs, the unexpected glimpse of himself in a glass window front, taxis and buses honking as they passed.

At the local shops he bought boxes of soap and other supplies that were rationed in Durban and Leiden. One day he shopped for himself at Macy's, the biggest department store on earth. He spent $55 on a black overcoat and $16 for four white Van Heusen shirts. Admiring himself in the mirror, he wished he were taking Helen to dinner and a movie instead of Captains Timmer and Sorensen. Later that night as the movie theater dimmed and *Brief Encounter* began, he imagined Helen in the seat beside him. He slowly balled his hand, imagining hers inside. He leaned his head towards his shoulder, sure hers was fitted beneath.

Sam settled into a routine. He regularly rode the Highline overhead railway to 34th Street and then descended the steps for the subway to Central Park. There he sat on the same bench by the pond. From that bench he watched the colorful spring unfurl and progress into lush green summer. Purple and white crocus bloomed, then bright yellow daffodils and red tulips emerged through dark dirt, pink azalea buds burst into glorious color followed by blue hydrangea on rounded green shrubs. All around him people lived their lives. Mothers pushed babies in prams, couples walked slowly with heads bent together and arms wrapped around each other, old men played bocce on the grass. The first warm Sunday, a group of children set their miniature yachts on the pond for a sail. As one little boy jumped and pointed excitedly to his boat, Sam's heart ached for Henry, and he pulled the little compass from his chest pocket and studied it. He wondered how tall Henry had grown, how he was faring in school, what sort of things he enjoyed with his friends. He wondered if he were being kind to his mother, and he hoped he thought well of the far away sailor he called Cappy. The needle pointed north, but his heart, always south.

On a sunny summer afternoon, Sam rode the elevator up, up, up to the top of the Empire State Building. He stepped onto the observation deck and braced himself against the wind. Awestricken, he spent nearly three hours walking around and around, smiling awkwardly to changing tourists and absorbing the view. He wrote on panoramic postcards for both Leiden and Durban. *I am standing atop the 86th floor of this building! Never have I been so high off the ground. I am convinced the guide planes flew lower than where I now stand!* He posed for a photograph, the Atlantic sprawling into the distance behind him, and sent the snapshot to Helen along with a copy of *The New York Times* newspaper. *What a large piece of work this newspaper is!* he wrote. *I am amazed that a new one is produced each day!* In the evenings he settled contentedly into his stateroom with the BBC broadcast, the *New York Times*, and his writing pen. He wrote to Helen weekly, usually late Thursday evenings, glancing up occasionally to smile back at her photograph on the dresser top. However, letters from Helen became few and far between.

At the same time, with a knot in his stomach he read weekly letters from Ger and the children. Though they usually sent thanks for his parcels of clothing and provisions, they also complained about nagging sickness. Trudy never failed to mention Mom's persistent cough. He'd read her words and set the paper down. The image of Ger's face filled his mind—her thinning hair, sallow skin, the deep dark circles under her eyes. He rubbed his forehead in a futile attempt to erase the vision. Since becoming reacquainted with his family, Sam could no longer read these accounts with the detached attitude and contented ignorance he had acquired during his years down south. Now he vividly saw their hunched frail bodies, too easily recalled their pale expressions. He hated to know his family was ailing, and he was ashamed at his inability to help.

Ger kept Sam informed about the children through her letters written with obvious pain. Her scratchy handwriting revealed her desperation to include him again as their father. In the months since he'd left for New York, the older two had become a huge disappointment. Sam couldn't help but share the blame. Once she was free from the fear of soldiers at every turn, Marike turned into a rebellious young woman. She stayed out late, refused to turn off the lights, snuck more than her fair share of food—all the things she couldn't dare attempt during the occupation. She became so difficult that Jenke sent her to live with a teacher's family in town. Though Ger didn't want her to go, Jenke convinced her it was best for everyone. Marike would gain the discipline she lacked; Maud, who would be repeating the school year, had a chance of becoming more independent without her overbearing sister. Most of all, the family would be rid of the unwanted tension Marike's antics created. Eventually, Ger agreed. She had to admit, if only to Sam in her letters, that the atmosphere became instantly more palatable after Marike left. But her heart ached for her oldest girl. She hoped they would remain in friendly contact. Trudy, however, continued to do exactly as was expected. She worked hard at school and faithfully tended to her mother. *I don't know what I'd do without her*, Ger wrote continually. Sam could feel Ger grinning from the page.

Months passed quickly. Sam celebrated his first Thanksgiving with turkey and all the American trimmings with his fellow officers at a restaurant on 42nd Street. Sinterklaas and Christmas slipped by unnoticed. He sent packages to Leiden and Durban, but he began feeling isolated, and it weighed on him. Often in the late afternoons, between the lunch and dinner crowds, he'd sit alone at a table by the window, drinking a beer and imagining he was seated instead on the metal chair at Merriwold. He'd reach into his chest pocket and take hold of the H pendant. He'd turn it over in his fingers, allowing the cool metal that once touched her skin to soothe him. All the while he'd stare out at the Atlantic and pretend it was the Indian. But as the months dragged on, his tricks no longer soothed his aching heart.

He looked forward to welcoming the New Year, the one that would return him to his hilltop down south. He was determined to repeat the grand New Year's celebration of the year before at the Nederland Club, complete with champagne toasts and fireworks displays. But on New Year's Night, 1947, Sam sat alone in his sparse room in the boarding house. Instead of big band music and hot hors d'ouvres, Sam ate cold soup from a can. The only sound was the radiator's intermittent hissing. The city had been paralyzed by more than twenty-six inches of snow from a fast and unexpected blizzard. The storm barreled through abruptly, stranding cars and buses in their tracks. Sam was devastated. Rather than greet the New Year alone, he opted to go to bed early.

Sometime during the night the radiator quit, and Sam awoke shivering. Curses shot from his mouth in short white puffs, especially when his bare feet hit the cold wooden floor. After a futile attempt to bang the radiator to life, he pulled on socks, spread another heavy wool blanket over the bed, and ducked under. His teeth chattering, he realized this burst of inconvenience was merely a small taste of what his family had experienced for far too long. This tiny annoyance paled miserably in comparison to what they must have endured all those long, miserable years.

TWENTY-TWO – Durban

1947 While Sam was in Holland, Helen found little encouragement in the hurried and sporadic telegrams and brief letters he'd sent. Her world nearly shattered. Without Sam's assurance, she could only assume his reunion with his family was too much to refuse. Day after day she dragged herself through ugly dark periods, lying awake at night, allowing her mind to drift to terrible conclusions. To her, their beautiful spell had been broken. Helen was convinced he had chosen his family over her. Until he had gone home, she easily dismissed his family. But once Sam was there with them, they became real in her mind. She pictured him playing with his girls; holding his wife. On the one hand, she could hardly blame him, imagining what they'd gone through and knowing how protective Sam was. On the other hand, she had devoted years to this man. She knew she would love him forever, but she would never forgive him, she decided, if he chose them over her. Certain that he had, she bundled all their correspondence into a kist and sent the boxful to him in a fit of imagined rage.

Weeks later on a particularly dreary Saturday, though, reassurance arrived in the form of a package from New York. She ripped open the box and found Sam's letter on top, folded around a photograph. Her heart leapt when she saw Sam smiling at her. Touching the photo gently, she said aloud, "You look thin and so very worn, my love," and kissed the picture. All doubt was immediately erased, and she regretted feeling otherwise. She would deftly avoid his questions about returning his letters until he quit asking, as she knew he eventually would.

She lifted *The New York Times* from the box and called to Henry, "Come see what a New Yorker's news looks like!" Henry immediately sprawled out on the lounge floor and devoured the sports section. The two enthusiastically combed every inch. "Mmmm, you like cheesecake, don't you!" Helen remarked as she tore out a recipe. She handed it to James when he brought tea. "This sounds yummy," she said. "Let's give it a go!"

After a while, Helen turned her attention to Sam's letter. She gently turned the paper over in her hands, knowing he'd touched it, attempting to feel his presence. He seemed to be enjoying himself, exploring the different areas, the Club, Central Park. "He's actually enjoying living in the most impersonal and pitiful city on earth!" she laughed to Henry. "My goodness, it's a *human ant heap!*" She showed the photo to Henry. "This was taken on the 86th floor! Look at the people below—ants!" She silently read excerpts from his letter.

"Yes, the view from atop the Empire State Building must have been lovely, but I cannot imagine spending three hours on a rooftop!" she exclaimed, obviously amused. A few hours later they had read every bit of the newspaper. "Is it true? Another just as large is made every day?" Henry and Helen looked at each other, incredulous. "Marvelous!"

While Sam's occasional packages did much to lift her spirits, Helen knew a visit was out of the question. Her routine became dreary and tedious. She'd ride the bus to town, head down, as the beautiful scenery sped by unnoticed. At work she kept to herself, ate lunch out of a paper sack alone on the park bench. At the end of the day she'd ride the bus and then watch her feet as they took her up the hill to home. Slowly, she withdrew into a solitary life, refusing invitations to join friends at dinner or parties. "I just don't feel up to going out," she'd say. "Please forgive me? Another time?" But eventually, people stopped asking.

At home she was surrounded by memories and physical reminders of Sam everywhere she looked. Grannie often caught her holding a framed photo or gazing at her tea lights. She offered her daughter a sherry, and Helen offered her an attempt at a smile. "Our life has been suspended in time, like Henry's butterfly pinned on display," Helen explained. "My life is at a complete standstill— that is, all but Henry. He is growing away from me at fantastic speed." Having turned fifteen, he was well into secondary school. She sipped her sherry. Her eyes welled as she said, "In a blink he will be off to university..." Emotion caught in her throat, and Grannie slid in beside her. She squeezed Helen's hand twice.

"It's always darkest before the dawn. Have you heard that expression?" Helen nodded she had. "Everything's going to be fine, I promise you. You like to be in control," she squeezed her daughter's shoulders. "Time to learn to take things as they come. Open your heart and allow people to reach you. Cutting yourself off from the world won't do you any good." She didn't wait for a reply. She finished her sherry and kissed her daughter's cheek. "Good night," she said patting Helen's leg. "Tomorrow is a new day."

But life continued to darken. Late in 1947, Durban experienced torrential rain and violent storms. Houses leaked, walls collapsed, and streets flooded with turbulent sandy water. Havoc was widespread. At 3 A.M. a crash woke her. She wrapped herself in a cotton robe and ran into the blinding rain to find the syringa tree split in half. The heart of the tree had been hollowed by white ants and could not hold up under the sustained heavy rains and winds. Her beautiful and treasured reminder of the life she and Sam shared lay broken and destroyed. She stood in the pouring rain and cried, arms taut at her sides, fists clenched. After a long while she dragged herself up the steps, stripped off her drenched clothes, and climbed into bed, praying she'd never wake up.

Helen went about her daily routine as lifelessly as possible. Everyone noticed. People stopped asking about Sam, assuming the distance had brought about a typical end to their wartime romance. Dr. Stuart finally wrapped an arm around her shoulder, escorted her into his office, and closed the door. He sat her down for a long talk and sent her off with special vitamins. His concern comforted her. Grannie's and his words made her realize she needed to get busy. She turned out closets and drawers, cleaned cabinets, and gathered enough clothing in need of mending to last through the hot season.

Just outside her miserable existence, life continued. As autumn approached, April routinely invited Grannie, Henry, and Helen to her home. Helen softened with each gesture until she finally gave in. Before long, she eagerly anticipated the visits with her family at April's house. Feeling rejuvenated, Helen decided to focus on the relationships at hand and ease off the one she'd hoped for with Sam. She took a renewed interest in the gardens, and devoted more and more time to digging in the dark brown earth. It was all very therapeutic, and she reemerged, months later, stronger and more confident.

After a spate of unpredictable weather swings, Helen came down with a nasty flu. About three weeks into her illness, she'd become thin, weak, and bedridden. Grannie had done her best to care for Helen, but climbing up and down the stairs became increasingly difficult for the aging woman. April moved in to care for her mother. It was the greatest act of kindness April had ever been permitted to show. Helen gratefully accepted, but in the back of her mind, Helen wondered if April were avoiding problems at home. Their more frequent visits made the burgeoning trouble tough to hide.

April knocked on Helen's bedroom door. "Tea time," she called. Helen placed her bookmark in *Brief Encounter* and welcomed April inside. Setting the tray on the bedside table, April first crossed to spread apart the sheers and open the veranda doors. "Let's have some fresh air and sunshine in here," she said. Then she sat on the edge of the bed and fixed their tea, two lumps of sugar for each. "You're looking much better this afternoon, mum," she said with obvious relief.

Helen pulled herself more upright, and April fluffed the pillows behind her. April had changed the sheets the night before, and this clean, crisp set still had the clean scent of the detergent. "I feel this dreaded flu is finally leaving me, thanks to your efforts. I am truly grateful, dear, you know that," she said laying a hand on April's knee. Her tone was serious, so April braced herself. "I am ready to listen if you are ready to talk, April." Helen searched her daughter's face. "Is there something amiss between you and David?"

April looked at her own hands in her lap and prayed her mother would not remove hers. A knot began to tighten in her stomach. She hadn't realized her problems were obvious. Growing up she had never been allowed to confide in her mother, but April felt—hoped— that now was the time. She had nowhere else to turn. David was no longer the faithful confidant he had been since adolescence. Slowly, April exhaled the words that had been pent up too long. "All I've ever wanted," she whispered, "is to be...loved." She rubbed her thumb in her palm as she spoke, trembling. Anguish caught in her chest. "I wanted someone to love me desperately and deeply. As Joseph loved you. As Sam loved you." She lifted her head just far enough to peek at the words registering on Helen's still, pale face. "I thought David was that someone." She hugged herself tightly and looked to the ceiling. "The promise of our happiness carried me through life until we married. When we moved into our home, I thought at last we could settle into a life—our life—like you had made here, one with parties, friends...children." With that her voice broke, and the tears fell. "Oh mum, nothing is going as planned!" she blurted, dropping onto the bed. "I haven't fallen pregnant, David works all the time...he doesn't even pretend to miss me...then Buddy died. I'm just so...lonely," she cried. Words continued to tumble out between sobs, "And I don't...think he...loves me...anymore." She buried her face in her hands, and her body shuddered. "Am I so...terribly... unlovable?"

Helen pulled April to her chest and pushed her hair from her face. She held her weeping daughter and wondered when she had last comforted April. Had she ever? "Love treats all ages with equal brutality," she said. "Here I am an old woman surrounded by people. There you are so young and vibrant. Yet we both suffer."

April cried harder. "It's worse than just that, mum," she said in a low voice as though she didn't want to hear what she was about to say. "I think," she stumbled, "David may have a mistress." Helen rocked her crying daughter in her arms, witnessing too closely the destruction of infidelity. *A mistress.* The words slipped from April's mouth and lodged in Helen's throat, choking her. Helen had never seen first-hand the impact of that pain, and she felt like a monster. April rambled on. "...Oh he says no, but I found a key, and now it's gone, and I don't know what to think. I want to believe him, trust him. Oh mum," she cried, "I couldn't bear it if he left me," she sobbed.

Quiet tears streaked Helen's face. Her darkest secrets illuminated, she felt flayed, raw. She wrapped her arms tightly around her daughter. "Hush, my darling," she whispered, patting her hair. "We'll get through this together, you'll see." And she meant every word. Helen vowed then to mend the bond with her daughter. Perhaps if she worked to repair this relationship, God would forgive her for the one she hoped to destroy.

April became Helen's focus, and the ground rules were no prying, no criticizing, and no expectations. Simply love her. April, the ever-forgiving, approval-seeking child, reveled in her mother's attention, and over time, blossomed as a result. The two made a point to visit and call a few times each week. Helen offered general tips on being a good wife and maintaining a healthy relationship, and April took her instructions to heart. And to Helen's delight, whenever David had occasion to work in Durban proper, April would ride along and arrange to meet her mother for lunch and discuss their progress.

Several months later, David received a last-minute call to work in Durban, and April decided to surprise her mother at the rooms. April leaned against the wall in the hectic hallway, waiting outside Dr. Stuart's office. At last Helen rounded the corner, her white lab coat buttoned, head down, writing notes on a clipboard. April stood in her path, and when Helen finally looked up, she let out a squeal. The two embraced easily and then popped in to say hello to Dr. Stuart.

"April, you look radiant," he remarked, pulling her in for a hug. "You remind me more and more of your mother!" he said, resting his head on April's and looking to Helen. He could see Helen mulling the comment over in her head, deciding how to take it.

The women invited him to lunch at the Playhouse Grill across the street, but he refused, citing paperwork and opting for the lunch Elizabeth had packed for him. "You'd best be on your way then. I'll have lots to hand over to you when you return, Helen," he warned. Then he took April's hands in his and thanked her for stopping to see him. "You've made my day," he told her. George watched as the two walked in the shade of the leopard trees across the park. April's arms waved as she spoke, and Helen's head pulled up in laughter. George felt blessed to witness the latent emergence of this duo.

They ordered lunch at the counter and then slid into a booth along aqua vinyl benches, chatting like old friends. Eventually, April grew more serious. "I think David and I have reached a new level of understanding," she began. "I feel more appreciated, I mean, when I make an effort to prepare a nice meal or fill the house with flowers from the garden, he seems to take notice. More than notice, really, he's...touched." She lifted her chin and smiled at her mother. "And that makes me want to please him all the more." She finished her sandwich and licked the tips of her fingers.

Helen reached across the table and covered April's hand with her own. "I am so happy for you, dear," she said, relieved. April simply smiled into her mother's approving eyes. They talked more about April's garden, Henry, and Merriwold, but Sam was not mentioned, as usual. Perhaps April adhered to the same unspoken ground rules. After lunch they walked leisurely across the park, arm-in-arm, and hugged goodbye, promising to see each other on Sunday at either house. April hurried to catch the bus toward Merriwold, where David would then retrieve her. Helen watched her skip along, thankful for her daughter's ability to forgive and gratified by the strides they'd made in mending their relationship. She knocked on George's door and entered the wood-paneled interior.

He handed her the stack of paperwork as promised. "I want to tell you how wonderful seeing you and April getting along makes me feel. These visits from her over the past few months have cheered my very soul." His eyes twinkled as he spoke, his ever-present grin broadening across his weathered face. "I can only imagine what a welcomed relief this must be for you!"

"I am filled to the brim, George. I don't have the words to describe the peace our renewed relationship gives me." Helen adjusted the stack on her hip. "Love conquers all, George, you know? Mending things with April has filled a gap, the missing stitch in the seam that now holds me firmly together." Her eyes danced. "And I think you're right," she added, "April has become more like me as she's grown. Um, on the inside anyway," she said, sharply tugging on her lapels.

At Merriwold, April heard David's car and opened the door as he approached. "David!" she called, throwing her arms around his neck and peppering him with kisses. Following her mother's advice, April focused more on her own actions than on David's reactions. His half-hearted response went unnoticed. Unwittingly, April was less focused on her marriage than on mending her relationship with her mother. Now that their relationship blossomed, all was right in her world. Or so it seemed.

TWENTY-THREE – Leiden

1948   In the space between wake and sleep, Trudy's teeth began to chatter, riveting her mind back in time. She heard the bomb's whistle, felt the house rattle, and, just before the bomb hit, she bolted upright, sweating. The room was deafeningly silent, save for the pounding of her heart inside her chest. Just another nightmare. She hurried to the window, pulled back the curtain, and was immediately blinded by fresh mounds of snow that had fallen throughout the night. Although she wasn't happy about the snow, she was gratefully reassured the war was over.

"Trudy, you're still in your nightclothes?" Mom asked, moving over to make room in her bed in the drafty old dining room.

"No school, remember, Mom?" Trudy slipped in beside her mother. The winter had been so bitter cold that the school's heat couldn't keep up. Finally, they'd sent the children home. They would have to trade their summer holiday for this winter's time off. The two automatically snuggled close, knees behind knees. "This blanket Pop sent is quite warm!" Mom opened her mouth to speak but coughed instead. Trudy gently tapped her back until she stopped; pulled the covers up to her neck. "I'm glad he sent this blanket, Mom. You really needed it. Maybe you can ask him for another next time you write?"

"Or maybe you can just share mine. I miss your body heat, Trudy," she teased. "And I have been missing our talks." Their minds drifted to frightened nights and shared hopes. Mom raised

Trudy's hand to kiss her palm, happy that awful time was behind them. They lay together in contented silence until Mom chuckled. "I'm guessing you haven't been missing Marike..."

Trudy smiled and thought only a moment, "True!" she laughed. "But I am surprised at how much I miss Maud. I do hope she does well in the Amsterdam School."

"Your father will have her head if she doesn—" coughing took over suddenly.

Trudy fetched a glass of water from the kitchen. "Come on, Mom. Up you go," Trudy said, helping her from the bed. "Let's have some eggs, real eggs, and a pat of butter on bread. Doesn't that sound lovely?"

Mom sat at the table sipping water while Trudy set to work. Jenke stumbled out of the pantry-turned-bedroom, wiping the sleep from her eyes, yawning. Instead of moving upstairs, she'd opted to stay close to Ger just in case she needed anything in the night. "Good morning," she called, stretching a lanky arm over her head, yawning to the ceiling. She started the coffee for herself and boiled tea water for Trudy and Ger. She padded over to Mom with a piece of paper and a pencil. "Make a list for me, Ger," Jenke began, "I'm going to the market today because I'm in a mood to cook!" The stores had been fully restocked, and Jenke needed no prodding. She brought Ger her tea. "How would you like a nice pheasant, or a leg of lamb?"

"A whole leg of lamb! I don't..." Ger coughed a little. "...mean to discourage your efforts, Jenke, but we are only three people! What will we do with a whole leg of lamb?"

"Well you'll need to eat it, of course. We need to add some fat to your bones, Ger!" she remarked, placing a hand on Ger's thin shoulder. Jenke smiled as she added real cream to her coffee and continued smiling when Trudy placed a plate of eggs and toast in front of her. "Trudy, you're a good girl, you've always been a good girl and done just as you were asked," she said more to Ger than to Trudy. Trudy brought two more plates of food and, placing one in front of Mom, joined the women. "Not like your sisters! Good Lord they were a handful." Ger shot Jenke a look, and the subject was dropped. They'd agreed to not negatively discuss the Ms in front of Trudy.

"Aunt Jenke, I don't think you'll make it to the market today. Have you seen the snow?" she asked, washing the dishes and looking outside. Remembering the surplus still in the refrigerator, she opened it and rummaged through. "But don't worry, you still have much to choose from—sausages, liver and onions, potatoes—"

"Potatoes! I swore I'd never eat another potato, or soup for that matter, remember?" huffed Jenke.

It was true. They'd all sworn off many things—going to bed hungry, worrying over tomorrow, complaining. But little by little they went back on their word, or at least Trudy did. Though she was sure she'd never long to eat a tulip bulb diced, shredded, or otherwise, things like soup and potatoes now represented something much more than desperation. They represented Survival. Day after day, month after month, year after desolate year, she had continued. And she'd helped to keep her mother aloft. She didn't own the words at six, eight, or even ten, but looking back now she clearly identified resilience, fortitude, courage. And she was filled with the self-confidence that came alongside. She was more fortunate than many.

The town of Leiden didn't blossom easily in the years after the war's slow close. People continued dying from starvation, malnutrition, and disease because relief came, in many cases, too late. Many healthy Dutch chose to emigrate rather than face the difficult task of rebuilding. Many of those remaining wanted retribution. They rooted out fellow countrymen who had sided with the Germans. Women who had taken German boyfriends, regardless of their reasons, had their heads shaved and were publicly humiliated as they were paraded through the streets along with other non-criminal collaborators. But the worst collaborators, the ones who'd actively turned against their countrymen, were arrested. Some collaborators were deported; others were shot or hanged; still others were forced to clear minefields. It wasn't until Arthur Seyss-Inquart was captured and tried for war crimes that people began to feel retribution had begun. He and several cronies were imprisoned and/or executed. After a very chaotic eighteen months, life began to settle down and fall into place. But the winters were brutally cold, even colder than they'd been throughout the occupation. And there was so much to rebuild; refresh.

"I don't think I'll get dressed today," declared Trudy. "No school, too much snow outside to even play in...I may as well work on my maths. When we're tired, we can have a nap," she said smiling at Mom.

"I'd forgotten they closed the schools for the month. January as well," added Jenke. "Poor children will have to give up their summer holiday in return," she said shaking her head.

"Seems terribly unfair, doesn't it?"

A knock on the front surprised them all. "Who would be out in this snow?" wondered Jenke aloud.

Leah! was always Trudy's first thought when caught off guard. She didn't realize how much she depended on her return. Of the 140,000 Dutch Jews that were either shipped to their death or forced into hiding, barely 15,000 survived. Years later, Trudy would allow herself to acknowledge that Leah was not among them.

"It's another package from Pop!" called Trudy returning to the kitchen. With a sharp knife she slit open the box. "*Time* Magazine!" It was the October 27 issue with a multi-armed monster on the cover. Beneath the colorful image read *INDIA Liberty and death*. She fanned the pages briefly and dove back into the box retrieving a small egg-shaped plastic. "Silly Putty?" she read the label. She popped open the egg and was surprised to find a small ball inside. It bounced high when she dropped it to the floor and then caught it. "Huh," she said returning it to the egg. "I'll have a look at those instructions later." Back into the box she dove and found tulip bulbs. *More tulip bulbs?* She didn't understand. She then pulled out the radio. "Ohhhh look, Mom! This must be for you!" She let her mother see it before whisking it away to the electrical outlet and tuning it in. The BBC had resumed local broadcasts, and Rodgers and Hammerstein's "You'll Never Walk Alone" came in beautifully clear. Trudy pulled Mom to her feet, and Jenke couldn't resist. They danced and giggled until they actually heard the lyrics, and then the giggles included sweet tears. "Walk on, walk, with hope in your heart, and you'll never walk alone..." When the music ended, the three stood wrapped in each other's arms, beaming through tears. From that moment the radio stayed on. In the daytime they heard intermittent news and wonderful musical broadcasts. In the evenings, they'd often hear a story or be content with classical performances. But the whole mood lightened as a result. And they were very grateful despite that long cold winter.

After supper—liver and onions—while the radio aired Vivaldi's "Four Seasons," Trudy sat on Mom's bed reading excerpts aloud from the magazine while Mom dozed. Pop had talked about his ports in India, so the connection heightened their interest. Turning the pages, she landed on an ad for a big egg-shaped car, reminding her of the Silly Putty. She carried the magazine back to the kitchen and spent hours flattening the putty onto the colorful pages—a wrist watch, a man in a handsome fedora, a razor—and then pulling back the flattened blob to reveal a mirror image. Then she flipped the page and saw it. The radio was as big as the seated woman beside it, a hundred times larger than the one they'd just received. She closed her eyes and imagined the tremendous sound it must make. She decided some day she would buy one for Mom. That desire alone would fuel Trudy's commitment to excel in school. "Mom!" she called, taking the magazine into the dining room. But her mother was sound asleep. Trudy hadn't noticed the time or the cold or that the house was quietly sleeping. That package turned out to be the greatest gift her father had ever given her. It had arrived just after Sinterklaas. Trudy wondered if he'd intended it to arrive for Christmas. Had he sent a similar package to the Ms, especially to Marike for her favorite holiday?

Trudy, Mom, and Aunt Jenke had allowed Sinterklaas and Christmas to slip by as they'd done easily in preceding years. Money was tight, and they needed basics—toothbrushes, clothes that fit, new boots—hardly the stuff of gifts. But saying goodbye to the old year and welcoming the new was something they refused to forfeit. They would forever celebrate distancing themselves from the war and all its misery. Mom was too sick to leave the house; she could barely walk from kitchen to dining room unassisted. So Trudy and Aunt Jenke did their best to bring the celebration to her.

On the morning of Old Year's Night, the radio blared "Old Devil Moon" while the two hung paper streamers from the ceiling in the front room. They danced and hummed along in tune. Trudy had taken colorful pages from her *Time* magazine and cut them into snowflakes. She was stringing them from doorjambs and the banister when she heard Mom's coughing and stopped to help. "Here you go," she said, offering Mom a glass of water. "Drink slowly." Trudy smoothed her hair as she drank. "How about a nice bath? Wash out the old and welcome the new?"

Trudy helped her frail mother into the tub and washed her hair in the warm water while Jenke changed the bed linens. "While Holland is going crazy tonight, we'll have our own celebration," Trudy said wrapping Mom in a towel and using another for her wet head. "You know Aunt Jenke is making a fat leg of lamb?"

The aroma had already started filling the house and made their mouths water. But Mom rolled her eyes and teased. "We'll be eating lamb for a week," she whispered. "But that's fine with me. As long as she doesn't make soup from the bone!"

Trudy laughed, "Oh I don't think you have to worry about that! Now let's get your hair nice and dry before you catch cold." Mom sat on the toilet lid dressed in a clean thick flannel nightgown while Trudy did her best to dry and comb Mom's thinning patches. Trudy couldn't help but remember the dark, thick braid that used to reach down her mother's back. Now her thin gray strands were too sparse to braid. She gently gathered them into a tiny bun and pinned it at the nape of her neck. Then she helped Mom into bed, pulled the warm blanket under her chin, and kissed her forehead. Before she could say "sleep tight," Mom was snoring quietly.

"Dinner is ready!" Jenke called an hour later. Trudy stopped fixing paper snowflakes and helped Mom out of bed. Jenke had already raised the volume on the radio. Ralph Vaughan Williams's piano music flooded the room. Jenke pulled the sizzling lamb from the oven. The aroma made Trudy ravenous immediately. Juice from the browned leg mixed with sliced potatoes, carrots, and onions. Jenke heaped a mound of cabbage salad onto each plate and then sliced off portions of the meat and added the vegetables. Meanwhile, Trudy scurried back and forth covertly carrying items to the front room from the kitchen. "You get the radio; I'll bring the dishes," whispered Jenke, winking at Trudy.

"And who's going to bring me?" called Mom, obviously delighted by the secrecy.

"I'll be right back for you, Mom," Trudy assured her. Seconds later the music was emanating from the front room. Trudy returned, offered her bent arm to her mother, "May I show you to your table, my lady?"

As they entered the front room, Jenke popped the champagne cork. Mom gasped, "Jenke! You naughty lady!" she grinned as she hobbled to her chair. The two had transformed the room into a celebration hall. Trudy's colorful paper snowflakes of all sizes hung everywhere, slowly turning in the slightest wisp of air. Jenke had slid the kitchen set there and draped an old pale yellow doll quilt over it. The three sat close and raised their coffee mugs to toast. Mom looked each one in the eyes for a long while before clearing her throat. "You two are my angels. I don't know what I would have done all these miserable years without you—" a cough rattled her chest, and she turned her head, covered her face with her napkin. "We have been through a lot," she stated. "Hopefully the bad memories fade a little more each day. But," she took a sip, motioning to her throat and winking at Trudy, "I will always remember your selfless dedication to me and to each other." She placed a hand on each of theirs. "I am truly and forever grateful." Then they raised their mugs and gently tapped them together before sipping.

Trudy immediately laughed and coughed. "Bubbles up my nose!" The women laughed, realizing that was her first taste of champagne.

"I thought we deserved to celebrate in style," Jenke explained, wiping a laugh tear from the corner of her eye. "Now my turn," she said holding her mug aloft and rocking on her bottom. "To you, Gertrude. You fought right alongside us, sick as you were, never complaining." She raised her chin in the air, looking from Trudy to Ger. "You handled these awful years with grace and elegance. You are a fine example to us all." Emotion caught in her throat. She didn't want to cry, so she downed her mugful and poured some more. "C'mon, ladies, drink up!" she urged with a giggle.

"And another thing," Jenke added. She was not the type to compliment, and Mom was surprised she was about to add to her sentiment. "I know we'll eat this for a week because I spent the week's allowance on this one meal alone!" she listed side to side as she laughed.

The three burst out laughing. They enjoyed their delicious dinner and drink while listening to the antics of Dutch partiers being broadcast on the radio. Between snippets of news, the classical music played on. Mom stayed awake for several hours that night while they all welcomed 1949, making a new memory to replace some of the dark reminders lurking in the corners of their minds. About 10:30 Jenke heated the oil. She could see Ger was tiring quickly and wouldn't last until the traditional midnight. She and Trudy dropped the oliebollen into the hot oil. The result was the most wonderful apple pastries they'd ever had.

TWENTY-FOUR – Durban

1949 Helen's days were spent working at the medical rooms for Dr. Stuart. Needy patients made the work emotionally draining. In the evenings she cared for her mother who was aging rapidly, both physically and mentally. Full days became weary weeks and developed into lifeless years.

Henry had blossomed into a seventeen-year-old man and declared his intention to become a lawyer like his father. His studies were as demanding as his social life. Helen's once dependable companion now had a full life of his own. In an effort to see him more often, Helen began a Wednesday tradition. On her way home from work, she'd stop at the market for fresh produce and cod for Henry's favorite, fish and chips. April was invited to join in this mid-week ritual, and to the family's delight, never missed. The routine continued uninterrupted for months, the yarn that helped knit them together.

While Helen cut flowers for the table, April approached, right on schedule. The two embraced, and April commented on how tired her mother looked. "I am very tired, dear, but I am well, honestly. I am middle aged, don't forget," said Helen, patting her hair. She slid her arm through April's as they climbed the porch steps. "And you, my dear, look as though you've swallowed a cat."

April stopped short at the doorway and turned to face her mother, smiling. "Oh, Mum!" April squealed, clapping her hands. "I have not had the test yet, but I have a very strong feeling that I'm finally pregnant!" The two stared at each other in disbelief, cupped hands over mouths, tears welling, speechless. April threw her arms around her stunned mother, and they laughed and cried and jumped up and down together. "I am only a few weeks late," she cautioned, but neither wanted to contain herself.

"My baby is having a baby!" Helen finally found words and screeched with delight. "Let's tell the others!" But April was reluctant just yet. "Nonsense! Be positive!" Helen glowed. "Besides, I am sure to burst if I have to hold this inside any longer," Helen said leading April inside by the hand. Once everyone gathered at the table, a beaming April shared the news. Henry immediately poured the champagne, and the group celebrated throughout dinner and into the evening while records blared on the phonograph. Grannie repeatedly told everyone she would soon be called Great Grannie, or Grannie the Great, she couldn't decide. Henry vowed to spoil the child once he became a wealthy lawyer. And James silently dabbed his eyes while visions of April as a child streamed in his memory.

The front door closed with a loud thud, signaling David's arrival. "Must be Daddy!" called Henry, retrieving another flute. David appeared in the dining room, looking more handsome than ever. "Guess you told them our happy news, hon" he beamed at his wife and ran a hand through his slick dark hair. He kissed the top of April's head, and she smiled up at him. The couple appeared more blissful than the day they married years earlier. At Henry's urging, April promised to continue to come for fish-and-chips Wednesdays so he could monitor his nephew's progress. (Of course the child would be a boy and named for his favorite uncle.) Helen and April huddled over calendars making plans to shop, knit, sew, decorate, and prepare for the blessed event. This pregnancy would provide Helen with the much-needed diversion from an otherwise dreary life.

At the rooms, news of Helen's grandchild spread quickly, but it was Helen's excitement that thrilled coworkers and patients the most. For the past few years they'd witnessed her steady emotional decline. The promise of a grandchild quickly restored Helen's personality and zest for life. Helen was back like a driving wind, and the rooms and Merriwold were happily swept up in her motion. For a brief time, all was right in the world again.

The following Wednesday Helen surprised April with her first baby shower. Mother Williams, Aunt Anne, Mrs. Peterson, Mrs. Milne, Elizabeth Stuart, Muriel Wilke, and Emma Roberts all enthusiastically joined the celebration, engulfing April upon her arrival. April basked in the attention. Henry kissed his sister and quickly escaped to his room for his studies. But through his closed door he heard the oohs and aahs as April opened each gift. He imagined his sister beaming, soaking up every morsel of joy and happiness sent in her direction. He smiled for her, knowing she had waited a long time to feel this good.

April opened each package with unrestrained delight. She laid the tiny clothes in her lap, imagining her baby inside them smiling up at her. She blinked back joyful tears, overwhelmed in knowing everyone there shared her joy. Helen served white cake with pink and blue frosting, and all the moms shared their stories of pregnancy and birth, some of which April wished she'd never heard. When the guests were gone, April and Helen sat on the floor among the gifts. April inspected a tiny one-piece outfit, and then hugged it against herself. It covered her torso from neck to lap. "However will this child fit inside me?" she asked in amazement. She dropped her hands and beamed at her mother. "I've waited so long, mum," she began. "Already I love this child! I can hardly wait to hold her or him!"

"And I can hardly wait for you to know the joy your child will bring you. Will bring all of us," Helen promised, tilting her head and beaming at her jubilant daughter.

That night Helen climbed into bed thoroughly elated and completely exhausted. The baby shower brought tangible evidence that her grandchild was indeed on the way. Helen closed her eyes and thanked God for providing this special joy. *I'll have to plant a tree in his honor*, she decided. She wanted to write every detail to Sam, but she simply could not muster the energy. Instead she drifted into the most unfettered, restful sleep she had enjoyed in months. When her alarm clock sounded the next morning, she felt refreshed and went about her routine with a skip in her step. She found James in the kitchen, and they laughed about his easy tears when April first announced her news. Before leaving for work, Helen climbed the steps once more just to kiss Great Grannie, or Grannie the Great, goodbye.

Dr. Stuart hung up the phone and walked across the street to the park bench where Helen had taken her lunch. The day was glorious, and Helen wanted to soak in every healthy breath. She spotted him as he approached and called out, "George, how wonderful of you to take a break with me on such a simply perfect day. Come sit here," she said patting the wooden bench beside her. All at once she noticed the concern in his face; he seemed old and worn. "Is everything all right, George? What is it?"

Instead of sitting, he took Helen's hand and helped her up. He gathered her things and loaded them into her sack. "Walk with me," he said quietly, and they headed across the park towards the parking lot. He slid an arm around her shoulder. "I hate nothing more than to tell you this, Helen, but April is in hospital. David took her there this morning. She was in a lot of pain, Helen, and they discovered that the embryo was caught in the fallopian tube." He stopped; his face to the ground. "I'm afraid it could not survive there."

Could not survive... "What do you mean?" she cried. "What will they do? What have they done?" Helen pulled frantically on George's arm, but he couldn't meet her eyes. "Surely they can do something—George? Could not survive? What are you saying?"

George led her to his car and opened the passenger door. "I am so sorry, Helen," he said at last, his voice breaking. "But I am afraid hopes for this baby are gone." He helped her into the car and closed the door. He climbed in behind the wheel and headed to the main road. "She is in Westville Hospital and asked that you come right away."

As the car raced towards the PMB, Helen sat mesmerized; her eyes wide and staring, seeing nothing. "But just last night—" her voice trailed off.

"If all goes well, she may still become pregnant, barring complications with the other tube. They had to perform surgery, Helen, but it could provide answers as well. Hopefully, the doctors will be able to tell April why it's taken so long for her to become pregnant." As George spoke, he covered her hand with his on the seat between them. "Hopefully, they'll be able to try again." But in Helen's head George's voice was muffled and distant. Her mind was too muddled to respond.

Helen squirmed in her seat, panicking as the hospital came into view. She was afraid to witness the toll this disappointment would have on April. At the front desk Helen and George were directed to the waiting room, where Helen paced near the window, rubbing her forehead while trying desperately to find the words April could tolerate hearing. George stood at the nurse's station wielding his medical profession as a tool to obtain answers. After a long ten minutes April's attending physician solemnly approached Helen with George in tow.

"Mrs. Dean," he began softly, bending slightly to become eye-level, "I am Dr. Mark Carroll, the surgeon who operated on your daughter. I am afraid I have bad news." He shoved his hands into the pockets of his stiff white lab coat.

Helen stopped listening. "Dr. Stuart already told me this pregnancy could not survive, doctor. But there still is hope for another, isn't that right?" Helen's speech accelerated, blocking Dr. Carroll's opportunity to speak. "How long must they wait before trying again? You see, we only just learned the wonderful news a few weeks ago, and...they are so happy. You see, they tried for many years...we were all so happy. Why just last Wednesday a week..." Helen finally slowed to a whisper, dropped her head, and finally stopped talking altogether. She began to cry. George wrapped an arm around her, and she buried her face in his chest, sobbing.

Dr. Carroll reached an awkward hand to Helen's shuddering shoulder. "I am terribly sorry, madam, but this tubal pregnancy has destroyed the fallopian tube. It seems the other tube had long been occluded, which may explain her difficulty conceiving in the past." He paused to assess whether or not the information he was feeding

Helen was being absorbed. He shifted his glance to Dr. Stuart, who nodded. He would make Helen understand when she was able to comprehend the news. "There is always the possibility of adoption, Mrs. Dean. Perhaps your daughter will consider that option at some future time." Dr. Carroll rubbed his neck. Dispensing bad news was an uncomfortable part of the job, but less so to those in the waiting room than in the hospital bed. Breaking bad news to the patient was the more difficult task, and one he artfully avoided in this case. George helped Helen to a chair and fetched some tea. As Helen blew on the tea to cool, she searched for the threads of optimism in this dismal situation. She vowed to take this opportunity to be a comfort to her daughter, to make up for the times she might have missed in the past.

April's anesthesia had worn off, and they were told she was awake. Helen knocked quietly and entered the semi-private room. A cloth curtain suspended from a track in the ceiling surrounded April's bed. Helen tugged at the curtain slightly and found April curled like a baby, whimpering. All color, and seemingly all life, had drained from April's face. Puffy eyes looked up to Helen from dark circles. Helen reached to caress her shoulder, and April relaxed a little under her touch. "I am so sorry, April," she whispered. "You have waited so long..." her voice caught in her throat as tears freely streaked her face.

April scolded herself. "Maybe next time I will be more careful..." she cried, convinced as usual that she caused this awful situation.

Helen sat beside her daughter and stroked her hair. "April, this is not your fault! No amount of caution could have prevented this. Do you understand?" She ran a soft palm down the side of April's face. "And as for next time, April, I am so terribly sorry to have to tell you... But the doctor said there...won't be a next time," she whispered, her heart breaking. She explained further.

The news shocked April, and she searched her mother's face for verification. "Nooooooo," she wailed, curling tightly into a ball and rocking slowly, sobbing. "I...wanted that...baby...mum...I wanted...him so...much," she spurted between sobs. "He was going...to love me," she whined.

Helen gently held her daughter, rubbing her back. "I'm here," she reassured April, crying along with her. When at last April fell asleep, Helen tiptoed to the hallway where David had just arrived. She hugged him and searched his sad, haggard face. "You still have each other," she offered. "And you can always adopt." David promised to keep Helen informed, and Helen swore she'd help them both through this difficult time. "Anything at all," she assured him, clutching his forearm.

George and Helen rode home in silence. His heart ached for her, and he knew she needed Sam more than ever. He wondered how much more sorrow this woman could endure. She had already experienced more than her fair share. Soon he would help her focus on the bright side, but for now he thought it best to let her be. They reached Merriwold after dark, and he helped Helen out of the car and up the steps to the porch. He wrapped his arms around her and assured her of what she already knew: he was there if she needed anything.

Telling the news to Grannie, Henry, and James was a difficult task. Sadness covered the house like a storm cloud. By the time Helen fell into bed, she felt nothing but deep, relentless sorrow. *If only Sam were here,* she thought. But the thought of Sam only heightened her pain. Alone now, she let herself cry. Though she'd vowed to help April through this time, she was convinced her own life would never be right again either. She felt completely lost, without purpose and without hope.

TWENTY-FIVE – Leiden

1949 The remodeled Janus left the Brooklyn shipyard as dawn crept into gray skies. An engineer from Todd's Shipyard sailed with them to note any oversights in the ship's overhaul, and already the list was lengthening. Sam, relieved to say goodbye to the New York metropolis, offered a final salute as they left the relatively calm Hudson River and entered the rolling waves of the Atlantic. Playing tourist for so long made him antsy, eager to be productive again. Although he enjoyed his extended holiday, he'd grown to feel useless. And he resented himself for it. After a few days in, they were blessed with warm summer weather, and Captain and crew easily made their way through the Florida Straits and into the Gulf of Mexico. In Corpus Christie, they loaded gasoline and retrieved discharge orders for Humber on Tyne. The convoy was going home again. The Janus was heading north in the English Channel when Graham received the radio message. Ger had taken a turn for the worse, and Sam was needed in Leiden as soon as he could physically manage.

Nearly three years had passed since Sam was last home, yet he was unhurried. And he was frightened. Jenke met him at the door. Placing both hands on his arms and setting her eyes on his, she whispered, "You are here in time. Thank heaven you are here in time." Straightening, Sam inhaled deeply, mustering his strength, and followed her into the former dining room.

The room was stifling quiet and warm; a putrid odor hung in the air. The pale faces that turned to him blended into the walls. Trudy lay across the foot of the bed propped on an elbow. Marike and Maud sat flanking Ger, their sad eyes haunting. Ger tapped their hands, and they rose wordlessly to greet their father, hesitating momentarily before folding into his arms. Sam rested his head on top of Maud's while stealing glimpses of his fragile wife leaning against pillows. Marike willingly relinquished her spot in her father's embrace to Trudy, who gave his waist a squeeze before leading him to Mom. Sam timidly lowered himself onto the bed's edge and smoothed gray tendrils of hair from Ger's face. Her emaciated chest rose and fell with each labored breath. Carefully, he scooped his broad warm hand under her cold frail palm and placed his other gently on top. She was but a wisp of her former self. As she smiled, her chapped lips stretched blue lines into hollow gray cheeks. The dark eyes that used to light up the room were sunken and flat.

Ger spoke first. "I am so pleased you are here," she whispered with obvious difficulty. "It's been a long time since..." she drew a deep breath, her boney chest rising, "...we were all together." The words tickled her throat forcing a cough. Sam eased her forward holding a glass of water to her lips. After a small sip she settled back against the pillow. "Our girls have grown into fine young women, haven't they?" she smiled at them before turning back to face him. He strained to avoid her eyes, his guilt evident to them both. He had no right to be considered part of this family. He had relinquished his place many years ago, yet he was never more fully aware of that fact than at that moment. Eyeing her husband, she whispered, "You know me, Sam," searching for his eyes to meet hers. "Oh, I may have changed on the outside, but I am still me." Studying his face, she slowly reached her hand to his cheek. "You've grown thin, Sam. And you have aged a little." She cocked her head and held his gaze. "Strange though...I hardly recognize you." Sam couldn't bear to look at her any longer. He lowered his chin to his chest and wept.

The family stayed close to home the following three days. Sam felt hopelessly out of place among his daughters, especially the older two. He purposely remained in the background, observing them all from his perch on the radiator under the window. He admired their easy way together. Just as much was said among them with as without words, and the girls chatted endlessly while Ger soaked them in. They laughed at incidents that had occurred over the years, imitated Ger humming and swaying to music, and teased each other about long-forgotten crushes—all while Ger dozed intermittently. Sam felt every bit the stranger he had become. Everything they referred to was unfamiliar. He was not part of a single shared memory. He wondered how his life had become so fractured; his loyalty, so diluted.

Trudy insisted on sleeping on the foot of Ger's bed. She wanted to be there in case her Mom needed anything at all—a drink of water, a warm blanket, a story. Early in the morning of 6 September 1949, Trudy woke, her back stiff and feeling groggy. One look at her Mom, and she knew. Of course Mom hadn't complained or cried out but rather passed quietly in the night. Trudy gathered her mother's reedy lifeless body in her arms, rocking gently and quietly weeping. She found herself inhaling deeply, desperately trying to contain the lilac scent of her skin, her hair. She wanted to draw in the whole of her, fill the widening, aching fissure in her chest. Loneliness settled into her heart like the ominous scent of smoke in a dry spell. Would she be able to breathe without her Mom? All her life, Trudy and Mom had been a team, a duality. Without the sun to illuminate it, does the moon continue to exist? She continued to rock and weep for a long while, until the morning sun forced itself into the bleak room. The others stirred above her. Trudy kissed her mother's forehead and smoothed her hair one last time. "You'll always have the biggest part of my heart, Mom," Trudy whispered into Mom's beautifully serene face. After so many years of suffering, Trudy couldn't help but find comfort in knowing her mother was finally at peace.

The funeral attendance was small. Sam wore his dark uniform and held his white hat following the casket into the nave of the church. The girls followed him, naturally clinging to Aunt Jenke and each other until Trudy realized her father was walking alone. She hurried ahead, slipping an arm through his. After the service they proceeded into the cemetery behind the church, lining up to bid Gertrude a final farewell. Dappled sun poked through the rows of shivering Aspen trees, and the sky was dotted with puffy white clouds, just as Ger would have preferred for her final outing.

Sam stayed at the house while the Janus was repaired. During their trek to Rotterdam, Todd's engineer finalized a long list—including a defective propeller and several faulty instruments. Repairs would take six months. But the Ms would be home for only two weeks. He hoped to take this opportunity to know his grown daughters before Marike needed to return to her teaching responsibilities, and Maud, to her school in Amsterdam. He tried his best to initiate conversation, but Marike and Maud were evasive, busy. So his default was Trudy, who willingly gave up her time and seemed eager to be with him. She asked questions and hung on every word he offered. She wanted to know how the war impacted him, how the sights he'd seen changed him, and about the life he'd led absent from hers. He told her the highlights—the views, the crew and pilots he'd relied on, the glorious Mediterranean. He was impressed she still remembered his early route by heart. The other two remained within earshot, always hovering but never joining. When they had to leave, he sadly realized he didn't know them any better than when he'd arrived. Sam rode the bus with Marike and Maud to the train station. He hoped to talk with them, corner them in the confined space if necessary. But the two sat together across the aisle from him and hardly looked in his direction. When the bus pulled to the curb, they gathered their things and darted out ahead of the crowd. Sam climbed out of the bus for a proper goodbye, only to see them heading away from him towards the station entrance. He called their names. They turned, waved, and continued on their way as the bus took off behind him.

Hurt and angry, his mood continued to worsen while he waited for another bus home. He sat on the bench and thought about his current situation. Since the war's end, the value of Dutch currency plummeted while family and medical expenses mounted. Ger's medicines had grown increasingly expensive. Trudy had to repeat the first year of the Leiden Lyceum. Maud chose a school in

Amsterdam, incurring additional living expenses on top of school costs. Although Marike was living on her own and working as a teacher, she continued to wrangle whatever funds she could from him. All the medicine, schooling, books, and extra lodging put a tremendous strain on Sam fiscally. He felt financially choked and wondered how he'd catch up. Even so, he felt compelled to send what little money he could spare to Helen for Merriwold's upkeep.

The holidays passed unnoticed. No one was in the mood to celebrate after Ger's passing, least of all Trudy. And Sam had no desire to reunite with old friends and neighbors at the festivities in the town square or at the parade in the canal. On Old Year's Night, Sam, Jenke, and Trudy sat reading books in the front room while fireworks exploded outside. Sam's mind wandered to Helen and Merriwold. Their future unclear, he ached for her. All he wanted was to continue their life together. He prayed 1950 would bring him closer to that goal.

Sam continued to press the Caltex offices at The Hague for money through Mr. Neilsen, Sam's contact there. Whenever time allowed, Sam took the train to see Mr. Neilsen, armed with fistfuls of invoices and receipts illustrating how difficult life had become for him. He'd start cordially pleading his case as Mr. Neilsen quietly wrote notes, listening with his head down. Inevitably, Sam grew agitated, even pounding his fist on the conference room table. Still, the promised wartime bonus went unpaid. And although retroactive yearly increases were allotted, the four-fold devaluation of the Dutch guilder meant that in reality, Sam was earning less in 1950 than when he'd begun in 1930. Even with all the skimping, Sam couldn't possibly get ahead. Instead of taking any leave, Sam took extra pay. He felt like a hamster spinning in a wheel. This stressful treadmill existence left him miserable.

After a fitful night's sleep, Sam woke at 5 A.M. The Janus was ready to run. He showered, collected his things, set them in the foyer, and made a pot of tea. He took a cup out the back door to the garden area. He had put a lot of work into that garden the last summer he was at home, tilled the ground with healthy soil, carefully planted cucumbers, broccoli, beans, and lettuces. Now he bent to pick up a handful of dry, barren dirt.

"I had my hands full caring for people, Sam, myself included. That didn't leave much time for plants." Jenke stood with her hands on her hips, looking for an argument, but Sam didn't bite.

"You spent your energies wisely, Jenke, and I am indebted to you." He stood and let the dirt fall from his hand. "I need to get back to my ship," he said passing her. He let the back door close behind him and placed his empty cup in the sink. Jenke followed. Without looking at her he said, "I thank you, Jenke, for all you've done here. I don't know how Ger would have managed without you."

He climbed the steps to find Trudy in her room, ready for school and studying. "The Janus is ready to go," he said, sitting on the bed. "I wanted to say good bye."

Trudy sat down beside him. She had so much to say to him but didn't know where to begin. After a few moments, she found the words. "Mom talked about you all the time," she began, avoiding his eyes at first, watching instead as her pencil bobbed up and down between her fingers. "Ever since I was a little girl, Mom told me stories about you, well..." she paused, "maybe they were exaggerated, I don't know." She turned to fully face him, her legs folded in front of her. "She painted this larger-than-life picture of you for me, Pop," she explained, drawing a large box in the air and searching his face. "You know she was convinced your return would make her well? She was so sure that all she needed was your loving attention, and presto," she snapped her fingers, "she'd be healed?"

Sam didn't know what to say. Though he could well imagine Ger's saying that, he couldn't imagine she continued to believe it. Especially not after he'd behaved so pitifully with her.

"How I prayed that were true," Trudy continued, clasping her hands together, her voice cracking. "I miss her so much," she whispered. Sam patted her shoulder. With a long finger he lifted her chin to wipe a tear off her cheek.

Checking his watch, he saw he was running late. "You don't want to hear this, but I really must go now." Her shoulders slumped with obvious disappointment. But Trudy was clearly not surprised. "I'll see you soon," he suggested, hugging her and kissing the top of her head. "Do well in school, and be good to Aunt Jenke. I'll see you soon," he blurted, hurrying towards the door. Like a wind gust, he was gone.

But Trudy would fail out of school and then enroll in the Leiden Household School. Maud would be expelled from the Amsterdam School, though she would never explain why. Instead she gave up on school altogether and took a nanny position with a young Dutch family heading to Oslo. *...where she'll be someone else's headache,* Sam told himself.

After a three-hour commute, Sam greeted Graham on deck, and the two inspected every inch. When they were satisfied that all repairs were complete, they set off for Bahrain. After six months on land, Sam appreciated the salty sea air filling his lungs. Once under way, Sam returned to his stateroom and clicked on his radio. The BBC aptly aired "It's a Lovely Day Tomorrow" by Irving Berlin. After unpacking, he retrieved his stationery and sat at his desk. It was 17 February 1950, and Helen's ever-present smile beamed at him from the frame on his dresser as he wrote a long and overdue letter.

For the next few years, Rotterdam served as Sam's home base. He continued to collect crude in Bahrain, but his discharge ports were limited to Thameshaven, Stockholm, Fredericia, and Copenhagen. He never went south of the Gulf of Oman. Caltex's benevolent efforts to root him in the north only strengthened his resolve to return south. Instead of traveling to Leiden from Rotterdam, he chose to remain on board, even during the occasional dry-dock periods. Time permitting, he would take the train to The Hague where he'd meet with Mr. Neilsen and plead his case.

At last Mr. Neilsen had some good news: Caltex intended to offer him a pension at the age of sixty, only a short seven months away. Though the details had yet to be defined, Mr. Neilsen assured Sam he was working on his behalf. Cautiously, and in spite of himself, Sam began to hold out hope that life would fall into place in 1953.

TWENTY-SIX – Durban

1953 Helen lay on a chaise reading a book in the shade of the frangipani tree when April arrived with an armful of homegrown flowers in a variety of colors. She stooped to allow her mother to inhale their sweet fragrance, dotting her cheek with a kiss. Helen shielded her face from the sun with an upturned hand and smiled into her daughter's grateful eyes. April went inside to find a suitable vase.

The scene had become routine. This mother-daughter duo had flourished much like a married couple becomes attuned to and tolerant of each other's shortcomings, dependent upon the other's strengths instead. They'd grown past expectation and, in their individual ways, allowed old wounds to heal. Like the twisted trunk of the fig tree, their lives intermingled and grew stronger because of the other's influence and support. Sam's years of absence opened a space in Helen's heart, and April eagerly stepped inside. Never too late. For April, Merriwold became the welcoming home she'd always wanted, its contents still mercifully intact—Henry, Grannie, James, even Ashes the cat. And because of April's added expertise, the garden grew more glorious than ever. She cultivated golden yellow and orange Namaqualand daisies in her spacious home garden and transferred cuttings to Merriwold, maintaining a constant presence in both. Though their connection had grown beautifully, April never allowed herself to become complacent. After a lifetime of effort, April couldn't bear the thought of being shut out of her mother's heart ever again. So she tended both the gardens and the relationship, for she knew uprooting either one would bring overwhelming devastation.

The work paid off at Merriwold; however, at home she seemed to be losing ground. While her gardens flourished, her relationship with David grew more strained. The failed pregnancy left April feeling resentful and completely inadequate as a female and as a wife. While they'd dated through school, David provided the acceptance April never felt at home, and that alone was the basis of their connection. Communication had never been their forte, and their relationship proved immature. In his own way, David did his best to assure April he was content without children. April would have rather believed David was hurting also, desperate as she for a child. She wanted to adopt, but she didn't know how to broach the subject. She refused to forgive herself, and her perceived failure hung like a foul stench in the air between them.

At the same time, David's father grew ill and had to be placed in a nursing home. For the first time in her life, Ann Williams, David's mother, was alone, and she did not fare well with her forced independence. She insisted David, without April, join her for dinner routinely and take her often to the home to visit her husband. David felt obligated; April felt ignored. To make matters worse, Ann Williams sold her in-town house and contracted to build a home not 500 yards from April and David's. The situation became overwhelming for April, who increasingly took refuge at Merriwold. David would drop April there when he had business in town. If he did not, April often made the long bus ride to downtown Durban and intercepted Helen on her way home from work.

April returned with the flowers and placed the vase on the metal table, a collection of sun drenched color. She tilted the book in her mother's hands to read the title. *"I Chose Freedom?"*

Helen held the book to her chest and took a deep breath. "Excellent! What an ordeal Victor Kravchenko went through! You can have it when I finish, which won't be long; I can't seem to put it down!" Helen replaced the dragonfly bookmark and closed the book, eyeing her daughter. "Are you well?" She learned to read her daughter easily, once she'd begun paying attention. "You seem a bit down."

April dropped herself into the chair. "My mother-in-law is making me crazy! She is building her home just up the road from us, right there," she waved her arm for emphasis. "As her new house takes shape, so does the lump in my throat...I'm choking!" she tried to joke, holding her hands around her own neck. "Honestly, can you imagine? We'll have no life of our own then." She shoved her hands into her pockets and pushed the soil at her foot. "Not that we *have* much of a life... She insists David be with her constantly." She leaned her head back and searched the sky. "Between his ever-increasing work commitments and her, I never see him anymore. And when I do, he's exhausted." She crossed her legs and furtively glanced at her mother. She regretted venting now, overshadowing their time with her complaints. She was usually mindful to make their time together pleasant, well aware that her mother welcomes cheerfulness and dismisses anger.

"But enough of that. How are you feeling, and how are you managing without Grannie here?" The suggestion that Grannie's absence hindered Helen in any way made them laugh. Grannie was spending a few days in hospital for minor surgery. After months of an open wound's refusal to heal on her leg, the doctor decided a skin graft was in order. It was Grannie's first trip to the operating room in her eighty-four years, and she had needed Helen, April, and Henry to calm her through the process.

"Quite heavenly, I dare say. And the idea of a sherry after dinner hasn't even crossed my mind." The two laughed aloud. "Poor old woman. I know she's had a hard time in such an unfamiliar place. But when Dr. Stuart offered to look in on her today, I decided to take the day off. That's not so terrible of me, is it?" She leaned her head back, closed her eyes, and smiled. "I actually dozed here earlier." She held her eyes shut for a bit before looking again to April. "Ah, but Henry and I will go fetch her tomorrow."

"You mean the barrister," April corrected. "I would remind him he has another few years to earn that title, but he's so much bigger than I am, and I tend not to argue with anything he says anymore."

Easy laughter warmed them both. "David is afraid to wrestle with him now." James brought out a tea tray and set it on the table next to the flowers. He fixed their cups as he knew they preferred them— two sugars for April, two for Helen.

"April," James began, "David called. He said for you to spend the night here at Merriwold. Said he's got to go out of town for a few days and won't be able to pick you up today as planned."

April forced a smile. Helen straightened. "I know you're disappointed, dear, but we're happy to have you. And won't Grannie be delighted." She found April's evasive eyes. "Henry will be here for dinner. Stay. It's all right, wonderful really." April searched the ocean below and stirred her tea. She welcomed the chance to stay at Merriwold, but she gagged on the suspicion rising from her chest.

Helen was inspired to cook. She prepared chicken fritters, cauliflower, and a creamy white sauce with chips. The following morning they drove together to retrieve Grannie, who was more than ready to come home. She had been waiting on the edge of her bed for two hours, her leg propped on a wheelchair. When her family finally arrived, she scolded them.

"Wonderful to see you as well," teased Henry. "We've missed your complaining and have come to take you home. You look tired, Grannie, didn't they let you sleep?" he teased.

A nurse arrived and gladly helped Grannie into the wheelchair. Helen pulled the car around, and Grannie was helped into the front seat, backside first. She complained throughout the ride home— she'd been poked, prodded, awakened, fed *poison* and denied sherry. She could not wait to get home; Helen was driving too slowly. At last Grannie was seated in the lounge, a tray of lunch in her lap, and more than ample sherry within reach. When the sherry put her to sleep, Henry suggested he and Helen ride April back to Westville. The house would be quiet for Grannie, and they'd save David the effort.

The drive to Westville passed quickly. The evergreen hilly terrain was naturally beautiful, a perfect way to spend a sunny afternoon. They arrived about four and agreed to go inside for a cool drink before making the return trip. Surprisingly, David greeted them in the foyer, dressed in khakis and a wrinkled jersey. He ran his fingers through messy dark hair. "April, I...didn't expect you. Hello Henry, Mother Dean," he offered nervously, avoiding their eyes.

April stopped short. "I thought you went out of town," she said flatly.

"They, um, changed their minds at the last minute," he said scratching the back of his head. As an afterthought, he brushed a quick kiss on April's cheek. His cologne was woodsy and sweet. "Everything was rather confusing. They finally told me not to come, but after I had called you...much later in fact." David rubbed his hands together as he spoke and then quickly turned to Henry. "Henry, old man, how is university?" He wrapped an arm around Henry's neck and led him towards the kitchen. "Let me get you all a drink," he called over his shoulder. Helen and April followed.

April ran out back to her garden and returned with some lettuces for her mother. "These are delicious," she promised and put them in a sack by the front door. Everyone returned to the lounge where they stood sipping their drinks and awkwardly chatting about nothing specific until Helen announced it was time to go. David collected their glasses, returned them to the sink, and caught up to them at the front door. He gave a quick hug to his mother-in-law, rubbed his sweaty palms on his pants, and shook Henry's hand, punctuated with a poke to his shoulder. In one swift motion, Henry had David pinned to the floor.

April hugged Henry then held onto Helen a bit longer. She offered her mother the bag of lettuces and promised to be at Merriwold for dinner on Wednesday. Helen turned her attention to her fidgeting son-in-law. "Perhaps you'll join us again someday, David." She didn't wait for a response; she believed his mother wouldn't allow it.

Henry drove so Helen could rest during the ride home. Slanted sunlight cast long, deep shadows on the roadside, and the vast ocean was in view for most of the ride. Normally Helen would keep her eyes on the ocean and daydream of Sam. But instead Helen kept her eyes shut, reviewing the scene they'd just left. Something gnawed at her, left her uncomfortable, but she couldn't pinpoint the source. David was rude, she thought, to leave them standing instead of inviting them to sit in the lounge. She felt hurried and unappreciated when in fact they had saved him the drive.

Wednesday came quickly, and as April approached Merriwold's door, she was met with sounds of Tommy Dorsey emanating from the lounge. She let herself in and found Helen in the kitchen, apron-clad and wooden spoon aloft, humming alone while she cooked. Her feet danced quietly in place as she swiveled her hips in tune. This was not the scene April had expected; in fact, this was wildly uncharacteristic. Her mind jumped to Sam. Could he possibly have anything to do with her mother's lightened spirit? She was afraid to ask.

April raised her voice over the music, "Hello, Mother! Where's James?" she yelled, startling Helen.

"Oh Aaaaaprilll, you're here!" Helen opened her arms wide and wrapped April inside them. Helen smelled of sweet apples and cinnamon. "I was hoping you'd arrive soon." Her eyes sparkled and her skin was luminous. "I gave old James the evening off," she giggled.

The music lowered, and then Henry appeared, beaming. He wrapped a large padded arm around both women, squeezing them together. "My two favorite women in the world," he announced. Helen squealed in delight.

"Want to tell me what this is all about?" April asked.

Helen spun herself around, obviously elated. "I have the most wonderful news from Sam." Helen placed both hands on April's crossed forearms and beamed into her solemn face. "He plans to retire next year!"

The words sprouted a dull ache in the pit of her stomach. "Here?" April blurted. "Well, of course here," she corrected herself. "Mum, that's...that's wonderful. Really wonderful." She tried to make her voice enthusiastic. "After so many years, you never gave up hope?"

Helen was too delighted to notice anything negative at all about April's reaction. She had grown to expect only mutual joy, and failed to see April's deeply buried emotions resurfacing. Helen grinned, "Hope is the only thing I *could* cling to." The music ended, and Helen froze mid-step, her arms aloft like the ballerina on a jewelry box. She let out a giggle and sat at the table, tapping the seat of the chair beside hers. April obliged, and Henry left the room to change records. Helen collected her thoughts, turning Sam's ring on her finger. "At times I am tickled as a schoolgirl," she said throwing back her head and tensing her shoulders with anticipation. "But then I realize we have been separated over seven years already, and things won't be as they were. I have become more settled in my ways, and I'm sure he has as well," she said, patting her graying hair. "And I'm certain I will appear terribly old, especially in comparison to the image he must carry in his mind." She looked down at her hands. "I almost hate to imagine that recognition in his face when he sees me."

"Oh, Mum, a few gray hairs have toned down the red, that's all," April quickly offered what her mother wanted to hear. After all, compliments were the route to her heart. "You are still as beautiful as ever. And I'm willing to bet he is sporting a few wrinkles himself." She eyed her mother cautiously. "A lot changes in seven years. How can you be sure he'll come? Even more importantly," she lowered her pleading voice, "are you sure you still want him to?"

Helen clasped her hands in her lap and smiled at them, noting every line life had etched. "How do I make you understand...? I believe in the notion of true love," she began. "When I think back on my life, even when I was quite small, it seems that Sam has always been there. He has magically spread himself over all time, so I scarcely have a memory that doesn't include him in some fashion." Helen rested her forearms on the table. "Yes, the years apart have been difficult, but I cannot imagine my life without him. I think of him constantly, and I feel his presence in my heart." She cocked her head to one side. "And I miss him terribly." She flashed a glance at April and smiled. "But I am never lonely," she said reaching to touch April's arm. "I think this is why we live, April: To love and to be loved. Once you have found each other, and you build a strong foundation, you can handle anything life throws your way." She studied April's face. "I can finally say that with confidence," she said smiling. "But I think you already know that, hmmm?" Helen stood, cupped April's face in her hands, and kissed the top of her head on her way to the stove.

Do I know that, April wondered? She marveled at her mother's confidence. After so many years of wonder and worry, her mother's hopes and dreams never waned. What kind of relationship not merely survives but strengthens over years of separation? Were she and David forced apart for years, would she soon be forgotten? In a heartbeat, she suspected. After eight years of marriage, she sadly realized she still didn't know the meaning of true love.

Big Band music sounded again, and April watched her mother, hips swaying and humming cheerfully, reeking of confidence and contentment. The love of her life was returning. April wondered what that meant for her. Was there room in her mother's heart for them both? Familiar pangs of panic seeped into April's consciousness. Her chest grew tight. She'd worked for years to carve herself a place in her mother's heart. Step by tedious step the two had forged a relationship based on need and strengthened by trust and compassion. Only in the last few years did she truly feel her mother could love her; did love her. And much of April's pride had been swallowed in the exchange. When the Captain returns, and she is no longer needed, will her mother cast her out again? She wanted to expect otherwise, but she had been through this routine more than once. *What about me?* She couldn't help but wonder. These emotions caught her off guard, and she felt ashamed of herself on the one hand. She and her mother had come so far together, how could she so easily doubt her? On the other hand, she had always been so easily cast aside in the past. Panic sprouted in the pit of April's stomach, and she felt nauseated, shaky. She needed time to sort out the flood of emotions clouding her mind. "Next year," her mother had said. April had a little more time to firmly secure her place in her mother's heart. While she prayed she could, deep in the recesses of her mind she knew better.

TWENTY-SEVEN – Leiden

1954 Early in the year, Sam began counting the days to retirement from his perch by the porthole behind his desk. While working there quietly most days, he saw the rime of early spring cloud the view, and heard the heater's intermittent hisses. But he didn't mind. He felt nearer to Helen just being there.

Sam heard a knock before his door opened, and Mr. Neilsen let himself inside. The Dutch director, Mr. Smits, was in tow, and both were dressed in full uniform under heavy wool coats, their hats quickly tucked under their arms.

"To what do I owe this pleasure, gentlemen?" asked Sam, shaking their hands. Sam motioned for them to sit on the settee while he pulled his desk chair close.

"Sam, your polite, albeit constant, shall we say... badgering about wartime allotments and back pay have finally raised some eyebrows in New York," Mr. Neilsen began, patting Sam's knee as he spoke. Smiling, he turned his gaze to Mr. Smits, who leaned forward, resting his elbows on his knees.

"Captain VanEck, we have reviewed your very detailed and lengthy paperwork outlining your grievances over the years. You must understand that wartime circumstances put a tremendous financial strain on everyone, Caltex included." Sam waved the air with a dismissive hand and crossed his arms over his chest. He had already heard all the excuses. "First of all," Mr. Smits continued, "we want you to know your pension has been raised from £50 to

£65 per month, commencing with your retirement, of course, on 27 May 1954." Sam's mouth dropped open. "And secondly, for your years of unfailing service, we are prepared to offer you a grant, amounting to eleven months' wages as evidence of our appreciation, again presentable upon your retirement. Until then, go home, with full pay, and plan the rest of your life, Captain." The room felt suddenly charged as though a bomb were about to explode. Sam realized he wasn't breathing. The two officers exchanged a cheerful glance. "Sam, take a breath, man!"

Caught completely off guard, Sam was speechless. Fighting with the management had become so routine that Sam was completely unprepared for truce, let alone acquiescence. Shock was evident on his face, and the two men finally exhaled a laugh that delightfully broke the tension. Sam struggled to regain his composure as Mr. Neilsen pulled him to his feet with a handshake and embrace. Sam's mind raced. Almost stumbling, he headed for the whiskey, and poured them all a tumbler full. Sam remained speechless as their glasses clinked. Finally, Sam found his voice and thanked them for their efforts and for traveling to tell him the news in person. "But," he continued, realizing he may never have another opportunity, "what if I told you to keep your money in exchange for a position in South Africa?" The men stopped short, baffled. Sam spoke quickly, "You see, gentlemen, there is a great little lady waiting for me there, and I feel I would be more attractive to her were I employed..." Sam brought them through a synopsis of his life in Merriwold.

Mr. Neilsen understood for the first time Sam's continued persistence. In the end, though, the men agreed they would like to help more, but they could not. Company policy prohibited employing anyone over the age of sixty as well as rehiring a pensioned officer. The men rose to leave and shook hands. Sam and Mr. Neilsen again embraced. Their partnership had come to a fruitful conclusion at last. Mr. Neilsen looked into his friend's eyes. "We may not be able to employ you, Sam, but I'll help you get home to Helen any way I can," he vowed. Sam fully intended to hold him to that promise, and he told him so very clearly. Fate had once again unlocked the door. Now, Sam realized, pushing that door open was completely up to him. Their ongoing correspondence had kept them connected over the years, yet Sam still hoped Helen would welcome him with open arms. He was planning now not just a long visit but to stay a lifetime.

Sam's replacement arrived at the Janus the very next day. He had been third mate on the Shell and was well versed in the workings of the ship as well as the cargo routes. Three days later, feeling fully confident in his replacement's abilities, Sam packed his belongings. Into his satchel he loaded personal items—photos of Helen, civilian clothes, Henry's compass, and the kist full of letters among them. He left all of his uniforms behind. Though it served him well, that life was over. In order to prepare for the next, he needed to return to Leiden. He took a last look around the small room that had been his sanctuary, the settee, his desk, the skylight over his lonely bed. He put on his hat, and opened the door. He stepped one foot over the coaming and paused abruptly. Turning, he removed his hat and tossed it onto the settee before closing the door behind him.

Sam clutched his satchel on his lap as he rode the train and then the bus to Leiden. A few times he caught himself smiling. He leaned his forehead on the window to make onlookers believe the scenery was appealing when, in fact, he saw nothing. His mind was busy traveling to the other end of the globe. He arrived to find Jenke had, justifiably, taken over the bigger bedroom upstairs. She half-heartedly offered to move in with Trudy, but Sam insisted he move into the old pantry instead. He assured himself he'd be sleeping in the child-sized bed for a very brief time. Sam finished unpacking and cleared a shelf where he then arranged his reminders of Merriwold—his radio, an alarm clock, his Zululand calendar. He held the compass Henry had given back to him. They had been apart more than eight long, often unbearable years, but now their reunion seemed just around the bend. The absence floated away, and lost time already began to dissipate. He prayed nothing would jeopardize their life together, now that he could almost taste it.

In the morning Sam rose early, made a pot of tea, and sat at the kitchen table. He stared briefly at the blank paper in front of him;

then set to work. He wrote *Helen* across the top, and then listed everything he needed to accomplish before joining his other half. He numbered the items as he wrote: 1. Emigration Office; 2. Termination of house lease; 3. Meet with notary; 4. Arrange transportation to SA. Satisfied, he downed the last of his tea, rooted out the necessary paperwork and took the bus to the Emigration Office. Hours later he was seen, and the process begun. How quickly, can they expedite his request, to whom could he speak—all his pleas landed on deaf ears. They would be in touch; he would have to wait. He was directed down the corridor where he filed immigration request papers to Pretoria, South Africa. Again, they would be in touch. He pulled his "Helen" list from his pocket and drew a line through Number 1.

In the evening he sat with Jenke for a review of bills and expenses. She was particularly bothered by his abrupt return home. Perhaps she assumed he had been let go and was worried about finances. But as usual, Sam laid money on the table to cover all anticipated expenses and added what he could to cover peace of mind. He assured her his presence at home would not burden the routine costs, but she was skeptical and had the nerve to suggest he move out. "On the contrary," he told her. "It is you who will be going...in due time."

Alone in his room he evaluated his daughters' current situations. Marike, now twenty-eight, had been the least trouble for him, earning her own keep for years. But she suddenly traded her learned profession as a teacher for a job as a stewardess for Royal Dutch Airlines without consulting with him in any way. He added her name to his "Helen" list and promptly drew a line through it, completely dismissing any responsibility.

When Maud failed at her nanny position in Norway, she hadn't returned to Leiden as instructed. Instead she went to Alkmaar to live with her boyfriend's family. Soon after, Sam learned the pair had eloped and were living in a flat in Bussuyn, not far from Leiden. Her husband, a newspaperman, had apparently been saving money for years. Their lack of gratitude amazed him. He hadn't received so much as an announcement. He retrieved the "Helen" list and wrote *Maud*, and then drew a line through that addition as well.

And Trudy. She was the only one to show him any affection. Little did he know it was all Ger's love shining through Trudy, all Ger's efforts holding Sam's undeserved place in Trudy's heart. With her Pop home, Trudy excelled at the Leiden Housekeeping School. It was with the school that she was now on a ten-day excursion to the Harz region of Germany. Trudy hadn't wanted to leave her father, but Sam encouraged her to go. He hoped to accomplish much while she was gone. He wrote *Trudy* on the page and beside her name wrote *Take to SA*.

Sam met with the town notary regarding the insurance policy that would mature upon his retirement. Though his older daughters had sorely disappointed him, he wanted to be fair. He added clauses providing a sum of £500 each at his sixtieth birthday, Trudy's sum to become payable on her twenty-first birthday next year. Sam and the notary drew up papers specifying liquidation and partition of property and securities upon his departure for South Africa. Upon completion of her schooling, Trudy would be considered an independent adult, and at that time, Jenke would receive notice of eviction. She would be given six months to find alternate housing, and money was apportioned from the insurance policy to cover all expenses during that time. The house would then be sold, and the funds forwarded to Sam's account in South Africa. However, if at any time Trudy opted to join her father in South Africa, the closing of the house would be accelerated.

Sam paid the notary for his time and included a little extra in his remittance. He was feeling generous. The pendulum of life was finally swinging his way. Stepping into the crisp sunshine, he stretched his arms to the sky. He closed his eyes and let the sun warm his upturned face. He imagined Helen sitting in the garden mending Henry's clothes, the frangipani tree heavy with fuchsia blossoms above her. His heart beat faster at the thought of holding her again. He reached into his pocket and took great delight in crossing out Numbers 2, 3, and 4.

In the evenings he and Jenke had very little interaction. Both preferred it that way. He prepared his own dinner and made himself scarce. While Trudy was away, he worked on the house in the early morning hours, repairing loose shingles in the roof, patching the dining room ceiling where the chandelier had hung. In the afternoons, he'd tackle his list. Passage to South Africa would be difficult to arrange, and he realized he'd need help. Sam traveled via tramcar and train to The Hague and met again with Mr. Neilsen.

Sam was delighted to see Mr. Neilsen who had come to represent improved relations with Caltex. Through him Sam felt appreciated for years of personal sacrifice, and because of him, aptly compensated at last. Mr. Neilsen greeted Sam warmly and invited him into his office. They sat on black leather armchairs, chatting like the old friends they'd become. Sam was very appreciative of his confidant, the only person he could share his hopes with face-to-face. The men discussed Sam's possible timing for emigration and compared scenarios against tanker schedules. Nothing could be confirmed until Sam's emigration was approved, and Mr. Neilsen promised to make arrangements when the time arrived.

Sam made the trek home, feeling refreshed. In two days Trudy would return. He had made good progress; the only thing left to do was wait. He wrote long letters to Helen outlining his progress.

His departure imminent, Sam felt increasingly unrestrained. He retrieved a bicycle from the attic and set out for a long ride in the countryside. He had had his head down in such deliberate focus since arriving in Leiden that he hadn't noticed the dazzling spring countryside in his midst. He passed aspen forests trying desperately to rebuild themselves. The white bark of each defiant sapling gleamed in the brilliant sunshine. Sprouting wheat had colored distant hills golden while once struggling tulip fields emerged in spotty swaths of red and brilliant yellow. The scenery calmed and delighted him, and the physical exercise was sorely needed. He was eager to take a ride with Trudy when she returned the following day.

Sam heard the girls' chatter long before he saw the bus. He watched the enthusiasm spill out with the riders. The girls collected their belongings and hunted for waiting families. Trudy looked right past him, searching for her Aunt Jenke and was stunned when her father stepped in front of her. "Pop!" The word surprised and melted his heart. "I didn't expect you," she explained, grasping the handle of her satchel with both hands and smiling broadly at him.

"Well that's quite obvious. I stood before you for a few minutes until you actually looked at me," he teased, taking her bag. They began walking home together. "Did you enjoy your holiday?"

While they walked, Trudy amused him with an animated monologue that lasted the entire way home. She glanced at him as she spoke, flashing her bright blue eyes, and touching his arm for emphasis. As the stories dwindled, she slipped her hand in his, and they walked the last bit in comfortable silence. The interaction would become one of his most memorable snippets as a father.

Sam created a daily routine to help ease the burden of his habitual waiting. In the early mornings he worked in the garden, determined to ensure it provide for the two women of the house. Then he would clean himself up and travel to whatever office that might expedite his departure. Early evenings were reserved for leisurely bike rides with Trudy, the favorite part of his day. Nighttime was spent alone reviewing his paperwork or writing to Helen.

He had expected to hear from the Emigration and Immigration Offices quickly, but weeks turned into months. While he waited, he packed parcels and sent them on ahead to Durban. He prepared a box containing various rugs and woolen blankets. He wrapped tools in green coconut matting and tied them with logline. He placed photo albums in a cane picnic basket inside another insulated box. The exercise left him wishing he could fold himself into a box marked for delivery to Merriwold. The delay in his paperwork processing crept under his skin like biting red ants and turned him irritable and impatient. All he wanted was to leave this country, this home, this life as soon as possible. He longed to sit in the hilltop garden with Helen and let their life together unfurl.

Finally, on 14 October 1954, Sam received confirmation of his expatriation/immigration. He immediately phoned Mr. Neilsen, who tended to his transportation as promised. On Friday the 21st, Sam received a telegram. He scurried to his makeshift bedroom and closed the door. Shaking, he ripped open the envelope and read the news he'd waited so long to receive: *The Caltex NY office is most happy to assist Capt. VanEck with a tanker passage to SA via the Persian Gulf on Mr. Neilsen's request.* Enclosed with the telegram was a KLM airline ticket from Amsterdam's Schiphol Aerodrome to Newcastle on Tyne via London. Another ticket was included for passage on the Caltex Saigon to Bahrain, where he would wait for the next South Africa-bound tanker. South Africa. His fingers turned cold as he studied the large envelope, his pulse racing. Pressing the tickets to his chest, he tilted back his head, and closed his eyes.

Then Trudy appeared in the forefront of his mind. "Pop," she had called him so sweetly. She had tolerated all his parental shortcomings, allowed his presence now to brush aside the empty years. She had forgiven as only a child can forgive. She loved him anyway.

As if summoned, Trudy knocked on the door. Sam quickly folded the tickets into the telegram and slid the bundle into his pocket. Trudy sensed the tension as soon as her father let her in, and the smile disappeared from her face. Closing the door behind her, he then took her by the shoulders, leveling his eyes to hers. "I'm going away," he blurted nervously, "But I want you to come with me this time, Trudy."

"I don't understand, Pop." She stared up at him, saw beads of sweat forming at the top of his brow. "You mean on a trek? To Bahrain?"

He directed her to sit on the edge of the bed. "My dear sweet girl, please try to understand. My travels on the Janus took me to many new places." He stayed on her wide, questioning eyes. "You realize I was not allowed to come home during the war. At least Mom and Aunt Jenke made that clear?" Trudy nodded, obviously confused. "Trudy, for years I didn't know if or when I'd be allowed to return to Leiden. Or ever." He paused, searching her eyes. "Everyone needs a home, Trudy, would you agree?" he asked nodding, his eyes intently focused on hers. "So I...I made a new one."

"What do you mean, *a new one*? You mean another one, like when you stay on board the Janus instead of coming home?" The trust and love in her eyes tugged at his heart.

"Trudy, my love, try to appreciate how I must have felt. For years I didn't know if I'd ever be here again, ever see you again." He quickly pulled her to his chest, touched his chin on the top of her head. "My darling, Trudy," he whispered. "I hate to leave you. But I am going away for good this time."

"But Pop, I thought you were retiring now. And that you were then staying home. With me."

Sam cleared his throat and adjusted to face her squarely. Taking both her hands in his, he searched her pleading, blameless eyes. "I have made too many mistakes in my life, Trudy. I was a rotten husband and a lousy father. I let my sense of duty overrule my heart and conscience. I came back here because you were so young..." He cupped her chin in his hand. "My plan was to stay here until you were finished with your schooling, an official adult." He slowly pushed her hair from her shoulder, trying to calm himself. "You are nearly finished now. And you don't need me...have never really needed me. Of all the girls, you leaned on me the least." He rubbed his forehead, searching for the right words. "Please understand me when I say I must go now, Trudy. I have a chance to start over, do better. To be a better person. And I am so eager—" Emotion caught in his throat, and he lifted his face to the ceiling. "At the same time, my sweet daughter..." his eyes locked on hers, and he tilted his head sideways. "I am having so much trouble with the thought of leaving you."

A smile slowly stretched across her face, melting his heart. "Well that's simple. Then don't leave me, Pop. Not now when we are finally getting to know each other." She sat on the bed and leaned back on straight arms. Her stomach was flat between bulging hip bones, still skinny from years of hunger.

"Knowing you has been an undeserved privilege. You have been more than gracious," he said, slowly lowering himself on the bed near her. "But Leiden is no longer, eh, home to me. And you are old enough to make your own choices." He leaned toward her, resting his hand on her knee. "I've been given a second chance, Trudy, and I want to take it." He searched her eyes. "Please, please, my little one, won't you come with me?"

At last she was beginning to understand what he was trying to say. Betrayal pricked at her skin. "Are you saying you already have somewhere else to go?" she let the words fall out though she couldn't imagine they were true. *How could he? How could anyone?* She thought further, and the volume of her voice rose to a shrill. "Where?" She stood near the window, facing outside and crossed her arms, hearing again his words—*needing a home, going for good, a new chance to do better.*

"Another life?" She turned to him abruptly, her heart racing. "Have you made another life...*Pop*?" She spat the last word as though it were venom.

"No, no, Trudy," Sam tried to calm her. He stood and attempted to take both her hands in his, but she pulled away. "Not in the way you may be thinking, Trudy! No!" He waited until she was again ready to listen. "But I know where I want to spend the winter of my life, Trudy. And I want you to come with me. There's a town in South Africa that pulled me in from the moment I saw it from my ship's deck." He could not contain the excitement in his voice, and she was outraged. "It's rugged and majestic, cosmopolitan and country—"

"So?" interrupted Trudy, flailing her arms in the air. "What does that matter? Go visit. Have a vacation, but pick up and *move* there?" She was pacing the floor, her mind whirling.

Sam searched the ceiling and clasped his hands. After a moment, he began. "Please allow me to explain?" He patted the bed, and she reluctantly sat down, but as far away from him as possible. "We discharged and dry-docked there often, Trudy. I made friends; learned my way around. "One family in particular, the Deans, made me feel quite welcome. Joseph, Helen, their son, Henry... You'd like Helen, really you would." His voice barely a whisper, he rubbed the sweat from his palms. "We could all be...be a family..."

"What are you talking about, be a family?" She glared at him as though he were crazy. "I am your family! Marike, Maud, Aunt Jenke! What do you mean, be a *family*?" She glowered at him, her heart beating in her ears. She became aware of the taste of bile on her tongue.

He reached for her then, grasped at the space between them. "Please try to understand, Trudy. I never intended any of this to happen, but I can't deny that it did. They took me in. Theirs became my *second* home." He ran a hand through his hair. "And now I'd like to—am going to—make it my permanent home." He continued to relay bits and pieces of the life he'd made in Durban, reminding her throughout his story that he "never intended for life to turn out this way," offering excuses until his stories made him sound more like the victim than the perpetrator.

When he started blaming the "situation" on Providence, suggesting God played a hand in his deceit, she stopped listening. His could not have been the same God she'd prayed to night after night to bring her father home and heal her mother. She looked around the tiny room that had housed abundance a lifetime ago, recalled in a miserable lump all the years the shelves held a meager amount of food, and then only Aunt Jenke's belongings and no food at all. She thought about the hungry agonizing winters that seemed to stretch on interminably. She fumed.

"We waited forever for you to come home," she said in a low, steady voice. "Mom waited. We prayed every night for your safe return. Because she believed she'd recover once you were here with us." Standing, she looked down on him. "But that didn't happen, did it? Dreaming to be a family again—the family you planned and were blessed with—kept us all alive. And now you have the gall to tell me you had another cozy life all the while? While we were living in—" Trudy's anger boiled over. "How could you? After all my efforts to learn you, memorize all Mom's stories of you, always you. She loved you so mu—" emotion caught in her throat. "I realize now I don't know you, never knew you at all!" She turned away from him to the window, pushing the blackout curtain aside and leaning her forehead on the glass. "I need to learn to be more careful about what and whom I choose to believe," she stated coldly, arms wrapped tightly around herself.

Her mind wanted to escape this conversation, and she needed to calm herself. Outside, hazy sunshine settled onto the vegetable garden struggling to take shape amid brown patches and yellow grass. She was a child again, watching her mother unfurl the blue blanket and guide it gently to the ground, where Trudy was the center of her mother's attention for a precious pause from the day's chores. Trudy slid a hand down her hair, imagining the soft touch of her mother's hand, the sweet sound of her voice telling stories about Pop, always about Pop. Through her stories, Trudy learned to idolize the man she hardly knew and rarely shared in person. She realized she had grown to love the idea of him, adore the image her mom had conjured. Now she had to make a choice. She had clung so desperately to the image of her father, loved him dearly only because of her mother's words. If she acknowledged this lying, spineless man slowly revealing himself now in person, she'd have to forfeit the father she'd maintained all her life. She had already lost her mother; Trudy decided she couldn't bear to lose him too. She opted to keep the image of the man Mom had beautifully painted, push aside all she had just heard about another home, another life. Believing him capable of such deceit would be disrespectful to her mother somehow. She missed her mother desperately, especially at that moment.

Trudy let the curtain fall and turned to her father. "I want to love you, Pop," she began, watching the hope rise in his eyes. "Maybe not you, personally," she corrected, "but the version of you Mom made for me." She couldn't help feeling smug as that flicker of hope in his eyes extinguished in an instant. "My life is here," she stated, crossing her arms in front of her. "And Mom is still here for me." She moved toward him, and as he stood, she kept her eyes on his and her arms folded. "I don't wish to start over, Pop. I have just barely begun." She let him wrap his arms around her, but she remained stiff, unresponsive. "And, Pop," she whispered, "please don't say any more about it." She turned to leave.

Sam was heartbroken. He chastised himself for not making her understand. Surely he hadn't explained himself well. He realized there was a better way to plead his case, make her understand why he had no choice but to resume his life in Durban. "Wait! Trudy, don't go just yet. I have something I'd like you to see; to read, actually." He lowered himself to his knees and reached under the bed, producing a carved wooden rectangle about the size of a bread box. "Your mother told you who I was," he began excitedly. "These letters will better tell you who I've become and why I must go now." He handed her the box, and she reluctantly took it. "I hope you'll read these, Trudy, all of them, and learn why I'm choosing to leave now. Please. Try to put yourself in my shoes? My life is waiting for me in South Africa." He tried to look into her eyes, but she wouldn't allow it. "I'll continue to pray you'll forgive me. Someday I hope you'll join us in South Africa where we could all be a family." He put his arms around her shoulders, "at least consider visiting us there? In the meantime," he kissed the top of her head, "make yourself proud."

Before dawn the next day, Sam packed the rest of his belongings into his worn leather satchel and waited on the front stoop for his taxi. Morning light peeked through gray wet skies. Sam snapped up his jacket collar and inhaled Leiden's autumn fragrance for the last time. Trudy stayed in her room as her father had requested. Saying another goodbye would be painfully inconvenient. She handled the sealed letter her father had given her to open later, when she was ready. The letter held the answers Trudy would eventually ask—his new address, money, his briefest summation of the life he felt Providence had led him to find.

Jenke stepped onto the front stoop and, seeing the suitcase, surmised the situation. She panicked. "How dare you leave us!" she seethed. "There are unpaid doctor bills, what about the fees," she yelled, waving her arms. "What will become of us—?"

He raised a hand to silence her. "The £73 I handed you on the first of the month will more than cover any bills, and the fees are paid until Trudy graduates," Sam replied in a deep, low voice. "You will receive instructions from the notary shortly." When the taxi arrived, Sam stepped into the mist and stowed his luggage in the boot. Jenke continued shouting. He set his gaze on her, and she instantly fell silent. "I leave with a clear conscience," he stated firmly. Then he waved his arm in a final salute and folded himself into the taxi. He did not look back.

Trudy observed this from the upstairs dormer window, in the room she'd shared long, long before with her two sisters. Those had been the best days of her young life, she realized, and she had clung to them despite the unexpected twists and turns. All her life people told her she was the picture of her father, especially since she'd grown tall and broad shouldered. She couldn't deny she was him on the outside. But now she knew she was all Mom on the inside. Because as she watched her father drive away, she felt a piece of herself go with him too.

TWENTY-EIGHT – Durban

November, 1954...I am housed mid-ship in an extra cabin marked "pilot" with your portrait over my old faithful Philips radio. What a relief to feel enroute to you at last. You might tell Dr. Stuart in confidence that your future husband is coming home. After all, it takes time to find your successor and get the person acquainted with her task! I wonder how a 22-year-old stinker will like his old Cappy now returning for keeps. I pray that my Merriwold family will not find me too old and shrunken after this horribly long absence...

Helen stopped reading aloud and pressed the letter to her chest, closing her eyes. "He is on his way at last," she exhaled, ready to burst. They were seated at the metal set outside in the garden.

April gulped her iced tea and fanned herself with a magazine, suddenly bothered by the summer heat. She had grown more agitated with each line. Sam was on his way. She could almost feel the shove from her mother's life. Fidgeting in her seat, she offered, "After so many years, will you even know him?"

Helen smiled with her eyes closed, her face towards the sun. "I thought I told you, dear. I've known Sam all my life."

April's head began to throb, and she tried to rub the pain away. Each passing year had given April more confidence that he'd never come. Claiming her spot in her mother's life had not been an easy task; becoming comfortable there, perhaps even more difficult. Piece by piece April had put down her armor and become vulnerable, loving every bit of the evolution. They had achieved an easy rapport, become welcomed in each other's homes, lent support in subtle ways. Would April be expected, again, to step aside to make room for the man in her mother's life? How could she expect otherwise? April continued to shift positions, crossing her legs one way, then the other; placing her hands on her thighs, then folding her arms in front of her. "He didn't say when to expect him," she said, fishing for a timeframe. "How can you plan his homecoming without a date?"

Helen dismissed her daughter's concern with an easy laugh. "Sam doesn't want a party, dear. All he wants is to find me still here waiting for him."

April snapped to her feet. She felt nauseated, and she preferred to leave on her own before her mother subtly dismissed her. "I really should get going," she announced.

Helen shielded her eyes from the late afternoon sun. "I thought you were spending the night while David is out of town," she objected.

"I've thought better of it. The weeds have taken over the garden, and I want to attack them before the heat of midday tomorrow." She collected her shoes and purse.

"Won't you at least stay for Sunday dinner? We'll make it a celebration."

Celebration indeed. April fished the car keys from her purse. "I am not yet confident to drive David's car in the dark. If I leave now, I'll be home by dusk. I'd feel safer." With that she found her keys and started towards the car. Attempting to sound cheerful, she called over her shoulder, "Congratulations on your good news, Mum." She turned fully towards her mother, walking backwards, "And please tell Henry I am expecting him on Saturday?" It was more of a command than a request. She wasn't about to relinquish that relationship.

Helen checked the date of Sam's letter once again, quickly calculating his arrival to be at least two weeks away. Henry could certainly be available this Saturday. "He'll phone you, dear," she called after April.

April drove home slowly and carefully. Hot, humid air whipped through the car messing her hair making her feel a bit rebellious and, oddly, a little better. She pulled onto her long driveway just as dusk settled and looked forward to a cool evening bath. She unlocked the door and dropped her keys and purse on the foyer table. The house was dim and quiet, and hinted oddly of garlic and onions though she had not cooked in days. She headed to the kitchen for a drink and let the tap water run cold before filling her glass. As she raised the glass to her lips, she saw the outside patio awash in candlelight. Her iron table, draped with a white cloth, and a pitcher of her yellow flowers in the center. Their chairs were close together, positioned so they could look out on April's well-tended gardens as the sun set. David's arm hung loosely on the back of her chair. A glass of wine poised aloft in her hand; her head thrown back exposing her long neck, giggling. Stunned, April's glass slipped from her fingers and crashed in the sink. A large shard of glass bounced up and gouged April's forearm, which immediately spouted blood.

David, hearing the noise, hurried inside and snapped on the light. He saw her standing motionless at the sink, blood streaming down her arm, glaring at him wide-eyed. "April, I, I didn't—"

"How could you," she seethed. Odd recollections collided in her head—the strange key, his constant travel—what else had she been overlooking? "Was any of your travel for business? How long have you...how long has this—?" He stepped towards her, tentatively reaching his hand to her shoulder, but she shot it away. "Don't you touch me!" she snarled. "You will never touch me!"

"April, let me help you, you're bleeding," he pleaded, motioning to her arm.

She felt the pain then and opened the spigot. The water ran deep crimson. April propped herself on her forearm, plucked a clean dishtowel from the drawer, and wrapped her arm tightly. Blood immediately drenched the towel.

"You need stitches," declared David. "At least let me take you to the hospital," he pleaded. In the distance a car's engine roared to a start.

"Why? Because now you have nothing else to do?" she spat.

She cringed at his touch while he helped her into the back seat. She refused to sit near him in the front. Questions flooded her brain—*who is she, how long, who else had conspired against her?* But they rode in tense silence. The bleeding was difficult to control. She squeezed the area and raised her arm above her head. Immediately, the throbbing became more painful, and she loosened her grip, lowering her arm to her lap. Blood oozed through the towel and crept onto her pale cotton skirt. All at once, she stopped caring whether she lived or died. What's the point? She let go of her arm and watched her blood spread into the fabric of her skirt, a growing blotch of red. She began to feel lightheaded as though her body might drift out the window, and she wondered if this was how it felt to bleed to death.

The waiting area was not crowded. April curled up on a vinyl sofa and rewrapped her arm while David filled out the necessary paperwork. He crouched to be eye-level with her, keeping awkwardly distant. "April, I—" he began. But she shot him a devastating glare and rolled away from him.

Dr. Carroll was again on duty and escorted them to an examination room. He didn't readily remember them, but the sight of him brought back the miserable experience of losing her child. She fought new tears. He pulled back the thin white curtain, covered the exam table with a clean cloth and helped April onto it. He washed his hands and unwrapped her arm. Blood pulsed from the gash. He summoned a nurse to help stem the flow while he plucked tiny shards of glass under a magnifying glass with giant sterilized tweezers. He worked on her wound for thirty minutes. "You're a lucky girl," Dr. Carroll said as he finished sewing. "Twelve stitches. A little deeper, and we would have had a real problem on our hands."

"Wouldn't that be just horrible, darling?" April offered sarcastically, seething at David. Squirming, he smoothed back his dark, slick hair.

The doctor scribbled on his prescription pad and tore off the paper. "Take these when you are ready to sleep very soundly. One, two at most, is all you'll need. There's enough here for four good nights' sleep if you take two a night, more if just one stems the pain. Rest is all you need now; then come back and see us in two weeks to take out those stitches." He glanced at his watch. Nearly midnight. "You may be groggy in the morning if you take these tonight, but that's fine. The sleep will do you good, young lady." He helped April from the table and directed himself to David, handing him the prescription. "I'm afraid the pharmacy down the hall is your only option at this hour." He shook David's hand, "Take good care of her," he instructed before leaving to find his next patient.

April paced near the entrance waiting for David. With her bloodstained skirt, bandaged arm, and exuding anger, she appeared to be the victim of attempted murder. When David finally emerged, she snatched the drugs, glaring at him with such loathing that onlookers would have surmised he was the assailant. They would have been correct.

All the way home David offered various explanations, but to April his words became monotonous babble. She sat fuming in the back seat and stared out the window into the black sky, recounting the clues she had overlooked. She wondered when had David started traveling more often, when was the last time they had made love? For how many years had their marriage been a lie? How could he intentionally hurt her like this?

When they arrived home, April's anger flared. "How could you do this to me? To us? How long has this been going on?" She picked up a vase full of flowers. "Nice touch. I do hope she appreciated my garden!" she yelled before hurling the vase at him. David quickly dodged it, and the vase crashed into the floor. "To hell with you!" she screamed, ran to the bedroom and slammed the door. She flicked on the light and saw the unmade bed. "That's *my* bed!" she yelled.

Meanwhile, David gently knocked on the door, "April, let me explain?" He tried the knob and knocked again harder. "April, honey, open the door. Let me help you. C'mon, I know this looked bad, but..." he continued banging on the door, but when she refused to answer, he retreated to the lounge and sat on the sofa, his head in his hands, devising his explanation. *She'll calm down tomorrow,* he assured himself.

April ignored David's pleading until she didn't even hear it, not noticing when he finally gave up. Anger fueled her. One-handed, April stripped the sheets, gathered them into a ball, kicked them into the hallway, and locked the door again. Her clothes reeked of dried blood. She struggled to get out of them, bathe, and remake the bed. She chose the yellow flowered sheets, the ones David disliked most. Every movement was difficult—unbuttoning her skirt, removing her bra, cleaning her teeth. As she struggled, angry tears flowed, and she cursed David, Sam, and Helen, her enemy troika.

Finally she slipped her nightgown over her head and sat on the edge of the bed. She plucked the bottle of pills from the bag, but she was too angry to sleep, so she paced the floor instead. *Was our life together one big lie? Had he been just pretending to love me all along? Does everyone just pretend? And for what? Why? Do I know that woman on the patio? Were there others? Had people seen them together? Why hadn't someone told me?* April suddenly stopped. *Oh my God, was David planning to leave me?* The thought made her cry again. She hugged herself with her good arm. *He did love me once,* she assured herself. *But when did he stop?* She had to know. She unlocked the bedroom door and walked deliberately to the lounge. The room was dark and quiet, except for David's slow, rhythmic snoring from the sofa. She approached him gingerly, intent on asking. Trembling, she knelt beside the sofa and gently nudged his shoulder, unsteady about hearing his answer. "David," her voice barely a whisper, "Did you *ever* love me?"

David rolled onto his side, his back to her. "Wha?" he mumbled before slipping back to sleep.

April nudged him a little harder. "Do you love me, David?"

David snorted and rubbed a hand over his closed eyes. "Yes, Melanie, now lemme—" again he was asleep.

April reeled away from him, muffling a gasp. The room spun, and cold perspiration began at her hairline. Shaking, she tiptoed back to the bedroom and locked the door. She paced in circles, hot tears streaming down her face. "He doesn't love me?" she repeated in an unfamiliar high-pitched voice. "He doesn't love me." And then she suddenly realized it all made sense. She froze. "Of course he doesn't love me," she whined. "No one does, not really." She sank to the floor. "Where will I go? Oh God, where can I go now?"

Memories of Merriwold ripped through her. She would surely not be welcomed there once Sam returned. Of course her mother would have no room in her life when the Captain reclaimed it. She had been a fool to hope otherwise. "So unfair!" she wailed. "What about me?" She gathered herself into a ball, wrapping her free arm tightly around her knees. The sobs began slowly and erupted into heart-wrenching shudders. Eventually, April cried herself to sleep.

Pulsing pain in her arm woke April mid-morning. She slowly uncurled her body until she lay flat on her back, feeling the pang of stiffness in her neck and shoulder. She prayed the night before had been a terrible dream. But as she ran a hand over her bandaged arm, she felt the genuine misery of the night before. Each recollected tidbit triggered more pain. She felt abandoned, completely alone. Deep down she had known the day would come when she would discover everyone she held close had lied. Everything she'd clung to had been fake—her father's love, Joseph's interest, Helen's assurances, David's vows. These had been the pilings on which she'd steadied herself. Now they collapsed beneath her, as she always feared and always knew they would. At the same time, though, she found the truth oddly liberating.

She pulled herself first to sitting and then slowly worked her way to her knees, her feet. Trancelike, she unlocked the door and padded into the lounge. David was gone. She crossed to the window to make certain the car was gone as well. She exhaled in relief and began to weep. With each tear, April became increasingly unburdened. The charade, she realized, was finally coming to an end.

Back in the bedroom, April stood before her reflection in the full-length mirror. Her eyes were two red mounds. An imprint of the carpet's pattern was faintly evident on half her face. She let out a long sigh, and grasped the mirror with both hands. "Your father ran from you immediately. Your own mother never really loved you. Oh, she pretended for a while..." she held her own gaze. "...And that felt good, didn't it? And you let yourself believe that she could. Tsk, tsk," she shook her head. "You foolish, foolish girl. You loved her with all your heart. After all she did to make you miserable, you still loved her. All you wanted was for her to love you back." She sank to the floor, pulled her knees to her chest. "You are such a fool," she said resting her head on her knees. "Now your husband has made a fool of you too." She ran a hand along her bandage and glanced again into the mirror. "He never loved you either, stupid," she spat, leaning forward on both arms, ignoring the pain. "Good God, you are completely useless and utterly unlovable! You can't even produce a child to love you." She was surprised to feel the tears on her face; she hadn't sensed them coming. "The reason we live is to love and be loved, according to my dear mother. Why, then, do you even draw breath?" Her mottled, puffy face was almost unrecognizable, even to herself. She stretched her legs in front of her and leaned back on her arms. The pain in her arm throbbed, and she welcomed it. She believed she deserved it.

April crawled over to retrieve the pills from the bedside table, then headed slowly to the kitchen. She took a glass from the cupboard and stood at the tap, gazing out the window at her colorful expansive gardens, seeing only the weeds. Her eyes shifted to the waxy remains of the candles on the table. The scene from the evening before repeated in her mind as she swallowed one pill after the other until they were gone. She set the glass in the sink and brought the empty prescription bottle back to the bedroom.

She climbed into bed and smoothed her hand over the sheets. "I love these yellow flowers," she said pleasantly, pulling the coverlet to her chin. She began to drift. Before long her body grew heavy as though the coverlet were made of lead. April didn't fight the deadly onset but rather welcomed the escape. She thought of her mother. She imagined her face beaming down at her, arms outstretched to welcome the toddler. "Aaaapril," she heard her sing, and April smiled. "Maybe you did love me once," she said, rolling with effort to her side. "I always wanted to believe that." Sometime later she was at Merriwold, reliving the scene when her mother's delight was precipitated by Sam's news. April knew then her own hopes were foolish. Drifting in and out of consciousness, her thoughts landed on Henry, and her heart ached. "I am so sorry, Henry," she slurred. "You did love me, I know. But you are the only one. And I needed more. But because I was his daughter, I guess, I didn't deserve it."

David returned home late that afternoon. The house was quiet, so he assumed April had gone to Merriwold and he was alone. He sorted the post, took a magazine to the lounge, but his mind was on April. He needed to make her believe his excuses for last night. Once she'd had time to cool off, he would call Merriwold. First he'd win over his mother-in-law; then he'd enlist her help with April. Of course she would willingly cooperate. He was well aware that the last thing Helen wanted was for April to become a permanent houseguest at Merriwold. A headache crept up the back of his neck, and he grabbed at it. He was still in the clothes he'd worn the night before and decided a shower might help clear his mind and help him feel refreshed. He unbuttoned his white short-sleeved shirt as he headed to the bedroom for fresh clothes. The door was locked. He rattled the knob, surprised that April had not yet left. "April? Are you in there?" he called. "I thought you'd gone out." No answer. "April, open the door," he groaned. "Come on now, you can't keep me out forever. I need to get my clothes!" He banged on the door, growing increasingly agitated. "April. Open this door! I need to explain about last night. You jumped to conclusions, you know. Honey, it's not what you think." Angry now, he banged harder. Still no answer. "Such a child," he mumbled.

He found a screwdriver in the toolbox and dismantled the doorknob. Minutes later, wet with perspiration, he stood horrified at the sight. April lay on the bed, her skin ghostly pale. "April!" he shouted, shaking her. She was unresponsive. He hit her face, and she let out a low moan. He spotted the empty prescription bottle on the table. "Oh my God, April, what have you done?" He snatched back the covers and rushed her listless body into the car. As he sped to the hospital, he continued calling her name, shouting at her to wake and hear him. "April, last night wasn't what you think.

Melanie is just a business associate of mine. April, do you hear me? She had been working really hard on a project for me, and I asked her to stay for dinner, that's all." He tilted the rear-view mirror to glance at his wife sprawled across the back seat. Her ghostly appearance was unchanged. He yelled louder. "I can see why you're upset, now that I think about it. We must have looked pretty cozy. But you should know better, honey. April?" He parked at the emergency entrance and gathered her listless body in his arms. Once inside he screamed, "Help! Someone please help me!" until nurses rushed to calm him. April was whisked away on a gurney, and David was quizzed for details in its wake.

Dr. Carroll was still on duty, and remembered the couple immediately. He shot an inquisitive glance at David, who averted his eyes. "She downed the whole bottle of your pills," David said scratching his head. Nurses swarmed around April like drones to the queen. Machines and trays of instruments appeared from all directions. David was pushed out of the way. The doctor gave quick orders in what sounded like another language. "She has a pulse!" cried the nurse leaning over April with a stethoscope. Another nurse forced a tube down April's throat. Completely oblivious, April did not gag or resist in any way. A milky substance eventually flowed through the tube and filled the clear bag. From his vantage point in the corner, David wished he were living a bad dream. Dr. Carroll placed a hand on David's shoulder. "Is there anyone you should call?" He bent to eye-level. "Son, who else would want to be here?"

"Why? What are you saying?" David asked, his voice quivering.

"Better hurry, son," he said.

Helen didn't understand much of what David was saying, but the desperation in his voice sent a chill through her body. The car ride was interminable. Helen, Grannie, and Henry rode in silence, afraid to speak. At last they arrived and were directed to the ICU. They burst into April's room and stopped short at the sight of her lying limp, pale, and tiny on the bed. April was still holding on. The machine rhythmically sounded her slow, steady heartbeat. The line to pump her stomach protruded from her mouth, and a bag of liquid hung from a steel post, condensed into a small tube, and punctured her left arm. Bloody bandages wrapped her right. Amid the network of protrusions, Helen didn't know where to touch her. She sat on the edge of April's bed. "We were having a chat just yesterday," Helen whispered, keeping her gaze on April. "David, the doctor told me she took a bottle of pills? Why? What is going on here?" The scene was difficult to comprehend. Helen touched the bandage on April's forearm. "Did she...do this to herself?" Helen finally turned to David, her expression, painfully pleading.

David jumped from his chair. "No, no, Helen. She dropped a glass in the sink, and the chards sliced her skin. We were here for stitches just last night." He tentatively reached his arm to touch her shoulder. "He gave her the prescription then to help her sleep, and we filled it before going home. He said sleep was important for her to heal. He said we were lucky. Had the cut gone any deeper..." his voice broke. David returned to his chair and buried his face.

Henry pulled a chair from the hallway for Grannie, who let out a sigh as she fell into it. Henry leaned over his sister, cautiously reaching a hand to her forehead. "Mum, do you think she hears us?" She smelled foul, like lettuce left to rot. "April," he called sharply. "April, why did you do this?" His stomach twisted. He wiped his forehead with a trembling palm and leaned close to her face shouting, "April! Wake up!" He held her shoulders and shook her. When she didn't flinch, Henry collapsed onto the bed and cried. Helen moved to him and rubbed his back, but he was overwhelmed. He walked from the room, and just outside the doorway, slid against the wall to the floor, burying his face in his hands.

Minutes dragged into surreal hours. The room was windowless, so any time of day was possible. Nurses came intermittently to check the machines, squeeze the bag of liquid. Helen fired questions at them—"what is happening, when will she wake, what are you doing for her, can you wake her, does she hear me, does she know we're here, wake her, dammit, why can't you wake her?"

The doctor appeared occasionally, touched April's head, forced open the lid on one vacant eye and then the other, and carefully avoided Helen's gaze. "Wait and see, we're doing all we can, we need more time—" was all he offered. Time continued in slow motion. Grannie remained in her chair, quietly weeping. Henry drifted back into the room. He and David took turns pacing and fetching hot tea. When the staff offered no answers, they turned to God. Bowing their heads, they prayed together for her life. Independently and silently, Helen and David begged for forgiveness.

The four remained vigilant watchmen at their posts, three slumped in chairs, and Helen at April's feet. Nurses changed shifts. Different doctors repeated the same words. April remained unchanged. When the watchmen inevitably fell asleep, the staff tiptoed around them repeating their routine checks. Then like a dreaded alarm clock, a constant tone pierced the air, startling Helen from sleep. She rubbed her forehead, forgetting for only a moment where she was. Instantly, the doctor and nurses stormed the room. Helen was lifted from the bed and placed firmly at the wall. The doctor lifted April's limp wrist briefly; let it drop. He barked orders. April was injected; no response. A nurse held open April's eyelid and ran a small beam over an unmoving eye. Another injection. All the while the deafening tone split the air. The doctor placed his stethoscope in his ears and leaned to April's chest. He shook her body violently and leaned in closer. All eyes were on him, cheering him on silently. Slowly, he stood upright and removed the instrument from his ears. Returning the gaze of one nurse, he shook his head, and lowered his chin to his chest. Someone halted the monitor's tone, and the ensuing silence was even more deafening. All activity screeched to a halt. Dr. Stevens ran his hand along April's cheek and briefly touched her shoulder before turning away from her. He crossed to Helen and placed a hand on her forearm. "I am so very sorry," was all he could offer. The nurses soberly followed him from the room.

Helen tried to speak, but her body was paralyzed. The words echoed only in her head. *Wait! Come back! Save her! You're mistaken! She's alive! Don't stop!* Helen doubled over in pain. April was gone. She had purposely taken her own life. Henry crossed to his mother and lifted her tiny frame to his. He wrapped his arms around her as she sobbed, muffling her painful howls with his chest. Grannie wept openly, shoulders shuddering. They cried in their incomprehensible shock. They cried for the lonely pain April must have felt. And they cried guilty tears for being completely unaware of April's private suffering.

Helen's accusing eyes landed fully on David. "You!" she seethed, pointing her finger. David cowered, shrinking into his chair. "You must know why she did this to herself! What have you done?" Helen loomed over him, and he covered his face. "You must have known something was wrong. She is your wife! You are supposed to know—" David slumped, crying soundlessly, while Helen continued her attack. "Why didn't you take better care—" Henry took hold of Helen, and she buried her face in his chest, gripping his shirt with clenched fists. She closed her eyes and saw April's face, her eyes puffy from crying on so many occasions. As she pushed one image away, another immediately replaced it. She couldn't bear to share the blame. Again she lashed out at David, hurling herself at him. "You weren't paying attention!" Her fists found his shoulders, his chest, and when he turned away from her, his back. "You were supposed to pay attention!" Helen pleaded, hitting him relentlessly. "You didn't love her enough...never enough...it wasn't her fault..." At last Henry succeeded in containing her. He wrapped his arms around her tightly until she finally grew limp in surrender. They all searched their memories for clues they had missed. Their unanswered questions would haunt them the rest of their lives.

David slipped into the hall. He couldn't bear to hear their weeping, knowing he was to blame. If there were a way to take it all back, relive the last few days, he would. Helen was right. He didn't love her well, but he thought he had loved her enough. She seemed content with the pittance of affection he threw in her direction. She hadn't complained anyway. And she had shown more interest in her garden and that mutt than in him, he assured himself. Anyone in his shoes would have done the same. No one else would have noticed her sadness, let alone anticipate *this*. No, he was not fully responsible he promised himself. It was his monster mother-in-law. She was the root of April's trouble. Always has been, he assured himself.

The service was held inside the small white church where Joseph had been honored. Very few gathered. They followed the casket down the center aisle. Helen sat in the front row flanked by Grannie and Henry. David sat behind them with his mother. He would spend the rest of his life in shameful penance.

"How do we say goodbye to someone who had barely begun to live?" the pastor began. Though her body sat still, rooted to the pew, Helen's mind raced anywhere else to evade the inconceivable present. She caught a glimpse of Henry's worn sole and thought of clothes that needed mending; the scent of carnations had her replanting the garden in her mind; a muffled sniffle brought her to the medical rooms. The most tragic trial for any parent is the death of a child. Helen would avoid that bleak reality as long as her practical mind would allow.

Henry's touch startled her, and he helped her to stand. They followed the casket outside to the graveyard where she was placed beside Joseph. Helen leaned on Henry's steady arm. He took her hand and squeezed it twice. "We will get through this, Mum," he assured her through red-rimmed eyes. She clung to him as an infant clings dearly to its mother. The two had come full circle, and she would rely on him to keep his word.

TWENTY-NINE – Merriwold

January, 1955 With the help of Grannie's sherry, Helen slept soundly for the first time since April's funeral. She awoke mid-morning; hours later than usual and with a persistent ache behind her eyes. Stretching her arm across the bed, she yearned as always for Sam's companionship. The prior three weeks had been unbearable, and she desperately needed his comfort. She slipped into her robe and called down to James to bring tea to her veranda. The morning was already hot, and the ocean breeze brought little relief. James knocked on the door before he entered.

"Good morning, Nkosi," he offered, attempting to be cheerful. But James had known April since she was a child, and he felt the pain of her passing as strongly as a parent. With slow, labored actions, he placed the tray on the small table. Helen had no words of comfort to offer. He pulled an envelope from his pocket and handed it to Helen. "I hope this makes you feel better. It just arrived."

Helen eyed the letter, acknowledging Sam's handwriting. But she couldn't open it. Living through April's suicide was proving to be the most difficult time of her life. The grief, guilt, and unbearable sadness left her paralyzed. Now, after so many years of joyful anticipation, how could she welcome Sam to this house of misery? Turning the envelope in her hands, she was struck by all the possibilities for disappointment the letter could possibly contain—emigration difficulties, unmet immigration requirements, problems with Trudy, an unexpected snag, or perhaps, a change of heart. She couldn't endure a disappointment of that magnitude. She placed the unopened letter on her bedside table, deciding to open it when she felt stronger.

Again she stayed in her room all day. James dutifully brought her food and drink, making himself as inconspicuous as possible. As evening fell, Helen sat on her veranda and watched the blue-green ocean as it rhythmically receded, curled, and overlapped onto the shore. Occasionally the waves reared violently into foamy eruptions. She felt as though she were seeing an illustration of her life and all its hurdles. For the most part, she had weathered small, foamy rises with fair consistency. The more turbulent waves represented her more difficult challenges—an unfaithful husband, Joseph's sudden death, April's suicide. These ripples left her gasping for air, and each recovery proved increasingly difficult. Her life had vacillated with the tides, and like the ocean needs the moon, she needed a magnetic tug to draw her back into life. As the sky darkened, the moonlight's silver path to her veranda brightened. And she ached for Sam. If only he were here, she assured herself, all would be right in her world going forward.

The next morning was hazy and warm again. Helen woke feeling somewhat refreshed, a little more eager to recover. Stepping onto the veranda, she caught sight of her overgrown garden below and decided it was the perfect place to begin again. In the past, getting her hands into that dark, rich soil tilled her aching heart, renewed her spirit. She knew this was what she needed. She bathed and dressed in a dark cotton shift, and allowed James to coax her into eating a banana and toast before heading to the market.

Rows of plants and possibilities overwhelmed her at first, but she cautioned herself to start small. She needed a task to master, not a project. She bought four daisy plants and a confetti lantana vine and went home. The outing left her exhausted, but she fought the urge to nap because she was eager to begin the process. She changed into slacks, donned a straw hat and canvas gloves, and retrieved her garden tools from the garage.

The sun shone directly overhead, burning the morning's haze. A warm breeze was barely noticeable. Taking a deep breath, Helen lowered herself to her knees. Before she could plant, she needed to clear some weeds, cut back overgrown foliage. She began digging, tentatively at first, then forcefully yanked stubborn roots and slashed nasty growth. She pulled on a weedy vine and followed it to its source. Before long she tugged off the gloves and plunged her hands into the cool dirt. She continued to dig and weed, plant and thin, all the while thinking about April and the understanding they had reached, the good times they had shared. How much more difficult this time would be without loving memories to treasure, she realized.

Hours later the planting process was finished, and Helen's healing, begun. She was exhausted, both physically and emotionally. James pulled a lounge chair into the shaded area of the garden for her and brought some iced tea and a *Life* magazine. "Rest now, Nkosi." She thankfully obliged. Helen downed her tea and stretched out on the lounge chair, asleep before turning the page.

The sound of the taxi didn't wake her. Sam unfolded his long legs and fixed his eyes on Merriwold. Beaming, he stood rubbing his eyes, pinching himself for assurance that he was really there. During his trek he had tried desperately to speed the process along. He sprinted through the Amsterdam Aerodrome, and while on deck, he paced like a caged animal. Now he wanted to slow down, soak in every bit of the thrill of returning home after so many years. The driver retrieved his bags from the boot, and instead of kissing him, Sam paid him generously. Most of his life he enjoyed the sounds of the ocean as his backdrop. He felt serenely content knowing the same sounds would accompany him the rest of his life. He bounded up the steps and set his bags on the porch. Giddy as a schoolboy, he searched for Helen and found her sleeping in the garden. His heart leapt at the sight of her. Overcome with emotion, he quietly approached and knelt beside his sleeping *engel*. With a shaky hand he timidly ran his forefinger along her soft languid arm.

Helen stirred slowly. When her sleepy eyes saw his face just inches from her own, she knew she was dreaming again and closed them tightly to continue. He brushed her arm once more. This time she woke fully. Slowly, she reached to feel the side of his tear-streaked face. He cupped his hand over hers and kissed her palm. Wordlessly, he helped her to her feet, his eyes never leaving hers. Her hands worked their way up his arms to his shoulders to his face. "Sam," she whispered. He wrapped his arms around her waist and lifted her off her feet for an embrace he'd dreamed of for nearly a decade. They wept silently, and he gently kissed away each tear.

Through each other's smiling eyes, they saw nothing had changed. Though time had etched some wrinkles here and there, the span they'd spent apart evaporated into the welcoming air around them. "I am home, Helen," he whispered, squeezing her close, "I am home at last." They held each other weeping, while their hands took in every available inch, assuring what their eyes saw was real.

Despite their late start, Helen and Sam enjoyed a lifetime in twenty-two years. Once reunited, they spent months holding tightly onto each other, making up for lost time. Gradually, they began to share themselves again with friends who had waited patiently in the wings.

Henry became a prominent lawyer and married Marianne Ernst, a paralegal in his first office. The two were madly in love. Before long their daughter was born. They named her Joelen after the parents he adored. Joelen became the center of Helen and Sam's universe. They poured themselves into the beautiful redhead child. Each time the little family arrived for a visit, Sam would hurry to take JoJo from the car and hoist her into the air. "My de vreugde van leven," he called her, his *joy of life*. And just like that, Merriwold was filled to the brim with the best kind of happiness again.

Helen and Sam grew old comfortably together and died quietly and painlessly, Sam leaving first. When Helen died, no one was surprised that her beloved Merriwold was left to Joelen. Helen knew Joelen would honor the tradition of Merriwold and continue to fill the home with parties, love, and laughter.

Epilogue

The house sold in the spring after my father left. Jenke and I took a flat just on the other side of town. The walls are painted a sunny yellow, and the large front windows welcome the sunlight and the moonlight because they are never covered. Instead, they are flanked with white sheers that move easily with the breeze when the weather permits. Through those front windows the town square is visible across the street. This is the park where we came to play as children, where neighbors continue to gather on holidays. After the war the pavilion was rebuilt, and the choir began singing carols again for Sinterklaas. On summer days, Jenke and I would sit for hours, sipping tea and watching children run and play in the sunshine. We'd marvel at their carefree lives, how fortunate they are to have been born when they were, to learn about the war only from stories or history books. After many years when Jenke grew feeble, we moved her bed to the front room where she could continue to watch the children play or simply admire the view. I cared for her until her death, doting on her in the same loving way she had doted on Mom all those years. How I miss them both.

Once a year I travel to Bussuyn for a long visit with Maud and her husband; Marike and her current husband. (She's had three.) At first our get-togethers were awkward, more so for the Ms. In their own rebellious grief they'd abandoned their little sister, and when they looked back on their actions, felt terrible guilt. But I always viewed their leaving as taking their chance to create their own lives.

I didn't blame them for wanting to put the ugly past behind and start fresh. Now I welcome our meetings as a way to preserve the good in our collective past, and a way to keep Mom alive in our hearts. When we are together, we repeat loving memories of her, her steadfast courage, and her remarkable resilience. None of us had children, and the realization that Mom's memory will die with us is bittersweet, a treasure we get to keep.

I've had many acquaintances and went out on dates occasionally, but I never found someone I wanted to share my life with. Now I guess I'm too old to change my ways or adapt to another's. I like my life. I am perfectly content to chat with neighbors over mid-morning coffee, help anyone in need, or have lunch with friends at the corner café. My closest friends tell me I keep people at bay, and I suppose that's true.

Despite his continued requests, I never visited my father in his new life. There was a time when I wanted to forgive him completely, reunite with him and embrace his new life. I'd eagerly await his posts and hang on every word. But always something would emerge from the depths of my subconscious, haunt me in my dreams, and I'd awake feeling cold and flat towards him. After a few years I allowed life to be my excuse to impede a visit—a needy friend, lack of funds, the weather. Then Jenke's illness took over, and I didn't need to fabricate my excuses any longer. As I aged, the desire to see him again faded, and I began reading his letters to me as excerpts of a fictional tale doled out piece by piece. When his correspondence slowed to a stop, I completed the story as I saw fit.

On warm sunny days when the sky is a brilliant cerulean blue, I still walk across to the town square, unfurl my worn blue blanket, and lie on my back. I never tire of feeling the cool breeze on my face or mussing my silver hair. On that blanket I can close my eyes and sense Mom's lilac-scented presence, hear the song in her voice, feel her warmth as I hug myself tightly. And I can't help but smile. After a while, I open my eyes and search the expansive sea above me. And in the white puffy clouds streaming overhead, I find a hat, an oil tanker, and its long lost captain.

Book Club Question Suggestions

1. Can a child ever "remove his or her own color" when evaluating a parent's actions?
2. How and why was Trudy's reaction to the occupation different from her sisters'?
3. The treatment of Holland's Jewish population is rarely discussed in American history books. Compare/contrast theirs with other countries, i.e. Poland's.
4. Put yourself in Sam's shoes. If you thought you'd never see your old life again, would you adopt another?
5. Can you understand Sam's willingness to allow his family to slip into the background?
6. Ger's ability to "read" her husband is uncanny. Are you able to "read" your spouse simply by his or her expression?
7. April tried all her life to be important to her mother. They did enjoy a close relationship. Why was she convinced Sam's return would end her relationship with her mother?
8. How does a mother's reassurance set the basis for a child's confidence?
9. Have you ever wanted to step out of your life and start fresh?
10. Which characters did you love, hate, admire and why?

Made in the USA
San Bernardino, CA
07 September 2019